CW01020457

Copyright ©2024 by Jon Sparks (including text, cover design, and original photographs).

No part of this publication may be reproduced, distributed, or transmitted in any form or by any means, including photocopying, recording, or other electronic or mechanical methods, without the prior written permission of the publisher, except as permitted by UK and international copyright law. For permission requests, contact jon@jonsparksauthor.com.

The story, all names, characters, and incidents portrayed in this production are fictitious. No identification with actual persons (living or deceased), places, buildings, and products is intended or should be inferred.

No generative AI was used in the creation of text or images for any part of this book.

For Richard and Marion

Vows and Watersheds

Book Three of The Shattered Moon
Jon Sparks

Jon Sparks

CONTENTS

Part One

Families

JON SPARKS

Chapter 1

Jerya

"Just think," said Embrel, "If we could really fly like the birds, then making maps would be easy."

That was an acute observation for one so young, thought Jerya. "It would... They say the ancients could fly." Perhaps *that* was a way to get him interested in history.

"Really? They had wings?"

"Not wings like the birds. But they could build machines like carriages, but that moved on their own, without horses, and some of them could leave the ground and fly through the air." The lad was looking at her sceptically. "That's what the stories say."

"Stories?"

"That's what history is," she said. "Stories. Stories about when things were different."

"When people flew through the air?"

"Some of them." *Really*, she'd often thought, *what do his tutors think they're doing?* There had been a succession of them, at least four that she could immediately name, and all had complained that it was hard to keep the lad's interest. Well, he wasn't patient, and he wasn't good at sitting still for long periods, but then he was nine years old.

So now... It was her own fault, really, failing to conceal her disdain for the latest of those plodding young men. Lady Pichenta had asked, "So you think you could do better?" and she had rashly responded, "I'd think it was hard to do worse." And now here she was, in addition to all her other duties, acting as interim... what would the word be? Governess? She had never heard of a female tutor, not on this side of the world; but she had never heard of a governess having authority over a male pupil either.

She collected her thoughts. "Let's go up to the attic. The end window... let's see if you can draw a map of the yard."

※

"That's very good," she said a little later. "But here's a question. Do you think it's a good idea to put the carriage in?"

"Why not?"

"Well, it's not always there, is it? It's only out because Whallin washed it and it's still drying off."

He wrinkled his nose, a sure sign of deep thought. There was one other person in the household who did that, and it wasn't either of his parents. *His official parents.* Really, it was a good thing Railu's hair had never come back, that she couldn't grow the Crest to which she would undoubtedly have been entitled. Jerya was certain that her hair would be black and curly, just like Embrel's. His official parents were both grey, but there wasn't a curl between them... *Choss, I can hardly blame the lad if his attention wanders, when I'm woolgathering myself!*

"Look," she said, "Remember the map on the library wall, the one that shows all the fields?"

"We looked at it earlier."

"Yes. And it has all their names, doesn't it?"

He nodded, but she could make a good guess at his thought. *I know the names anyway; why would I need a map?* She could have given him an answer; *because you have a map in your head already.* Maybe she would come back to that. "And what's growing in... UnderKnowe, this year?"

He barely needed to think. "Beets."

"Yes, quite right. But did they grow beets there last year?"

"No, it was clover, for fodder."

"Aye, and it's good for the soil, too. Then next year it'll be different again. But it's always called UnderKnowe and the hedges and gates are always in the same places..."

His nose wrinkled again for a moment, then his face brightened. "And tomorrow the coach won't be in the yard, but the coach-house will be in the same place."

"And the stables..."

"And the pump, and—" He broke off. "Someone's coming."

She could hear it too, hooves on the gravel, changing to a harder clatter as the horse entered the yard. Together, woman and boy peered through the open window.

"Do you know who it is?" asked Embrel.

"Don't think so."

She gained only a rear view of the rider as he dismounted. A man, undoubtedly, and young, by the slim build and lithe movements, in well-fitting but unostentatious riding-clothes, with splashed boots and a dark green jacket. He handed the reins of the horse—a fine-looking bay of maybe sixteen hands—to Whallin, pausing for a brief conversation before striding off, presumably to the boot-room.

In that moment, as she watched, Embrel was gone. She heard a bustle in the house: Railu, announcing the arrival to the Master and Mistress; the unmistakable sound of Embrel descending the stairs two at a time; Lady Pichenta chiding him; a stranger's laugh. The men moved off, but she heard Pichenta giving instructions to the slaves.

Jerya sighed and made her way back to the library.

❋

It was no surprise, ten or fifteen minutes later, to hear small feet running up the stairs; still less of a surprise when Embrel knocked on the door but entered without waiting for a reply. He stood beside her, looking down at the ledgers and invoice books and papers spread on the desk. "What are you doing?"

"What are you doing, Miss Jerya?" she corrected, softening the stern tone with a fond smile.

"I beg your pardon. What are you doing, Miss Jerya?"

"Accounts."

"What's accounts?"

"It's how we keep a record of how much money comes in, and how much goes out." *And how you find out when someone's embezzling*, she thought, remembering the months between first suspicions and finally delivering the proof of Grevel's peculation.

"It sounds boring," he said, the easy response of one who had never yet needed to think about money, beyond a coin that found its way into his hand to buy a cake at a fayre.

"Money sounds boring... until you haven't got enough of it. Then it's not just interesting, it can be positively terrifying."

"Have we got enough?"

"Well, that's why I'm doing this, so we can be sure. But I would think so." *Though not as much as there would be if Grevel had been honest...*

"That's all right, then." He smiled, and she saw, as she all too often did, the echoes of Rodal in his face; the overall shape, especially the angle of the jaw, and more than anything the slightly crooked smile. The likeness was becoming more evident as he grew up. It was—she supposed—a good thing that no-one would ever see them together.

"You'll have to understand all this one day," she said.

"One day," he said. "Not now."

"Well, unless you came up specially to learn about accounts, no, not now." She gave him a quizzical look. "I presume there *was* a reason you came up? Tell me you'd finished your map, perhaps?"

"No," he said, and then brightened. "I would have, but a visitor's arrived... why are you smiling?"

At how cunning you think you are, she could have said, but instead she just said, "I know... So tell me, who is he, what's he like?"

※

His name—which Embrel had rendered *almost* correctly—was Hedric of Kirwaugh. What Embrel had failed to report was that he was *The Honourable* Hedric of Kirwaugh, and therefore not merely gentry, but nobility. Jerya had long resolved to remain unimpressed by such distinctions, but she needed to be informed about them. 'Honourable' indicated that he was the heir to a title, but Kirwaugh was not a name she had heard before. It lay, he said, in the woldlands to the North-East, most of a day's ride away.

Hedric himself was around her own age, perhaps a little younger. As she'd already observed, he was of slim build, and no taller than herself: a tidy figure, but not a particularly imposing one. It was impossible not to notice that his face was rather dominated by round, heavy-rimmed, eye-glasses. She had seen eye-glasses before, going right back to her days in the College; Tutor Yanil often wore them, and many of the older Tutors, a few of the younger ones, even one or two Novices. However, the lenses had always been much smaller. Glasses of this size would give a broader view, but must be very expensive, she thought. And heavy, she added to herself later, noticing how more than once he shifted them to rub at the bridge of his nose or over an ear.

He bowed politely as Duncal finished the introductions. "Miss Delven," he said with a warm smile, "A true pleasure to meet you."

She had heard that before, and it was generally no more than a polite platitude. She had too many memories of guests who had turned cool on learning that she had been freed; but Hedric was not like that. The very next moment, he said, "I have heard of you, of course, and hoped to make your acquaintance for some time. But it is awkward for me to get away as often, or roam as far, as I would like."

"That seems most unfortunate, sir."

"Unfortunate? Yes, to me it is."

They were interrupted by the dinner-gong, which came mostly as a relief to Jerya; people who were keen to meet her were often also keen to enquire about her history. Though she had grown expert at parrying such questions, it was never easy to do so without appearing rude, and she was already keen not to appear rude to this particular guest.

Fortunately, the conversation over dinner was very much focused on the campaign for the betterment of slaves. Jerya was able to make a few modest contributions, but mostly she sat back, enjoying the food—Rhenya had excelled herself—and observing. From occasional remarks and asides she gathered a good idea of why Hedric's freedom of movement was constrained. His Uncle, the Earl of Skilthorn, liked to keep his nephew and heir close to hand. She could see that this frustrated him, that he chafed against the restrictions. Unspecified 'business' in Denvirran had been the ostensible reason for his current journey, but it almost seemed as if he had come to Duncal in search of moral support, or reassurance.

But perhaps there was another reason. At the end of the meal, just as coffee was being brought in, he turned smilingly to Jerya. "I gather this house does not rigidly enforce the custom of gentlemen withdrawing after dinner, and neither the Squire nor myself are smokers, but I hope you will forgive us if tonight we do leave you? The Squire's telescope is an uncommonly fine instrument, I have heard, and tonight is a clear one."

His impatience was clear, and she could well understand it. How often she had gazed upon that same telescope? (How often, as a slave, had she dusted it?) How rarely had she enjoyed the opportunity to gaze *through* it?

Tonight was just the same. She was obliged to follow Lady Pichenta into the drawing-room, face her across the hearthrug, and talk of whatever Pichenta wished to talk about. At least things were easier than in the early years, when similar situations had been close to excruciating, stilted snatches of conversation punctuating long awkward silences. As Jerya had become more embedded in the life of the house, and the estate, they gained more common ground. And then, as Embrel grew, they gained a whole new topic of mutual concern, to which Jerya's role as governess gave added depth.

Tonight, not for the first time, their discussion centred on sending the lad away to school. Custom was rigid on this; sons of the gentry were sent away to be 'educated'. Only the timing permitted some variation. Some of Embrel's age would already be away at preparatory school. Twelve was as late as any family would leave it, and boys who went to school later than others were often thought to be at a disadvantage, socially if not intellectually.

The problem was, everyone in the house hated the thought of losing the boy's sunny presence, and Embrel himself was passionately opposed. It was almost the only thing that made him miserable. It was all familiar stuff, but they aired it again anyway, united in the faint hope of finding some way to reconcile the dictates of custom with the demands of everyone's heart.

They chewed over the question as they had several times before, but to no better resolution. "He needs friends of his own age," was the best argument Pichenta could come up with.

Hedric and Duncal had been out on the terrace for around an hour, when the Squire came in, rubbing his hands together. He hurried over to the fire, stood as close to it as he dared.

"'Pon my soul," he said, "That young man's made of sterner stuff than I am. A very devil for observing, hm." He glanced at Jerya. "I'm sure it would be a kindness to send out a pot of hot coffee. Would you be so good as to ask Rhenya to see to it?"

"Of course," she said, rising. "But perhaps I might take it out myself? Rhenya was up before any of us, probably hours before, and I've no doubt it'll be the same tomorrow."

"By all means, if you are happy to do so."

"Ah, Miss Delven. How very thoughtful..."

"It was the Squire's thought, sir."

"But you who enact it, so I give thanks to you both... You must think me a very mannerless guest, loitering out here all evening like this."

"Loitering, sir? Is there then no purpose to your remaining out here?"

A soft sound, perhaps a chuckle. "A poor choice of epithet, perhaps. 'Loitering' might be exactly how many see it, but astronomy...

"I must make a confession, Miss Delven. I am second to none in my admiration for your employers and their endeavours on behalf of the enslaved. And it would grieve me to think that you might have any cause to doubt my commitment to support this great work in whatever way presently lies within my powers. But..." This time, a distinct chuckle. "If they desired my undivided attention, the Squire should never have shown me this fine instrument—" He laid a hand on the casing of the telescope, delicately, so as not to disturb its alignment. "And most particularly not on such a night as this. It is most noticeable how a rise of even a few hundred feet improves the seeing, escaping the heavier airs of the Vale... 'Twould be interesting, some day, to make comparative measurements of pressure and humidity. And you have such a wide horizon here, especially of the Eastern sky."

He laughed again. "Pray forgive my ramblings. But perhaps you will discern that—notwithstanding my adherence to our noble cause—my true passion is science, and first among sciences, astronomy."

She lowered her coffee-cup. "May I ask what you have been observing tonight?"

"Why, of course—do you know something of astronomy, Miss Delven?"

"A little," she said. "A very little." *I might have learned a great deal more if I had stayed West of the mountains*. Might-have-beens were bittersweet, an indulgence she seldom allowed herself.

"Then may I ask if you know what is meant by the word 'nebula'?"

She thought; recalled a chapter of a book, and a single glimpse, under less than perfect conditions, of the Swordsman's Nebula. *I probably remember every single object I've observed through a telescope*, she thought. "A nebula appears to the unaided eye as a small fuzzy patch, like a wisp of cloud."

"Just so. But through a telescope, especially a fine instrument like this one, and on a night like this... well, Miss Delven, perhaps you would care to take a look for yourself."

I thought you'd never ask. "I should be very glad, if you do not mind."

"Not at all. When one has a passion such as mine, one delights in sharing it. 'Twould be a miserable soul who wished to keep the heavens to himself... I must only stipulate that you must feel no compunction in speaking out if you become too cold, or too bored.

"Now, you will need to adjust the focus significantly. I observe that you are fortunate enough not to require spectacles, and from that I deduce that your vision is far superior to mine."

He moved to show her how to make the adjustment, but Jerya was ahead of him. She might have enjoyed a mere handful of chances to observe through the telescope before, but she had dusted it any number of times, and studied it carefully while doing so. She knew exactly where the eyepiece was, and the little knurled wheel alongside it that provided precise adjustment.

The image swam, shimmered, sharpened, blurred again. She had over-adjusted the focus slightly and had to back the wheel a little. Then... "Oh, my word..."

"You have it clear? Magnificent, is it not?"

"It is... but please, sir, what exactly am I looking at?"

"We call it the Great Nebula."

Hedric mentioned something that she had first heard ten years ago, in another life: nebulae seem to be of different kinds. Even from just two observations, she could begin to grasp this: the Great Nebula she had just seen was clearly ordered, while the Swordsman's appeared ragged and chaotic. Therefore, he suggested, astronomers were bound to ask: are they different in kind, so that it becomes misleading to refer to both by the same term? And are they at different distances, in different regions of the heavens, perhaps? How could we tell, when we can barely measure the distances to the moons with any confidence of accuracy? Are they closer than the stars, or scattered among them, or even, hard though it may be to imagine, at a yet greater distance?

A little later, she became aware that she was growing cold.

"I should excuse myself," she said. "I have presumed upon your time long enough."

"Not at all, Miss Delven. Believe me, it is with the utmost sincerity that I say it is a true pleasure to share the experience with such an enthusiast. But if you are chilled, you must of course withdraw."

"Well," she said, emboldened. "I could, instead, go and fetch a warm shawl, and change my shoes. And perhaps I should inform my employers; if you intend to stay out here much longer, they might wish to retire."

"Of course. Truly, Miss Delven, it would bring me nothing but pleasure if you should wish to remain."

"Then I shall leave you for a few minutes only. Oh, and sir..."

"Yes?"

"I did not bring that coffee out merely for it to grow cold in its pot."

Having informed the Master and Mistress, she went on to the kitchen, where Railu and Rhenya were still sitting with hot drinks. She advised them to go to bed as soon as they wished; anything else that required doing she would manage herself.

It was nearing one of the morn when she and Hedric carried the telescope and its stand back inside. They left it in the drawing-room, as carrying it upstairs without waking any of the sleepers would be difficult. "How I should love to have a permanent observatory..." Hedric murmured wistfully as she locked the windows and closed the curtains for the final time. She was not sure how to answer this, so merely wished him a quiet, "Good-night—and thank you."

※

It seemed that Hedric, too, had risen too late for dining-room breakfast, and in the end they ate ad hoc at the kitchen table, Rhenya fussing over them. Jerya noticed, approvingly, that he seemed perfectly at ease with the informality. Then, somehow, it became the plan that they should take a walk together.

'That Knowe seems like it might give some view over the Vale," he said a moment after exiting.

Jerya did not particularly wish to go up to the Knowe with him. She seldom went there, in company or alone, preferring not to be reminded of her parting from Rodal. But she could not think of any good pretext for avoiding it, and he was already bending his steps toward it.

When the path narrowed, he deferred politely, leaving her a few paces ahead of him as they came to the fence that encircled the base of the Knowe. Without thinking she climbed over the stile. He was smiling as he followed her. "Forgive me if I presume, Miss Delven, but I say this as a scientist, as a dispassionate observer: you are a most unusual young lady."

"How so, sir?"

"What other young lady would willingly stay out half the night—in temperatures rapidly approaching freezing—to observe stars and nebulae? What other young lady would join in carrying the instruments back indoors, having sent the slaves to bed at a civilised hour? And what other young lady would spring over a stile like that without waiting for a gentleman to assist her?"

I've crossed the mountains, with a load on my back; fifty pounds or more, when we set out. I've descended steep, soaking wet rock—and helped Railu do the same. Why should I balk at a simple stile?

She said none of it, merely, lightly, "And how do you suppose young ladies manage when they go walking without young gentlemen to leap to their assistance at every obstacle?" She had lived almost ten years at Duncal, and she had established a simple principle: *watch; listen; learn*. She had also read, or at least begun, a number of novels deemed suitable for the genteel female, which she found as substantial as meringue but far less digestible. She had a very good idea how young ladies were supposed to talk with young gentlemen, the euphemisms and circumlocutions and allusions that might be artfully deployed. There was even a kind of artful satisfaction in the crafting of an elegant phrase.

She did, however, have a suspicion that she had let her guard slip a little, last night, caught up as she had been in the joy of observing. But that, surely, was all the more reason to be circumspect and ladylike today. Still, she would not pretend to infirmity or ignorance she did not possess.

"Well," he was saying now, with a lightness to match her own, "How I might imagine it is one thing. But you ask a question which seems to admit of scientific scrutiny."

"How so?"

"You imply, Miss Delven, that young ladies may behave differently when gentlemen are present, and when they are not. As a scientist, I ask how we should verify this proposition, and observe with precision what form these differences take. But this poses a conundrum; as a scientist, I may hypothesise; as a gentleman myself, I cannot observe how young ladies behave in the absence of gentlemen. One might perform some observations clandestinely, I suppose, but that seems somewhat... unsavoury."

They started up the slope, Jerya picking up her skirts where dew lingered in the longer grass. "It seems to me that there is an obvious solution to your conundrum."

"There is? I confess it escapes me."

"Why, sir, you merely employ one of the young ladies as your observer."

He stopped, laughing too much to continue. He was laughing at himself, she thought, and that was admirable. "My word, Miss Delven, you completely confound me. And you shame me, that I should not think of it. Why should not a young lady—a keen-eyed and observant young lady, such as yourself?—yes, such a person would be the perfect observer."

"She would," she said, as they began to climb again, "But I would not."

"Why not, pray? You seem admirably qualified, in my estimation."

"You are too kind, sir. But why not? Because I am rarely alone in the company of other young ladies." There had been Nielle, but Grevel's dismissal had meant the loss of Nielle too. Her wounded look as the carriage rolled away still haunted Jerya, far more than her husband's baleful glare. What Nielle had not known was that the Squire had been inclined to press charges, and that it was Jerya who had pleaded for clemency. Repaying all he could, and being dismissed without a character, would make it hard enough for the man to provide for his wife and family.

Hedric broke in on her brief reverie. "Well, that is indeed a considerable impediment in this particular case. Though I should say it might be less so for an aspiring astronomer."

She said nothing. They climbed the steepest section, where the path became a clear slash angling across the slope, in silence. Then, as they met easier gradients just below the first of the trees, he said, "Miss Delven... I should like to ask you something. You may, however, find this intrusive, if not impudent, and you must feel free not to answer."

"Please, ask your question."

"Well, it is... I am not mistaken, am I, in thinking that you were once a slave?"

"*That* is your impudent question? It's a matter of public record."

"True, of course." He bowed his head. "But I did envisage that you might prefer not to be reminded of it."

"Sir, I am reminded of it every day. Every day I see, I speak with, I frequently work with, those who were slaves alongside me—and who are enslaved still."

"Yes. Yes, of course. Forgive me, Miss Delven. I failed to anticipate... one so rarely meets a freed slave, excepting those of an advanced age."

"Were I of a cynical disposition, I might suggest that this is because few owners see fit to free slaves who are still capable of sustained work."

"Quite so... indeed I have never met a freed person of my own age, or even close to it, before. Yes, Miss Delven, a penetrating observation."

"You flatter me, sir," she said, and meant it. To her it seemed blindingly obvious. But then she had not grown up in a slave society, and perhaps one should give credit to those, like Hedric, who were prepared to question even a portion of its assumptions.

"No flattery, I assure you," he said firmly.

On the drier ground beneath the trees there was no obvious path among the litter of old leaves and strewings of beech-mast, but she knew with a heavy sense of inevitability that he would be drawn to the same clearing where she had once parted from Rodal. *Well, I suppose I must go there some time.*

"My circumstances are unusual," she said, in the most neutral voice she could manage.

"Well, indeed. One might even venture to describe them as unique. As you yourself are, in my estimation, unique. Though both, perhaps, should be less so..."

"You intrigue me, sir..."

"I own slaves, of course," he said, sitting down on the very stump where Rodal had once sat. Reluctantly, she hitched her skirts to sit on one of the great logs, facing him, a couple of yards away. "I endeavour to offer them every possible consideration, just as your employers do here. But... this is something I have said to very few, Miss Delven. I have no doubt that you understand the delicacy, and will be most circumspect about speaking of it to others... I should like to do more."

"More...?"

He shrugged heavily. "But I am constrained... would you indulge me? I know I alluded to my circumstances last night, but may I offer a fuller account?" She nodded. "Thank you, Miss Delven. My late father was a liberal-minded man, as well as a man of science; he believed much as your employers do. But now I am dependent on my uncle, my mother's brother, and he is a man of very different stripe."

She understood dependency. She might be free—she certainly had more freedom than Railu or Rhenya—but she was dependent on Duncal. There were few opportunities for employment for independent women; fewer still for those who bore the label 'freed'. Still, how a man like Hedric, who could ride in on his own horse, who owned slaves, might be dependent, was not so clear to her.

"My father was a liberal-minded man, as I say, but also a cautious man, and not a wealthy one. His estate was—is—no larger than this one, perhaps even a little smaller. And, being a cautious man, he left it to me, but in trust until I am twenty-eight, that being the age at which he inherited. Before that day, still the best part of two years away, if I do anything that my uncle disapproves of, he could very easily tighten the restrictions under which I am allowed to enjoy the benefits and income of the estate.

"But that is not all, Miss Delven. I am also my uncle's heir, as his will stands presently. He is not an elderly man, he is still in his fifties, but he is not in the best of health. As well as suffering from gout, he is apoplectic by nature; his own father was carried off by an apoplectic fit before he was sixty. His doctor advises him to avoid occasions of anger and, as a dutiful nephew I counsel the same, but..."

He smiled slightly. "As a scientist, I must question the theory of the four temperaments, yet my uncle does fit the description of the choleric: quick to anger, impatient, impulsive. A man who might easily change his will were his nephew to do anything of which he disapproved—such, for example, as *publicly* espousing any movement for the betterment of slaves, or evincing any disapproval of his treatment of his own slaves... I walk on eggshells, Miss Delven, whenever I am around him, and that is one reason why I travel as much as I am able, though far less than I might wish. Naturally, I send back reports of my meetings with fellow men of science, of our discussions and experiments and observations, but I say nothing of my *other* discussions."

He smiled again; a brief, shy, almost sad smile. "I have no doubt he would be distinctly perturbed were he to learn of this meeting, or of the time that we spent alone last night. A freed-woman—let alone one so young, or so recently freed—"

"—Nine years does not seem so recent to me."

"Perhaps not; but had you been ninety years free, it would not be enough for my uncle. No, he would not consider such a one to be a suitable companion. I am sure he would be more than perturbed were he to know anything of the direction of our conversation.

"I think, Miss Delven, I can safely presume that no word of our encounters will reach him, or I should feel that I am taking a profound risk in speaking to you. Perhaps some residue of that feeling lingers anyway. Perhaps that accounts for my sense of—" He broke off, looked away. She thought she detected a faint heightening of colour in the cheek now presented to her.

After a moment he looked at her again. "Well... it would of course be despicable to wish for the early demise of any man. And yet... and yet, Miss Delven, against that, is one not obliged to consider the changes that might be wrought in the wake of his passing? One need think no further than the condition of the slaves on his estates—slaves numbering, in all, almost two thousand. A new owner, a more liberal owner, could swiftly implement profound changes for those benighted souls. Is it, then, wicked of me to contemplate the likelihood of a second apoplectic seizure? In the light of the consequences that might flow from it?"

She considered this. She was not much disposed to think in terms of 'wickedness'. In Delven they had used simpler terms: truth, lies, right, wrong.

"If you're asking me for moral counsel, sir," she said at last, "I fear I may be of little help to you. But I am minded... when my friend and I were taken by the freebooters, we were all but starved for more than a day and a half. On the first day we were carried for hours on the backs of horses, face-down behind the saddle; on the second, we were strung behind them and forced to follow, day-long, at a pace faster than any natural walk. When we arrived in Drumlenn, late in the day, we were thrown behind bars. We were fed at last, after a fashion, but we had no place to... to relieve ourselves save in a bucket, and the only privacy for this was for one to stand before the other and shield her as best she could. And both the freebooters and the men of the Slave-market would repeatedly remind us that there was a great deal more that they could do to us and that they only restrained themselves to preserve whatever market value we might have.

"You look horrified, sir, as well you might. But throughout all this I told myself, and I told Railu, that it would pass. It was hard to believe it myself, many times, but I held to that belief... and, in the end, it did pass. And I remember it now, all of it, the rough hands, the rougher words, falling to my knees in the road and being dragged along before the horse could be halted... I remember it all, but only as images, as sounds. I do not remember exactly what the pain felt like."

"Perhaps the mind has mercy," he said quietly, clearly shaken.

"Perhaps it does, sir. But that is not... The agony passes, but what does not pass... On the day of the sale we were paraded on a platform. When no-one offered a bid, they stripped our clothes from us, exhibited us stark naked. Naked but for our chains, of course, and for the placards that declared we were Lot Four. And had not Squire Duncal and his lady put in a bid we would have been sold to some youths who... well, I leave to your imagination what they wished to use us for.

"And yet, all that—that too, passes. But what does not pass—" She could contain herself no more, sprang to her feet, paced about the clearing. She stopped, looking out through the trees over the Vale, dappled with cloud-shadows; the same two trees between which Rodal had stepped, nine years ago, into the misty rain.

"What does not pass," she said, not turning her head, "Is that the two of us were *sold*. Sold, and bought, for less than the price of the clothes I am wearing now."

"Miss Delven, I..." He faltered.

"You said that you would wish to do more," she continued. "More than merely treating your slaves as kindly as you could. I would know what you mean by that. Do you mean that you would free more slaves..." She hesitated, half-turning to look at him. It was the thing that she had begun to believe no-one else in this land had even conceived of. "Or do you mean that you would wish to abolish the institution of slavery itself?"

He sat silent for long moments before he spoke again. "Indeed you intrigue me, Miss Delven. It is.... how long did you say it was since your manumission? Nine years, I believe?"

"Indeed." It was easy to remember; just a little longer than Embrel had been alive.

"Well, nine years is a good time, and many a man counts his entire schooling shorter than that. But you have not had the benefit of school, have you?" *Four months in the College of Dawnsingers*, she thought, but she could not speak of that, to him, or to anyone. Even Railu was reluctant to speak of it, these days. "And no-one has tutored you?"

"My employers have helped me with some things. And I have been reading my way through the Squire's library, and have gradually acquired a few books of my own." Only this year, the tally had passed twenty-three: the total number of books that Delven had possessed.

"But most of your time has been taken up with your secretarial duties, I am sure. And governess to the boy, too... It is evident to me that you are central both to the running of this estate and to The Work. Yet, had I known nothing of the—ah—unusual... your unusual background... I should have had no reason to suppose that you have not enjoyed an education the equal of any young lady in the province."

She pondered how to reply to this. Modesty might counsel saying nothing, but that might seem impolite. And she found that she did not want to seem impolite to this eager, earnest young man.

"You used the word 'unusual', sir—and I believe I have said before, my circumstances are unusual."

"Indeed, Miss Delven, but... well, I can conceive of but two explanations. Either you have learned at a quite prodigious rate since your manumission—or you have somehow acquired some prior education even as a slave."

Oh, there's a third, she thought. *Can you not see it?* But she really dare not speak it. Not yet. She would know him a great deal better before she risked any such revelation. That she could even contemplate such a possibility was itself novel, and unsettling—though also strangely exhilarating.

Instead, thinking to deflect the conversation at least a little, she said, "I believe I am right in thinking that the law forbids any free person to teach a slave to read and write and calculate."

"Quite so."

"But am I also right in thinking that the law makes no other prohibition on educating slaves?"

"No," he said. "Again, you are correct." He looked at her with what she took to be surmise, and she thought, *not deflected enough*. Quickly she went on, "I have, for instance, seen and heard slaves who are—to my ears, at least—accomplished musicians. And I wondered, sir, believing as you do, whether your slaves receive a deeper education than the average?"

"As to that," he said, "It can hardly be said that 'a deeper education than the average' means anything at all, when the average is as close to nothing as makes no real difference."

CHAPTER 2

HEDRIC

There were several matters that required consideration, but his thoughts would keep straying to one particular subject. *Miss Jerya Delven*.

He could not help it; she was, as he had remarked, a most unusual young woman. Perhaps it had been indiscreet to say so, but she had not seemed to mind.

Of course, she was as tall as he, though hardly unique in that. She was, he thought, also a few years older. Neither were generally reckoned desirable attributes in a potential... he checked himself. It was far too soon to be thinking along any such lines. And yet...

He was almost twenty-six years of age. He had a reasonable property of his own, and there were many young ladies to whom Mistress of Kirwaugh would be a most appealing title. But there was the prospect of one vastly more imposing: *Countess of Skilthorn*. Twenty-six, and single, and heir to an Earldom; he knew very well that in all likelihood he was presently the most eligible young man in the Principality of Denvirran; indeed, one of the most eligible in all the Principalities.

His uncle's insistence on seeing him regularly had many disadvantages, but there was this to be said for it; it kept him away from Society. No one would blame him for paying due attention to his uncle, who was well known to be ailing. He might hope that his diligent attendance was ascribed to the sincere concern of an affectionate nephew, but he had few illusions that many people would suspect more mercenary motives.

In a way he could hardly blame them. Whatever might be said of his motives, he did very much want to inherit. It felt more like a duty than any cause for pleasurable anticipation, but still...

He knew that if he displeased his uncle in any way—and who could be certain what might do that?—his cousin Ferrowby could be named heir in his stead. Ferrowby, being older than Hedric, believed the title should be his by rights; but Hedric's mother had been the elder of the Earl's sisters, and in the absence of a brother (or, of course, a son) the Earl had taken the view that her descendants had precedence. It had not stood in Ferrowby's favour that his mother had complained loudly about this while her sister, Hedric's mother, was scarcely cold in her grave.

Hedric felt less that he wanted to inherit for his own sake, more—much more—that it was imperative that cousin Ferrowby not become the next Earl. Ferrowby was a man in much the same mould as his uncle; and that, exactly that, was why it would be such an unwished-for outcome. Fortunately, if the Earl had ever felt true affection for anyone, that person had been his older sister; and Ferrowby's mother's ill-timed and utterly ill-judged plaint had offended him deeply. Far from advancing her son's cause, she had retarded it severely.

But now the Earl was sick, and his temper more volatile than ever, and Hedric was no longer sure that an offence more than twenty years old still carried decisive weight. His hold on the inheritance could not be reckoned secure, and therefore he had to do everything he could to stay on the right side of his uncle. And with that in mind, any association with Miss Jerya Delven demanded most careful consideration.

The Earl might be virtually bedridden these days, had certainly not been out of doors, except in a wheeled chair, for many months; but there were plenty who would be pleased to feed gossip into his ear: Ferrowby's mother was still not welcome at Skilthorn, but Ferrowby himself was received on occasion. There was also a certain young lady who was known to entertain hopes of Ferrowby, and to her, and her extensive family, any possibility of a revision of the will was of surpassing interest. They, and their friends, and others whose motives might vary, would surely all take an active interest in any suggestion that Hedric might have blotted his copybook.

Too obvious an association with Squire Duncal might itself be risky. The Squire and his Lady were open, in a way Hedric dare not be, in promoting the amelioration of the condition of the enslaved. Being gentry rather than nobility, their names might not be known to Ferrowby or his circle, but even that was not a certainty.

Fortunately visits could be justified on scientific grounds. The Squire did have an uncommonly fine telescope, for an amateur, and Duncal's elevation genuinely offered better seeing than most places. It was not actually much higher than Kirwaugh, but something about its position between the Vale and the foothills of the Dividing Range seemed to give more clear nights.

Hedric did also have genuine reason to travel to Denvirran on occasion, and Duncal was conveniently placed on the natural route between Kirwaugh and the city. Who was to know if he chose to break the journey there rather than one of the inns in Drumlenn? Duncal and his Lady understood his situation, and were hardly disposed to gossip anyway; and he felt sure Miss Jerya Delven was not the gossipy type, nor that she had any connection, however tenuous, with Ferrowby or any of his associates.

That visits to Denvirran also exposed him to social obligation was a more mixed blessing. Hedric hardly considered himself an unsocial man, though no one would call him gregarious. Quiet conversation with like-minded men, men of science and learning, over a decent meal and a glass or two, was much more to his taste than balls or parties.

Here he paused to reflect that quiet conversation with *women* of learning had previously been conspicuously absent from his life. For the first time he asked himself why that might be; and he was sufficiently a man of science to conceive several plausible hypotheses.

Returning to his prior train of thought, he acknowledged the less comfortable side of social obligation, especially as his conspicuously eligible status made him an object of great interest to numerous young ladies, not to mention their mothers, and often, in consequence, their fathers, brothers, uncles, and sundry other relations.

It was not that he had any essential objection to young ladies. A fox might have no objection to a hound if they met as individuals; but when there was a whole pack of them being worked up by huntsmen and whippers-in... Perhaps an overwrought metaphor, but he had always felt more sympathy for the fox than gentlemen were supposed to admit.

He thought again of the words he had used, just a few hours ago: *You imply, Miss Delven, that young ladies may behave differently when gentlemen are present, and when they are not.* It was quite true but, for himself, he could only observe how they behaved when he was present. And it was his undeniable observation that young ladies, in general, behaved as if they knew nothing of science. For the most part, they seemed to make a point of flaunting their ignorance; even to delight in it—and, still more bamboozling, to behave as if they fully expected *him* to be equally delighted.

He had almost resigned himself to the thought that the most he could reasonably hope for in a wife was one who did not cherish her ignorance but humbly submitted to instruction. It was encouraging to find that there was at least one young woman who not only already knew what a nebula was, and how to adjust the focus on a telescope, but showed an unembarrassed appetite for further learning.

Quite how she, a former slave, had acquired the learning she already possessed was quite a mystery. How had she even learned to read in the first place? He had gained no inkling that the Squire had given significant instruction; allowing her free run of his library seemed to be the extent of his contribution. If he, or Lady Pichenta, had done much more than that, Hedric thought that Miss Delven would have acknowledged it.

Clearly she was remarkable, but was it to be supposed that she was entirely unique? Perhaps, he conjectured, what set her apart was not her appetite for learning, but rather her willingness to let him see it. She herself had hinted at this in saying that other young ladies might be equally capable of negotiating a stile when not constrained by the presence of a gentleman.

He supposed that was encouraging. It suggested that there might be other young ladies who shared her appetite for learning. Perhaps they might not already know what a nebula was, but they might be both keen to find out *and* capable of grasping the scientific background.

And some of those (currently hypothetical) young ladies would surely be more *suitable* than Miss Jerya Delven.

Remarkable as she was, and admirable as she was, he knew those qualities would count for naught with his uncle. They would count for little enough anyway, but would be entirely negated by her social standing, or lack of it. A woman of common birth, even freeborn, would already be a lot for the Earl to swallow; nobility should marry nobility, or at the very least the better sort of gentry. Hedric was perfectly entitled in law to marry any free woman he chose (*were she to accept*, he qualified carefully). But were he to announce that his intended was a *freed* woman, he had little doubt that the Earl would change his will just as soon as his attorney could be summoned to Skilthorn.

He sighed. He thought, not for the first time, that life would be simpler in many ways if he never married at all. It would not please the Earl, who had oft expressed a wish that his heir wed 'while I'm still here to see it'. Besides, he rather thought he should marry, and for exactly the reason that he had heard cited a thousand times; his responsibility to produce an heir.

Supposing he became Earl, he could not then leave the estate to just any-one; certainly not without protracted legal struggles. Various entails from the wills of past Earls, perpetuated in marriage deeds, stipulated that only incidental bequests could be made outside the Skilthorn bloodline. Apart from some distant cousins he barely knew, that line's only living mem-bers were himself, the Earl, Ferrowby and Ferrowby's mother. Ferrowby pursued similarly unhealthy habits to their uncle, so Hedric, younger and more temperate, thought his odds of outliving his cousin were pretty good; but if Ferrowby married and produced an heir, the picture would change.

Even a female would do at a pinch, though a proxy would have to hold the property. Unless he himself also produced a legitimate heir, his wishes would be overridden and the estate would, eventually, land in the hands of a man he knew and—to put it at its mildest—did not trust, or in those of some other, unknown, relative.

In fact, he thought now, if Ferrowby were to wed while Hedric still showed no sign of impending nuptials, that too could very plausibly prompt the Earl to change his will. And if Ferrowby and that hypothetical bride were to produce an heir, it would go from plausible to racing certainty.

In a galling irony, the present Earl, so ardent an advocate of marriage for his heir-apparent, had himself never married. Indeed, he too must once have been the most eligible young man in the Principality. But then it was his wont to expect others to live by standards from which he freely exempted himself.

Beyond doubt, he had fathered numerous children, all slaveborn. Some owners had been known to acknowledge their paternity, confer favoured status, to free their progeny when they came of age. However, Hedric had never heard of any such person being named as heir, and though he paid little attention to gossip, such a thing would surely be a prodigious scandal and widely talked of.

The Earl, however, had never acknowledged such offspring, except in the negative sense that any girl who had the unmitigated gall to find herself with child would be dismissed from the household and redeployed in the fields, the mill, or some other outpost; even, sometimes, sold to another estate. Even so, Hedric knew enough about probability to recognise a statistical certainty. He would have met some of these progeny in his visits to Skilthorn, and they were his first cousins, just as closely related as Ferrowby himself.

One more question to worry at; if and when he himself became Earl, could he, should he, seek out those cousins? Would it be of any benefit to them, especially if they were unaware of their parenthood, or would it merely make them uncomfortable? Perhaps this was a question he could refer to Lallon, assuming him to be fully recovered when he got back to Kirwaugh. Lallon had been bent on attending Hedric as usual on this trip, despite the streaming cold he had contracted, and had only desisted when Hedric had cited the increased risk that he himself would also catch it.

Lallon, usually, was as close-mouthed a man as Hedric had ever known. It made him an ideal confidant, innately trustworthy and vanishingly unlikely to let slip any secrets by accident. He said little, but listened always. Not only a confidant, he was, really, Hedric's closest friend; not a thing many men would say about a slave. It crossed Hedric's mind that it might have been fitting if Lallon were one of those cousins; but he knew Lallon's parentage and both were Kirwaugh slaves.

He came to a cross-roads and almost laughed out loud. It seemed all too pointed a metaphor for where he stood in his life.

He could do nothing about those cousins unless and until he became Earl, and they could hardly be more than a few handfuls. There were fifteen hundred enslaved on the Skilthorn estate, and he could make a profound difference to the lives of every single one; but to do so he had to inherit.

Hedric steered his horse onto the left-hand road, thinking that nothing seemed more likely to imperil his standing as heir than pursuing an association with Miss Jerya Delven.

But... *Damn it, does a man not have a right to a little happiness? Is it unreasonable to wish for a congenial companion in the endeavours that lie ahead?*

He had convinced himself, a mile or so back, that Miss Delven was proof that a woman could be the kind of companion he had scarcely dared dream of. Well, he argued now, if she could, surely others could too?

But there was the rub. Hypothetically, there must be others; but where were they? He had never met anyone like her. Was it simply that other young women, especially the fine ladies to whom everyone was so anxious he should be introduced, felt obliged to hide their light under a bushel? Were they merely awaiting the right words of encouragement to throw off their disguise and emerge like a butterfly from a chrysalis? (A process he had first watched, spellbound, as a boy of seven or eight; a memory that stood undimmed.)

It was a consoling notion, but he could not help thinking that if they were concealing their true natures in this way, they were doing a very thorough job of it. Still, it could do no harm to consider how he might best offer the required encouragement to engender such a revelation. It might, at least, add interest to those social obligations.

And, viewed in that light also, it could do no harm to maintain his regular visits to Denvirran city. At least monthly, so that he could keep up his attendance at the principal meetings of the Denvirran Society for Natural Philosophy. If other business occasionally required additional trips, or that the regular visits be extended, that would be well enough also.

And if he was to continue travelling this road regularly, what could be more reasonable than to break the long day's journey at Duncal? There was that telescope, after all, and last night's sky had been as clear as he had seen for a long time.

CHAPTER 3

JERYA

SIX MONTHS LATER

"How's yowr courtin' goin'?" asked Rhenya.

Jerya laughed. "Courting? No, we're just friends." *And maybe collaborators*, she added to herself.

"Just friends? Tain't how he sees it, ask me."

"You think so?"

"I seen how he looks at yow."

Jerya thought about this—*how* does *he look at me, then?*—but only for a moment. With a knowing smile, Rhenya added, "And I seen how yow looks at him." That was an order of magnitude more confounding.

"Under the mentorship of Ernespie himself, who measured the distance to the singular moon, Cintilla. Look, it's here, in the *Proceedings* from '94."

Jerya looked at the journal, skimmed the opening page, turned it carefully. Here there was a diagram, showing just how the observations had been made. The basics of triangulation, she had understood since her first lessons with the Cartography Tutor—what was her name? Skarat.

She had learned about the principle of parallax with Jossena. The distances to the planets were gauged this way, but then you had a baseline as wide as the diameter of Earth's orbit, many millions of miles. That created new problems in calculation, because of course the planets also moved, but it was possible, and repeated measurements allowed for further refinement.

There were sections devoted to each of the considerations the experimenters faced: synchronisation of chronometers, for example: for ultimate accuracy it was essential that observations be precisely simultaneous... Allowance for the curvature of the Earth (but that, she thought, assumed in turn that you had an accurate figure for that dimension!)... Calibration of measured angles by observation against the fixed stars...

She looked up, aware that in another moment she would have been entirely absorbed. "It occurs to me that there is a good reason to repeat this experiment."

"And what is that, Miss Jerya?"

"It is generally said, is it not, that Cintilla is a fragment of what was once a single moon? But it moves much faster across the sky than the other remnants, the Three. And the general belief—supported by these observations, I suppose—is that this means it's much closer."

"You *suppose*?"

"Well, this gives us a distance for Cintilla. I haven't seen a comparable distance for the others, the Three. And if they are much more distant, then presumably it would be harder to achieve a reliable figure for their distance."

"Yes," Hedric said, nodding, looking delighted. Delighted with *her*, she felt somehow. She wasn't quite sure exactly how she felt about that. "If they are, as we assume, so much more distant then... to achieve a precise measurement, we would require a correspondingly longer baseline. Which, admittedly, creates obvious difficulties."

"Well, how long was the baseline they used?"

She skimmed the article again, but Hedric had the answer already. "Eighty miles."

Jerya knew where to lay her hands on most things in the library, and the general map of the Five Principalities was no exception. In a moment she had it spread on the table, and between them they weighted the corners to stop it re-rolling itself. "Look where we are—and look here. On the coast, a little North of Sessapont. It's on the same line of latitude, but what's the distance? Must be close on three hundred miles."

She turned to another drawer, found a pair of dividers, walked them along the grid-line. "More than two hundred and ninety, at any rate. The better part of four times the original baseline. I have to ask why the revered Ernespie did not avail himself of the opportunity."

"As to that," he said, "I have a suggestion. The length of the baseline can be determined only as accurately as maps allow. I suspect when he performed his original observations accurate maps of other Principalities would not have been readily available."

Jerya nodded. That made perfect sense. The Five Principalities had not always lived in harmony.

Already her mind was running ahead to the next issue. "Presumably the observations also need to be synchronised. The moons move, after all."

"Indeed."

"So we would require the most accurate chronometers we can get." She sighed to herself. *Railu and I had Guild-made watches that were better than any I've seen here. Did those ruffians who took us even realise what they'd stolen?* Well, that was a question whose answer she was highly unlikely ever to discover. Better to focus on something where answers were achievable.

"If one were setting up observations three hundred miles apart," she said slowly, thinking it out, "One could at least attempt readings for the Three as well."

Hedric nodded. "Though one imagines that might be more suited to a baseline of, say, three thousand."

Three hundred miles was one thing; it was feasible within the borders of the land. Three thousand, however, would be a voyage into the unknown, or the rumoured. Jerya tried to recall maps of the Sung Lands that she had seen, ten years ago. That study hadn't been a high priority during her time in the College; she had learned more about how maps were made than what they actually depicted. Still, she had looked at maps, and she had a sense of the distance between Delven and Carwerid. She'd been interested to compare that against the overall scale of the Sung Lands. Now, she had also perused maps of the Five Principalities, and had a sense of how the two lands were situated. Even *one* thousand miles, she thought, would take you beyond the Westernmost point of the one, or the Easternmost extremity of the other, into the realms of sailors' tales, of the barely-known, or the unreliably-reported. *Three* thousand miles would take you far beyond anything known. At this latitude it was getting close to a quarter of the way around the globe.

You don't even know what lies beyond the mountains fifty miles West of here, she thought, looking at Hedric. Sometimes she felt she understood exactly why the Dawnsingers had kept so much knowledge secret. Now, though, she found herself wondering how he would react if she blurted out the truth. A truth only she and Railu, in all the Five Principalities, were aware of.

Instead, she just said, "If only that were possible, sir. But I was only thinking of the value there might be in repeating the original observations."

"Because...?"

"Verification, of course, and with a baseline the best part of four times as long we can hope for greater precision. But also... we've said that both the One and the Three were once part of a single Moon. In which case, either the Three have since moved further away, or the One has, by some means, come much closer to the Earth."

"And which possibility do you think more likely?"

"I couldn't say... But supposing that the One, Cintilla, *has* moved closer, is it still approaching, or is its orbit now stable?"

"My word! Of course. Why did I not think of that?"

Why did not the great Ernespie think of it, for that matter? she wondered. But Ernespie was a great man, and dead, and therefore probably unassailable.

"And this can be done within the borders of this land," she said. "If Ernespie could obtain clear differences in angle over an eighty-mile baseline, then surely we can over three hundred."

Hedric looked at her, the reflection of the window sliding across his lenses. "We?"

"Well, sir, if I am competent to plan such a proceeding—even to critique the methods of the great Ernespie—I am surely competent to carry it out in the field."

"Oh, Miss Jerya, rest assured that I have no doubt about your competence. No doubts whatsoever; you are the equal of any observer I have worked with, and better than most. No, the difficulties which present themselves to my mind are of another order entirely. Mundane, beyond question, and no doubt regrettable, but nonetheless significant."

She gave him a severe look. "Miss Jerya," he said. "You understand that there are people who would find fault in our sitting alone together like this. Who would certainly object to our solitary walks, unobserved by any other; who would no doubt think it scandalous that we spend long hours together, alone, under the stars, *in the dark*... You understand that it is only possible for us to do these things because of the liberal and tolerant ways of your employers, my kind and frequent hosts, and because there is no one here who will blab about our doings."

Yes, she thought, his visits had become frequent in the past months. She realised suddenly how much she had come to look forward to them.

And she recalled what Rhenya had said.

But he was still speaking. "Such liberalism and tolerance are, alas, the exception, not the rule, across this land. It is simply not done for a respectable young lady to travel across the provinces alone, or accompanied only by a young, unrelated, man."

She almost laughed. How, by what tortuous route, had she become 'respectable'? Or, indeed, a 'young lady'? She wanted to say this, to say that she cared not a fig for the opinions of pinched old women and narrow-minded writers of letters to newspapers, but she saw that another thought had seized him.

"Of course..." he said, sounding suddenly breathless. "There is one way that you could accompany me on such a journey—on any journey."

"And what is that?"

"Why, Miss Jerya... were you my wife it would be perfectly simple."

She stared. An expression she had heard somewhere jumped unbidden into her mind: 'swept off her feet'. But this—it was more as if Hedric had swept himself off his own feet. He seemed even more dazed than she.

It did not last long. He shook his head, then laughed softly, "Oh, a fine idea, but there is one problem, is there not?"

"Only one?" she said, with a smile, but he was not to be deflected. She straightened her face. "Your uncle."

"Just so. My uncle. Were I to marry—or even to become betrothed to—a former slave, he would surely disinherit me in a heartbeat."

He turned his gaze full on her. "For myself, I could live with that. But when I think of the good that could be done with the wealth and prestige of the Earldom... and weighing what I know of my cousin Ferrowby... have I the right to throw up that responsibility in pursuit of my own happiness?"

She reached for his hand. They had not touched very often, and always decorously. Now the touch felt different.

But still... *wife*. It was not a word she had ever imagined applying to herself. If she had remained in Delven, never been Chosen, then it was possible she would have ended up as Rodal's Own; but that prospect had been wiped away almost before she had even considered it.

And this, too... well, it was surely out of the question while his uncle still lived. After that... but that might be ten years yet. And Hedric would surely be under pressure to wed someone more *suitable*. She smiled wryly to herself. *Could there be anyone* less *suitable?*

No, it was but a momentary fancy. Ten seconds later he had laughed at it, and begged her to forget that he had ever even mentioned it.

Jerya had laughed too, but she was not so sure that his words would be quite so easy to forget. Nor Rhenya's. *'I seen how he looks at yow. And I seen how yow looks at him.'*

✳

"Of course, in purely practical terms, the thing requires one observer at each end of the baseline."

"Synchronous observations..."

"And thus you would have no need to travel far."

"Does it not occur to you that I might want to?" she said with a snap that obviously dismayed him. "Why should the woman always be the one who stays?"

"Miss Jerya," he said, hastily seeking to smooth ruffled feathers, "Far be it from me to say that it should be so. I merely observe that as we are presently situated, it *is* so. Both my sex and my station in society—"

"—Yes, I know how this society works." She knew her tone was still peevish. "That doesn't mean I have to be happy about it. Listen, Hedric. For the first nineteen years of my life I never roved farther from home than a day's walk. For the last ten my range has hardly been any greater. But in between, for a few months, I travelled. And it chafes me to be told I can't do more..."

"Miss Jerya," he said solemnly. "You know that it is not I who tells you so, don't you? On the contrary, were we both free, I would like nothing better than to travel the length and breadth of the land with you."

"I thought we *were* free," she said.

"We are not slaves, that is true. We are called free. But we aren't, really, are we?"

She understood what he was trying to say, but she could not simply accept it, not at this moment. "Your freedom is not without limit, no, but it seems to me that you still have a great deal more than I do; the freedom to travel unaccompanied, for example. And at the same time I have a great deal more freedom than Railu or Rhenya."

He accepted the correction, casting his eyes down. It was one of the things she liked about him, that he would accept amendment from one whom society would brand inferior, by both rank and gender. Few men, she thought, would take it so graciously; even the Squire was apt to frown and to become testy for a while. But then there were few men like Hedric.

And still the thought came back, sidling again into her mind as soon as her thoughts weren't fully occupied with baselines and synchronisation of observation. *How* does *he look at me?*

CHAPTER 4

JERYA

J erya was not a dutiful reader of newspapers. It was something she did when she had time, and often a day or two after the papers arrived, when they had found their way from the morning-room to the kitchen. Rhenya would use them for lighting fires, and for packing around anything delicate that must be transported.

It was just so this particular morning. She had wandered into the kitchen, hoping for coffee. Rhenya, busy with preparations for the midday meal, only nodded at her. *You can make your own but stay out of my way*, Jerya translated. Halfway through spooning grounds into the chamber of the coffee-maker, her eye was seized by a word on the front of the paper in the kindling bin. It wasn't even the largest type on the half-page she could see, but somehow it snagged her attention.

A word you did not normally see in the headlines. *Mountain.*

She hurried to get the coffee on, then extracted the paper, brushed off the sawdust, and unfolded it.

His Grace Plans New Mountain Venture ran the headline.

The piece below was brief, but lost nothing in impact.

We have today learned that His Grace the Duke of Selton is making final preparations for a new expedition into the Dividing Range. Our informant assures us that this expedition will be bigger and better-organised than any-thing before. We are as yet unable to confirm whether His Grace intends to attempt the fabled Crossing; as our readers will be well aware, many eminent persons have declared that this feat is impossible, while others have stated the opinion that entry into the Western lands would be perilous in the extreme for the health of any person foolhardy enough to attempt it.

Our readers may rest assured that we are making diligent endeavours to obtain further details and that we shall convey these to you as soon as may be.

Jerya turned, intending to run to find Railu, the only other person who would fully grasp the significance, but fortuitously she had just entered the kitchen. She brandished the paper under Railu's nose. "Read that."

They moved aside, to give Rhenya more room, then Railu lifted the paper close to her eyes. *I wonder if she needs eye-glasses?* was Jerya's sudden thought. Railu read quickly, a slight widening of the eyes the only sign of comprehension. "It doesn't say they are definitely going to attempt the Crossing."

"True, but... what time does the the afternoon diligence pass the end of the road?" she asked with sudden urgency.

"How should I know? And what are you going to do anyway?"

Rhenya had no more idea about coach-times than Railu, but Jerya decided to trust her recollection that the afternoon diligence left Denvirran at midday. It could hardly pass the Duncal turning before two of the afternoon. There was time—barely.

"Have you got paper and envelopes in your room?" she demanded.

"Of course."

"May I borrow some?"

"Gladly, but what for?"

"I need to write to Hedric."

As she scrawled a hasty note, she was debating whether it would be quicker to run down to the road-end, or ride. She decided the time it would take to saddle up outweighed any subsequent gains. It was pleasing to find that she could still run a decent pace, though she cursed the need to hold up her skirts.

There was just time to restore her breathing to something like normal before the diligence came swaying and rumbling into view. The driver pulled up with a heavy hand on the brake; any passengers would feel that, for sure. "Where goin', m'lady?"

"I'm not, but will you take a letter for me? It's to go to the Earl's house, at Skilthorn?" She fumbled in her pocket, thrust all the coins at him.

"I c'n hand it on at Blisco, m'lady. There'm a coach to Skilton from there." The man pocketed the letter, then accepted the coins. Peered at them, handed one back. She looked at it as the coach grumbled into motion again: a silver. *Bless me, an honest man...*

She returned to the house in twice the time and with a deal more than twice the decorum.

He came in the afternoon three days later. As soon as they could snatch a minute alone together she showed him the paper. Since seeing that first story, she had checked each morning, but there had been no further updates.

"All those times I've avoided talking about where I came from..."

He was quick, but his mind didn't take him all the way. "You came from somewhere up in the mountains?"

"No, I came from *beyond* the mountains. Railu too."

He stared, his face quirking oddly. Perhaps he was struggling not to laugh. She knew that anyone claiming to have come from beyond the mountains would generally be laughed out of court.

"Everyone knows there's no life West of the mountains," she said, then took a deep breath. Speak it, or not? It was surely now, or never. "And everyone on the other side knows there's no life East of them."

He was still gazing fixedly at her. But he wasn't laughing. "Can it really be true?"

"It can," she said, "But I only know one way to prove it to you."

"Then you would have me seek to join Selton's expedition?"

"No," she said. "I would have us stage our own."

"But how... *why* should we hope to succeed when many others before us have failed?"

"Because I've done it before." She wanted to shake him. He was not a stupid man—very far from it, in general—but sometimes his mind strained to grasp ideas which were obvious to her. She supposed it was a matter of different experiences; he, after all, had lived all his life in one land, one culture; she had known two. *Three* cultures, you might almost say, if you counted her few months at the College of Dawnsingers, a time which always seemed to glow with particular intensity in memory. "I know the route."

Something about the plain way she said this seemed finally to reach him. "Well, it is clear to me that you believe what you are saying. Therefore either it is true, or you are quite mad." He paused a moment, smiling, teasing by delay. "And I cannot believe that you are mad."

"Oh, thank you so kindly for that, sir."

He grinned. She never called him 'sir' any more, save in company, or in raillery.

"Well," he said, finally reaching for a chair and drawing it up to her desk. "I suppose at least that explains a few things, like how you initially learned to read. But now... what is it that you propose? And I suppose I must also ask, why the urgency?"

"I'll explain it all," she said. "But there's something I need from my room upstairs. Perhaps while I'm fetching it you could find us some drinks? This may take a while."

She had meant tea or coffee, but he had fetched wine. *Oh well*, she thought, *maybe he's right. This may go easier with a little help...*

She cleared everything from the desk, stacking account books in a corner, tipping pens and rulers and other impedimenta into the centre drawer. First she spread out a map covering the area North and West of Drumlenn.

"We have a chance; they've not started yet, and they're trying too far South anyway. Too far South for the Crossing I know, that is. For all I know there could be another route..."

"Though there have been attempts there before..."

"Under-funded and ill-prepared, they say... But, look, it says that if they are unsuccessful there this year they intend to try again in a different area. Which probably means further North."

"And that is...?"

"That is where we crossed before."

CHAPTER 5

HEDRIC

Hedric could hear the Earl long before he reached the bedroom, though he could decipher little of the tirade, distorted as it was by echoing off several walls. In any case, it was generally hard to make full sense of his uncle's wilder outbursts even when you were in the room with him.

Before he reached the door, Doctor Aiskin emerged. "Ah, Hedric," he said with easy familiarity; he had been the family physician since before Hedric was born. He was only a few years younger than the Earl, but carried his age far more lightly. "I'm glad you're here. No knowing whether he's heard a word I've said, still less whether he'll heed any of it."

"Then tell me, and I shall see what I can do."

They spent a minute or two discussing matters medical. The Earl continued to rant, making it clear there was still someone in the room with him. As the Doctor took his leave, there was a final shout and then silence. Turning towards the bedroom Hedric saw a slave-girl scurrying out. She appeared ready to flee, but stopped when she saw him.

The girl was young, sixteen or seventeen at most. The Earl still liked to surround himself with nubile females, though he could do little more than look these days. She was whey-faced and trembling. Tears tracked down plump cheeks.

"Here," he said, fishing out a handkerchief. "Dry those tears."

"Thank yow, sir," she said almost inaudibly. "But I surely couldn't." Couldn't take a gentleman's handkerchief, he supposed.

"You surely could. You surely *can*. Do you want to tell me what happened?"

"I don't know as I should, sir..."

"You know who I am, don't you? I'm his nephew. His closest living relative. I need to know, for his sake as well as yours."

"Aye, sir, but... well, it's hard to say. Shoutin' this and shoutin' that, and I can't make out half'n it... so... I's a good girl, sir, I does as I'm told, but how's I to follow orders if I can't und'stand what I's bein' told to do? And so I... I asked him, yow see, sir, asked him what he meant for me to do 'cos I hadn't understood, and he yelled at me for a stupid trull an' this an' that... I din't und'stand half on it but seemed like he was sayin' terrible things. And then he tol' me to get out."

Hedric essayed a smile. "At least you could understand that, eh?" He got the merest flicker of a smile in return, but it was progress.

Then came a new volley from within. "Who's that muttering out there?"

"It's me, Uncle!" he called.

"Hedric, is it? What're ye doing out there? Who're ye muttering with? Can't abide muttering. Skulking in shadows..."

He wanted to laugh. It was a good deal brighter before the tall window in the passage than it would be in the Earl's bedroom. "One moment, Uncle."

He turned back to the girl. "I have to go. But you take a little time to recover yourself before you go on. Sit there if you wish." He pointed to one of the chairs spaced between windows.

"I couldn't, sir, we's told not to sit on the furniture."

"And *I'm* telling you you may. But it's as you wish...."

His eyes took a moment to adjust to the dimness of the bedroom. The Earl was sitting in a high winged chair in nightshirt and dressing gown, a swollen foot propped on a stool before him. A coverlet, which presumably had been over his legs, had been thrown halfway across the room. Hedric noticed all this and more—the brandy glass on the table within reach, but the bottle removed to a sideboard—in the space of four strides across what he had long held to be the vilest carpet in the world. Surely purple and yellow were the last colours that should be seen together. *There's something to be said for closed curtains, after all.*

"Good morning, Uncle."

"What's good about it, I'd like to know? That pestilential fool of a so-called doctor telling me to lay off brandy, and then a stupid trull of a slave refusing my orders—numen, if I could stand I'd have given her a thrashing!" All that was clear enough, if you were familiar with the Earl's typically slurred delivery.

"She was only trying to understand what you require, Uncle."

"Is that what she says? Pah, they can all wrap you round their little finger. You have to let them know who's boss, boy."

Let them know who's boss: Hedric had heard this particular pearl of wisdom a thousand times. It seemed to him that in his own modest household the slaves knew perfectly well who the master was, without resort to bullying and bluster. And as often as not they knew what needed doing better than their master did.

But he bit his tongue, only saying gently, "She was trying her best."

"Trying? I don't want slaves who try, I want slaves who do as they're told."

He endeavoured to make allowances. His uncle was frequently in pain, and his body would no longer do what he wanted it to. It must gall him particularly to see the Doctor—a contemporary—still striding about like a man half his age. But the Doctor practised what he preached; moderation in all things. Moderation in anything was foreign to the Earl's nature. Besides, he had hardly been a model of sweetness and light ten years ago, when his health was still good. What allowances should have been made then?

Still, he was resolved not to alienate his uncle, so he held his peace.

"Anyway," the Earl went on, "Don't stand there looking over me, bring yourself a chair and sit down. And bring that damn brandy bottle over while you're about it."

"The Doctor says it's brandy that causes your gout."

"How would he know? Eh? How would he know? Brandy don't cause the pain; it's the only damn thing that eases it."

"If you won't take your Doctor's advice, I don't know why you bother consulting him at all," he said, but he brought the bottle.

"Neither do I! Ha, there's an idea, lad! Save myself all his fuss and bother, and save myself a small fortune on his wretched bills, too. He won't look so high and mighty when half his income dries up."

Hedric said nothing. There was plenty he could have said, but he had to tread so carefully, especially with the request he had come to make. He watched for a moment as the Earl struggled with the stopper on the bottle. He even felt a stab of pity. The attacks of gout were agonising, but intermittent; the arthritis in the hands was chronic, and getting worse.

"Here, allow me," he said. It was always a gamble whether the Earl would acquiesce, even fumble a thank-you, or rebuff him with an indignant assertion that he was 'perfectly capable, damn you'. Today it was acquiescence, though there were no thanks, only a sullen, "You do it, then."

Stopper removed, he poured a modest measure. The Earl sniffed, but said nothing. With the bottle once again in reach, he could always pour for himself. His hands worked well enough for that, as long as the stopper was loose. He raised the glass, inhaled the aroma, then took a long sip. "See? I'm not glugging it like small-beer. Moderation, like that damn fool Aiskin's always blathering about." He lifted the glass again. "A toast! To moderation."

"To moderation," Hedric echoed, though he had no glass to raise.

"Feels better already. Told you, brandy's the cure, not the cause."

Hedric, of course, didn't believe this for a moment. Even if that were true, the spirit had barely reached the stomach, never mind having time to reach the bloodstream. But his uncle believed what he chose to believe.

"Well, boy." By comparison with earlier, the Earl looked almost benign. "Did you just come to parrot Aiskin's nonsense and stick up for useless slaves, or did you want something of me?" *You usually do*, his tone implied, though Hedric thought that profoundly unfair.

On this occasion, however, he did want something. "Yes, there was something I wanted to discuss with you. An exciting prospect, but it would take me away from home for a few weeks."

"What is it? More damn stargazing?"

"No, not astronomy. I can do that very well at Drumlenn, and it fits in with trips to Denvirran."

"And I'll drop down dead on the spot, tumble flabbergasted into my grave, if you tell me you're courting a rich young lady."

"Not that, either." *Not rich, for sure... But courting? Am I?*

"It's about damn time you *were* courting someone. What are you, twenty-five?"

"Twenty-six, in fact, Uncle."

"Twenty-six! Well, never mind. Stop flammering about and tell me what it is you're proposing."

"A journey of exploration."

"Exploration? And is there any profit in it?"

"There could be. It's not certain until we get there." *That's rather in the nature of exploration, you know.*

"Hmph. A gamble, then." The Earl sipped brandy.

"Well, I suppose, but it would cost very little. And if nothing else there could always be a book of our travels. A well-received book can earn a goodly sum, and travelogues are perennially popular... You have shelves of them in your own library."

"Do I now? Never read any."

You never read anything but account books and slave registers. "Perhaps not, sir, but you *bought* them, and that's where authors earn their money."

"Got to keep up appearances. A well-stocked library, mark of a gentleman. But Dykes takes care of all that. Still, I take yer point: authors earn money, and it's a fitting occupation for a gentleman." He sipped again, then cradled the glass in both hands, looked over the rim at Hedric, eyes narrowed. "So where're ye planning on venturing? Southron Sea? Nay, you said it wouldn't cost. Chartering a ship ain't cheap."

"Indeed, sir: an enticing prospect, but expensive, as you say. No, we plan to head West. You may have seen in the paper, there are plans for a large expedition into the mountains. To look for a way across, you know."

"And ye want to join 'em?"

"No, sir, I want to *beat* them. I believe they're looking in the wrong place. I've heard some... intriguing reports that lead me to believe that the prospects are better further North. North-West of Drumlenn, in fact."

"Reports?"

Carefully, now. He could hardly reveal the true nature of his source, but then again he didn't like to tell outright lies, not even to his uncle. Not if he could possibly help it. "There are those who go a fair way into the mountains, as you know. Hunters, trappers. Crystal collectors. They know the valleys, the lower heights, better than any learned society. And I've seen a map which appears to suggest there's every chance of finding a pass."

"Hardly sounds a certainty, though."

"No, sir, but sometimes one must take a chance." Gambling was something the Earl did understand. "And, whatever the odds may be, the stake is low. Horses, warm clothing, tents, food. I have little doubt we have most of our requisites already. The main risk is that it simply turns out to be a waste of a few weeks. But imagine if we succeed... It would be all over the papers. A best-selling book. And..." He paused. This, he hoped, was the clincher. "It would be one up on His Grace of Selton."

The Earl scowled. "That jackanapes! But what's he got to do with it?"

"He's leading the other expedition."

"The one that's heading in the wrong direction?"

"Yes, sir, I believe that's exactly what they are doing."

"Well, then, damn me, what are you waiting for?"

CHAPTER 6

JERYA

"There is a difficulty, however," he said.

"I never said it would be easy."

"No, I'm sure... but that is not what I am thinking of." He gazed at her and she saw his olive cheeks grow pinker. "I am thinking of... sleeping arrangements."

"Sleeping arrangements?" It took real effort not to laugh.

"Yes, because there will be three of us, but surely it makes no sense to carry more than one tent. One quite small tent."

We didn't have a tent at all, the first time. But she said nothing, because she wanted to see where this was leading.

"And of course there would be concerns about... decorum. You might well say that no one else need know anything about it. But there are perhaps reasons why—underlying reasons—what can happen when young men and young ladies are in overly close proximity."

"We have been in close proximity before, surely," she said lightly. "Indeed, we are in close proximity now, are we not?"

His blush deepened. She wanted to take his hand and tell him, *it's all right: it's quite all right.* Was it 'decorum' that held her back?

"We are, Miss—Jerya. And I think you have no idea how much I would like to... I think you have no idea how very... *appealing* you are."

It was even harder, now, not to laugh, but she knew it would hurt him. She looked down at her lap, concentrated on her hands. She had had practice, one way or another, in hiding her feelings. As a girl of Delven, a Postulant, a Novice, a slave...

"We could take two tents, I suppose," she said when she could control her voice.

"We could," he said, but it was obvious that was not the solution he was thinking of.

"I hope you're not suggesting I don't come at all."

"It would make things simpler, in so many ways."

"*Simpler*...!" She had to move, sprang up, spun away from him.

"And yet," she said when she could speak more calmly, "You have not suggested leaving Lallon behind."

"If we did that," he said from a few paces behind her, "Then we would be two to carry the tent, rather than three."

"If it's a small tent for three, then it would be more spacious for two. Would that satisfy your need for *decorum*?" He said nothing.

"I am trying to consider all possible ..."

"*Considerations?*" she said acidly.

"Jerya, please..."

"You evidently do not realise how... offended I am. That you should consider, even for a moment, proceeding without me... how do you suppose I should feel? Do I have to remind you that this was my suggestion in the first place? Do I have to remind you that there are only two people in the Five Principalities who have made the crossing before, and you are not one of them?"

She left the room without a backward glance.

❀

He found her, half an hour later, in Duncal's little Wilderness. His face as he approached was so humble, so pleading, that her resolution to dismiss him melted away. She even acquiesced to his request to join her on the stone bench.

He pulled off his glasses and wiped them carefully as he spoke. "Please, Miss Delven, hear me out. Suggesting you don't come was *not* what was in my mind. Even if we could find the route just from the map and from your description, well, it would surely go easier to have one with us who's been there before. And we will need you even more when we reach the other side."

He was holding her hand. How had that happened? "That's all perfectly true, beyond question—but it's not... it's not the most important thing. The most important thing, Jerya, is that I *want* you there. The greatest adventure of my life..." He seemed lost in thought a moment, presumably thinking about those six words. Then he shook himself a little, almost like a wet dog. "But all of life is an adventure, is it not? I dare say you know that better than I. No, Jerya, even to contemplate crossing the mountains without you... I would not, *could* not do it...

"But merely thinking about that possibility for the merest moment showed me... and then feeling estranged from you, even only for half an hour... it all made it clearer. I don't wish to be parted from you, ever."

His grip tightened, and suddenly he was on one knee before her. "Miss Delven... Jerya... my dearest Jerya... would you do me the ineffable honour of consenting to be my wife?"

She stared, and because she did not speak, he was babbling; it would solve all the problems of the journey (which she had never seen as major obstacles anyway)... of course it would have to be secret at first... his uncle could not know...

She finally recovered the power of speech. "Wait a minute. And get up. That gravel can't be good for your knee." She matched deed to word, pulling him up by his hand. "Sit with me again.

"I thank you for your offer," she said when they were settled. "No, wait, please, do not speak. I have a few things to say and maybe none of them will make sense until I have finished them all. Make sense to *me*, at least...

"I've been a slave. Not for many months, but still... I've been paraded on a platform, I've been bought. Then I was given my freedom—but the crucial word is *given*. Only it wasn't really a gift. It was a bargain. It was freedom, yes, but... but partial, conditional. Maybe freedom is always like that—"

"Yes, but as my—"

"*Please*, I haven't finished. What does it mean, to be your wife? In a land where a woman cannot own a house, or a horse, save under some convoluted proxy arrangement; where even her own name is surrendered upon entering into marriage... in such a land, it seems to me, being a wife can't be so very different from being a slave."

She held up a hand against the protests that were surely seething inside him. "I do not mean that you want me to be that kind of wife. I think I know you better than that. I know that what you want—and, yes, what I want, too—is something different. But there's what we want and then there's what the world expects.

"So, then, what *is* marriage? I've been in this land for almost ten years but, you know, the only weddings I've attended have been slave-weddings. And we all know that marriage between slaves means as much or as little as their master allows it to mean. If it suits him, a master can dissolve a slave-marriage and sell either spouse. He can take their children and sell them. There is a man not two hours' ride from here who has done so more than once to settle a gambling debt.

"No, I know, you would never do such things. The Squire and Lady here would never do such things. And it's a prime tenet of the campaign that such practices should be outlawed.

"But you may say you and I are not slaves, and the marriage of free people is different." She shrugged. "Well, perhaps it is. But sometimes I see things that make me think it is not always so very different. Anyway, what is marriage? What is the heart of it, the core?"

Now she looked at him as if to say *you may speak*. He seemed almost startled, for a moment, then collected himself. "I suppose... the heart of the ceremony is the vows. I suppose they are the heart of the marriage as they are the heart of the wedding."

"Yes," she said, pleased; that was exactly the answer she had been looking for. "The vows... But I took a vow once before—Not a marriage vow," she added hastily, seeing his face. "But a vow that I suppose must be considered equally binding, a vow for life.

"I have said very little of my life before. Maybe more than I have said to anyone else on this side of the world—bar Railu, of course, who knows already—but still very little. And I need to rectify that before we reach the other side. There are many things you'll need to know. But the thing I must tell you right now is that I took a vow, a solemn, lifelong vow... and within a few months I broke it. Tore it to shreds and let it blow away on the wind. You need to know that about me before you ask me to make any vow to you."

He stared at her. His mouth was open but no words issued forth.

"Well," she said, "Does that make me fickle, faithless? I hate to think so. I can very easily say that vow was thrust upon me, that I had no real idea what I was undertaking. And I certainly intend never to make any such commitment again without knowing exactly what I'm committing to...

"But in the end I think... to break that vow was an act of dishonesty. And to... escape; that involved other acts of dishonesty, other deceits. All of which I hated. But it seemed—it seemed very clear to me, then, that to stay, to act as the vow required... that doing so made me part of a greater deceit. It was as if, without ever knowing, I'd made a prior vow, and when the two clashed I had to choose."

She laughed; heard herself. It sounded unreal, forced. "Well, that's how justify it all to myself. I still don't really know if I was right, but also I still don't see how I could have done anything but what I did."

"And it brought you here," he said.

"Well, so it did."

"Then I would find it hard to be sorry you acted as you did."

"Thank you." She contrived a smile. "I'll tell you more; I'll have to, soon enough. And then you'll see for yourself. But now... now, I'm trying to give you some sort of answer to your offer. And I think..."

She took his hand again. "I'll marry no other, I promise you that. But I'll not marry you, either, not now.

"Hedric... if marriage is just the vows two people make to each other, we could do that right now. We wouldn't need anyone else. To love each other, to work together... Whatever words we need, we choose. But marriage *isn't* just that. If only it were...

"Marriage, though. In this land, in this world, it is something else. It's public. It's a contract. That is the word, isn't it? A contract of marriage. So asking me to wed you in secret... does it even make sense? I can't see it."

"I would wed you tomorrow," he said. "In public. In the sight of all five Principals, if they cared to attend. But I can't. You know why I can't."

"So we wait until we can. The marriage, the contract, the public side. We wait. But that's not—oh, yes, it's all important; in this land, under these laws, it's very important. It means we can do things together, things we've talked about. But really, Hedric, the vow that matters to me is not some prescribed form of words in front of a Reeve. It's the promise in the heart. And I... Actually, that's enough words."

She released his hand, but only to link her own hands behind his head, draw him closer.

※

Then she had to tell Railu.

In the early part of their life at Duncal, Railu's attitude had oscillated between resignation and resentment. Jerya had little difficulty understanding either. It was hard to imagine a more invidious position than being required to act as wet-nurse to your own child. At the same time, Railu had to see, every day, how Jerya's life was becoming wider; and she could not fail to be conscious that Jerya was the only reason she was in the Five Principalities, in the life she had.

Once Embrel was weaned, things began—slowly—to improve. As her skill as a healer became more widely acknowledged, to the point where slaves from neighbouring estates would seek her out for clandestine consultations, Railu began to rediscover purpose and pride in herself. If there was resentment now, its object was the laws that made it impossible for her to practise more openly.

Curiously, the less Embrel actually needed her, the fonder she became of him. As nurse to a suckling, she had been grimly dutiful. As nursemaid to a toddler, merely dutiful. As housekeeper, only occasionally required to offer personal care, she doted on him like every other member of the household. Even Whallin, whose general demeanour only grew more irascible as he aged, revealed a softer side where the boy was concerned.

Railu, nearly a decade into life in the East, was a calmer, more contented soul than she had been in the first years. Even so, she had never quite regained the blithe quality, the almost unfailing cheerfulness, that had so attracted Jerya in those distant days of their beginning. It sometimes seemed as if that side of her had been drained away and poured into Embrel.

Just occasionally there were hints that her general equanimity was more fragile than it appeared. Some little local tragedy—the death of a kitten, or the separation of a slave couple she barely knew on a nearby estate—would wreck her balance, and for a day or two everyone would walk on eggshells. On those days Jerya would be longing for some ailing or injured slave to present her with a case; nothing would bring Railu back to herself more certainly than the chance to be valuable, and valued. More than once Jerya had been strongly tempted to contrive some minor injury to herself, or feign sickness, just to restore her friend.

It was Railu's fragility that preyed on her mind as she contemplated how best to tell her about their plans.

❋

She found Railu in the kitchen, seated at the table, poring over some papers; household accounts or order-books, Jerya couldn't tell at a glance. Embrel stood on the chair next to her, one hand resting on her shoulder. *His mother's shoulder*, she thought, with the usual stab of tangled emotions; the old anger, the desire to reveal the secret, but also tenderness, and simple pleasure at the mutual affection she saw.

Embrel's eyes were not on his mother, but firmly fixed on Rhenya, who was evidently making a cake, and making a show of it for his benefit, whipping the batter with gusto, muscles showing clear under dark skin. Jerya's mind flashed back to her first sight of Rhenya; what a slender, almost wiry, little thing she'd been back then. Of course she had been—by their best estimate—barely sixteen years old. Rhenya in her mid-twenties was an altogether more substantial being, both taller and more solid.

Railu, Rhenya, Embrel. *My family*, she thought suddenly.

Jerya smiled at Rhenya, then at Embrel as she slipped into the free chair at the end of the table. Railu glanced up but her eyes seemed hardly to focus. "I could do with a chat, sometime soon."

Finally Railu gave her her full attention. "Now, if you want. My eyes are getting tired of these anyway."

We really need to think about glasses for you, thought Jerya. She filed it away. "Would you care for a stroll round the Wilderness? The rain's stopped."

"I'll get a shawl."

Embrel looked after them wistfully, as if he would like to join them, but the moment must be fast approaching where he would get to scrape the remnants of the mixture from the bowl. And then it would not be long before there were fresh cakes to taste.

A few years into their time here, Railu had grown distinctly stout. She had always been what Delvenfolk called comfortable, but after Embrel's birth, her life had mostly been in a few rooms, and she had been the prime object of Rhenya's urge to feed everyone. Even as she mourned old Cook, Rhenya had been intoxicated at finding herself in sole charge of the kitchen. This, combined with an innate generosity of spirit, meant she was forever loading every plate just a little too full, not to mention urging treats on anyone who entered her domain between meals; which, first and foremost, meant Railu.

Railu had steadfastly ignored various hints that she might be getting a little too big for her own good, until an accident to one of the field slaves. Rushing to the scene, she had become so breathless she almost collapsed, and Jerya had feared she might need medical attention herself. "If that man had lost his hand," said Railu afterwards, "I'd never have been able to forgive myself." She had steeled herself to decline most of Rhenya's treats and second helpings, and from avoiding 'unnecessary' exercise had made a point at least of walking every day. This coincided with Embrel's becoming increasingly mobile, which was all to the good. To Railu now, an invitation to take a turn or two around the Wilderness was welcome for its own sake.

They had often shared a chuckle at the silliness of the title. Both had seen real wilderness; Railu sometimes said she'd seen enough to last her a lifetime. Wilderness it was not, far from it, but the informality of its ivy-draped trees and wandering paths made a pleasing contrast to the rest of the gardens. And it was closer than the Knowe, and held fewer difficult memories.

Also, as Railu said, the paths were gravelled, and there was no need to trail their skirts in wet grass.

They walked briskly down the side of the main lawn and through the rose garden, but slowed their pace when they came under the trees. "Now," said Railu, "What's so important?"

"I never said it was important."

"You didn't need to. I know you, Jerya. Come on, out with it."

Jerya sighed. She'd thought she knew exactly how she was going to begin, but somehow, now they'd come to it, she'd lost her certainty. "Well, you're right. You do know me." She smiled, to show she was glad of it. "And it *is* important."

"So stop procrastinating and tell me."

"You remember that story in the newspaper the other day?"

"When do I ever have time to read newspapers? My eyes get tired enough with accounts and whatnot."

Jerya made herself a definite promise: *I'll do something about glasses for you.* But raising that subject now would most surely count as procrastination; and Railu might be prickly about it, which would not be a good lead-in to the subject she needed to talk about. "You know, the one I showed you. How the Duke of Selton is preparing an expedition into the mountains."

"And what's that to do with the price of—oh, but wait." She hadn't lost her wits. "When you say 'into' you mean 'across' don't you?"

"He's confirmed it now, aye." There'd been a longer story just yesterday.

"Are they looking where we came over?"

"No, further South."

"So maybe they won't find anything."

"Well, we know the peaks are higher there, sharper. They may fail, besure." Railu smiled at Jerya's use of the Delven dialect word. "But they may not. We don't know; we can't know. And if they do... then what?"

"It's bound to happen sometime, I suppose."

"Besure," she said again. "We know there's one feasible route."

"Aye, and if *I* can do it, in boots that didn't even fit..." She didn't need to finish the thought. It wasn't exactly a route that you could take pack-animals on, but there was really only one difficult place. Jerya knew from her own girlhood of several ways steep rocks could be made easier: ladders, knotted ropes, even steps hewn from the rock itself.

They walked on a few paces, past rhododendrons that were shedding petals all over the path. "I know you, Jerya," said Railu again. "And there's more..."

"Aye... well, let me ask you... you said, it's bound to happen sometime. And then what? What do you think about that?"

Railu gave her a sidelong look, as if she counted this, too, as procrastination; but she also gave the question serious thought. "Not so sure it'd be good news for the Sung Lands," she said eventually.

"Worse if they've had no warning, d'you reckon?"

Railu stopped. They faced each other under the fanning branch of a larch tree. "I might have known," she said. "Soon as you mentioned it."

"Known what?"

"Don't pretend, Jerya. Do I have to keep reminding you, I *know* you? Though I'd hardly need to, to put two and two together. You're planning something. *We know there's one feasible route*, you said, and *worse if they've had no warning*.

"And...?"

This time Railu did amaze her. "Were you planning on asking me to come with you?"

"Would you want to?" she managed after a moment.

"Well, that's the question, but it might be nice to be asked."

"You keep saying you know me... it cuts both ways, Railu. I know you. And I couldn't imagine you wanting to repeat that journey."

"Maybe not... but still, nice to be asked."

"Of course. I'm sorry, Rai."

Railu only shrugged, and after a moment began to walk again. The path narrowed, holly trees encroaching. To preserve their skirts they had to go single file. When they could again walk abreast, Railu gave her another sideways glance. "Have you thought about what happens when you get there? The College, I mean—where else would you go?"

"Aye."

"And what happens when Miss Delven presents herself there? Are you supposing they won't recognise you? Your precious veil ain't going to do it there."

"I hadn't even thought of the veil."

"Well, no one wears 'em in Carwerid. Hardly the way to pass unnoticed. And even if they'd admit you to the College... stars, Jerya, there's people there wouldn't need to see your face, they'd know you just by your voice."

"True, I suppose. But I hadn't even thought of trying to go incognito. Why would they listen to some anonymous woman prattling about visitors from nowhere?"

"But will they listen to *you*? Or will they just... draff, I don't even know what the penalty is for breaking your Vow."

"Seems to me it's a chance I have to take. What else am I going to do? Write them a letter? What chance they'll take that seriously? Remember, Rai, everyone there *knows* there's no life this side of the mountains, just like everyone this side *knows* there's no life on the West. But *I* know. I've been here best part of ten years. I'm living proof..."

"If they'll listen."

"I have to take the chance."

"Aye, because who else is there?" That was almost exactly how Jerya had expressed it to herself; but she saw in a moment that Railu meant it differently. "Because Miss Delven has to be the centre of the drama, doesn't she?"

"Is that how you see me?"

"Are you really going to tell me different? Come on, Jerya, why are we even here, in the East, in the first place? Because nothing would do but the most dramatic gesture you could conceive of."

It always comes back to this, she thought. Railu might have forgiven her; she might be reconciled to this alternative life; she might even be, or appear to be, content. But forgiving was not forgetting.

And she could not say she didn't deserve the rebuke.

"You're right, Rai. I'm not really sure what else I could have done, but I didn't have to drag you along with me. But it was ten years ago. I was nineteen, not twenty-nine. I'd be a sorry sort of a person if I hadn't learned a few things in that time."

"Not enough to stop you going and sticking your head in the noose, seems to me."

"All right, you tell me, what else can I do?"

"Have you thought about doing nothing?"

"Nothing? Really? You said yourself, *not good news*; and you didn't question *worse if they've had no warning*."

Railu's jaw was set; she was silent. They completed the circuit, and without a word turned to begin again.

"Remember what happened to us," said Jerya. "When those... when we were taken. Everyone took one look at us and thought 'slaves'. Can you contemplate that happening to Analind, or Veradel? Jossena? Yanil? Everyone else we knew, and the ones we don't, Postulants of ten or eleven... I can't think about that and... if it's in my power to do something and I do nothing... how could I live with myself?"

"So, what? You're just going gallivanting off on your own?"

"No, not on my own."

"Ah. You and the Honourable Hedric, then."

"He *is* honourable."

"I'm not denying it."

"Then what...?"

"What do you mean, 'then what'?"

"There was something in your tone. Either you don't approve of Hedric, or you don't approve of me crossing the mountains with him."

"I don't know him like you do, but what I've seen I like well enough. Seems like a good man, for an owner."

For an owner... Jerya thought about that, wondered why she hadn't given it more thought already. As a woman in the Five Principalities, she couldn't own slaves herself, but as the wife of an owner... There was no avoiding a sense of complicity.

She didn't have time to pursue it, as Railu was still speaking. "Last time it was me—and Rodal—who got dragged in to your adventure. This time it's Hedric. And I'm just wondering if he has any better idea what he's letting himself in for than I did ten years back."

"There is a difference, though, isn't there?"

"Is there?"

"Besure. Last time, none of us had any idea what we might find this side. If we expected anything, it was just wilderness and more wilderness." They both smiled, again, at the 'wilderness' around them. "This time... I *do* know what to expect. Delven, the journey to the city, the College: none of it's new to me. I'll do my best to make sure he understands. In fact... you could talk to him too, if you like."

"Would he listen to me?"

"Why not?"

"I'm just a housekeeper. *And* I'm a slave."

"Rai, really, he's not like that. Besides, you're *not* just a housekeeper, not just a slave. That may be what the world at large sees, but we know better. Just to start, you're the best healer for miles around; stars, if you could practise openly, if you had the same access to medicines and equipment, you'd put Doctor Feldreth out of business."

Railu grunted, as if sceptical, but Jerya knew she was pleased. However, mere compliments couldn't deflect her entirely. "Maybe I will talk to him, if he'll listen. Still, does he really have a choice?"

"Why should he not?"

"Because you always know best," said Railu. There was no rancour in her tone, just a plain statement of fact. "When you set your mind to something... might as well try and change the orbits of the moons."

"Tell me I'm wrong, then. Tell me how I'm wrong. 'Cause if there's another way..."

"There has to be another way."

"So what is it?"

"I don't know, Jerya!" Railu spun around as she halted. "Do you want to know the truth? Do you want to know why I'm not jumping up and down cheering?" She fixed her gaze on Jerya. "Comes down to this: I'm terrified I'll never see you again."

At first Jerya could only stare. Then she closed the distance in a swift stride, flung her arms round Railu, and hugged her harder than she had in years.

CHAPTER 7

JERYA

"You ask us to swallow a great deal," said Duncal. "Not just that there is life beyond the mountains. That much... hm, the general view has always been otherwise, but it seems His Grace of Selton, for one, thinks the matter at least worth investigation. That, perhaps, I can consider, hm. But to accept that the first to cross that barrier were two girls not even out of their teens... That is indeed straining all credibility."

Would it be more credible if she revealed that those two girls had not been alone? With a man to help them... It prompted another question: *would we have made it without Rodal?* It was possible, she thought, but not certain. In any case, mention of Rodal would draw them closer to the question of Embrel's parentage, and the Squire and his Lady never appreciated reminders that the boy was not their trueborn son.

It grated, as always. But now, of all days, she must be diplomatic. Only, what to say instead? "I do understand how unlikely it must seem. And I don't see how I can prove it to you. We had things with us, from the other side, which might have helped, but everything was taken by the freebooters or at the slave-market. Though there is always the question of why Railu's hair has never grown back. You know she has been here ten years and never needed to shave."

"Aye" said Lady Pichenta. "We told her she might grow the Crest, but there's never been any sign of it."

"It's hard on her, but there's nothing to be done." *Unless*, she thought suddenly, *the Dawnsingers have an antidote to their own preparation.* "But if you want proof, you have only to wait for our return."

"Well, that's another thing. It's one thing for you to meet with him here, in our household. It's quite another for the two of you to go gadding about the wilds with no chaperone but a slave or two."

Duncal sighed. "You may care little for your own reputation, Jerya. I can even understand that you have little regard for common gossip. But you surely have regard for Hedric... You know what is at stake if his uncle should learn of this, hm. And it will be hard to conceal your setting out together."

"We have considered that." It wasn't quite true; *she* had considered it, in the last few seconds. But as fast as she saw the problem, she saw a solution. "We'll travel separately at first. I can go on my own, until well beyond the last habitation. And I'll wear my veil, of course."

"A veil is scant protection," said Lady Pichenta. "A young woman on her own, out of reach of civilisation... Why, you know yourself... I hesitate to remind you, but you did fall foul of those freebooters last time you were in that region."

"I'm hardly likely to forget," she said, but she was thinking: *Draff, I can't go with Hedric because I'd compromise his reputation, and I can't go alone because a woman needs a male protector. It's a wonder any woman ever travels at all.* Because she wanted their support, or at least acquiescence, if she could possibly get it, she kept that to herself. "I suppose someone could accompany me? A slave... perhaps Whallin...?"

"By the spirits, Jerya, you presume," said Duncal. "You ask a lot just in requesting an indefinite leave of absence."

"I hope it need not be more than five or six weeks," she said.

"But you cannot promise... and six weeks is no small time anyway." His tone turned wheedling. "Perhaps you don't appreciate how valuable you are to this household, hm, and to the Work. I should say invaluable, even indispensable."

"And for Embrel, of course," added Lady Pichenta. "Need I remind you, it was your own opinion that you could do better by him than the tutors he'd had before."

For a moment Railu's words rang in her mind: *because you always know best*. Aye, and she didn't always make life easy for herself.

"I did say that. And I... I love the lad with all my heart. I will miss him more than I can say. Believe me, if I could see another way...

"I wish I could adequately explain this to you, but it would take hours. Let me just say this. I left the Western land because... well, the reasons are complicated, too. I left because I could see no other choice. But there are still people there I care about. And they need to know... it's past time that they knew... what lies on this side. They need to be prepared. If the Duke's expedition doesn't find a crossing this summer, he's already said they will try again next year; and there are rumours of others planning attempts too. The people on the other side need to know, to have time to prepare. And there's no one better placed than I to carry that message."

She took a moment to settle her breathing. "Sir, madam, I'll never forget what you did for me, and for Railu. Had you not been in the slave-market that day, had you not stepped in, I dare not contemplate what our future might have held, if indeed we'd have had any future at all."

This was all true, though she could wish he was less inclined to congratulate himself on it. That always grated; but the debt remained.

"And that is only the beginning of what I owe you. None of what I have now would I have were it not for you." That was the literal truth, she supposed, but still it threatened to curdle on her lips.. "Words cannot express how much I owe to you. And so, believe me, I dearly hope that I may go with your blessing... or, at least, with your acceptance. But I owe it to you to speak plainly, and the fact is that I believe I *must* go, with or without your consent."

Duncal drew breath, but Jerya went on quickly. He wouldn't like being interrupted—and that *was* how he would see it—but there was one final thing she needed to say. "There's one more debt I owe you. Nine years ago—nine and a half, near enough—in this very room you gave me my freedom. And freedom includes the right to act as I feel I must, even if it disappoints you."

She had braced herself, or thought she had, but telling Embrel was still the hardest part. She tried to break the news gently, to introduce the idea that she might be absent 'a few weeks' before saying anything of where she was going, but there was still that one hard moment when he grasped the import of her words.

Then he simply could not speak for several minutes. He threw himself face down on the chaise-longue, shuddering with silent sobs. When she ventured to lay a hand on his shoulder, he threw it off with a violent gesture.

When finally he did sit up, his face was red and contorted almost out of recognition. At first he struggled to get any words out. "Jer... Jerya, you *can't* go."

"I have to, my darling."

"I'm *not* your darling. If I was your darling you wouldn't go off and leave me for the whole summer."

"Now you know that's not what I said. I said 'a few weeks'. A whole summer's three months."

"Then why don't I get three months off lessons?"

She dared a brief smile, a teasing note. "Time off lessons means less time with me, you know. Would you rather keep going with lessons, if I were here?"

He frowned. Maybe such hypotheticals were too hard for a not-quite-ten-year-old mind. *Better change the subject.* "Railu and Rhenya aren't going anywhere. Maybe Railu can give you some lessons. She knows more about healing, about how bodies work, than I'll ever know."

He looked doubtful, almost as if he couldn't credit that there were things Jerya didn't know. But there was something else on his mind. "They won't let me do lessons with Railu. They'll get one of those smelly old men back."

"Smelly?" She couldn't stop herself repeating it; it was hard enough to keep from smiling.

"Stinky. 'Specially that old Stencoose. Stink-goose I called him."

"Not to his face, I hope."

"Might be I did, once."

"I ought to tan your hide for that." It was an empty threat, and he knew it. The fact was, not one of them had ever raised a hand to the lad. Jerya knew there were many who would consider this laxity shocking, that the boy was bound to be spoiled by it.

It wasn't that the household had collectively resolved against beating or smacking. It was much simpler: the occasion had never arisen. There had never, in all her memory, been an offence that might warrant corporal punishment. When four-year-old Embrel had pulled at the tablecloth and sent most of the second-best tea service crashing to the floor, the heavy milk-jug had cracked him on the brow. After that it was Railu's doctoring he needed, not further injury. When another prank had resulted in a burned hand for Rhenya, her scream, and then her silent but tangible suffering as Railu treated the wound, had left Embrel ashen-faced and trembling with shock and guilt.

Simply put, there was an essential goodness in the lad. Beside, the fact that he wasn't beaten didn't mean there was no discipline. Nine times out of ten, just seeing that those he loved were disappointed in him made him more wretched than any whipping. On the tenth, being sent to bed early, or—even more effective—having an empty plate placed in front of him while the others tucked into a tasty supper, or some of Rhenya's celebrated scones, was punishment enough, Embrel being Embrel...

Here was a lad halfway through his tenth year, and the worst physical 'punishment' he'd ever had to endure was having a hand slapped aside when he reached inquisitively towards a candle-flame. But... she knew, and he surely knew too, that any school he was likely to be sent to would have a very different approach to discipline.

It seemed his thoughts had followed a similar path. "If you're not here to teach me, and they don't want to bring back any of the smelly old men—"

"—That's not fair." She smiled. "Some of them weren't *that* old."

He wasn't to be deflected so easily. "They'll send me away to school." The voice quavered, the bottom lip trembled; all the signs of a fresh outbreak of tears impending.

She reached out, gripped his slender shoulders. This time he didn't throw her off. "Embrel, listen. You know, don't you, that whatever I say or do, and however much you like my lessons—which I'm very glad to hear, by the way. Because there've been a few occasions when you haven't seemed quite so keen..."

"I'll always be there on time, from now on."

She wondered how long that promise might hold, but there were bigger fish to fry. "Embrel. If it were up to me... but you know it's your Mama and Papa who decide. And you know they've always said you'll have to go away to school by the autumn after you turn eleven. But that's a long time yet."

"But if you're not here to teach me..."

"I'll talk to them." *One more difficult conversation, another hour used up. But if it has to be done...* "But listen... About what Railu can teach you. It's not just doctoring. You'd be surprised what else she knows."

"I bet she's not as good as you."

"You can't know that till you give her a chance." *And she is your mother.* Though that was the one thing that must never be said. Embrel's 'Mama and Papa' would never forgive that; and neither, she suspected, would Railu. "Anyway, I'll talk to them. I'm sure they have no idea of sending you away so soon."

"You promise?"

"I promise I'll talk to them. It's they who'll have to promise not to send you away."

"I still don't want you to go," the boy said glumly, but at least he was no longer tearful. Another moment, and he crept into her arms.

"I don't want to go, either," she said. "But, you know, we all have to do things we don't like, sometimes. It's part of being grown-up."

"Maybe I'll never grow up, then."

"Well, that would be fine, if you can manage it," she said, squeezing him tighter. "You're pretty near perfect just as you are."

CHAPTER 8

JERYA

S he had a long day of riding ahead, and had planned an early departure, before the usual breakfast hour. She had just finished the bread and preserves Rhenya had provided and was savouring her good coffee, when Railu came scurrying in. One glance at her face was enough. "What's the matter?"

"Embrel's gone missing." Jerya's heart seemed to drop into her boots.

She asked a few quick questions—when was he first missed, where had they looked already—then sent Railu to the Wilderness while she set off, running, for the Knowe. Fortunately her divided skirt was less of a hindrance than a regular one.

"We have all the field-slaves out searching the estate," said Pichenta when she returned empty-handed.

"He can't have left the house before Railu unlocked the yard door," added Duncal. "He can't have gone far."

"There's nothing more you can do," said Railu. It was brave of her, Jerya knew, given her still-mixed feelings about the whole venture. "You're already later than you meant to be."

"But how can I leave like this? It's my fault..."

"How is it your fault?"

"He doesn't want me to go. He *hates* the idea."

"Well," said Railu, who now seemed to be the only one thinking rationally, "The best thing you can do for him is come back as soon as you can—and *safely*. You've a long way to go today, and if you're not there before dark..."

Somehow she let herself be persuaded, climbed up into the saddle, made her farewells.

"Please," she said. "Don't send him away before I get back."

"We've made it quite clear," said Pichenta. "We have no immediate plans of that kind... but if you can't give us a sure date for your return, we can make no indefinite promises."

It was hard to swallow, but Jerya knew she could hardly ask for more.

"I will return," she said. "And as soon as I can."

She set off, but every hoofbeat on the road felt like a drum of doom. Every stride felt *wrong*. The horse sensed her mood, and its gait dragged. Yet she never reined in, never turned her mount's head around, kept plodding forward, unable to make that final decision.

Then she saw a small figure sitting on the bench by the junction, and her mind cleared in an instant.

She stopped the horse a few yards back, approached on foot. He watched her warily, but made no attempt to run off.

She sat down beside him on the rough plank. "Waiting for the diligence?" He nodded.

"You have money for the fare?"

"I have twenty pence." He pulled a few coins out of his pocket to show her.

"How far do you think that will get you?"

"I don't know."

"I'm not exactly sure myself, but it might get you to Denvirran. Not further. Is Denvirran where you want to go?" He shrugged. "And then what? What are you going to do in Denvirran, on your own, with—I guess—only two or three pence left in your pocket?"

He didn't answer.

"Embrel," she said. "Look at me." She waited till he met her gaze. Those umber eyes, the long lashes... how could anyone *not* see he was Railu's child?

People see what they expect to see... or want to see. "Travelling's a great thing. You know I've done it before... and now I'm doing it again, but... When I was your age, and for many years after, I never went further from home than I could walk and get back by nightfall." ·

She'd said very little about her childhood, to him or anyone. A little more to Hedric, lately, but still not much. Embrel was just at the age when he'd surely want to know more. And his curiosity was stirring now. "Didn't you have a horse?"

She laughed. "Never even rode a horse till I came here—even after that, in fact. There were none where I grew up." His eyes widened; horses, to him, were simply part of life, no more to be questioned than Rhenya's baking. "Embrel, listen. I never left home, that small patch that I could range on foot, till I was nineteen years old. Nineteen. And when I did, I was terrified." Maybe that was a little exaggerated, over-simplified. Truth be, she had felt a mix of... of almost everything it was possible to feel.

She held his gaze. "I'm not saying you need to wait till you're nineteen, I know that's a very long way off. But don't you think, really, ten is just a *little* bit young? Especially to be heading off with nothing but twenty pence in your pocket? If you're going to go travelling, you really need a better plan than that. You know how Hedric and I have been planning and preparing for weeks." *Though I had a lot less of a plan the first time I crossed the mountains...*

"Take me with you," he said suddenly. He couldn't know, of course, what that sparked in her... *and I could take him to meet his father.*

"I can't," she said. "It's a lovely idea, but I really can't. But, listen, one day. I'll make you a promise." Again she snagged his gaze. "You do trust me, don't you?"

"Yes," he said, with all the solemnity a ten-year-old can muster.

"You know I've already promised that I'm coming back from this journey, as soon as I can. And here's another. One day, when you're a bit older, we will go on a journey together."

"A real journey?"

"A real journey."

"Just you and me?"

"Well, we'll see. If that's what you want, at the time."

"All right," he said.

A distant sound. She looked up, and saw the diligence lumbering down the far curve of the road. "Look," she said. "It'll be here in ten minutes. Do you still want to catch it?"

He thought a moment longer. "I suppose not."

"No, save your money, you'll need a bit more than that... Maybe we'd better move. If the driver sees us here he'll stop, and then the poor horses'll have to strain to get it moving again."

The interests of the horses swayed him, as she'd known they would.

She put him up on the horse and climbed on behind. He was still light enough to lift, but for how much longer? She let him hold the reins, kept her own hands on his upper arms. They were still thin, almost frail. Doubtless he would fill out in time—his true parents were both sturdy enough—but not yet.

By the time she'd got him home and said her goodbyes all over again she was more than an hour behind her intended time of departure.

※

As she rode away she lowered her veil to hide her tears from anyone she might pass.

She kept it in place as she passed through Drumlenn. This had always been the plan, to go incognito, as far as possible. She might still be recognised; there were, after all, few women around Drumlenn who rode astride, and even fewer who ever rode veiled. There might even be some who recognised, not the rider, but the horse. But there was no reason why anyone should think it anything out of the ordinary, unless someone noticed that she rode all the way through without stopping. And even that should hardly provoke more than momentary curiosity.

Long after the outskirts of Drumlenn had given way to fields and woods, Jerya kept her veil down. A misty drizzle had set in, and the gauze kept her face dry. That was true enough; but there was more to it. She had discovered long ago that there were times when she simply *liked* wearing it. She'd never quite understood why, but with a day's riding ahead, there was plenty of time to consider the matter.

And others.

Embrel, first of all. She could hope, now, that the lad was somewhat more reconciled to her absence; but in the process, she'd made him a promise. *Almost a vow... and I haven't a good history with vows. I should know better than to bind myself like that.*

Well, she had to keep the other promise first: to return safely. She had made that commitment not only to Embrel but to Railu, and others. Until then, the second one was moot. And she knew that, however solid her resolve, circumstances could make it impossible to meet the first.

Meanwhile, the promise she had tried and failed to extract from his parents. She knew they didn't relish the prospect any more than the rest of the household, but they could not shed the conviction that it was necessary. Duncal himself had been sent away to school ('of course', he always said). *And so was I*, thought Jerya suddenly. *Why did I never think of that before?*

True, it was never called a school, always a College, but what was the difference, really? She had been there for just a few crowded months, but Railu had gone through a full eight years. Jerya found herself grinning behind her veil at the thought that intruded on her unruly mind. How would Embrel cope with the kind of education delivered at the College of Dawnsingers? And how different was it from what he might get at a school here? There was one very obvious difference to start with...

Part of her problem was that she knew virtually nothing about boys' schools—and if there *were* any schools for girls, she'd never heard of them. As far as she knew, girls, if they were educated at all, were educated by governesses, who might well be even less qualified than herself.

The only people who could enlighten her would be the Squire, who had never shown any inclination to speak of the subject, or Hedric. *Well, we're going to have lots of time to talk in the coming days...*

And another question: were all schools alike? Might some be more to Embrel's liking than others? Contrary to the damning verdicts of his tutors, he was perfectly capable of learning if you saw a way to engage his interest; and he was much better at concentrating on lessons if he'd had an hour or two of running around first.

He could hardly be the only small boy like that. Were there schools which made allowance for such a disposition, rather than trying to bend all boys to a set way of doing things, as the tutors had been wont to do? That seemed like a potential line of enquiry, at least.

She looked around, only then realising that she had barely observed her surroundings for the last hour. The veil offered no real impediment to her vision, unless she deliberately tried to focus on it. Now, doing so, she saw how beads of moisture on the gauze refracted the scene into strangely distorted miniature worlds.

When it was introspection she wanted, the veil helped, giving a sense of detachment from her surroundings. Still, she dare not lose track of where she was. She had been this way before, but face down across the back of a horse. *Not ideal for sightseeing,* she thought with a suppressed snort of laughter. Better to laugh than think too deeply about that dark time.

For distraction as much as anything, she pulled out the map from her jacket. Seeing no one around, she lifted the veil. It had little effect on distance vision but was less conducive to close study, as she had discovered the first time she wore it to the book-seller's in Drumlenn.

The map was the same edition, but not the same copy, that she had shown to the former freebooter, Barek. That one, she had given to Rodal; where was it now? *Perhaps I'll find out.*

She didn't need reminders of Barek. She *did* need to know where she was going, and memory would not suffice. Yes, the left at the next main junction. That would not be for another hour or so. After that she would need to pay more attention to the route. Until then... she slipped the map back into her jacket and lowered the veil, because the introspective mood was on her.

Marriage, now... On his uncle's death, provided he kept in the old man's good books, Hedric would inherit not only a vast estate and untold wealth, but also a title. He had never mentioned it, but Jerya was no fool. *Well, I hope not.* Hedric's wife, one day, would become Countess of Skilthorn.

She would have laughed out loud, but she saw a group of slaves loading logs onto a waggon just ahead. A veiled lady riding by was not something they were likely to gossip about; a veiled lady riding by and laughing aloud might be.

But, really, *Countess*... What could be more ludicrous? She had been a simple village girl for nineteen years; then, briefly, a Dawnsinger. Later, equally briefly, a slave... and then, well, whatever she was now. Secretary, governess, freedwoman... all were true, but none seemed to adequately describe herself, or the life she had managed to carve out.

She could, just about, imagine herself as Hedric's wife. Even then, she supposed, she would be a Lady... That was far enough for her mind to stretch. Mistress of Kirwaugh, a place of similar scale to Duncal. A place of which Hedric spoke with a warmth notably missing when he spoke of Skilthorn. Kirwaugh had always been his home, and she could imagine making it her home too. She knew how an estate like that worked. She knew, more or less, what was expected of the Lady of such a place, though she had made it clear to Hedric that she did not mean to conform to all of those expectations.

But he was heir to an Earldom. What did it even mean? What did any of it mean? Dukes and Counts and Princes... Countesses...

And why, she thought, muffling another laugh—though she was quite alone again now—why, if the wife of a Prince was a Princess, the wife of a Duke a Duchess, why in the name of all seven planets was the wife of an Earl called a Countess?

If her own comfort was all that mattered, then she knew she would far rather ask Hedric to renounce the title. Let them be Master and Mistress of Kirwaugh, let Kirwaugh be another small beacon for the enlightened approach to slavery...

But there was the rub. If Hedric didn't care about the title and the estates, he need not carry on tiptoeing around his uncle's prejudices. He could acknowledge her publicly, marry her at once... and his uncle would disinherit him.

The rub indeed. Because he was a good man, a man of conscience, he could not countenance that possibility. Not, she was sure, for himself; she acquitted him of such vanity or ambition. No, his concern was for the slaves, thousands of them, whose future lives could be lived under a master (and mistress) who would do all they could for them... or under his cousin Ferrowby, whom Hedric painted as, if anything, even more odious than the current Earl.

There was all that. But he was an owner; as Earl, he would be an owner of thousands. He would have the power, and he would surely have the will, to make a great difference to their lives.

And his Countess would be part of it... Was that not a good thing?

There was more to it, though, she thought; Hedric's dislike—loathing was hardly too strong a word—was too raw, too personal. He had suffered, in some way, at the hands of this Ferrowby. She knew, because she had come to know Hedric well, but he had never spoken a word of any such issue. It was all in a tone of voice, a tightening of posture, the way his eyes shied away from hers.

Hedric, she knew, would do almost anything to keep those thousands of souls out of Ferrowby's hands. How could she blame him for that?

The position and wealth of an Earl gave him the power to do a great deal of good—or ill—to a great number of people. And surely a Countess had some power, or at least influence, also. Great ladies were patrons of many causes, she knew, from orphanages to orchestras.

A new thought arrived, and it brought her full circle, back to Embrel again.

Was it possible... could a Countess establish a school that would be congenial for boys like Embrel?

But then... might a Countess even establish a school for *girls*?

She thought about that until the fingerpost at the junction loomed into view.

She knew full well that the left way was the one, but she lifted the veil and checked the map anyway. From here on there would be more frequent branches, but most were marked as dotted lines, not continuous ones; tracks, not roads. She left the veil pushed back as she continued.

Twice she stopped where her course crossed significant streams; a good check on progress against the map, but also a chance to water the horse, let her crop whatever grass she could find. She knew she hadn't made up the time lost in the morning, but there was no sense in pushing her mount too far. Truth be, she was glad to take a break for herself too. She rode regularly enough, but her trips into town were eighty minutes each way and almost every other ride she did was shorter, an hour's hack or a tour of inspection around the estate.

Well into the afternoon, when she had seen nothing but trees for the better part of an hour, she was surprised to see chickens in the road ahead. They belonged, she soon saw, to a cottage in a clearing, a scatter of thorn-fenced fields behind, a yard pecked bare in front. The thatch was green, overdue for renewal.

She stopped, swung down from the saddle, and stretched. The cottage door was ajar, but no one appeared. "Hello?"

A face peered round the door. Jerya thought quickly. "Hello. I wondered if you might have a couple of carrots for my horse? And perhaps I could get a cool drink? I... I'm happy to pay, of course."

She knew that poor frees were often proud people, likely to refuse payment, even to be affronted by the offer, but her immediate impression was that the folk here could use every penny they could get. When they emerged, she thought she was right. The woman might have been no older than herself, but looked worn down. All of them were threadbare. There were three girls, and a toddler of indeterminate sex.

The woman gazed at her, eyes surprisingly clear and blue, then muttered to the older girls. The tallest disappeared round the side of the house, the other within.

"It's only goat's milk, m'lady," said the woman as the first of the daughters returned with a brimming birch cup, a rougher version of the one Jerya herself carried.

"Goat's milk will be fine," she said, smiling. The woman could not know, but goat's milk was the only kind Jerya had known for the first nineteen years of her life. One sip and she was right back in Delven.

Growing up in Delven, she had never thought of herself as poor. She had never gone hungry, except by her own fault, staying out too long and missing meals. All she had owned was a few items of clothing, but they'd never been allowed to grow threadbare. Poverty had been a concept mentioned in a couple of the village's books.

And now this woman called her 'my lady'. She tried to imagine how she must look to these people, stepping down from a fine horse... but her own clothes were hardly grand. Her riding-skirt was almost as old as Embrel, and a lot more worn, its original indigo faded to a paler slate hue, and patched more than once, by her own hands. It flitted across her mind that it had been one of the first purchases she had made with her own money. Money had not been used within the community in Delven, and it had been much the same as a Dawnsinger; Dawnsingers also had few possessions they could call their own. Her jacket was—what? four years old?—but looked well enough on cursory examination.

None of the family had approached close enough to look closely, bar the second girl, and she'd stepped back to her mother's side as soon as she'd handed up the mug. The eldest, who might be anywhere from thirteen to sixteen, was feeding carrots to the horse. A streak of soil marked one cheek, pale against her skin. The youngest was tottering on fat little legs in fruitless pursuit of a scrawny chicken, supervised by the third girl, who looked to be five or six.

She drained the mug and handed it back with another smile, hoping it looked as warm as it felt. "Thank you. That was delicious. Fresh today, I'm sure?"

"Yes, thank yow, m'lady," said the woman. She seemed surprised that Jerya was partial to goat's milk, or that she knew enough to gauge its freshness. Jerya longed to tell her *I've milked goats a thousand times. I know when it's fresh.* She was sure that, if she only had time to overcome their shyness, she could show these people how much they had in common.

But time was one thing she did not have. She handed over a few coins, anxious to give fair payment without it appearing too much like charity. It was lucky, indeed, that she'd absent-mindedly left a few pennies in the pocket of the skirt last time she'd worn it. The coins in a purse in her saddle-bag were all silver, for use in the Sung Lands.

As far as she could tell, the woman's thanks were sincere. She wished for something else to say, but could not think of the right words. She swung up into the saddle again, tapped with her heels. The horse gave a distinct snort as she stepped forward. There was no mistaking the tone of resignation.

Behind her, one of the girls laughed. Jerya looked round, grinned. "Aye, she's had a long day, and a few miles left to do." She leaned forward, spoke a few encouraging words, and they rode away.

※

Jerya had never seen inside the cottage, knew next to nothing of that family's life, not even if the girls had a father or brothers. All she could say was that their clothes were worn almost to the point of falling apart, and that neither apparel nor wearers were overly clean. The woman had worn crude wooden clogs; the girls had been barefoot. But she didn't know what they had been doing before her arrival. There were some tasks for which any person of sense wore their oldest clothes. Some people could leap to judgement based on nothing more than a glimpse out of a carriage window; Jerya had often had to bite her lip at some of the things guests in the house said.

Still, she could not help wondering. Slaves at Duncal were not dressed in rags, didn't have a rotting thatch over their heads. She thought it very likely they were better housed, better clad, better fed, than the family she had just seen. Did that mean they were better off as slaves? She had heard the argument; the 'degraded' condition of many poor free folk was clear evidence that they could not manage their own lives. They would be more comfortable as slaves—'on a well-regulated estate, of course'. Thus did some 'altruistically' justify the creeping extension of enslavement to more of the population.

She had heard it said that giving poor frees charity was doing them no favour at all, only perpetuating their ill-omened state. Those who could not fend for themselves would always have the option of voluntary enslavement. She had even heard that some people would sell a child to pay off a debt—or, it was darkly hinted, for less savoury reasons.

Political economy was hardly Jerya's preferred field of study. She had heard the arguments, and rebelled inwardly, but rarely felt herself fully equipped to contest the case; and, as a humble secretary/governess, it was hardly her place to do so anyway.

Still, one thought came clear to her. *If poverty's the problem, that doesn't mean slavery's the solution.*

She might not have much grasp on the finer points of political economy, but she did have what she considered a decisive advantage over every one of those opinionated gentlemen and ladies. *I know what it feels like to be a slave.*

She had been taken as a slave, sold by a brute, bought by a gentleman. She had lived as a slave for barely six months, but she knew what it felt like.

Railu and Rhenya, two of the four people in the world she felt closest to, were still slaves.

She knew both, and she knew beyond all doubt which she preferred. But did that give her the right to decide for others?

✳

Another hour, and she hadn't seen another dwelling, nor did the map show any more along her route. The track was barely wide enough for a single cart, and there was a green band down the middle, rough grass with a sprinkling of flowers; trefoil, scarlet pimpernel, eyebright. Occasional cruder tracks, churned by hooves and wheels, led off into the forest: logging trails, no doubt. She saw areas scarred by clear-felling, but also spreads of new planting, neat rows of all-but-identical little trees.

All of these grew fewer as she went on. The sky had cleared but there was no hint of sun even in the tops of the tallest trees; it must have dipped below the skyline of the mountains. The forest crowded shadowy alongside the track.

She hadn't prepared herself for the way the memories came back. She might have been upside down behind the saddle rather than upright in it, but there was too much that was the same. The trail was clearer than she remembered, had presumably seen more traffic in the ten years since, but the soft thudding of hooves on compacted sand was the same, and so was the forest, filling with encroaching night just as it had that first time.

The track a pale band between black masses of forest. Horse and rider both tired. And then something reaching her ears between her own mount's hoofbeats. A shadow on the road, a lone horse and rider...

A sudden memory of Lady Pichenta's words. "*It's hardly safe, a young woman on her own, out of reach of civilisation. Why, you know yourself... I hesitate to remind you...*"

And then, a voice out of the dusk, calling across fifty yards that still separated them.

"Jerya, is it you?"

"It is me."

"Thank the stars."

CHAPTER 9

JERYA

"Somewhere around here," she said, reining in.

"Around here?" repeated Hedric.

"We were taken by the freebooters."

"I would have thought you might rather ride on by," he said quietly, coming up beside her where she stood on the flood-bank. She looked around, saw that Lallon, Semyon and Catlow had remained with the horses, about fifteen yards away. The latter two would not be coming much further: it would be their responsibility to take the horses back. They'd discussed leaving someone there all summer, as there was plenty of water and grazing, but decided it was far too likely to draw attention. "Ah well," she'd said, "We'll just have to walk, when we come back."

"I can't be sure this is the exact spot," she said now. "Near enough ten years… Things change. Trees fall, new ones grow, the river shifts its course."

"Much has changed for you, too, I think."

"Aye, and in ways I could never have imagined. You know, until that moment, we had no notion there were people this side of the mountains. Never even considered it."

"I wish that knowledge had come to you less brutally."

She thought about this as her eyes swept the flats, the dry, braided, channels left by spring floods. "I don't know," she said finally. "Perhaps it's better to learn hard truths right away. It can be more painful if you start out believing things are good, only to have your illusions shattered later."

"Yes," he said, in his thoughtful way. "I can see how that could be."

"Well, if it wasn't here, it was somewhere close, and looking much like this." She turned to him, summoned a brisker manner. "And it *was* ten years ago. I'm hardly the same person I was then."

"Aye," he said stoutly, "And none, now, shall treat you as those ruffians did back then."

No, she thought, *For myself, I have no such fears. But such treatment is meted out to slaves every day in this land.* She didn't need to say it. He knew it perfectly well, and his abhorrence of it was scarcely less deep-rooted than her own. Impulsively, she reached out, gave his arm a firm squeeze.

He looked at her in surprise. In general they eschewed demonstrations of affection in front of others. She only smiled. "You're a good man."

"I try," he said. "To be as good as the world allows me to be, anyway."

"That's all anyone can do."

As they rode on, and the valley's opening curve allowed the first glimpses of the greater slopes ahead, she thought of another thing. Somewhere near here, Embrel had been conceived.

She saw the boy every day, of course, and his mother—his *true* mother. She might not think of Rodal daily, but she recalled him often enough, and as Embrel grew she saw more hints of his father in looks or mannerisms. Hardly ever, though, did she think about Rodal and Railu together, still less contemplate that moment of passion they must have shared on that sun-warmed mossy bank.

Passion—at least passion of that kind—was not a presence in her life now; nor, she thought, in Railu's.

They rode on, moving down to the stony flats when the forest grew too dense. Another hour, she thought, and they would leave the trees behind. That would be a good place to rest and water the horses, and take some lunch for themselves. For now, they rode on, single file, each with their own thoughts.

She looked ahead. For a moment, Lallon's broad back denied her any view of his master's slighter figure, but their course bent to skirt a stand of fireweed, and she had a clear view again. As if sensing her eyes on him, he glanced round, flashed her a brief smile.

Would there be passion, she wondered, when—if—she and he could finally be together?

Of course, using the word a little differently, there was passion aplenty already. A passion for learning, for the stars, and for a better world. Those were fine things to share. Perhaps it would be greedy to ask for more.

That afternoon, she took the lead. The bare strath was easy going for the horses—all five could have ridden abreast—and there was no trouble about picking the route. She wanted to lead simply to have an unobstructed view ahead.

What she saw first was that there was no more promising way out of the valley than the one she knew. On both sides there were crags, not always very high, but wherever she looked there was the shadowy presence of an overhang, or a band of smooth-looking verticality. To her, that was encouraging. Anyone else —such as the Duke of Selton—looking at this valley would not mark it as an encouraging place for further investigation.

Before departing from Drumlenn she had spent time trying to recall everything she could of their descent of the crags. After ten years, it was hard to capture anything more than fragmentary images of dark, slippery rock and the swirling mists that occasionally parted to reveal glimpses of the ground some incalculable distance below. Try as she might, she could not recall anything more, save a rough sense of the broadest outlines of the route. They had made it out the night before their descent, she and Rodal, perched on a promontory that gave a fair perspective of the upper part at least. There had been a long sweep out to the right, a gradual return to the centre, then an intricate series of smaller zigs and zags, like stitching on a blanket, sometimes so close to the falls that Rodal's hair was beaded with spray and the roar of the water drowned anything below a full shout. Finally they had straggled down a rough boulder-strewn ramp, away to the right again, spilling out onto the fringe of scree at the foot.

There was no convenient promontory from which to prospect their approach from below. From above, also, it was the weaknesses of the rock face, its ledges and ramps, that were apparent. From below, these were hidden, their edges hard to distinguish from any other seam or stratum. From below, what you saw were the steeps.

For at least two hours, as they rode closer to the edge of the map, she scoured the crags with her eyes. It was unfortunate that they were already in shadow. Perhaps it would be worth waiting a while in the morning, to see what they could pick out as the sun moved around. Some time before midday its light would rake acutely across the cliffs. Then, perhaps, they would learn more.

She mentioned this to Hedric when they had pitched camp. Lallon was building up a fire with a bundle of driftwood the two slaves had gathered lower down. Concern showed plain in Hedric's face. "You can't remember the route?"

"It was ten years ago. I recall the general line, not the details. Seeing it in better light might loosen my memory a little more."

"Well." He looked up at the shadowy crags again. "I guess you came down it sight unseen."

She didn't say anything about the way they'd sighted the route from above. She sensed that he hoped for reassurance, not to be told how they'd had an advantage coming down.

Anyway, she told herself, they'd got Railu down. Railu, who'd never climbed a rock before in her life. And who, like Jerya, had been wearing clumsy boots, two sizes too big, inadequately padded out with extra socks.

She looked at the boots she was wearing now. The cobbler in Drumlenn had been more than mildly surprised being asked to make such boots for a lady, but had been paid well enough to swallow any qualms. They were beautifully crafted, precisely fitted, and nailed all round with tricounis. For someone who for much of her life had scrambled up rocks in sandals and long skirts, to be equipped as she was now was luxury. That had to count for something.

CHAPTER 10

HEDRIC

"I should lead now," said Jerya.

Hedric said nothing, recalling the conversation over breakfast:

"Two reasons," she'd said,. "Maybe three. One, I've been this way before. I can't remember it all, but now and then something comes back to me. Two, I grew up among rocks. I was climbing almost before I could walk."

For a moment that made no sense, but then he thought: a babe goes on all fours, and a climber goes on all four limbs also.

"Three," she was saying, "I'm the lightest. If I should fall, the two of you have much better chance of holding me than any other way."

Grudgingly he admitted the truth of that, but... "I don't like to hear you speak of falling."

"I like the idea even less, believe me, and I don't mean to do it. It's a precaution, that's all".

Now, she said, "You remember I showed you, how the men of Delven guard the rope when they go after eggs?" She was tying the rope at her waist as she spoke, fingers deft and sure though her eyes were steady on him. "No, the twist round the other arm, on the side where the free rope is. Well, you can get the hang of it here. This bit's easy."

"Stand by me," he said to Lallon. "Both hands on my belt."

In that moment, Jerya had turned away to face the rock, her hands already grasping the first holds, and he'd lost the chance to give her a reassuring smile. Though in truth, he knew, he himself was in greater need of reassurance.

She glanced round. "Ready?"

As I'll ever be. He nodded, tried to smile, to look only at her and the thirty or forty feet of rock she had to climb for this first pitch. He didn't look behind, at the hundred or more feet of air that already lay below. The drop had accumulated gradually, almost unnoticed, as they picked their way up the first slanting terrace, where the only hazard had been disturbing a precariously balanced rock that might roll and crush a toe.

Jerya moved immediately on his nod, swift but unhurried. "Easy," she said after a few moments, feet already higher than his head. She went on steadily, never so fast that he had trouble feeding out the rope. There was little to be heard over the roaring whisper of the falls about twenty yards to their right, just the occasional click as her boot-nails found another little ledge.

In no more than two minutes she was up, disappearing over the edge. A moment later her face appeared. "I've hitched the rope over a boulder. You can let go now." He dropped the rope. "If you come up next and then the two of us can haul the sacks. Lallon stays below to tie each one on. Then we bring him up. Understood?"

He looked at Lallon, who only shrugged. He was a phlegmatic man—practically the opposite, Hedric had often thought, of his choleric uncle. It was not a difference between slave and aristocrat: there were choleric slaves and phlegmatic lords. It was simply a difference of character. If Lallon had any thoughts about the wisdom of any of this enterprise, or that it was the woman who was now firmly in charge, he kept them to himself.

"That wasn't so bad," said Hedric, a little breathlessly, as he joined Jerya on the ledge.

"I wish I could promise you it's all that easy." She smiled and squeezed his hand, but it didn't entirely soften the impact of her words.

The second pitch ran closer to the falls, and he had to stop a couple of times to wipe the spray from his spectacles, but otherwise the climbing was no harder than the first. The third pitch was further left, so his lenses stayed dry, but the rock was steeper, and he felt the beginnings of an ache in his arms as he worked his way upward.

"Try not to pull yourself up," said Jerya at the top. "Your legs are much stronger than your arms. Let them do the work."

He recognised the sense in that. She surely couldn't have a man's strength of arm and shoulder, but she had progressed up the pitch as smoothly as anyone could wish.

"You look like you're born to this," he said.

"Aye, well, I sort of was."

Things got a lot worse on the fourth pitch. It hadn't helped that Jerya, for the first time, had hesitated halfway up. He hadn't dared call out for fear of breaking her concentration, but after a moment she'd spoken anyway. "Just need to work out..."

After an agonising half-minute, she'd solved the problem by moving further right, even nearer to the falls, before continuing upward; but the conformation of the rock meant that he and Lallon could no longer see her, or only occasional glimpses, and with the roar of the water they couldn't hear her either. Only the rope, inching out through his hands, told him that she was still moving; even, he felt, that she still existed. Every time the rope stilled for more than a second, he held his breath; every time it moved again, he blew out a huge sigh of relief.

Finally, after what seemed an age, she was up, calling down to him. It was hard to make out words over the sound of the falls, but two sharp tugs on the rope, the pre-agreed backup signal, told him it was time to start.

He began too fast, and the worst of it was he *knew* he was climbing too fast.

"Miss Jerya weren't so far to th'right," said Lallon. "Not till a bit higher. I figger if yow took a long stride t'yowr left yow'd be back where she were."

"Thanks," he said, but then... 'a long stride' sounded easy but actually doing it meant stepping from one ledge that was half the width of a boot to another much the same, with precious little for fingers to grip. And stepping *across* rather than moving *up* demanded you look *down* to where your foot must go. And there was far too much *down* beyond that little jut of rock.

At least, he thought, looking up, *the rope's right above me. Even if I do slip I can't fall far.*

With that he persuaded himself to essay the move, and of course once he tried it it was, if not easy, straightforward enough. It was all a matter of transfer of weight, feeling where your centre of gravity was.

Then it seemed easy enough for a few moves, until he got to the point where Jerya had stalled. He could see why, as the rock above him reared from perhaps seventy degrees (which already felt quite steep enough) to vertical, or near as made no difference.

It was a matter of more 'long strides', but none quite so long this time, until he realised that the rope no longer ran straight up and down but slanted away to the left. If he should lose his grip, even assuming Jerya held him firmly, he would go swinging across like a pendulum.

And this realisation hit him just as he stood, on nothing much, at the point where the rock curved slightly, so that the next move would take him out of sight of Lallon. He would surely have no sight of Jerya either, and the ever-closer roar of the falls promised he would be out of earshot too. Alone.

He stood, absolutely unwilling to take that next step, wishing to be anywhere else but here, for he knew not how long.

Then a voice broke into the spiral of his thoughts. Lallon. Carefully, because his balance felt so precarious, he turned his head, looked back at his slave.

"Hedric!" he heard, barely, though Lallon must be shouting full out. And then... something... "...Grip on yourself!"

Get a grip on yourself. Any slave who spoke like that to a typical master would surely be flogged, but Hedric and Lallon had been playmates when he was too young to properly understand the distinction of master and slave. He laughed quietly to himself, and that settled his nerves sufficiently to make the step around the curve.

He found himself in a shallow niche, no more than a dimpling of the rockface. Just enough to give some hint, or illusion, of shelter. He pressed his forehead against cool smooth stone. *Get a grip on yourself.* He found himself smiling. He must remember to thank Lallon—when they reached the top.

The problem with the feeling of shelter is that sooner or later you have to leave it. *Can't stop here all day.* But when he looked up he saw that the shallow indentation in the rock continued above him, slanting gently to the left; and the rope ran that way too.

"I'm moving up again," he called, in the faint hope Jerya could hear. A slight footledge *here*, an angled facet *there*; a couple of moves passed without difficulty.

Then it all started to fall apart again. There was some spiteful shift of the wind, perhaps; or it was merely the configuration of the rock. He felt the chill spatter of spray on his face. The rock shone evilly; and, worse, all at once his glasses were beaded with moisture. He could see nothing in front of him but a grey blur. He tried brushing the water off with a sleeve, but that only gave a smeared vision that was scarcely better; and two seconds later the water was back anyway.

Sighing, he braced himself as best he could, trying to ensure his position was stable enough that he could—very carefully—remove his glasses and stow them inside his jerkin. Now he could only see the rock clearly out to about arm's-length away. *Well, that's all you need at any one time*, he told himself.

He looked down. The good thing about shedding his glasses was that he no longer had any clear sense of how far below the ground was. Less good, his feet were no longer clear either; but he could see well enough to see how he had, almost unconsciously, set them on rock-facets that, though both sloping, were opposed to each other. That opposing pressure must help to keep them firmly in place.

And that was something he could apply again and again.

Try not to pull, Jerya had said. *Let your legs do the work.* That made more sense now, but she hadn't said as much as she might have. *Think of it as a problem in physics. Opposing forces. Press* into *the rock. That must be how you maintained grip, especially on wet and sloping holds.*

He muttered to himself under his breath as he climbed on. *Press, don't pull. Centre of gravity. Opposing forces.*

When he reached her, Jerya's smile changed swiftly to a look of concern. "Hedric, you haven't lost your glasses?"

"No," he said, smiling back, and then had to check inside his jerkin to be sure. They were there, and the moments when his chest had scraped against the rock did not seem to have damaged them.

"I hardly ever see you without your glasses," she said as he slipped them back on. "You have nice eyes."

He didn't know how to answer that, and before he could think of anything, she was asking how the pitch had gone.

"Not so bad, in the end," he said. "You just have to think of it as a problem in physics."

CHAPTER 11

HEDRIC

Before them lay a vast shallow bowl—or would a topographer call it a gently dished plateau? Jerya was looking bemused. "Coming down, we were almost guided, like everything funnelled down, but coming up it just spreads out... The way lies somewhere to the left, besure, but now I'm not sure where exactly."

"Did you not have a compass?"

She smiled. "Not as such. Without a map, what would it have told me anyway?" She looked once more at the miles-wide slope that rose on the left, featureless but for a dozen or more shallow runnels, the courses of incipient, perhaps seasonal, streams. "We came down by one of those channels, but which one?" He hadn't meant to judge her; already he was somewhat in awe of the achievement of crossing this way, without a map, with equipment far more primitive than what they had now. Still, under his steady regard, she seemed to grow defensive. "We never really saw anything before. It was always snowing, or the clouds were low."

He considered a moment. "We could try them one by one, I suppose... or we could climb that peak over there. That might give us a better view." It was small compared to those beyond it, but it was still a mountain, with a sharp peak and rocky flanks.

And, as was soon becoming clearer by the minute, it was small only in comparison with the greater peaks. He quickly became glad they had shed everything except some spare clothing and their water-flasks. What he had thought might take ten minutes became an hour's solid trudging up a stony slope, little more than barely-compacted scree. If it was scree, he thought, remembering a talk he'd heard at the Society for Natural Philosophy a few years ago, then the angle could hardly be more than thirty-five degrees, but it felt steeper. It seemed easier to look down between his legs than over his shoulder, but after performing the experiment once, he decided not to repeat it. It would be bad enough having to look down when they came to descend.

He tried to occupy his mind by contemplating what their current altitude might be. Some of the higher peaks around them had been triangulated from afar, their elevation estimated with a high level of confidence. The highest stood around nine thousand feet, if memory served. The valley below the waterfall-climb reached almost four and a half thousand, assuming the survey had been accurate. To his considerable chagrin, the entire crag-band they had climbed could hardly be more than five hundred feet; never, on the four hard pitches, had Jerya run out more than half of their hundred-foot rope. They could not have gained more than another five hundred feet since the top of the rocks, so the spot where they had left Lallon with the bulk of the gear must be between five thousand and five and a half.

A barometer would have been a fine thing to have brought, he mused, slogging on up in Jerya's wake. A small aneroid would not have been too heavy or cumbersome. Of course a barometer could not give an absolute measure of altitude, but it would give a good notion of height gained or lost on any given day. He had no doubt the Duke's expedition would have barometers a-plenty, clinometers, every other imaginable contrivance for altimetry and surveying. But His Grace's priorities must be very different. He and Jerya had a single objective.

At the top of the slope, a line of crags girded the peak like a ruff. They were not high, maybe sixty feet, but that was more than enough; truth, *twenty* feet might be more than enough. And, just here, they looked impregnable, at least to his eyes. But Jerya went prospecting, briefly vanishing from sight round a bulge like a gnarled pilaster on the left, and came back grinning. "Easy round the corner."

"Your idea of easy and my idea of easy might be some distance apart."

"No, seriously."

And, he had to admit, she was right. A dark gully cut into the cliff, getting deeper as it ascended. There were a couple of awkward steps, but each above a substantial ledge. Higher up, the gully twisted to the right, and all sense of the sweep and tumble of the slope below was lost.

He was panting as he clambered out into the sunlight again; but he was grinning too. And it got better; the kink of the gully isolated a wedge-shaped segment of rock, its top a near-level platform perhaps four yards long and three broad, tapering to a blunt 'point' less than a yard wide.

"A magnificent belvedere," he pronounced.

"Is that the aristocratic way of saying it's a pretty spot?" teased Jerya. They were both a little euphoric.

"If you like." He pulled out his sketchbook. "Can you see which way we should go?"

"Reckon." She stepped close, so he could follow the line of her arm as she pointed.

They were about level with the top of the sprawling slope opposite. Beyond—some miles beyond, surely—more peaks rose, a tangled mass of axe-sharp facets. In just one place was there a gap in that barricade of rock and ice, a notch like a missing tooth.

"There," she said, no doubt in her voice now.

He settled down cross-legged, as far out on the rock wedge as he dared go. Their purpose might not be scientific or geographical, but it could do no harm to spend half an hour, while the weather was fine and settled, making a sketch of all he could see.

As far left as he could see—about Southwest by West—there was another gap between peaks, one that, given its distance, must be two or three miles broad. Something glinted there in the afternoon light. He indicated it to Jerya. "Ice, do you suppose?"

"Besure."

"That must be what the ancients meant by a glacier." He looked again, baffled as to how to sketch it, but also thrilled to have seen it. He felt the pull, to go and stand close, perhaps even to clamber onto that slippery surface. He might be the first man in this age of the world to do so. *That would be something...* But it was not why they were here now; even if they could spare the time, they were hardly equipped for side-trips.

Another time, he thought, and returned to his sketch, taking bearings to the prominent peaks and noting them down in his most minuscule hand. He also marked a spot on the opposite slope, a distinctive amber patch, where they must climb tomorrow, to take a back-bearing to where they stood now. Then he stood, shaking stiffness from his legs, and declared himself ready to descend.

Unexpectedly, Jerya pouted. "I thought we could go on to the summit. It's not far."

It surely wasn't, a few hundred yards perhaps, and the angle was certainly easier than the screes and fellfields below them, but... "It's ice."

She shook her head. "It's just a glaze on the surface. The snow's soft beneath. Look, I tested it."

It was true, he saw. Deep holes in the snow, at least twenty of them, marked where she had ventured. She could probably have been to the top and back in the time he'd been sketching, but she'd waited.

"We have what he need," he felt bound to point out. "What we came for. There's no reason..."

"No need, perhaps, if you're strict about it. Draff, there was no need for you to make that sketch either. No need, but surely there's a *reason*. You know, I grew up close to the mountains. Been looking at them, often as I got a chance, since I was old enough to slope off on my own." She grinned. "And that might not be as old as you'd think... Younger than Embrel, to be sure. But I never got to climb one, actually stand on top; never had the chance. And I might never have the chance again."

It was unwarranted effort, unnecessary risk; but the look on her face made it impossible to deny her.

The slope did gleam icy in the Sun, too dazzling to look directly ahead, but Jerya was right: it was just a fragile crust over a few feet of snow. And snow was familiar enough, even down at Kirwaugh. He had done all the things boys do in snow. Perhaps girls did them too, or some girls. It was hard to know; there had been no girls among his childhood companions. And precious few boys, too, really, save when he played, illicitly, with some of the slave lads, Lallon among them. Though, when he thought about it, his father must have known, and turned a blind eye.

So he followed in Jerya's steps, stamping the snow down more firmly, thinking it would make things easier and safer on the return. Within little more than ten minutes the slope was rounding off into a kind of shallow dome. If it wasn't the perfect pointed peak that a child might draw—that a child named Hedric *had* drawn—it felt a good deal safer because of it, and a lot easier to stand there both together.

Jerya threw her arms around him. "Thank you! Thank you, my lovely. Admit it, that was worth it, wasn't it?"

He looked around, and after a moment she drew away, though she kept a hand on his arm. Together they gazed at the panorama.

Vastness, dazzle, planes and blades of rock, the shimmer of ice. Air and space and a breeze freighted with cold as if straight from the glacier. No one could describe this, he thought. Oh, one could concoct a mechanical description, this peak and that pass and the sheet of ice sprawling along the horizon. But it was like trying to describe a human face in words. Every novelist tried that, and every novelist failed; whether you gave it ten words or a whole page, words could not do what ten strokes of an artist's pen might begin to achieve.

But... words could not come anywhere near this feeling, and he wasn't sure if even the greatest artist, an Isteban or a Falovas, could do more than hint at it.

He looked into Jerya's eyes and thought *she knows it too.*

He could have stayed an hour, but the thought of the descent grew niggling and nagging in his mind. After maybe fifteen minutes he ventured to suggest it. Jerya was surprisingly agreeable, only insisting on a final hug before they turned to go.

✳

He never knew quite how it happened; a patch of ice under the snow, or a loose stone? He only knew that all at once he was sliding, head-first, and though the slope hadn't seemed particularly steep, he was gathering speed at an alarming rate. The thin glaze-crust was smooth and slick; it was ice, after all. It had seemed flimsy enough when they were stamping out steps on the way up, but it was bearing his weight now.

The rim of the crag-ruff was rushing closer all too rapidly. He could too easily imagine how he was about to go flying off there, cartwheeling through a gulf of air, before crashing into the scree-slope somewhere far below. A man might survive such a fall, but it seemed a slim prospect.

And then, somehow, time itself seemed to slow. He knew he was still hurtling down the slope, still gathering speed, and yet there was time to think, a hard cold clarity in his mind. He even had a moment to wonder at this change, before telling himself there were more urgent matters.

He could see no way of stopping himself, and even kicking his boots against the slope to try and break the crust was having no discernible effect. But perhaps he could affect the *direction* of his slide... A few feet to his left was the dark dotted line of the steps they had made for themselves on the way up. But to the right of his direct trajectory, the crag-rim poked up, a blocky little tower, above the foot of the ice-slope.

He could steer to the left—if he could steer at all—and perhaps where the crust was broken he would slow. But would he slow enough to stop? Or he could steer to the right. Those rocks would surely stop him. No doubt it would still be painful, but the odds of survival seemed vastly better.

He aimed right, pressing his right boot against the slope, stretching out his right arm and rolling slightly to increase pressure. At first he couldn't be sure if it was working, but then... the jutting rocks were definitely closer to his line of travel. A moment later he began to worry that he might veer too far to the right and miss them on the other side. He dug in both toes, threw out both arms.

Perhaps this began to slow him. Perhaps the ice-glaze was softer here. In the last few yards, as the rocks loomed, dark and suddenly all too close, he knew that he was decelerating. At the very last, he thought to protect his head, wrapped his arms about it and curled up in a convulsive attempt to interpose a shoulder.

The impact was still enough to knock all the breath from his body. For a moment he lost all sense of where he was, perhaps even who he was. He was the small boy who'd fallen from his pony; the larger one, at school now, who'd found the temerity to throw a punch at a persistent tormentor and got a dozen in return.

His vision seemed to swim. He realised that his glasses were hanging askew, that he was seeing clear from one eye only. But before attempting to right them, before attempting to move at all, he began to gather some sense of how his body had fared. There was a broad dull pain all around his left shoulder, but everywhere else seemed unharmed, at least in comparison.

Very slowly, inch by inch, he began to roll over and work himself up into a sitting position. The battered area grumbled but there was no sharp flare of pain, and he began to believe nothing was broken. With his right hand he resettled his glasses on his face, and for the first time since coming to that crashing stop, looked around him.

Jerya was about thirty yards away. He could see at once how two impulses warred within her; the urge to rush down to him, and the patent need to go carefully, to make sure she too did not slip.

"I'm all right," he called. His voice cracked weakly. In case she hadn't heard, he waved his right hand.

Then she was beside him. Her face was almost grey, stricken.

"Gossan, I thought I'd lost you," she said, breathless, close to tears. "I couldn't have borne it."

"I thought for a while I'd lost myself," he said, then coughed.

"Careful, you might have cracked a rib."

"I don't think anything's broken."

"Well, let's not rush to conclusions." Her hand strayed toward him, then halted. Afraid of hurting him, he thought. He caught it with his own—his right. He wasn't ready to risk the left just yet.

"I'm sorry," he said.

"What for?"

"Stupid of me to trip like that."

"My fault for dragging you up the peak when we didn't need to."

"All right, let's agree that we're both complete fools. Does that make you feel better?"

She didn't laugh, but she did manage a small smile. He counted that progress.

"Draff," she said then, "I wish Railu was here."

"Aye," he countered. "I wager she'd love it."

Then she did laugh, but only for a moment, before springing to the defence of her friend. "Don't underestimate her. Don't forget she crossed these mountains too."

"Aye, you're right, of course." He freed his hand from hers long enough to push himself a little more upright. Several bits of his body grumbled, but none screamed. "I really begin to believe nothing's broken, but I imagine there's a lot of bruising."

"D'you think you can use that left arm at all?"

He could flex the fingers, work the wrist and the elbow, but the shoulder was already stiffening.

"If you can," she said, "I reckon we should get you down that bit of gully before you stiffen up any more. Either that or I'll have to go fetch Lallon. We'd get you down there easy enough between the two of us."

He couldn't see how it would be 'easy', but he didn't argue the point. "Let's see about standing up first."

❋

Descending the gully involved a lot of shuffling over rock steps on his backside, Jerya bracing him from below as he slithered down each one. Easy it certainly was not, but they managed it securely enough without needing to summon Lallon.

He hoped his servant hadn't seen the fall, and wondered briefly about not telling him at all, but knew that would never work. By the time they got down to the camping spot, he couldn't lift his left arm more than six inches from his side: *that* was not going to go unnoticed.

Lallon had scoured the slope for clumps of heather, cut enough for a good fire. "Oh, well done," said Jerya. "*And* you've already got water on." She turned back to Hedric. "We need to have a look at you. I'd ask you to strip but you aren't going to manage it on your own, are you?"

"Miss Delven!" he protested like a scandalised dowager.

"I've helped Railu enough times. I've seen half the slaves at Duncal with their shirts off. I'm not going to faint at the sight of your ribcage."

It's a bit different, he thought, and then spent the next few minutes, as she gently extricated him from jerkin and shirt and undershirt, wondering exactly why he might think that. *Because they're slaves?* He hoped it was not that, and he did not believe it was. No, it was because he could imagine other circumstances which might involve her removing his garments—but there would be no onlookers then.

There was a sharp intake of breath when the undershirt came off, but that was Lallon. Jerya was already leaning close, examining his upper arm and the back of his ribs. "I wish Railu was here," she said again, but she didn't sound too fearful. "To me it looks as if you've got off fairly lightly."

"Not sure it feels like it. It feels like I've been kicked by a horse."

"*Were* you ever kicked by a horse?" she asked.

"Never on the shoulder. Caught one on the thigh once, couldn't walk for a—ow!"

She'd begun cleaning the injured area with a cloth that had evidently been dipped in the hot water. It couldn't have been boiling, he reasoned, or her fingers would not be able to hold it; but it felt like it where his skin was broken.

"Stop whimmering," she said. "That's what Railu always tells them. Have to clean the wounds so they don't get infected. Not that there's much. More scrapes than cuts, really. Good thing your jacket's sturdy. And there can't have been any really sharp edges on the rock just there... Nearly done. Then I'll bandage the area, just in case they weep. Don't want you sticking to your sleeping-bag in the night."

❋

It was Lallon who suggested they should think about going back.

Hedric was half-reclining with his right side against a handy mound of soft mossy earth. It almost looked like an anthill, but he'd seen no sign of life. Perhaps it was still too cold for them to emerge. He looked up in surprise.

"Go back? Why?"

"'Cause yow're hurt. And a long ways still to go, I figger."

"Four days to Delven," said Jerya. "Long as the weather doesn't turn nasty."

"Or one day back down to where we can get a horse for 'im. Even a waggon, if needs be."

Jerya shrugged. "I can see the sense, one way. But I can't see any way he can climb down five hundred feet of steep crag with only one arm."

"We could lower 'im, maybe."

"Have you—" she began, but Hedric cut her off.

"Excuse me," he said. "If you've quite finished talking as if I'm not here... I'll stay here till I can use my arm again before I let anyone *lower* me down that precipice. But if that's an option... Jerya, tell me again what we still have to do? There's no more climbing? No more crags?"

"There's a little, just going down off the moors into Delven. But it's easy." She met his gaze. "Proper easy."

"And the rest is just walking?"

"Aye. A day uphill, to the first pass, or close below it. A short descent and re-ascent to the second gap. The rest is mostly down or level."

"Well, then. There's nothing wrong with my legs."

She gave him a smile; as always, it lifted his heart. "That's the spirit. But there is one problem."

"Wha... oh."

"Aye, I very much doubt you'll feel like carrying a heavy pack tomorrow."

"I c'n tek more," said Lallon stoutly.

"I'm sure," said Jerya. "And so can I. But there's only so much we can fit in any one rucksack... Pity there's no trees up here."

He and Lallon both stared at her in bemusement. "Why?" he asked.

"There's something I've seen the men do, in Delven. When they've a heavy load to bring in, like they've killed a stag... They make a framework out of branches, drag the carcass on that. You can haul a lot more than you can carry on your back."

Hedric laughed, then stopped at a grumble from his shoulder. "And if we had a few more tools we could make a waggon and you could haul *me*... But there's no trees and there's no way of making a waggon out of stone... unless they have that art too, in Delven?"

"If they do, I never saw."

"Listen, then," he said. "I don't like it but I'm sure it makes sense for you two to take heavier loads tomorrow. So put the stuff that's bulky but light in my pack, like the sleeping bags. I'm sure I can carry that, taking what weight there is on my good shoulder and my waist."

Jerya considered briefly. "I can't think of a better plan. But let's see how you are in the morning. We could always consider stopping here another day, or even two. The packs get lighter every day, after all... though we might be hungry before we reach Delven."

"You don't want that," he said. "I'm not good to be around when I'm hungry."

Part Two
The Sung Lands

CHAPTER 12

JERYA

The approach to the final pass was not steep. She remembered it had been hard to tell where they began to go downhill. Then, the air had been full of snow, whirling and disorientating, but the ground had been clear. Now, the sky above was blue, scattered clouds shredding in the Northerly wind, but drifts of snow lay across their route. Breaking trail through these, when it was her turn, made it feel like the climb was much steeper than it really was.

As they neared the pass, a blue space between blades of char-black rock streaked with veins the colour of dried blood, the wind strengthened. The pass itself must funnel it, she thought, so that it would always be either at your back or in your face, never blowing across you. It had been in her face the first time, and so it was now, which seemed vaguely unfair.

Today it wasn't driving the fat wet snowflakes she recalled, but it was lifting grains from the lying snow, flinging them hard as hail. She pulled her hood lower, her scarf over mouth and nose, but still she had to cringe away from the scouring icy pellets, only glancing forward occasionally to keep a straight course. A word came to her mind, from some forgotten book: *spindrift*.

At last they entered the pass itself. The wind howled and moaned over the edges of the rocks, twenty or thirty yards to each side, but the ground between was clear of snow. Long since scoured clean, she reckoned, whipped into spindrift. Tears sprang to her eyes, but she blinked them away until she could look steadily ahead again.

They stopped at what seemed to be the highest point, or near enough, took out drinks and dried fruit. There was nowhere to sit, no handy boulders or outcrops. The crags here seemed to spring straight from the ground, with barely any scree below, as if even that had been swept away by the wind, so they stood, easing aches from their shoulders as always when they had the packs off.

Hedric had his glasses off too, was wiping them with his usual care; he could use his left hand enough for that now. Jerya was still faintly surprised each time she saw him without lenses, how different his eyes looked, even his whole face; younger, perhaps, and maybe more vulnerable. She wondered if the spectacles had offered any protection from the vicious spindrift.

Even in the Sun, the wind was too cold to encourage them to linger long. Moving on, there were renewed flurries of spindrift as snow-patches reappeared, coalescing into a broad band.

Then the ground grew clearer, and it was possible to thread a course between the remaining drifts. A few more minutes and they could feel that they were going downhill. "That's the watershed," she said. "Welcome to the Sung Lands." A sudden thought made her fix her gaze on Lallon. "You know there are no slaves here."

"Aye," said Hedric, "You're a free man, lad." Lallon's only reaction was a shrug.

Soon the ground steepened. The stony slope, dappled with snow, demanded care. They picked a zigzag course, a few yards apart, each with their own thoughts.

As the slope eased again, the first wan vegetation appeared, still flattened from a winter under snow. Hedric came alongside Jerya.

"From here there's no more difficulty," she said. He regarded her sceptically. "Well, we'll reach Delven. After that we might have difficulties of a different kind."

He accepted that, looking around, down the long sweep of the valley, closed off in the far haze by its own slow curve. After a moment, he said, "Thus far this Western land looks little different from the Eastern."

"It's not the land that's different. Or that's not the difference that matters."

"Aye... well, as to that, I think I need to know a good deal more of how this land is governed."

She laughed. "You think I know? I could tell you far more about the governance of the Five Principalities than of the land I was born in... though I doubt I'd be telling you anything you don't already know. I only knew Delven for my first nineteen years. I knew the College for a few months. The rest I barely glimpsed."

"Well, then, tell me how Delven is governed."

She considered how best to answer. "It often seemed to me... well, it is not like the farm at Duncal, where the steward tells the field-slaves what to do. More like the house, where Railu and Rhenya know what needs to be done. My memory of Delven is like that. It often seemed to me as if things just happened. People knew their responsibilities, what was needful. Of course, the Headman oversees all, and makes decisions when decisions must be made, but mostly, as far as I saw, he would lead discussion rather than issuing orders like a slave-owner."

"And the Dawnsinger works via the Headman?"

"He speaks with her often; most days, I think."

"To what end?"

"I often wondered exactly what they spoke about. As far as I was concerned, the Dawnsinger was a complete mystery. Until I saw her close I hardly even knew that she was human."

"But you knew she made the sun rise," he said, tone almost teasing.

"Truer to say I feared the sun would not rise if she didn't Sing."

"Isn't that the same thing?"

She shrugged. "Perhaps. But I must have known that the sun did shine on Unsung lands also. As if something else happened, or did not happen, there... The truth is, it wasn't one of the questions I thought hard about, because there was already an answer. If I asked, 'why does the sun rise?', they knew what to tell me. When I asked, 'why do sticks float and stones sink?', they told me not to be a bother, so I had to worry at it for myself."

Her mind flitted to another track. "If you want to know about the duties of a village Dawnsinger, you should have asked Railu. She had that training; I wasn't there long, and they had other things in mind for me."

"I often forget that Railu was a Dawnsinger, too."

"She doesn't talk about it much." *Hardly at all, truth be told.* "Anyway, you'll see Delven for yourself soon enough."

"Aye... What do you think? Two days now?"

"On the way up, we camped once at the foot of the pass, somewhere not too far below us now. And before that, where the valley widens, beyond where you can see. We'll get well past the first, but we won't get to the second without driving ourselves too hard. It seems to me if we camp at whatever spot seems best tonight, then tomorrow night we can find somewhere on the moors above Delven. That way we can reach Delven early the following day, just after Dawnsong."

"You wish to see the Dawnsinger first?"

"I need to, I think." *I need to know if she still lives*, she thought, but did not say.

He murmured acknowledgement, "Well, it seems to me what I may need to know most, in the end, is how the Guild of Dawnsingers is governed."

She smiled. "There too I may know less than you wish for. I can say, of course, that the Guild is led by a Conclave of Masters, under the Master Prime, but I never even saw them all, save when I said my Novitial Vow..." *The Vow that I broke*, she thought, and walked a few strides in silence. "I spoke my Vow to the Master Prime, as every Dawnsinger does, but as a Postulant and then a Novice, our lives were ruled by the Tutors, and over them the Senior Tutor. I could tell you much about *her*..."

CHAPTER 13

HEDRIC

Below the steeps of the descent, they threaded easily between scattered boulders, some huge as houses. A stream burbled gently beside them.

"Jerya," said Hedric, coming alongside her on an open stretch, "A thought occurs to me."

"I'd have imagined that thoughts frequently occur to you. I would certainly *hope* so."

He returned her grin. "I hope you're right. Very well, a *particular* thought occurs to me; one I would wish to share with you."

"Then what are you waiting for?"

"Well, you tell me that we will be in Delven tomorrow night, or the following morning. The place of your birth... and, as you reminded us not so long ago, there are no slaves here. I... I don't mean to suggest that I ever doubted your word, but I could hardly say to others, 'I know Jerya is freeborn because she told me so.' Now, however, it occurs to me that very soon, I will be able to swear on oath that I have seen proof that you are freeborn."

"But if my word is good enough for you, what difference does that make?"

"To me, none. To others, maybe a great deal."

"I suppose... but if all there is is your word, people will say... you have your own reasons to tell that particular tale. You're hardly an impartial witness."

He considered that. "Perhaps... but there's also Railu. I can tell Duncal that she too was never a slave." He chuckled suddenly. "Aye, and they could go to the market where you were bought, say they sold you under false pretences. Claim the money back..."

She laughed too. "I'd like to see that swine Keeving's face...!" But then she sobered quickly. "You could give Railu her freedom, but how much would really change? Her hair will never come back, she will always look like a slave."

"There are such things as wigs. Good ones are undetectable. They use real human hair." he hesitated a moment. "I have heard that when someone is taken into slavery, and their head is shaved, the slave-market will sell the hair to a wig-maker; a little extra to add to their commission on the sale."

She looked pensive. He supposed she was thinking about the time her own head was first shaved; one more shock, by the sound of it, in a day of shocks.

After a moment she said, "Sounds expensive."

"Doubtless, but I am not a poor man."

"It's good of you," she said, and gave his hand a squeeze. A rare touch; they were cautious whenever Lallon, or anyone else, might see. "You're a good man. And we shall ask her, when we get back... but be prepared for her to be less enthused than you might expect. I don't know if I could say she is happy with her life as it is, but I think she is... she has come to terms with it."

Perhaps an hour later, he happened to mention that Lallon had a wife and family, Jerya gave him what he was coming to think of as one of *those* looks. "Don't you think taking him away from them so much is a bit too much like the way other owners treat married slaves?"

"No, I do not," he said indignantly, "And neither does Lallon. Ask him if you doubt my word. But ask yourself also why so many of my visits to Duncal have been made alone."

They walked a little apart for a while, but then he came back to her side. "Let me tell you a little about me and Lallon. I don't even remember the first time we met; we ran about together from some very early age. That's not so very unusual, but there are many folk who don't think there should be intimacy even in youngsters. Turned out my father's steward was one.

"When I was eight or nine, I fell into a pond and Lallon hauled me out. The steward saw him—and had him flogged for laying hands on me. I—"

"—Wait," she said. "He flogged a boy who'd just rescued you from drowning?"

"I doubt I'd have drowned, in fact, but the sides were steep and slippery. I'm not sure how I'd have got out on my own."

"Still..." She shook her head, looking both baffled and angry.

"I was furious, of course, and made bitter complaint to my father. He wasn't a man who relished confrontation, but he must have said something. Aymesh—that was the man's name—couldn't do anything against me, and he didn't do anything to Lallon either, not for a while. Not till I went away to school in fact.

"When I came home for my first vacation, I went looking for Lallon, but he was nowhere to be found. Asking around, I learned he, Aymesh, had sent him off to some land my father owned fifteen miles away.

"When my father died I was in my first year at university. As soon as I was home for the summer, I called that man, Aymesh, into my fa—what was now my study, and dismissed him with immediate effect. Of course it took me some time to find a new steward, and for those months I had to oversee everything myself. But what I found, of course, was that the slaves knew perfectly well what needed to be done and when; for the most part I needed to do little more than sign documents and pay invoices. It occurred to me that I could almost have left them to it, but that would have been scandalous. I need only consider the consequences once my uncle got to hear of it. Still, it taught me that much of what is said and written about the incapacity of slaves to work without direction is nonsense.

"Lallon had been a great help to me in that time, a conduit between me and the other slaves. He cannot read, of course, but his memory is prodigious."

"Did you never consider freeing him, making him your steward?"

"Aye, I did." He gave a short laugh. "For about three minutes. And I have no doubt he had all the abilities—save literacy—to do the job. In many ways he would have been better than the first man I employed. It wasn't till I was fully home after taking my degree that I truly saw—I mustn't digress. To free Lallon, at such a young age, I am sure would spark envy, resentment, among the other slaves. And now the law makes it all but impossible to free any slave under thirty. Not to mention, again, how my uncle would be likely to respond."

That man," she said in a voice dull with bitterness. "I have never seen him..."

"Best hope you never do. "

They walked on with their own thoughts. The way must still be down-hill, he thought; the stream beside them flowed purposefully on; but the ground seemed level to his eyes and under his feet.

It was a grey dawn, the mountains behind only vague suggestions through swirling mist. There was no way he could tell if the Singer began on time. In fact it was hard to tell exactly when she began at all. The Song began soft as a lullaby, swelling gradually in one long crescendo. The melody was one of those paradoxical ones that seems to be entirely composed of rising cadences yet somehow remains within the compass of a single Singer's voice.

When it ended, he looked at Jerya. Her eyes were wet. He thought for a moment she was simply moved by the return to her old life, but then she shook her head.

"That wasn't Sharess," she said.

CHAPTER 14

JERYA

"The last time—the only time—I climbed those steps," she said, "I didn't know it, but my life was about to change forever."

Hedric looked at her, silent, as if he could not find the words. And then he did... "For myself, I cannot be sorry."

If Lallon had not been there, she would have embraced him, or at least grasped his hands. Her eyes prickled suspiciously. One last, almost pleading look, and then she turned away, squared her shoulders, and began to ascend. It felt as if memories were weighing her down quite as much as the pack she'd been carrying.

She had entered the chamber once before, but that had been at Holdren's bidding. Now she hovered on the the top step, almost transported back to another time, when all of this had been forbidden... not even forbidden, unthinkable.

Well, that was ten years past, and more. Another time, and she was another person.

She raised her hand and rapped firmly on the stout wooden door.

"Who is it?" The voice did not sound like Sharess. Well, the voice they'd heard in Song hadn't sounded like her either.

"My name is Jerya." Simply that: not Jerya Delven, or Jerya of Delven.

"*Jerya?*" Even through the oaken door-panels the incredulity was clear. In a moment the door was flung wide, and Jerya found herself gazing upon...

"*Marit?*"

"You remember me, then. Yea, and I remember you. But what... Wait, come in."

She hurried Jerya inside, shooting a glance at the deserted path below; Hedric and Lallon had retreated, and no one else was about. Jerya could understand: Marit might not want her unexpected visitor to be seen before she herself knew what was going on.

Marit had been taller than herself, she remembered, or that was how she had seen her. Had she, Jerya, continued to grow even beyond nineteen summers? Surely Marit could not have shrunk... she couldn't be more than forty-five at the outside. Then she saw that Marit was barefoot, while she was wearing boots. Perhaps that accounted for it.

For a moment they just stared at each other. Marit was the first to recover. "By the seven planets, *what* are you doing here?"

Jerya almost laughed. "I could ask you the same question."

"Oh, my answer's simple enough. I have a feeling yours is going to be more complicated. But come in properly. If you've a story to tell... sit there. I was just brewing coffee..."

"I'd forgotten..." said Jerya a minute later.

"Forgotten?"

"The taste of the Guild Blend. I haven't had any quite like it for ten years."

"Aye," said Marit, settling on a three-legged stool facing her. "It is ten years, isn't it?" She inhaled, then sipped. "Now, what's your story, Jerya? They call you a Vow-breaker, a renegade."

"You said your story was simple, and mine isn't. Could you tell first... and set my mind at rest about Sharess?"

Marit shrugged. "As you like. Well, not so long after you passed through Thrushgill—the second time—I had the unexpected pleasure of a Visitation. Two Peripatetics and their Master. Partly they were after clues to where you'd gone. But they also took a look at me..."

"You might have me to thank for that," said Jerya. Marit gave her a hard look, and she hastened to add, "I only mentioned that you'd said you hadn't seen a Visitation in a long time. Nothing more."

"Ah, well, they'd have had to be blind not to see how things were with me. Not that anything happened right away, they were more interested in chasing after you. And my drinking only got worse. Until one night, while I was drunk—I'd never have done it sober—I wrote a letter to the Masters. Hardly know what I said... Grabbed a bird and fumbled the ring onto its leg and sent it on its way. In the morning... well, then it was too late." She laughed. "What could I do, send another message? *Ignore my previous, I wrote it while drunk*?

"After that, they sent me here to cut off my supply of alcohol." For a moment her gaze seemed to turn inward. Her hands tightened on the coffee-cup. "Have you ever wanted anything so badly you feel like you'd kill for it?" Jerya shook her head. "That's how I felt. The people must have heard, stars only know what they thought. I'd probably have killed any of them for a drink, 'cept Sharess kept saying to me, 'you're still a Dawnsinger'."

She hardly dared, but she had to ask... "And what of Sharess?"

"Back in the College, last I heard."

"In good health?"

Marit shrugged. "Her hands trouble her. Her feet too, a little. Otherwise she's well enough, I think."

Jerya almost hugged her in her relief. Yes, it was sad that Sharess's hands were a problem—she remembered suddenly that her very first glimpse, up close, had been the old Singer's hand. Even then it had been warped, the joints swollen. She had a word now, a likely diagnosis: arthritis. She did not know how much relief the Healers of the Guild could give the condition, but she did know that Singers who could no longer serve in a village or town were treated with honour, accommodated in a wing of the College, and encouraged to continue with whatever work or pursuits their inclinations and abilities led them to.

Most of all, her mother still lived, and very possibly she would have the chance to see her again.

With her worst fears allayed, she was able to contrive an account of herself. "You'll have heard from Sharess what we intended to do. Well, we succeeded... crossed to the other side. And—"

"—And found no Blistered Lands," said Marit, laughing.

Jerya blinked several times. "How did you know?"

"Well, I knew the start from Sharess anyway. And then we had the news from that Rodal fellow, on his way back. So tell me as much as you like, but could be I've heard the main part anyway."

"Of course, Rodal..." How could she have forgotten? Only yesterday she had been reminding herself to ask after him. The shock of finding Marit in residence, the concern for Sharess, had thrown her off her intent.

And he had made it back across, alive and well. *I should never have doubted it*, she thought. *That climb by the waterfalls would be nothing to a man of Delven. I wonder if he climbed the ice-peak too, to spy out the way ahead?* Still, there had always been a niggling doubt, especially as he'd been obliged to tackle it on his own.

It was all very well thinking she should never have doubted. The relief of actually knowing silenced her for a minute. Marit waited sympathetically, quietly topping up her coffee from the pot.

Finally, Jerya said, "There's still a few things I need to tell you. Starting with the fact that I'm not alone."

"The other one's with you? What was her name... Railu?"

"Not Railu, no."

❋

There was one more person she needed to speak to, but privacy was always hard to find in Delven. Eventually they walked out together past the

Dawnsinger's tor—Marit's tor now—to the meadow where the nearest
beehives stood. There, among the murmur of a thousand bees, they faced
each other. Holdren was obviously older, his hair whiter and sparser, his
back not quite so straight.

"I know," she said straight out. They might only have a few minutes; best
not to beat about the bush.

"You know?" he echoed, his tone quizzical, but his eyes suggested he had
at least a guess at what she meant.

"I see Sharess every time I look in the mirror," she said. "It was clearer
when I was bald, of course. I couldn't truly see you until my hair grew back."

"And yet my hair was never black, nor had that glint of red like yours."

"No, but the way it falls, its shape around my face, something in the line
of the jaw... I knew, then, but I was sure before. Who else could it be, truly?"

"It was a great wrong that we did," he said, very softly, almost as if to
himself.

She shrugged. "Maybe so, maybe not. I don't feel that you wronged *me*."

He didn't answer. Looking at him, she saw that perhaps he couldn't.

Men of Delven didn't weep. There might be moments when a man had
to look away, hide his face, but no one called it weeping.

Finally he sighed. It might seem careworn, fatigued, but maybe it was
relief, that the secret he'd held for thirty years was finally free.

"I never could acknowledge you," he said. "Even now, before others...
you understand, don't you?"

"Yes, of course."

He smiled. "In a way it was almost funny. Everyone was looking around
at the maidens, even some of the younger wives... but no one ever guessed
the truth."

She understood that. Dawnsingers were different. Dawnsingers were,
almost, not women at all. "I wouldn't have guessed, myself. You know,
before."

"Before..." he repeated, looking at her. Grey eyes: like her own, but many
people in Delven had grey or hazel eyes.

"Well," he continued, "I gave you to my own mother's care at first. That would seem natural enough, I thought."

He went on, but she hardly heard him. She was staring. "Your *mother*...?" she managed at last. Holdren's mother, Pentrunne, had been the elderwife, always in the lead in councils and discussions... but Jerya hadn't seen her this time.

"She's not so strong any more," he said. "Don't get about so much." His face was sad, but Jerya's heart leapt.

"Hello, grandmother."

It needn't mean anything. Girls in Delven called any woman of a certain age 'grandmother', just as all of the intermediate generation were 'aunt'.

The old woman smiled. Her teeth were surprisingly white. The Delven diet was good for teeth, it seemed. "Come closer, child. My eyes aren't what they used to be."

Eyes... a thought flickered through Jerya's mind even as she was stepping forward.

"Bless me, where's your headcloth?"

"I haven't worn a headcloth these ten years, grandmother."

The old one tsked and tutted, but Jerya didn't believe she was truly shocked. Then she said something, and Jerya was the one who was shocked. "You call me grandmother, eh? Maybe you speak more truth than you realise."

Gasping, she sank onto the seat beside Pentrunne, feeling the absolute solidity of stone beneath the folded rug that served as a cushion. Solidity was what she needed, just then. "You *knew*?"

Pentrunne laughed, a sound like the rustling of autumn leaves blowing about the outer court. "I knew the first time I held you. It was like Holdren all over again. Maybe no one else saw it, but... every mother remembers the first sight of her firstborn, besure."

"And you never said."

"Not a word to anyone."

"Not even Holdren?"

"Least of all Holdren." She laughed again. "Can't an old woman have some fun? Not that I was so very old then, o'course."

Jerya thought about that a moment, about ages. She was almost thirty herself, and Holdren... it must have been after he became Headman that he and Sharess... he had assumed the role unusually young, but could hardly have been less than thirty-five. Looking at him now, yes, sixty-five seemed about right. And then... he was Pentrunne's firstborn, and girls in Delven often began bearing children in their teens. She might be eighty, probably a few years more, could hardly be less.

Perhaps mistaking her calculating silence for distress, the old woman reached out. The backs of her hands were wrinkled and spotted, but her grip felt like cool parchment.

Then she released one hand, raising it to stroke Jerya's hair, the long braid that had slipped forward over her shoulder. "I remember your hair. Looks black in the shadows, like now, but sunlight frees the fire in it. Besure, t'were a shame to cover it wi' a headcloth... But then they took you for a Dawnsinger, all those years ago."

Her gaze seized Jerya's. "I always thought once you become a Dawnsinger, you'd always be a Dawnsinger. But you ain't no Dawnsinger now, are you?"

Jerya shook her head tightly.

"Did you fail, then? Do something wrong?"

"I don't know, grandmother. To this day, I don't know if I was wrong or right."

✳

Jerya had thought long and hard about what she might say at tale-tell. Saying nothing hardly felt like an option, but there were pitfalls in anything she might say.

The only person she could consult was Marit, and Marit's strong advice had been to duck out altogether. "Soon as you say anything about the land in the East... listen, Delven folk are simple, but simple isn't stupid. You and Railu crossing over, they can reason it out: you took the Dawnsong with you."

Not for the first time, Jerya wondered exactly what Rodal had said when he came back. And what story had Sharess spun—or maybe Sharess and Rodal together? And what, if anything, had they passed on to the Masters of the Guild?

What Marit made very clear was that the truth was not generally known. "Might be it's not even known to the generality of Dawnsingers. I never heard a word of it from any but Sharess."

There was another warning. "You say you're going to the College, to speak with the Masters. Might be a risk for you, but I understand... But if they hear, if they get even a hint, that you've said anything to anyone outwith the Guild..." She hardly needed to voice the implication.

It all made sense, but, "How I can say nothing? You said it yourself. Folk aren't stupid. They know I went East. They know I've been gone ten years, all but a month or two. Now I'm back. They can see I'm healthy; they can see my clothes. They can see I haven't been living in a hollow tree for ten years.

"If we took the Dawnsong with us, what was there before? It's not just me, there's Hedric and Lallon. Where did they come from? *That's* what they're going to reason out; either there were Dawnsingers on the other side already... or life can prosper without the Dawnsong. For all we know someone's thinking it already."

"You're right," said Marit, shaking her head. "This isn't going to make my life easier, I know that... Well, it is what it is. The question is, what do you want them to think? Dawnsingers there already, or life without Dawnsong?"

"One's true and one's a lie."

"But the lie—if you must call it that—sustains the Guild, and the Guild has kept the peace in this land for at least four centuries."

"I know," said Jerya with a heavy sigh. "Peace... That's why I'm here. There's a challenge coming, maybe a threat to that peace. Even if I wanted to undermine the Guild, now's the worst possible time."

"*Did* you want to undermine the Guild?"

"I don't... no, I think not. All I knew was I couldn't be part of it."

"And now would be a bad time, you say. So what *are* you going to tell the people?"

That was a very good question.

※

"I've spent much of the day wondering what I'm going to say here tonight; but Rodal came back nine years ago. I'm sure he said something...?"

People looked at each other, and in a few seconds it seemed they were all looking at one man. She found the name in decade-old memories: Sardain. *Of course, Rodal's father.*

"Truetell," he said, "He never said a right lot. Not to us. Likely he said more to the Dawnsinger."

"I'm sure... but what did he say to you?"

He pondered briefly. "He said you were well, you and that other... that Dawnsinger what were with you."

"Railu," said Jerya. She understood his hesitation. She might have been a Dawnsinger then, or at least looked like one, but they had walked away, which was not at all what Dawnsingers did.

"Don't know as we ever heard her name. You don't ask, wi' Dawnsingers, do you?"

It was true. Growing up, she had never known the name of Delven's Dawnsinger; even as she pondered all manner of questions, she had never considered that one. Only when she reached the College had she learned the name: Sharess. *My own mother.*

She pulled herself out of reverie. "What else did he say?"

"Well, we asked, me and me Own—" He glanced at the woman by his side. "Asked if he'd done right, leaving the two of you alone there. And he... he sort of smiled to himself a moment, and then he said, "Don't worry, they're quite comfortable." I hope that's true, like..."

"True enough. In fact... We didn't exactly tell him to leave us, but we didn't hold him back. He'd made a promise, after all. And I guess he kept it...?"

"To Annyt? Aye. Seems he were back in the City in time. Likely Annyt weren't right happy about it all at first, but she come round in time, and now they're wed and got a young 'un."

"That's wonderful news. You hear from him, then?"

"Aye, now and then. Couple o'times a year, mebbe. When someone can carry a letter, like."

Jerya nodded. Mail service was, she thought, one thing in which the Five Principalities surpassed the Sung Lands. Dawnsingers had their own channels of communication, but everyone else, especially in out-of-the-way places like Delven, had to rely on whoever could be found going in roughly the right direction. Letters might travel by stages, and could wait weeks in one place or another for a trustworthy person to carry them onward.

She sighed. "I'd like to hear all his news, but I guess you all know it all already, and all being well I'll be seeing him in a week. Glad to carry a letter for you, by the way... But right now it's me you're hearing from." Heads nodded around the chamber. Away from the lanterns around the hearth, many were only dim shapes outlined by scattered rushlights. "I'm sure I can guess what you want to know: why did we leave? and where did we go?"

She sipped at the cup of mead. Hedric and Lallon had been handed cups, along with the other men, but none was offered to the women. This was the custom, and Jerya hadn't been inclined to make a fuss, but Lallon had wordlessly handed his on to her. Feeling the need of a drink, she'd accepted, hoping he'd get another.

"Why did we leave? I sometimes wonder about that myself, whether it was the right thing to do. Though..." She shrugged. "What's the point, really? I can't go back ten years and do it again, try it another way. I did it; *we* did it, and we have to live with it.

"All I can really tell you about why, the one sure thing in my mind, is that I couldn't be a Dawnsinger. Likely 'twould have been different..." She heard herself slipping into the comfortable vernacular of Delven, and smiled inwardly. "...If I'd been Chosen at the usual age, ten or eleven, instead of when I was nineteen." *Sharess herself wondered if she'd made a mistake there.* But she wouldn't say that.

"I couldn't be a Dawnsinger, and I knew that the Guild—someone in the Guild—was wrong to send Railu to be Dawnsinger here. You may wonder at me saying that, saying a Dawnsinger was wrong... but Dawnsingers are people too. People make mistakes." Privately she didn't think Perriad had 'made a mistake'; she had acted with deliberate, even malicious, intent. "I know that's not a proper answer to 'why', but it's as good as I can give. But I hope I can do better for you on the other question; where did we go?"

She sipped again. "I'm like you—'course I am—I grew up with stories about Unsung Lands, the Blistered Lands. But in the City, at the College of the Dawnsingers, I found out those stories weren't true. Not true in the way we'd had them, besure. No one there would say more than this: they didn't know what was beyond the mountains.

"Actually, that's probably another part of my *why*. I'd always looked at the mountains, all my life. Telling me *no one knew what lay beyond*, that was like... like setting a hound to a scent. I wanted to know, I felt like I *had* to know. So we went...

"And in the end crossing the mountains wasn't as hard as I'd thought it would be. Not saying it was easy, mind." She grinned. "Anyone who's been even half a day's journey over the moors knows how the weather can turn nasty, and we got a deal higher than that. Though we didn't go over the peaks, that *would* have been hard. We found a pass to go through them. Two passes, in fact.

"And what did we find when we started to descend the other side?" She grinned again, into rapt silence. "Crags and a waterfall, then a wide valley, and then a little lower down we came into forest. Not as tall a forest as around here, not at first, but not so very different. Birch-trees, bilberries, roe-deer and heather-cock, trout in the river. Seemed like these Blistered Lands weren't so terrible after all...

"But that was at first. Before we'd seen any other people."

There was a stir then, lots of whispering. Of course there was.

"That's a shock, bain't it? Not supposed to be people in Unsung Lands, are there? Not unless they had their own Dawnsingers... and they don't, nor anything like. And the first people we saw—the first *men*, 'cause they all were men—did they treat us with the respect due to a Dawnsinger, to a bald head? Truetell, they did not." She sighed, took another nip of mead. "I can't tell you all they did to us, because it'd take too long, and I don't much like recalling it anyway.

"Before we knew what was happening, we were each thrown across the back of a horse. Next day we were tied to ropes behind the horses and had to half-walk, half-run, to keep up." She felt the weight of the silence, tried to lighten it a little. "By the end of the second day I reckoned I'd seen all I ever wanted to of the back end of a horse... And what comes out of it."

There wasn't much laughter, but there were a few soft chuckles, a few appreciative murmurs. Most Delven-folk had never seen a horse, she knew, but they would know what they were.

But down in the front row, much in the same place she herself had frequently sat, a young girl—fifteen or sixteen, Jerya judged—was gazing at her with a rapt and serious expression. Catching her gaze, she spoke up. "May I ask you a question, Jerya?"

"Please do. But what's your name?"

"Emsalli."

"Ah, I do remember you. But you'd only have been *so* high when I left... anyway, what's your question?"

"Why? I mean, why did they treat you like that? Are you saying they'd never seen a Dawnsinger?"

"Yes," said Jerya, and then paused a moment. She knew the implications. If life could survive without Dawnsingers... "That's exactly what I'm saying—part of it, anyway. Here, a bald head means one thing; there it means something completely different." She paused again. "It means you're a slave."

Some faces showed shock; others only looked puzzled. Jerya kept her focus on Emsalli. "Do you know what that means?"

"Not rightly, no."

"Well, as simply as I can put it, some people are owners and some people are owned; they're *property*. And those people are called slaves."

She tried to explain further, but as she spoke she found herself looking again and again at the young face gazing up at her. How much freedom would Emsalli have? What did 'freedom' even mean to people, and perhaps especially to girls and women, in a place like Delven? She, herself, would have had precious few choices to look forward to if she hadn't been abruptly plucked out of one life and thrown headlong into another. Even then, freedom had meant uprooting herself a second time. *And look where that landed me...*

She looked into Emsalli's eyes, eyes again of colour akin to her own—well, they must be related in some way, at least distantly—and wondered how she could say all this, and perhaps if she even should. For some moments she was silent, suspended in indecision.

Emsalli rescued her, shyly lifting a hand. "May I ask you another question, Jerya?"

"Besure."

"Well, you said you were taken for slaves..."

"Yes, they assumed we were runaways."

"And you said a bald head is the mark of a slave..."

"Right again." She grinned. "Shows at least one person's listening."

"But you're not bald now. Fact, you look like you been growing your hair for years."

"I do, and I have." With difficulty she resisted the temptation to reach up and touch her own hair, as if suddenly doubting it was really there. She'd been bald little more than half a year, but her own reflection could still catch her by surprise, on occasion. "Most of the time I've been in the East, in fact."

"Do that mean you ain't a slave no longer?"

"Besure. Which leads on to the next bit of my story." She told, as concisely as she could, how she and Railu had been acquired by the most liberal owners in the region. "We were lucky in that, because it meant we had reasonably comfortable accommodation." *Indeed, some might think it a step up from a stone bed in a cave-cell...* "One other thing about being a slave. Slaves aren't supposed to read. The law says no free person may teach a slave to read... but of course I could read already. Fact, I learned right here in this chamber. Listening to Holdren and tracing the words as he read..." She caught his gaze, gave a quick smile.

"Soon enough my master discovered I could read, and he decided I'd be more use to him as a secretary—writing letters for him, keeping records—than fetching and carrying and cleaning. So he set me free."

Emsalli looked happy at that, but then, obviously, another thought struck her. "Jerya, what—"

"—Ems!" hissed her mother, almost slapping the girl's hand down. "No-one's here to hear you!"

"It's quite all right, Sheniza," said Jerya. "Go on, Emsalli."

"What about the other, your friend? The one who'd..." She stopped, but Jerya thought everyone in the chamber knew what would have come next. *The one who'd been meant to be our Dawnsinger.*

"Railu? I'm afraid she's still a slave."

"But surely—" EmsallI's mother grasped her arm, but the girl was determined, "—She were a Dawnsinger, she could read too?"

"Aye, besure. You know, that's a really good question, but it's a hard one for me. The simple answer is that our master only needed one secretary." *Simple, and true, and yet not quite honest...* "But it was hard... I mean, it was especially hard for Railu, obviously, but I felt bad about it too. For a while we weren't such good friends as we should have been, but it's better now. She's still a slave, at least in name, but her life... she's respected, she has responsibility, she's even able to practise, in a way, as a healer. Which was always what she really wanted to be." *For all the difficulties in her way, as a woman and a slave, she probably has more opportunity to practise there than she would have as Dawnsinger here.*

Though she'd avoided the other great fact of Railu's life, implications rolled through her mind. As Rodal's son, Embrel was related to most of the people present, just as she herself was. Sardain and Ashlem were his grandparents. But Railu had steadfastly resisted all arguments that anyone, including Rodal, should be told. If he could not know, it was unfair to tell anyone else.

She sighed. "Sorry, I'm woolgathering. Telling all this does take me back to some hard times... And I'm sure Emsalli isn't the only one with questions..."

There was a brief silence; no one wanted to go first. She had an inkling that Emsalli could have asked another dozen questions, but was holding her tongue for now. Then a young lad raised his hand to ask if there were goats in the East, and the reticence was dispelled. Some questions were weighty, others trivial. Inevitably, someone wondered how folk could live without a Dawnsinger. This was difficult, but at least she'd anticipated it. She wasn't prepared for a question about the fullness of her skirt. In truth, after ten years in the Five Principalities, she hardly noticed anymore, and the relative slimness of skirts in Delven had been what seemed strange. The irony was that her daily wear at home was closer to the simplicity she'd grown up with, but the skirt she'd brought, anticipating meetings with Dawnsingers, was more formal.

As the long evening began to wind down, she found Emsalli and her mother hovering near. "I'm sorry for all the int'ruptions," said Sheniza.

"Don't be." She grasped the girl's hands. "Really, Emsalli, you've helped me tell a better story." She thought a little more about Emsalli. All she really knew was that the girl had an inquiring mind. Some people—her mother among them—might think she asked too many questions. *And who else did they say that about?*

An obvious question sprang to mind now. She glanced at Sheniza, asking permission, then drew the girl a few paces away. "You know, when I was your age, and younger, my aunts—especially Vilina and Sarria—were forever telling me I asked too many questions. As you might guess, I never really stopped." Emsalli smiled, obviously delighted with the comparison. "Tell me something, do you ever have Dawnsingers coming here?"

"You mean from Outside? Not just our own?"

"Yes, visiting."

"Sometimes," the girl said. "Once when I were 'bout nine, once when I were thirteen, I reckon. And I think I remember once afore that, when I were mebbe six."

That was a better frequency than when Jerya had been a girl, but it was still pretty sparse. "Did they hold a Choosing?"

"They looked at all the girls that were... ten or eleven, reckon, if that's what you mean. They didn't take anyone."

"And you were too young the first time and too old the second..."

"Besure." Emsalli's tone was neutral; no telling whether she viewed the missed chance with relief or regret. She could hardly compare it with her own case, being Chosen at an outlandishly advanced age, never having even dreamed that she could be a Dawnsinger.

Her case was unique; she had realised soon after her arrival in the College that no one had known quite what to do with her, and now understood why. She thought it likely that Dawnsingers up and down the Sung Lands had since been firmly instructed not to send girls beyond the usual age. Emsalli's chance, if she'd ever had one, had passed; and that meant that the choices she would face in the coming years would be as few, and as narrow, as Jerya had seen open to her before that fateful day.

CHAPTER 15

HEDRIC

The journey to Carwerid was essentially uneventful, but endlessly fascinating, and sometimes confusing.

They left Delven early, soon after the Dawnsong. Jerya's concern was not so much for the first day, but to be in place to start even earlier on the second, and the crossing of the Scorched Plains. Her account of her first experience led him to think it a wise precaution.

That second day, they started as soon as there was enough light for the track to be discernible, and were out of earshot of Thrushgill's Singer before the sun had risen. Thanks in part to this early start, in part to stately clouds that began to mass overhead before mid-morning, the temperature remained tolerable throughout. Jerya had unearthed a battered, broad-brimmed felt hat, but it hardly seemed essential.

They rested briefly at the abandoned village in the middle of the Plains. "Third time I've been here," said Jerya as they moved on, "And only the first was difficult. And... people went to all the trouble of building houses, sinking a well, and then they abandoned it all. I have to wonder why."

"I've been wondering too. It does all look very dry, as if the whole district lies in a rain-shadow, and it all seems to be a shallow bowl, inclining to the South, which might accentuate the power of the sun on clear days."

"But you would think people would have been aware of all that; all the work they did here took time, and they must have experienced days like the one we endured. Could there be other reasons, things that revealed themselves more slowly, like crops failing to thrive?"

"To be sure. That river did not look healthy, did it? You say the well-water was sweet enough, but would it fill and refill fast enough to support the thirst of people and animals, let alone the irrigation of crops?"

She nodded, the gesture exaggerated by her hat. "And there could also be toxins in the soil."

"Indeed. I've read of areas in the far South, in Velyadero and inland Buscanya, that look much like this. Pale, gritty, earth, bare ground or stunted herbs and scrub. Where the soils have been assayed they turn out to have unusually high levels of lead, among other things."

"Left over from the Age Before, do you think?"

He shrugged. "No way to be sure, but it seems highly plausible."

There was no real difficulty completing the crossing, but they were both relieved to come into greener, healthier, country as they approached Stainscomb. Lallon, as usual, said nothing of his feelings, but even he seemed to have more spring to his step in that final hour.

Jerya made enquiries, but there were no horses to be had, nor any carriage or waggon expected. However, post-horses were available at an inn half a day's walk away, where the Stainscomb track met the main South Road.

The stable-master examined their Five Principalities coins dubiously. Finally convinced that they were indeed silver, he agreed to accept them, but Hedric was sure he'd offered well below their real value. Jerya's 'local knowledge' revealed a limitation here. "I never handled money in the Sung Lands before. Rodal did that, when it was needed. I've no more idea of true values than you." She suggested they exchange the minimum they need until they reached the city. "Rodal will help us then." A fine notion, he thought, assuming they could depend on tracking down a friend she hadn't seen or heard from in ten years.

The wrangle over coin took time, and they were only able to make it as far as the next inn, about three hours down the hard road. Here they were welcomed by a woman called Tresenka. She seemed no older than Jerya and stood no taller, but Hedric reckoned her a good forty pounds heavier. Still, she seemed the image of vitality, all smiles, almost skipping ahead of them as she showed them to their rooms.

Later, as they settled for their evening meal, Jerya laughed. "You're still looking for a father or husband, aren't you?" Her eyes sparkled impishly in the late sunlight slanting through the windows. "Did you not notice the sign over the entrance? At the very least it proves she holds the licence. And then she said *welcome to* my *humble house.* Anyway, just look, and tell me she isn't in charge."

"I see it." Indeed, he hadn't seen any male staff in the inn itself, only in the stables behind. "But does she own the place?"

"*My humble house,*" she repeated.

He nodded. "You tell me things are different, and of course I believe you. But knowing is one thing, seeing is another, and truly grasping the reality is a third."

"Besure," she said, dropping abruptly into the accent of Delven. "Your book-learnin's all vurry well. Ain't proper knowin', but-though."

But-though, which he heard everywhere, was just one of the obvious differences in speech between the Five Principalities and the Sung Lands. It was rarely truly hard to understand, once you'd had a little time to accustom the ear, but small differences abounded. Hardly a vowel-sound but was subtly different; and the final consonant of many words, not just '-ing' words, was often lost, so that Jerya's speech could almost have been rendered as "Your boo-learnin's a' vurry well. Ain' proper knowin', bu-tho'."

In dress, men nearly always wore full-length trousers rather than breeches and hose. Among women, skirts were not so full as in the Five Principalities, where even those of the lowest were gathered or pleated for a more 'becoming' silhouette, while many of the more prosperous favoured even more exaggerated outlines.

Livestock was simultaneously familiar and unfamiliar. Delven had goats, the next village also had sheep, and thereafter he saw cows, horses, pigs, geese, chickens: all the usual animals, but not the same breeds he knew.

The same with food, few major differences, many minor, like being offered something called mustard with his beef where he might have expected horseradish.

So many small divergences; some fascinating, some amusing, some simply puzzling. But he knew the one great difference between the two lands had been, so far, almost entirely invisible to him. In the Five Principalities, the power in the land was the Principals and their various cohorts. In the Sung Lands the power lay with the Guild of Dawnsingers; of which, as yet, he had seen nothing beyond a brief and stiltedly polite introduction to Delven's Dawnsinger.

He saw people in the fields every day. Inevitably they were working hard, and he didn't think they had much, but he saw far more laughter than he'd ever seen in slave-worked fields. Even, he thought uncomfortably, on his own land. Later, riding an empty road between empty fields, he asked Jerya, "I do my best to give them a decent life. If I gave it all away, would they be better off? Would any other owner give them a better life?"

She looked at him for a long time before she answered. "You're a good man, Hedric. I know it. But you still can't see past the world as you've always known it."

"What do you mean?"

"It's not giving it to another owner you have to think about. It's giving it to the slaves themselves. *That* is how you set them free."

It was his turn to stare at her. For whole minutes they rode in silence.

"Well," he said finally. "Even if there is any way under present laws, which I doubt... I cannot do any such thing while my uncle lives. He'd disinherit me in a heartbeat, and then I'd have no chance of doing anything for all his slaves."

This was incontestable, but he knew it suited him for his own reasons. It was one thing to be a good owner, to offer discreet support to the betterment campaign and hope one day to be able to do more. He had no doubts about that.

To give up being an owner altogether... that was quite another thing to contemplate. He wasn't ready to face that. He wasn't sure if he ever would be.

And... he'd thought many times about the life he'd be able to offer Jerya once they were free to marry. Not so much the title that would accompany his inheritance.... *Countess of Skilthorn.* He had never uttered the words to her, but she must have thought about it. He'd never been sure how she might feel. Would she really be comfortable with the title and all that went with it?

When he thought about it, when he imagined bringing her home as his bride, it was always his own much more modest estate at Kirwaugh that he saw in his mind's eye. He could see Jerya at home there. Skilthorn was a very different proposition. But that scenario rested on two hypothetical circumstances: marrying Jerya, and inheriting the title.

It was all too easy to see ways in which each could obstruct the other.

A day of rain, rattling on hoods, making conversation all but impossible. Barring half-shouted exchanges about which road or when to rest, they rode each in their own thoughts.

The next day began uncertainly, but within an hour the clouds were clearing. He looked at the blue that was gaining ground across the sky, then edged his mount forward to ride beside Jerya. "I've been thinking."

She leered. "Oh, you poor thing. Does your head hurt?"

He scowled ferociously, but in a moment he was grinning too. "I was wondering. The Dawnsingers keep a lot of knowledge to themselves, I understand that, but... what happens when other people ask questions, wonder about things? Men, of course, but not only men... you were one who wondered, too, weren't you?"

She gave it thought before replying. "When it's girls, the Guild looks out for those ones. I suppose local Singers get to hear, and then the Peripatetics get around every couple of years.... most places, anyway."

"But you were missed?"

"Yes, for some reason Delven had no Visitation in all the time I could remember. I've often wondered what I would have become if I'd been Chosen at the usual age... but it's bootless. I might just as easily have never been Chosen at all... and that's what you're asking, isn't it?"

"Part of it, anyway."

"I only see two ways it could have gone. Kept on as I was, wandering off on my own, wondering why sticks float and stones sink. Head full of questions and no way to get answers... There's only so much astronomy you can do with the naked eye. Not only did I not have a telescope, I didn't even know what a telescope was."

He'd seen Delven now, seen its one paltry shelf of books—at least two of which, he'd quickly concluded, contained far more false 'information' than truth. Hardly the best nourishment for a developing mind. The wonder was that Jerya had grown as she had. But... "You said two ways?"

"Aye. The other... I'd have been married, pushing out a babe every year or two, and then what time would I have had for sticks and stones and stars?" She rode on, looking at the road ahead, for a minute, then turned to him again. "That's what happens to women in the Five Principalities, you know: no Guild of Dawnsingers for the bright ones there."

He nodded, then realised it might be missed amid the natural motion of a rider. "You're right, of course. But then what becomes of bright boys here, if there's no Guild for them?"

"Truth be, Hedric, I don't rightly know. I knew Delven for nineteen years. I knew the College for a few months. I hardly saw more of the rest of the land than we're seeing now."

He saw how that must be. Much of her homeland might be less known to her, now, than the Five Principalities. The word 'exile' flitted across his mind. *But exile from where, to where?*

They rode on in mutual silence for a few moments. He saw a huge white horse, a simplistic outline like the drawing of a mountain-sized child, carved through the short turf to reveal the chalky bedrock. Rock that looked very like the stuff of the Wolds behind Skilthorn.

Jerya was looking at him again. "You said bright boys. You were a bright boy, I'm sure. So what did you wonder?"

"Many things..."

"Of course."

"But I do remember... I must have been about seven..."

She was smiling at him. "I bet you looked just the same... did you wear glasses then?"

"Not then. Not till I was about ten, I think." *Just in time to go away to school, where the boy with glasses was a prime target for every bully...*

"Still... so what did you wonder?"

"It was a day much like this, and I looked up, and suddenly I asked, 'why doesn't the sky fall down?'

She laughed aloud, fearless on the empty road. "Hedric, that's a wonderful question! Did you get an answer?"

"Not right away, as I remember. Maybe I got a bad one."

"*It's the way things are,*" she said.

"Is that what they told you?"

"All the time." She thought a moment. "Of course one answer wouldn't do anyway. You'd need one for the moons, another for the stars, another again for the clouds. Maybe yet another for all the flying things, birds and bats and butterflies..."

"All that and you still haven't told me why all that blue stuff stays up there," he said, trying to sound like a dissatisfied seven-year-old.

She caught the tone, and grinned. "But the 'blue stuff' all goes away when the sun goes down. Like it wasn't really 'stuff' at all."

"Stuff," he said. "A fine scientific word."

"As good as any, when you don't know the true answer. And science is all about pursuing answers. Besides, for a governess, there's no more useful word in my vocabulary."

Hedric looked ahead, and noticed that Lallon, whose enthusiastic mount kept carrying him ahead, had reined in, was now silhouetted against the Southern sky. They came up the rise beside him and stopped.

"I take it that's Carwerid," said Hedric, looking at a city that seemed like a watercolour rendering of itself in the afternoon haze.

"It is." Jerya's voice was strangely tight. He gave her a curious look. "First time I saw it was from just this spot. I couldn't have imagined all that was going to happen there." She tried to laugh. "Couldn't really have imagined any of it."

She shook herself, then straightened in her saddle. "If we find a posting inn on the outskirts... the horses won't make us any faster in the city itself. Stay there tonight, walk in early in the morning, we'll be outside the College before the morning's half gone."

"And then...?"

She shrugged. "I had no idea last time, and I've precious little now."

CHAPTER 16

JERYA

Everything looked the same: the wall with the fence atop it, the wide steps between verdant lawns. She turned to Hedric and Lallon. "I've no idea how long I may be. I may be here all day. I hope they will agree to see you too, but I can't know. It could be a long wait."

Hedric bit his lip. "What else are we to do?"

"Well, Lallon could explore the city..."

Lallon looked affronted. Jerya wouldn't have said she knew him; she had never quite penetrated his reserve, but this she understood. The idea that he would desert his master at an important time was offensive to him. She grinned to show she hadn't meant it seriously. But she also wondered if, even now, he had truly grasped that in this city, this land, he was a free man.

She pushed open the gate. It did not squeal as it had the first time. *They've oiled the hinges*, she thought, trying to amuse herself, to calm her nerves. Once before she had walked alone up this same path. She could not tell whether she had been more nervous then, or now.

The portress, not one she remembered, greeted her politely, but with a barely masked air of surprise: "How may I help you, ma'am?"

"Could someone kindly take this to Tutor Jossena? It's quite urgent."

"*Senior* Tutor Jossena." Jerya inclined her head to the correction. *Senior Tutor: that's good... but it probably implies Perriad is now a Master, which won't be.*

She handed the Portress a copy of the issue of the *Proceedings of the Denvirran Society for Natural Philosophy* containing their paper on the parallax observations, with a note inserted and clearly visible at the appropriate page. *I am sure this will interest you. Please take note of the authors' names—and ask yourself who J. Delven might be.*

✳

Jossena was, perhaps, a little plumper but otherwise unchanged, her face unlined. And with her came Yanil, looking older, eyebrows quite gone, but still brisk. They looked at Jerya, looked again at each other.

"'J. Delven'?" asked Yanil quietly.

"That's what I'm called now: Jerya Delven. Styling myself J.Delven in this publication obscured the fact that I'm a woman."

Again that quick look between the two. She was sure they understood the significance, or some of it. And she wondered at the same time: *Yanil and Jossena?* Had it been the same between them ten years ago? But there was no time for speculation now.

"And *where* is it that all this takes place, J. Delven?" Jossena, striking right at the heart of the matter.

"Please call me Jerya; it is still my name. And I think you know already where." The *Proceedings* could not have been published anywhere in the Sung Lands.

Yanil nodded. "Why now?"

"Because there are others on that side seeking a way across the mountains. It's much harder to find from the East than from the West, but they will find it. Maybe not this year, though it could be; maybe next year, or the year after. But I had to come now."

"Because...?"

"I need to talk to the Masters, I think."

Jossena and Yanil looked at each other again; then, with swift decision, Jossena turned back to Jerya. "Go back out of the gate and turn down to the left. In about a hundred yards, turn left, a narrow ginnel that widens after a few steps. Along to a blue door. Sometimes the Masters need to confer... inconspicuously... with certain men. Ring the bell and wait."

"Jerya," added Yanil.

"Yes, Tutor Yanil?"

"It's very good to see you."

The meeting wasn't five minutes old before Perriad broke in on Jerya's tale. "You are a renegade, a Vow-breaker. You deceived me and all of the Guild ten years ago. Why should we believe you now?"

She made herself stand straight and look Perriad in the eye. Perriad might have grown in power and influence, but she, Jerya, had grown too. "Tu—I beg your pardon, *Master* Perriad. We could argue half the morning about who deceived whom, and in what order, ten years ago. It gains us nothing. And, besides, I have proofs."

"A book and a piece of newsprint?"

"If you're suggesting I forged them, you're crediting me with far greater skill than I possess."

Jossena cleared her throat. "If I may, Masters?"

Perriad frowned, but the oldest of the three nodded at Jossena. "Masters, I have had but a few minutes to examine this document. Others may be able to comment on the paper, or the binding, or the printing. I comment only on the content, and specifically this section." She read out the title. "*Reiteration of Estimation of Distance to Cintilla*—which I take to mean the object we call the One?" Jerya nodded. "*By means of Observations of Parallax. Notes in Consequence and Suggestions for Further Study.* And already... I can only say it is *remarkable*. It is exceedingly advanced work, my Masters.

I should venture to say that the observational techniques described here easily equal anything we have accomplished, at least."

"But what you have," said Perriad, "Is merely a claim that such observations occurred. It is not proof that they did, still less that they were made in some fantasy land East of the mountains."

"With all due respect, Master Perriad, I disagree. I cannot on this cursory examination say that this report proves that such was the case, but I can say that it is eminently susceptible to scrutiny which *would* prove—or disprove—that claim. There's an appendix giving a full record of the actual observations. The calendar differs from our own, and no doubt their system employs a different prime meridian, but they do use the same units for measurement of angles—degrees, minutes and seconds of arc. I am sure that if we could establish the correspondence between the calendrics, we could show whether or not the the observed angles to the One are consistent with its position at the same date and time as shown in our own ephemerides. It would then be clear to us whether or not these observations were taken from locations East of our own latitude."

Perriad looked as if she would argue the point further, but the older Master spoke first. "Former Novice Jerya of Delven, I imagine you understand that the Guild does not look kindly on renegades, on those who break their Vow?"

"I do understand, Master."

"It's Master Prime, to be precise. I heard your Novitial Vow ten years ago. And indeed your presence here raises questions that we must—in due course—consider. However, I ask myself first, what does this girl—what does Jerya of Delven—or is it just Jerya Delven now?"

"The latter, if you please, Master Prime."

"'If I please'. Well, we'll defer consideration of what pleases me... No, my question is, what does Jerya Delven stand to gain by coming back here now, after—what is it? Nine years away? Ten? You risk much by doing so, it seems to me, but what do you gain? And, further, what would you gain by fabricating such evidence as you have laid before us?" Heavy-lidded eyes flicked down momentarily to the copy of the *Proceedings* lying on the table before her. "Even to fabricate such a thing would be no small undertaking, it seems to me." She glanced left and right; the small, and so far silent, Master on her left nodded agreement; Perriad shrugged, looking almost sulky.

The Master Prime unhooded her eyes, fixed them on Jerya again. "Please, then, satisfy my curiosity. What do you stand to gain?"

"With respect, Master Prime, that is not the first question before you. The question you need to ask yourselves is what does *the Guild* gain?"

The Prime continued to regard her steadily. "Very well, Jerya Delven, what do we gain?"

"Forewarning," said Jerya. The Prime merely inclined her head a few degrees, but the message seemed clear: *continue*. "In a couple of months I'll have lived beyond the mountains for ten years. I have a comfortable life there, but it is a very different land from this. It concerns me greatly to think that its ways might be imposed upon the Sung Lands. It would certainly spell an end to the influence of the Guild, for one thing."

"What do you care about the Guild?" asked Perriad. The Prime barely moved, but some slight shift in her posture suggested she was losing patience with Perriad's truculence.

Jerya turned her gaze to Perriad. "A fair question, I suppose, Master Perriad, but when I first read that piece in the newspaper, I found that I cared rather more than you might expect: more, indeed, than *I* expected... But it is wider than the Guild."

She nodded toward the slim leather-bound volume lying on the table. "I contributed to that paper which Senior Tutor Jossena says is remarkable; I was an equal partner in both authorship and the work which preceded it. My name is shown, however, only as J. Delven. Do you know why? It is to obscure the fact that I am female. Women cannot be members of the eminent Society which publishes those *Proceedings*. The first-named author of any paper must be a member, and as a non-member my name appears last. And had my gender been apparent it is quite possible that the editor would, to say the least, have been less kindly-disposed towards our work.

"That's but a small example. Women cannot own land, or a house, or any substantial property. And even that is not all. There is another matter, which you may find even more disturbing. The fact is that in that land there are slaves. I myself was taken for a slave when I first arrived. I did not endure it very long, but it was enough...

"So why, you may ask, am I here now? The way across the mountains that I found when I left ten years ago, and which I used again to return a week ago—it is much harder to find from the Eastern side, but... they're trying further South. They may find another way. They're certainly well-eqipped." She pushed the newspaper cutting forward. "If I may..."

"As Senior Tutor Jossena said, the calendrics are unfamiliar." The third Master spoke for the first time.

"This is recent, Master. I read it less than a month ago. It's what impelled me to make this journey... Being larger, the expedition may take longer to assemble than ours, and may move more slowly, but I'm sure they are in the field by now."

"Thank you. Please continue."

"I have no idea whether or when they may find a feasible crossing; maybe not this year. But if I found a route at the first attempt, how likely is it that it's the only feasible one? In any case, sooner or later, someone will look at the route I used. As I said, it's harder to find from the East, but it's not impossible.

"And, Masters, if anyone did make that crossing, the first place they would arrive is my former home, Delven. And... those travellers would almost certainly be 'gentlemen', slave-owners, and I don't like the prospects that raises in my mind."

She let them ponder that for a few moments, a few more ticks, before adding, "I am here of my own free will. As I said, I am no longer a slave. I will always carry the scars, within and without, but my life now is comfortable enough. I can even believe I do a little good in the world, over there, and perhaps in the future I may have the chance to do more." *As a Countess?* She had no time for that thought now.

"Masters, I did not return for my own benefit. I came because you needed to hear the news I bring. And I believe you need to include me in your counsels about how to respond. To talk instead about punishing me is nothing but distraction. And, unless you still fail to believe what I have told you, I am sure you must see that distraction is your enemy."

The Master Prime drew her gaze. Perhaps there was the slightest of nods, though she could not have said what it signified. "Your last point is well made: belief or disbelief is indeed the primary question, and we must reach a firm decision on that before anything else. I could wish, Jerya Delven, that you had brought more proofs of your tale."

Jossena stirred. "Master Prime, may I?"

"Speak, Jossena."

"Initial examination leads me to believe this document could not have been produced in our land. I think that within an hour I could draw a firmer conclusion. Perhaps, also, one of the Librarians might be able to glean something from the paper, the ink, the binding."

"Indeed, thank you, Jossena. Yes, please go, but be sure to return as soon as you have anything significant to tell us."

Jossena left at once, shooting Jerya the briefest of glances as she turned away. Her errand was undoubtedly necessary, but Jerya could not help feeling that it left her with only one friend in the room... and Yanil had no vote in the counsels of the Masters.

Well, if it comes to allies... "Master Prime, may I suggest something?"

"If it might help..."

"You spoke of proofs... well, I did not cross the mountains alone. I had two companions, and one of them is waiting in the anteroom even now. Perhaps if you were to question him you would get a stronger sense that this is... not merely some elaborate hoax of my devising."

"Him, did you say?"

"Yes, Master Prime, him."

"Well, it would not be the first time we have interviewed a man in this chamber."

CHAPTER 17

HEDRIC

She looked strained, he thought; more so than at any time on the journey, apart, possibly, from after his fall on the peak. "Does it not go well?" he asked quietly.

She shook her head. "I don't know, Hedric. They're still debating whether they can believe anything I say. But, listen... I've told them they should speak to you, too. Maybe you can convince them..." She hardly sounded convinced herself. Eyes and hands both sought his. "I'm sorry. Telling them you would, without asking you first."

"Worry not, Jerya. It cannot be entirely unexpected." He squeezed her hands.

His words provoked scant signs of relief. "Listen, best not keep them waiting, but remember... you're going to walk into that room and see nothing but bald heads, but you mustn't think of slaves, not for one second."

"I—" He got no further. The door behind Jerya opened and a woman slipped through: a compact figure, brown-skinned. Her eyes, behind metal-rimmed spectacles, took in the closeness of the two before her, their clasped hands.

Jerya slipped his grasp, turning to face the newcomer. "Tutor Yanil, this is my... friend, Hedric."

"I am pleased to meet you," said Yanil, half an octave deeper than he'd expected. "Jerya, they request to speak to your friend alone."

"Alone? Why?"

"I think the notion is that unprompted testimony will carry more weight."

"I could sit at the back and say nothing."

"Jerya, as your friend, I think it better not to cavil. You walk a knife-edge here, and any objection to their request might be sufficient to shift the balance. Also..." she glanced at Hedric. "They do not like to be kept waiting."

He took a step forward. "I'm ready."

Jerya turned a stricken face toward him. He wanted to kiss her, to hold her again, to say something... but Yanil's presence, even though she styled herself a friend, inhibited him, and he could only hope his eyes said all he felt.

Yanil pulled the door closed behind him. "I'll stay with Jerya," she said quietly in the last second before it clicked shut.

❋

You mustn't think of slaves, not for one second. It turned out that, at least, was easy to achieve. Bald they might be, but none of the women before him had the faintest trace of submissiveness about them.

Least of all the one who spoke first. "I am the Master Prime of the Guild of Dawnsingers. This is Perriad, Master of Records, and Syrtos, Master of Dispensation. And you are...?"

"My name is The Honourable Hedric of Kirwaugh."

"Is that a name or a description?"

He inclined his head, hoping they would see it as respectful. "That is how I would normally introduce myself among my own people, but you are right, Master Prime, it is more than a name. 'Honourable' indicates my rank, and Kirwaugh is my home. A plain name, I suppose, would be Hedric Pendeen."

"You men do like your titles," said the tall Master seated on the left. Perriad, he remembered.

He could not resist. "I suppose we do, Master Perriad." The slightest of stresses on 'Master'. Perriad narrowed her eyes, as if annoyed, but he was almost sure he'd seen a flicker of a smile tweak the corners of the Master Prime's mouth.

"Well, Hedric Pendeen," continued Syrtos, "You say your home is called Kirwaugh. And where is this Kirwaugh?"

There were many ways he could answer this. "It lies about eighty miles North-East of the city of Denvirran, in the Principality of Denvirran."

"Principality of what?" was Perriad's sharp demand.

"We mostly refer to our land as The Five Principalities. Sometimes The Principalities, sometimes just The Five. They each have a high degree of autonomy, you see, in laws and customs."

Master Syrtos was smaller than the other two, and darker. "It might be thought that you are striving to avoid the real question."

"You are asking which side of the mountains my home lies?" *Then why not ask straight out...* he knew better than to voice that thought. "To the East, Masters."

He was looking at Syrtos. One of the others made a small sound, probably of disbelief. "Perhaps you know," said Syrtos, "That is generally believed here that no human life exists East of the mountains. Even that no human life *can* exist."

He dipped his head again. "And the converse is generally believed on my side. However, Masters, from my certain knowledge, both beliefs are wrong."

"So you keep saying," said Perriad. "Why should we believe a single word you say?"

"Why should we lie? There's no profit in this, only risk. Especially for Jerya, I think."

"Why ? I can think of one reason, at least. Because you are male. Because there are males who have never accepted the pre-eminence of females, as represented by the Guild. Because there are males who, quite simply, *hate* the Guild, and would do anything to end its influence."

"Madam," he said, "I promise you, I do not hate your Guild of Dawnsingers. The plain fact is that I knew nothing of its existence until Jerya enlightened me a few weeks ago."

He saw the risk in saying that; that it might appear to belittle their Guild. But what could he do? It was the simple logic of the situation.

All the time he had been bandying words with Perriad, Master Syrtos had been looking impatient. He took another risk, spurning Perriad, turning his face to Syrtos. She didn't smile, but perhaps there was a hint of appreciation in her eye. "What manner of place is this Kirwaugh?"

"A country estate. Modest compared to some, about three hundred acres." This spawned some confusion, 'acres' being an unknown unit. Neither did they routinely use miles, but they had at least heard the term, had some idea what a square mile looked like; and three hundred acres was about half a square mile.

"And, apart from you, who lives there?"

"Three household slaves and fifteen field slaves, plus some children."

They all frowned, but they were not shocked. Well, they had spent the best part of an hour questioning Jerya already. He could not imagine she would have withheld the crucial fact of slavery.

"But you are not a slave, are you? You, in fact, are the *owner* of these... what did you say? Eighteen people, and their children."

He felt an impulse to deny it, but that would surely be unwise. "That is so."

"And how do you justify such a state of affairs?"

"I do not seek to justify it. I... inherited the estate, and most of the slaves. And to save you asking why I don't simply set them all free, the law prevents me." *And if I could?* Jerya had asked that, and he had not been able to summon a ready answer. "There are stringent limits on how many slaves any owner can free in a year; besides which, freed slaves, in general, find it hard to find any gainful employment, or to take any secure place in society."

"And yet *Jerya* appears to have achieved both..." said Perriad. Suspicion and sarcasm made an uneasy cocktail. *Jerya is unusual*, he wanted to say, but Perriad fixed him with indigo eyes. "Hedric Pendeen, what is the precise nature of your... relationship with former Novice Jerya?"

Former Novice, he thought. *An interesting choice of label.* But he was more concerned with her question. *what is the precise nature of your relationship? If I could give a precise answer...*

He kept his actual reply simple. "We are engaged to be married." It was not strictly true, at least in any formal sense. He still wasn't quite sure you could call their understanding, known only to the two of them, an engagement at all. But he saw no gain in saying that, nor did he feel Perriad deserved so much.

Perriad looked as if she had swallowed something sour; like tasting horseradish when she'd expected cream. But she was relentless. "Tell us, Hedric Pendeen, has this relationship been... consummated?"

Keep calm, he commanded himself, but his hackles rose regardless. "That's an an uncommonly personal question."

"And yet—" began Perriad, but the Master Prime's quiet tones cut through. "I must say, Master Perriad, I fail to see why we should require such intimate details of personal relationships."

"I am sure you do not forget, Master Prime, that it was to you yourself that Jerya made her Vows. And those Vows—"

"Place no specific prohibition on intimacy with any person, man or woman," said Syrtos.

"Not specifically, but they do say *I shall conduct myself at all times in accordance with the rules and practices of the Guild*, and those rules—"

"—Master Perriad." The Master Prime's voice was still softly pitched, but there was no mistaking the note of impatience that had crept into it. "We already know that Jerya broke her Vows. No one, including herself, disputes that. I genuinely fail to see what is gained by picking over details of what else she may or may not have done five or ten years after—"

"—*Details* which illuminate the full depth of—"

"—Master Perriad." The tone was firmer now, ripe with asperity. "I should be grateful if you would refrain from interrupting me."

"Your pardon, Master Prime."

"*As I was saying*, we know the fundamental fact. As to the minutiae of her subsequent conduct... even if it is relevant at all, of which I have yet to be convinced, there are more urgent matters for our consideration. To wit: do we believe the tale that Jerya brought us, and which Hedric Pendeen apparently corroborates? And, if we do, what do we do about it? It is my judgement that these are the questions we should be addressing."

Perriad inclined her head in token of acquiescence, but it was obvious that she was far from satisfied.

In that silence, the Master Prime nodded to Syrtos, who continued, "Hedric Pendeen, I believe I said to you earlier that many here believe that no human life exists beyond the Sundering Wall."

"You did, Master Syrtos, and I observed that the converse is true."

"Then how would you convince us of the truth of your assertion?"

"I believe Jerya has already offered you the most convincing proofs, such as the journal article we co-authored."

Perriad sniffed. "All of which can be fabricated."

"Madam," he said, forgetting 'Master' in his annoyance, "Anything which is made by one person can be 'fabricated' by another. This includes the cut of my clothes, the nailing of my boots, the coins in my pocket, anything else which I might produce in evidence. In fact, 'fabricate' is essentially a synonym of 'make', is it not?

"Stipulating, then, that it is *possible*, the question as I see it must be: is it plausible, is it even feasible, that we *fabricated* all these items purely for the purpose of deceiving you? Consider all the resources we would need. A printing press, the skills for setting type, the ability to forge typefaces unknown in your lands. I know a little about this, and I am sure there are some among you who know more, and they can confirm that font creation is no simple undertaking. Design, the creation of moulds, the casting process, all highly technical matters. You may also find that the paper on which the journal, the news article, and the map are printed is discernibly different from anything made here. I know that paper can be hand-made in small quantities, but I think you will find that this yields a very different end-product. Perhaps—" Here he reached inside his jacket. "—I might also offer you my pocket-watch. And my baggage could yield a few more items, including a compass which Jerya tells me is not similar to any she ever saw in her time here." He smiled. "I think she regards both the compass and the watch as inferior pieces of work. 'More ornate, but less accurate' might summarise her verdict.

"Taking all these things together... if you really wish to suggest that Jerya and I *fabricated* all our evidence somewhere in the Sung Lands, then you credit us with remarkable industrial capacity. Do you really think two of us alone could do all this? You seem to be positing a larger conspiracy—and where? Where in the Sung Lands could we do this unnoticed? In the smaller villages, nothing approaching this could escape the notice of the resident Dawnsinger. In towns, or in this city... I am a newcomer here, of course, but it is my understanding that every trade is regulated by the Estimable Orders and Companies... do I have that right? I am sure that printers, paper-makers, coiners, and a dozen other trades, are very alert to unlicensed activity in their demesnes." He took a breath, looked at the three women. "And, I ask again, what would we gain by all this?"

CHAPTER 18

JERYA

"This may be our only chance to talk alone," said Yanil, "So I'll say it right out. You know, we had high hopes of you. Quite a few of us, but especially Joss and I. So when we heard what you'd done.... I'll be frank, Jerya, 'disappointed' doesn't do it justice. It wasn't until I got to talk to Sharess, when she eventually got here, that I began to, well, reconcile myself to it. Not that it wasn't a loss, still, but I could understand."

Reflection made momentary blanks of her lenses, but behind them her gaze was direct and steady. "I suppose it never occurred to you, Jerya, but you're not the first to have... misgivings."

"Misgivings?"

"About the deception."

Jerya slumped in the seat. "I never thought..."

"I blame myself... we blame ourselves. Jossena told me you were clearly shaken when you learned the truth about Song and sunrise. If we'd taken you into our confidence earlier..."

Jerya was still too shaken to think clearly. She dug her fingers into the seat as if the ache of overworked muscles could focus her mind. *What if*....

What if, indeed? But 'what ifs' cut two ways. In the world in which Jerya remained in the College, she would never have met Hedric, and J. Delven would never have contributed to the *Proceedings*.

And the world would not have Embrel in it.

And, more pertinently at this moment... "If I hadn't crossed the mountains, I wouldn't be here now to warn you."

"Well," said Yanil. "There is that."

"I am sorry. That I disappointed you."

"I said I was disappointed... I did not say you disappointed me. I—we—maybe Joss more than I—we've often wondered if there was something we could have said or done that would have made the difference."

"You mustn't blame yourselves."

Yanil nodded, but abstractedly; she was thinking of something else. After a moment, she said, "I think I knew, right from that first morning in my classroom, that you would do something extraordinary. Which you did, of course... And now it seems you've done another extraordinary thing in coming back.

"But I must warn you, Jerya, if you haven't seen this already: Perriad sees it in a different light. Oh, I have no doubt she also thinks your presence is extraordinary, but not in the way I mean it. I think... understand, this is my inference, but I base it on things I've heard her say in the past, as well as how she has acted just now. I think she believes you want to destroy the Guild—"

"—That's ridic—"

Yanil held up a hand. "Whatever we think of it, it is, I am sure, what she believes. That she believes you hate the Guild, I have no doubt whatever. How she explains your reappearance... my inference is that she thinks you have spent the last ten years in hiding somewhere, *fabricating* a plan to sabotage the influence of the Guild by concocting fake proofs of a land East of the mountains. A land Unsung, but somehow thriving."

"How can she think that? Is she even *sane*?"

Yanil sighed. "I have never had cause to question her sanity before. But on this matter... in fact, on anything connected with yourself... well, perhaps her judgement is, shall I say, skewed?"

"You're saying she can't accept the news I bring... because *I'm* the one bringing it?"

"Sadly, yes. And the worrying part is, Jerya, she has influence."

"If you or Jossena were Masters..."

Yanil shrugged. "If wishes were fishes, no one would be hungry."

Jerya stared at the floor, thinking hard. "What about the Master Prime? She seems... even-handed."

"She is a good woman. She will seek to draw out all the facts, and make her judgement on that basis. But she is first among equals, a leader not a commander. If the Conclave of Masters is tied, she has a casting vote, but that's all. And from what I've seen, and things I've heard from certain Masters, she sometimes tries too hard to be, in your words, even-handed. She might believe you, but what will she do if the Conclave leans the other way?"

"Is that a real possibility?"

"It is certainly a possibility."

"You mean a majority of Masters might actually swallow Perriad's nonsense?"

"Or, more simply, they may find it hard to overturn a belief we have all held our entire lives."

"You know what's ironic? Ironic, but not funny... I grew up believing the tale of the Blistered Lands. I never questioned it, until... it was *Perriad* who first gave me the idea that life might be possible beyond the mountains after all."

Yanil snorted softly, a sound that was not quite a laugh.

Jerya's mind was already moving forward. "How does she explain my coming here? If I wanted to attack the influence of the Guild, surely I'd do that by spreading my story, disseminating the *fake proofs* that I've *concocted*? Why would I come here, and put myself—and my evidence—in the Guild's hands? I would have to be crazy, wouldn't I?"

"I suppose so... But that's another hypothetical, isn't it? It's not *proof*. We must hope that the proofs you have brought are sufficiently convincing."

Jerya sighed. "I wish I'd brought more. But, you know, the journey is hard, and when you must carry all you need on your back, including seven days' food... then you consider every ounce. I thought very seriously about dismembering the copy of *The Proceedings*, just bringing the pages that show our work. But now..." She tried to remember exactly what the other papers in that volume concerned. There was one on the curious occurrence of what appeared to be marine fossils in montane strata, she was sure. And there were, of course, also minutes of meetings and other notices, all the business of the Denvirran Society for Natural Philosophy. "If I'd thought, I would have brought a mathematical journal too, for you. But... there are things in there which may be of interest to other Tutors, other Masters. And, you know, it would be a prodigious feat to fabricate it all. How am I supposed to have done all that?"

Yanil said nothing. "Still, in the end," said Jerya, "I reckon the most substantial proofs are Hedric and myself."

She gazed at the door as if it could tell her how Hedric was faring in the chamber beyond.

"If your tale is true," said Yanil. Jerya looked at her. "I believe you, but belief isn't proof, no more than Perriad's doubt is disproof. And it occurs to me that—if your tale *is* true—proof will arrive of its own doing, sooner or later."

"But that's exactly what I hoped to forestall," said Jerya, feeling a first quiver of desperation.

"But there is another way in which absolute proof could be found."

Jerya stared at her, but only for a moment. Then it hit her. "Of course. *Why* did I not think of that?"

"Let someone else make the crossing. Someone trusted by all... perhaps, indeed, a sceptic; one who is not invested in your tale."

"It would have to be someone... They would need some skill in climbing. Some experience of rough travel. And they would need to be well-briefed, prepared, so they don't give themselves away." Her mind raced, trying to consider a hundred things at once. "We could give them money, at least. Coin that no one in the East would look askance at." Of all the things, that was hardly of first importance... except that maybe everything was.

"The first place to look would be among the Peripatetics," said Yanil. "And that says to me that we should speak with Master Evisyn. In any case, she is one who could be... whom I hope would be an ally. I am sure she will be fascinated by your tale."

Then she frowned. "But therein lies a problem: how to bring you and Evisyn together? It would be rash to get her into this room—not now—and we can't bring you into the College proper. Not yet, at any rate."

"Is there no way I could... could I enter guised as a servitor or something? I do remember an... *unofficial* way in and out."

"Hmm... it might be... or it might be safer for me to bring her to you. Is there somewhere... have you a place to stay?"

"I hope so." But that was not yet certain, and it came freighted with its own cargo of unknowns.

"There's one other thing," said Jerya. "I'd really like to see Sharess, if that's possible."

Yanil frowned in thought. "She lives in the Yandor Wing, adjacent to the Upper Infirmary. I suppose it might be possible to get you into... But can you wait a day or two? If the Masters accept your tale, then I imagine you will be able to enter the Precincts openly. And if they don't... then who knows?"

CHAPTER 19

JERYA

Just for a moment, Jerya had wondered if she had misremembered the directions. She had only been to Garam's twice, ten years ago. Assuredly the place did not look as she remembered. *But then neither do I*, she thought.

The walls, to the best of her recall, had been a pale brown, like coffee with too much milk added; probably once white, but discoloured by years of smoke from lamps and pipes. The barrel-vaulting of the ceiling had been unpainted blush-coloured brick. Now both walls and ceiling were painted a fresh yellow that made her think of primroses. Wooden panelling, painted bronze, clad the walls up to about hip-height. The place smelt fresh, and as she advanced she saw that on each table was a small jar—probably one that had once held preserves—holding a few flowers or sprays of lavender.

There was all that, but there was something else too. She was halfway down the room before she realised. When she'd visited before, her memories seemed to say, the only females in the place had been herself, and Annyt behind the bar; plus, on one occasion, Railu. Now she saw two women, around her own age, deep in conversation in a booth, never even glancing up as she passed an arm's length from their table. Another woman sat with a couple of men.

And then two more men moved away from the bar, taking first sips from brimming mugs as they turned, and she saw the figure they'd been masking.

He looked up, smiling what was surely a standard welcome. It took him a moment; she thought again how much she must have changed. *It's ten years, after all.* She could see exactly the moment he knew. His eyes widened. He mouthed a word, too faint for her to hear. Her name?

Three more strides brought her to the bar. She hardly felt more calm than he appeared, but at least she still had the power of speech. "Hello, Rodal."

"It really *is* you."

"Besure," she said, smiling. He threw back his head, a laugh fuelled at least partly by relief.

"Good grief... what are you..." He stopped, visibly mastering himself, then smiled. "Jerya. It's good to see you... you look well."

"You too... reckon you've changed less than I have." His hair was longer than she'd been used to, but perhaps no longer than it had been at their last parting, brushed back neatly from a face that was a little fuller.

"Life over there suits you, it seems," he said. "And how's Railu?"

He does not know, she thought at once. *Had he known, he'd surely have asked after his son, too.* So Sharess had chosen to leave him in ignorance. Railu, at their last parting, had been as adamant as ever, so she said nothing of Embrel. "She's well."

"And is she still...?"

"Still a slave? I'm afraid so." She watched the flicker of expression on his face. "I think if she—and I—pressed for it, they might grant her freedom, but it would be... well, you know how it is over there. I don't honestly know how much difference it would make. She is housekeeper now, a responsible position, trusted... and she has much work as a healer too. It has to be clandestine, but even as a free woman she couldn't practise openly. I ask myself, sometimes, would she have had a better life if..."

"If you hadn't..."

"If I hadn't dragged us all across the mountains; if she'd stayed as Dawnsinger in Delven. 'Twould have been a lonelier life, besure. Beyond that, it's hardly for me to say."

He nodded. "Well, for me... I had my year over there, the adventure of my life. It was hard, at first, when I came back. I'd kept my word to Annyt, I was back within the twelvemonth, but... well, it was a cruel trick I'd played on her. And even when she seemed to be coming around, her parents wouldn't have me."

"Rodal, I'm sorry. You, Railu... who else did I injure, being so sure that I knew best?"

He shrugged. "It flows under the bridges, as they say here."

"Then Annyt..."

"Give me a moment and you shall see for yourself."

Annyt, at first glance, looked much the same. What she saw first, though, was the child on her hip, a sturdy girl of two or three. *Embrel has a sister*, she thought, and had to blink back tears. And, when Annyt came closer, she saw: there was another on the way.

Much of the next few minutes was a recapitulation of her converse with Rodal. But Annyt handed the child—Sokkie, they called her—to her father, came round the bar to grasp Jerya warmly by the shoulders. "I was mad at you at first," she said frankly. "Even after Rodal came back... though then, mostly, I was mad at him."

"I told him already, I'm truly sorry."

"Life's too short to bear grudges; specially when things work out fair in the end."

"Listen," said Jerya, squeezing her hands. "I must talk more with both of you, and get to know your daughter, and explain why I'm here. And I don't know if there's time for any of it. But first, I must... there's someone I want you to meet." *They've been waiting outside too long already.*

Rodal was busy serving a few new customers; presumably he'd set Sokkie down somewhere. So Hedric was introduced to Annyt first. He, having had an account of Jerya's earlier travels, had some notion of who she was; but how to explain to her who Hedric was? "My friend, who's come with me from the other side," was wholly true, but far from the whole truth.

"Too much to say, and too little time," she sighed. "I'm sorry, may I talk business for a minute? Do you have any rooms?"

Annyt's face fell. "We don't let out rooms any more. More trouble than it was worth, with a child in the house."

"Besure," said Rodal, appearing beside her. "But the rooms are still there." He gave Hedric a wary sort of nod; Hedric responded in kind. "How many?

"Three, I suppose." Though that still left a question—and no time to consider it now. "If you're sure you can...?"

"Jerya, I haven't seen you for ten years. What kind of friend would I be to send you out into the night when we have the power to accommodate you? The rooms may look a little bare, but we keep 'em clean."

The place was getting busier, and Sokkie was looking as though she might be sleepy. At that age, Jerya remembered, Embrel could go from furious activity to fast asleep in ten minutes. Annyt excused herself, and Rodal was occupied with customers for a while. Jerya, Hedric, and Lallon settled into a booth against the right hand wall. Rodal appeared a minute later with three mugs. "I anticipated your order," he said, not very apologetically.

"I was always told this house served the best ale in the city," said Jerya.

"Besure, but who told you that?" He grinned. "Annyt's Pa runs the brewery these days. We bought out their interest in this place. Half th'taverns in th'city sell their ale now. And we're better friends not mixing too much in each other's business... Now, might you folks be hungry at all?"

Jerya and Hedric had been given some modest sustenance during the long day at the Guild, but it turned out Lallon, languishing all but forgotten in the streets, had had nothing. "Double helping for you, my lad," said Hedric. Lallon smiled, scratching under his cap. The brawny slave, always reticent, had turned shy in the new land, among new people, not knowing what his place was. In the East, his relationship with Hedric had been so easy they did not seem like master and slave at all, save when they needed to perform the roles in front of others. Here, unsure of his ground, the free man was acting more like a slave than he did where he was one.

"I'll bring a basket o'bread right away," said Rodal, already turning.

＊

She had barely finished eating, and Lallon was still mopping his plate with a chunk of bread, of which he'd eaten more than Jerya and Hedric together. Suddenly she became aware of someone looking closely at her, a couple of paces away, another figure almost hidden behind her.

"You are Jerya?"

"I am."

"I am Evisyn." The newcomer was bronze-skinned, tall, rangy, carrying a sense of suppressed energy. A sharp nose gave her a hawkish look. Drab skirt and blouse and bonnet, a Dawnsinger's incognito, could not entirely efface an air of authority.

Evisyn was looking warily at Jerya's companions. She realised the issue at once. Two could fit, easily enough, in the space beside Lallon, but these were Dawnsingers; it was hardly likely they'd be happy in such close proximity to a male.

Hedric seemed to read the situation, or intuit her thoughts. With nothing more than a glance he sent a message. Wordless as ever, Lallon grabbed his plate and the last of the bread, shuffled along the seat and out.

"And I should go too," said Hedric, waiting for her to rise and let him out.

Jerya held up a hand. "Master Evisyn, this is my... friend and colleague, Hedric. His knowledge of the Eastern land certainly exceeds my own. I understand you may be less than comfortable, but if you would allow him to stay, I am sure he has much to contribute."

Evisyn considered a moment. As a Peripatetic, thought Jerya, she almost certainly had wider contact with men than most Dawnsingers. "Let him remain."

She slipped into the space Lallon had vacated, and for the first time Jerya got clear sight of her companion. She was shorter by a handsbreadth, and notably darker of skin: Analind.

Jerya recognised her one-time roommate with a surge of joy, but her eager smile was not reciprocated. She sighed inwardly as she completed the introductions. "I know that you are Master of Peripatetics," she added to Evisyn, "But I don't know what your role is now...?" This to Analind.

"I am a Peripatetic, with particular responsibility for map-making and revision, but in the winter I also serve as Assistant Tutor in Cartography and Toponymy." Analind's voice betrayed a tension that Jerya had never previously seen in her. *People change in ten years...* But she suspected there was more to it than that.

"Under Tutor Skarat?" Analind gave a single grudging nod. Jerya had a sudden sense she would rather not be here at all. Whether it was the tavern, the male company, or whether she was, like Perriad, disinclined to forgive or overlook Jerya's offence... it could be any, or all.

Well, things will work out, or they won't. There were, regrettably, higher priorities than Analind's dourness. She drew her backpack from under the bench, fished out the oilcloth wallet containing the maps. As soon as she saw what they were, Evisyn sat up, leaned closer. "I assume Tutor Yanil told you our thought..." said Jerya.

"About proving your tale?"

As Evisyn assented, Jerya realised: *she wants to go, herself.* Whether a Master had the freedom to leave the College for so long, she doubted. But if anyone could, it would be the Master of Peripatetics.

"Well," she said, "There's much to think about before anyone makes that journey. And it's perhaps more urgent to consider where... if anyone does come from the other side, where they might appear."

"Of course," said Evisyn, sounding slightly Crestfallen.

"To start," said Jerya, "We can look at maps from the East, make comparisons with Guild maps. I remember ten years ago, Tutor Skarat spoke of plans to recruit Peripatetics to help improve the maps..." Indeed, it seemed as if Analind were engaged in exactly such duties.

"Just so, and much has been done."

"So, we make that comparison... what's the other word I'm thinking of?"

"Concordance?" said Hedric.

"Of course, thank you." She was already unfolding one of the Eastern maps, and Evisyn was leaning even closer. "It won't be entirely straight-forward. The scales are different, the units of distance, but it'll be a simple calc—"

"—How reliable are these?" asked Analind, peering suspiciously at the map spread across the table.

"I'm no cartographer," she said. "I had a few lessons with Tutor Skarat, and I enjoyed them, but—well, you know, there was never enough time."

"There would have been, had you stayed."

"I can't deny it. But I have learned other things, in the East. And..." She drew breath. "To answer your question, I did need to know that these maps are accurate, for some of the astronomical work I—we—have done." A brief glance at Hedric. She explained quickly about the need for a long baseline and precise calibration. "We received assurances that distances, across the breadth of the Five Principalities, were accurate to a fraction of one percent."

Evisyn was nodding. "So, clearly, we can try putting these maps together with ours to make a whole... but it seems likely there will be something of a void in between."

"We considered that," said Hedric. "And we don't know exactly where the Selton expedition is aiming to try... naturally he didn't want to show his hand ahead of time... but I've studied these maps, and I think there are two main approaches that would suggest themselves to them, with a third as a contingency. Once a concordance is established, that will surely suggest where they are most likely to appear on this side."

"*If* they appear," said Analind, evidently still sceptical about the whole scheme. She had never seemed like a particular admirer of Perriad—far from it, indeed—but time could change attitudes. Or maybe she was simply unpersuaded for reasons of her own. An open mind was an admirable thing, Jerya reminded herself.

Jerya focused on Evisyn. "As soon as the concordance is done, you... I beg your pardon, I don't mean to tell you your business."

Evisyn only smiled, showing white but rather uneven teeth. "It's obvious where you're going with this. Likely places should be watched... If we proceed, cautiously, as far as we can... At the very least, we may learn something more about our own land." Analind was looking at her: Jerya was sure it was the use of 'we'.

She thought it was unlikely the Conclave of Masters would attach great weight to the 'learn something more' argument. Everything still hinged on the Masters accepting the basic truth of Jerya's tale. The maps might carry some weight, but if Perriad continued to argue that the *Proceedings* could be fabricated... maps could be fabricated too, probably more easily. The Masters, she thought glumly, might think that much could be accomplished in ten years.

Evisyn was unfolding another of the maps. Hedric leaned forward, said something explanatory, and Evisyn responded with a question. One Dawnsinger, at least, was easy enough in male company.

Then she realised that Analind was looking at her. They had been close, once; Analind had been kinder to her than anyone, apart from Railu and Yanil. She had to at least try to bridge the gap that had grown between them.

"Look," she said, "I do know how much I—"

"No, Jerya, I don't think you do. I don't think you have any idea how we felt—how *I* felt—when we realised what you'd done. You'd lied to us all, let us believe you'd be coming back in a few weeks. I was looking forward to seeing you again, going forward into the future together. I'd even been hoping we might be roommates again."

Jerya knew tears were springing to her eyes. She made no attempt to brush them away; let Analind see. At the same time she was wondering exactly what Analind had been hoping for: had she thought they might become more than mere roommates? *Maybe we would...* It was impossible to know, now.

"You're right," she said. She reached for her tankard, but didn't lift it to her lips, just wrapped her hands around it, gauging its weight. "I *don't* know, or I didn't until this moment. I didn't think of you, or all the others who'd be hurt. Or not enough... I can only hope I'm a little wiser now, ten years on; better able to understand. To put myself in the shoes of others."

"You left," said Analind. "You turned renegade, and you lied to us all, and none of us could understand why."

"There is one person who might have given you some account of it. Not at the time, but some years before now."

"Who might that be?"

"Singer Sharess." There was no sign that Analind recognised the name. "The old Singer, from Delven, the one who Chose me. We told her, before we left Delven."

"She didn't try to stop you?"

"No, and if she had, I would have found it hard to go through with it... she said it grieved her to her heart, but she also said she was proud of me." Seeing doubt, she added, "You can ask her yourself. She lives in the Precincts now."

"In the Yandor Wing?"

"So Yanil said."

"Did you tell her *why* you were leaving?"

"I tried. I hope she understood."

"Can you explain it to me?"

"I can try." Finally, she raised her mug to her lips and took a drink. "You said I lied to you, let you believe I'd be coming back. I did. But that was because there was a greater lie that I couldn't stomach. The Guild allows people to believe that Dawnsong causes the sun to rise."

"*Allows* them to believe," protested Analind. "We don't actually proclaim—" She saw the contradiction, and stopped. Jerya thought of saying, *and I never proclaimed I was coming back*, but opted for silence. She lifted her tankard again, giving Analind a moment to think. The next question was hardly unexpected. "If that's what you believe, why did you come back?"

"I came back because I saw that there are greater evils in this world."

"What greater evils?"

"Slavery, for one."

Analind's obvious shock showed she hadn't been told that news. Jerya wondered exactly what she *had* been told—and by whom. "Slavery," she repeated after a moment. "Really?"

She looked around, spotted Lallon on a stool at the bar, speaking to Rodal. Jerya wondered what they were talking about. "He's a slave, over there. And..." She hesitated only a moment. "Railu and I were taken for slaves when we first crossed."

Analind stared, beyond speech. Jerya considered briefly. "I'm telling you this because... we were close, once, and you've shown me how much pain I caused you. But I would think very carefully... there are many Masters who would not be happy if any of this got out before they are ready."

"You have the right of it there," said Evisyn. Jerya started; she had not realised the Master was now listening. Hedric, too, but none of this would shock him.

"But, for me, please continue," added Evisyn. "Yanil gave me a very condensed account. I am eager to know more."

So Jerya waded through the tale of their capture and its aftermath; how their fates had hinged on the merest chance that Duncal and Pichenta had been in the slave-market that afternoon. To this day, Jerya had never been told *why* they had been there. They had not acquired anyone else that day, nor had they ever done so in all the years since.

And then, what was always the hardest part, she had to tell how it was that she was now free while Railu had remained a slave. "As a slave on Duncal's estate, she has a better life than many of the poor free folk; better than some of the poor here, I should think. But still..." She did not know how to finish. She studied Analind's face, hoping for some clue... hoping for some indication that she *understood*.

At last Analind released a long breath. "Oh, Jerya... I was so angry with you. In some way, I still *am* angry with you. But I never thought... never thought you might have suffered like that."

"It was horrible," she said. "No doubt of that. But compared to what might have become of us... and it was only three days. There's no need to pity me."

"I hardly know what I should feel."

"Maybe, then," said Evisyn with a sort of rough kindness, "You might distract yourself by looking at these maps and giving me your professional opinion."

CHAPTER 20

HEDRIC

Hedric was struggling to catch up, to understand the context of the questions he was now being asked. Since leaving Jerya on the threshold early that morning, he had wandered the streets of the city for several hours. He did his best to take it all in. By Jerya's count, he and Lallon were only the fourth and fifth people to see both sides of the world. Still, his mind kept returning to that room in the Annexe, and what was happening to Jerya.

He had been assured there would be no news before lunchtime… and there was no knowing whether it would be good, bad, or dire. Jerya had said little, but he'd seen enough on the previous day to know that some in the Dawnsinger's Guild thought she should not be heard at all; and that some of those also held that she should be seized and punished for her actions of ten years ago.

An hour after the noon-bells—a peal any city in the Five Principalities would be proud to own—he'd first returned to the narrow, kinked alley which led to the Annexe. Seeing no sign of Jerya, and under her strict orders not to attempt entry alone, he'd found a stall a few streets away selling some sort of mess of vegetables rolled up in a flat, floury bread. He ate it without really tasting it, knowing he needed to keep his strength up, wondering if Jerya was eating too. Another stall sold him a sort of watery buttermilk in a flimsy tin mug. "Penny back on th'mug," said the unsmiling stall-holder.

He drank enough to make it safe to carry without spilling, then returned to the alley. About twenty yards from the door, a large granite boulder, possibly a relic of the hill's natural state, protruded where two walls met at a curious angle. If anyone was watching from the peephole in the door, or the window-slits beside and above it, he was far enough away not to care unduly.

He settled down to nurse the rest of his sour-sweet drink and wait.

His heart sank when at last the door opened and a figure emerged. It was a woman in white, and bald: not Jerya.

When she came closer, he saw it was Evisyn's assistant... what was her name? Analyn? She had never spoken directly to him on the previous evening, and she didn't meet his the eye now. "The Masters require your presence," was all she said. *Require*, not *request*, he noticed, as if he were subject to their authority.

But he did not object, only asking, "Is all well with Jerya?"

This time she almost met his gaze, eyes shying away at the last. "It's not for me to say."

He left the mug on the boulder. If it was there when he came back, well and good: if not, someone else could have the penny.

It could not be the full Conclave: Jerya had said there were twenty Masters, but only a handful of seats at one end of the table were filled. Jerya sat halfway along. She gave him a smile he could not quite read. *She looks tired*, was all he could conclude.

They placed a seat for him at the other end of the table, setting him apart. Jerya met his eye with a rueful shrug. Evisyn introduced all of those present, including those he had met before; herself, Analind, and Yanil.

Apart from herself, the only Guild Master present was Skarat, whom Evisyn described as a 'pioneer' in cartography.

Introductions complete, Evisyn yielded to Skarat, a woman of stocky frame and ruddy complexion. "Hedric Pendeen," she said. "Our purpose is to assemble as much hard information as we can, to be laid before the full Conclave on the morrow. Jerya made the case—persuasively, I must say—that we should not ignore your potential contribution, and she was supported by Master Evisyn and Singer Analind." Startled by the latter name, he glanced involuntarily at Analind, but she dropped her gaze.

"For myself," said Skarat dourly, "I reserve my judgement." *I hope that's another way of saying you have an open mind*, he thought.

Evisyn moved to break the ensuing silence. "As you know, Master Skarat, it is my firm view that the Conclave can make no well-informed decision without at least initial outlines of the concordance we've spoken of."

"I have my best girls on it now," said Skarat, "And I hope to be able to join my own efforts to theirs before too long."

Hedric cleared his throat. "If there is any assistance I can give I should be happy to oblige. I can say without fear of contradiction that Jerya and I have unique knowledge of the Eastern side. And she would be the first to admit that I have travelled more extensively within the Five Principalities than she has." It chafed her sometimes, he knew.

"I don't deny your help would have value, but, practically, there is a difficulty. The work is best carried forward in the map room, on the great table, with all the drawing instruments and calculating engines to hand." He was instantly curious about these 'calculating engines', but that would have to wait. "The Masters have made considerable concessions to this unprecedented situation, but they are hardly likely to agree that you may pass into the College proper. No man has been admitted here since the walls were completed."

"They haven't even agreed that *I* might be admitted yet," said Jerya.

He sighed in frustration. The whole idea of the concordance fascinated him. To see the outlines emerging, to envision the gaps that would undoubtedly remain, was powerfully alluring—and he was sure he *could* help. Suddenly he recalled the sketches he'd made on the peak. *I could offer those... but not to be in the room...*

Perhaps his frustration made him speak rashly. "On my side of the mountains, men pronounce and women listen. Here, it seems to be the other way around. I cannot help wondering—" *if the world would be a better place...* no, he had sufficient self-command not to go that far. "—How it might be if men and women listened to each other."

He had gone quite far enough, he saw. They were staring. Evisyn, perhaps, looked like she could hear him without shock. The rest...

Only Jerya had the beginnings of a smile... but at the same time there was a warning in her eyes.

He made himself shrug. "Idle speculation, no doubt. If I cannot go to the map room, then I must give what aid I can remotely."

"We shall consider this," said Skarat. "In the meantime, there are other questions. What can you tell us about this expedition?"

"I know little—nothing, really—beyond what is in the newspaper report. Anything more will be conjecture, though I think well-founded."

"Well, let us see. This Duke of... of Selden?"

"Selton."

"What manner of man is he?"

"I have only passing acquaintance with the man himself, but he is well-reputed. And I have read some of his work. He is a true natural philosopher—a scientist, as I think you say here. He has done solid work in geology, and has advanced ideas in geomorphology."

"Then would you say his motivation is purely scientific?"

"Firstly, perhaps. He has that curiosity, no doubt of that. But *purely*? That I do doubt; and in any case, there are others with him, and more who might follow on behind."

"What about the others, then?"

He reached for a transcript, scanned the names again. "Rafforth I have met. Ortner and Gallard... I've heard them speak. Sound enough men, but amateurs. The others I don't know. Friends, probably, along for the adventure; plus one whom I think must be the Duke's son. If so, he's quite young."

"The report says an expedition of thirty or so, but it only mentions eight names."

"Those are the only *gentlemen*," said Jerya. "That is how society works in the Five Principalities."

He nodded acknowledgement. Left to himself he might have taken that for granted, as any Five Principalities native would. "And each of those gentlemen will be accompanied by a body-slave."

"A *body-slave*?" Skarat repeated in tones of distaste. He wondered briefly exactly what scenarios her mind might be conjuring.

"That is the common term, but it might be clearer to say 'personal attendant' or some such form of words. They are there to serve all their master's needs. In polite circumstances they would help him dress, for example." Faces showed what the Dawnsingers thought of this. "I should point out that gentlemen's formal attire in the Five Principalities is sometimes... complicated... I see Jerya nodding."

"That is one word. I might prefer 'ridiculous'." She smiled, in case he thought she was mocking him. "But perhaps we should discuss the details of gentlemen's personal arrangements at a later date."

"Agreed."

"The rest of that thirty, fourteen or so, will be assistants, camp followers. And that doesn't even consider the muleteers who doubtless serve the expedition's base camp. And there may be a number of slaves held in readiness to carry supplies when mules could be coaxed no further.

"The main point I draw from this is that an expedition of this magnitude will be cumbersome, and will move relatively slowly. At the pace of the slowest. But also that it will take a major obstacle to halt it altogether."

He picked up the transcript again. "These are the Duke's own words, at least as reported: *Last year I penetrated some way into these mountains, and I could see that it would be possible to continue further. I had no time then, because of the wedding of my eldest daughter. Had I failed to return for that it would have been safer for me never to return at all.* 'Yes, he's quite the witty fellow...' *This year, fortunately, my younger daughter is not getting married before the autumn. And if we do not succeed this year, well, I have no more daughters left...*'" The Duke's 'humour' seemed to pass them all by. Jerya, he thought, understood, but was unimpressed. "My primary inference is that he is prepared for a long campaign. If this year's attempt proves fruitless, he will regroup and try again. And, as Jerya has no doubt said, if he does not discover another feasible route, then sooner or later he is bound to stumble on one we used. At that point, if not before, success is assured."

CHAPTER 21

JERYA

A new day, some new faces in the room.

"Your name is Lallon, is that correct?"

"Aye, m'lady."

"And is that the entirety of your name?"

"Beg pardon, m'lady?"

"Is that your whole name?"

"In th'Register it'd be Lallon bey-Kirwaugh, m'lady."

"And bey-Kirwaugh means what, exactly?"

"Kirwaugh's th'estate, m'lady, where I belongs."

"Because you're a slave?" Syrtos's tone was still gentle, but Singers around the room sat a little straighter, fixed their gazes more firmly on Lallon.

If he saw this, he gave no sign, keeping his gaze on the table in front of Master Syrtos. "I am, m'lady."

Evisyn and Syrtos exchanged glances, and Syrtos made a 'yield' gesture. "Lallon," said Evisyn. "I think you're aware that there is no slavery in the Sung Lands, is that so?"

"Aye, m'lady."

"Then as far as we are concerned, you are a free man."

"Aye, m'lady, Master said th'same, and Miss Jerya afore him."

"But you stay with your Master all the same?"

"Aye, m'lady."

"May we ask why?"

Lallon shrugged. "Belike I owes him summat, m'lady. An'... I figger I has a better life'n most people I sees. Not just slaves, a lot o' th' frees, too."

Evisyn nodded, though Jerya wondered how far she could truly understand. She had struggled, herself, to grasp why people close to her—and there were few closer than Rhenya—could seem so completely content with their lot.

Syrtos resumed. "Would you tell us what makes most slaves' lives worse than yours?"

Nothing in Lallon's reply was news to Jerya, so she studied the faces of the Masters as they absorbed the litany of evils. There were relatively banal complaints like barracks living (which, she thought, might not sound too different from the dormitory life of Postulants and the younger Novices), and poor food. There were deeper abuses, like slaves being told whom they could or could not marry, and the splitting of existing families when convenience or profit required. And there was the violence, from routine whippings to punishments like tonguing. Jerya shuddered, remembering how she had once been threatened, by a brute named Keeving, with hot wax in her ear.

In finishing, Lallon took pains to emphasise, "Ain't none o'this-like on my Master's estate. Nor at Duncal, where Miss Jerya lives. Seen that wi' me own eyes, belike."

At this Master Berrivan gestured, requesting the floor. "You are familiar with the Duncal estate, then?"

"Dun't know about 'familiar', m'lady. I's bin a few times. I knows th'house-slaves, belike, dun't know the farm or the field-hands."

"And do you know someone called Railu?"

"I knows her, m'lady. I..." He hesitated.

"What is it?"

"I were goin' to say she's a puzzle, m'lady. Looks like a slave, but dun't seem she is one."

"She looks like a slave because...?"

"Because she dun't got no hair, m'lady. But all o' yow..." He faltered again.

"Be assured *we* are not slaves," said Perriad.

"Aye, I knows that, m'lady."

"Lallon," said Evisyn, smiling as if to counter Perriad's acerbity, "Would you be so good as to remove your cap?"

There were indrawn breaths and muttered comments around the room as he slid off his knitted cap. The topknot marked a clear difference from the pure bald of every Dawnsinger, but Jerya wondered what would happen to any man who dared to go about fully hairless. Men could lose their hair, and for a free man in the Five Principalities it was a source of shame... and an opportunity for the peddlers of dubious nostrums. For a woman complete alopecia was rare, but probably even more shaming. There were wigs, but they were expensive. The only alternative was to cover one's head; that must be what they did here too. Well, she'd worn a headcloth for ten years in Delven.

And I'm woolgathering... The questioning had not obligingly ceased.

"Now, I'd like to ask you about your journey to get here. Can you tell us when and where you started?"

"Aye, m'lady. 'Twere goin' on two week agone now. As to where, belike yow'd say we started prop'ly from Drumlenn."

"Drumlenn is the town nearest the Duncal estate, isn't it?" Jerya wasn't at all surprised Evisyn knew this, given how avidly she'd pored over her map.

"Tha's c'rect, m'lady. 'Bout an hour's ride, or a bit more."

"And this was yourself, Hedric Pendeen, and Jerya, was it?"

"Not th'first day, m'lady. We had a couple other lads wi'us, to tek th'horses back when we couldn't ride no farther. An' Miss Jerya rode up alone."

"Oh, why was that?"

Lallon fumbled some explanation about preserving the decencies; Evisyn had to refer briefly to Hedric before she decided the assembled

Singers understood well enough. She moved on, asking about the terrain they had traversed.

"It were mostly fields an' farms at first, m'lady, but by th'afternoon 'twere mostly forest. And we was riding up into th' hills all th'time, though we mostly couldn't see too much 'count o'th'trees. We made camp in a clearin' that night."

"And Jerya joined you there?"

"Tha's c'rect, m'lady. Quite late, she were; master were gettin' a bit worrit."

"Tell us about the second day."

Evisyn proceeded, never showing impatience with Lallon's propensity for giving bare-minimum answers. She drew out the story of the approach, the crag-climb, the passes. He mentioned the ascent of the peak, but not Hedric's slip. Jerya felt relief; doubtless Hedric was even more grateful.

The account reached the moors above Delven. "What happened next day?" asked Evisyn.

"Broke camp proper early, m'lady. We was movin' almost afore we could see. Came to some rocks, came down a bit—they was easy, not like on th'way up—an' then we stopped. Waited a bit. Waitin' for dawn, Miss Jerya said."

"And what happened when dawn arrived?"

"We heard some'un singin'..."

Normally, meetings of the Conclave took place in a dedicated chamber at the heart of the College. Since Jerya's presence was required, but had still not been granted admission to the Precincts, this one was held instead in the Annexe, in the same room as the previous meetings. Extra chairs had been brought in, adding several rows across the back of the room.

In theory, Jerya recalled, meetings of the Conclave were open to all Dawnsingers. In practice, since they took place on working days, almost everyone had other obligations; classes to attend or to teach, the demands of the Infirmary, research to pursue. She had never attended one in her short time here. Nor did it seem as if the exceptional nature of this session had been spread around. There were only a handful of observers, fully half of whom she recognised. Analind was there, and her senior, Skarat. So was Yanil... and with her...

Jerya felt as if her heart would stop.

Sharess sat slightly hunched, a shawl over her robe though the room was warm. But she caught Jerya's gaze, and her eyes were clear, as far as Jerya could tell across the width of the room. She raised a hand, fingers curled in toward the palm; another clutch at the heart. Her face felt stiff, almost frozen, as she tried to smile in response. She had wanted, more than anything, to see her mother again. Just once, to look her in the eye and call her that. But she could not cross the room now, could not speak to her, needed to put her out of mind altogether and give the whole of her mind to what was said in the coming hours.

Part of her almost wished that Sharess was not there.

There was no sign of Jossena. Perriad, of course, to state the case against. And, Jerya was pleased to see, Master Evisyn to stand up in her favour. Pleased, but really not surprised.

"My fellow Masters," began Perriad sonorously. Her voice was a fine instrument, Jerya had to admit. "This morning there will be much talk of proofs, of evidence, and I shall in the next few minutes attend to all of these that have been placed before us. But when all is said and done, it is for this Conclave to make a judgement on the authenticity, or otherwise, of these few items." She lingered fractionally over 'few'. "And when you do so, Masters, do be sure to remind yourselves who brought these things to us. I'm sure the historians among you will confirm that when you judge the authenticity or value of material, you take account of what is known about its provenance; about the author, if she is known." A couple of heads nodded.

"I need hardly tell you that the source of these proofs is someone known to us all. Shall I say 'notorious'?"

"Please confine yourself to matters of fact," said the Master Prime.

Perriad bowed her head, but only slightly and only for an instant. "Of course, Master Prime. The *fact* is that this person is a Vow-breaker and a renegade. We all know this. Not only did she break her own Vow, she—"

"—I think we are all well aware of these facts," said Master Evisyn. "I fail to see what's gained by raking over these particular coals."

"I'm inclined to agree," said the Master Prime. "Master Perriad, if you would be so kind, please turn your attention to the evidence."

"Of course, Master Prime, but may I call it 'alleged evidence'?"

"You may not," said the Master Prime. "It's evidence. Whether it's good evidence or bad is what we're here to decide."

To Jerya, watching closely, it seemed that Perriad was overplaying her hand. In doing so, she had already irked the Master Prime. Did she also risk alienating some of the other Masters? Thus far, she could not tell. Most of them seemed to be hanging on Perriad's every word, but paying close attention hardly proved they were convinced. No doubt she looked equally intent herself.

Perriad gave another grudging nod. "I proceed to the *evidence.* But may I just remind you all of the context? It has been ten years, very nearly, since this person absconded. Much can happen in ten years. If any should say—" She seemed to make a point of looking at neither Jerya nor Evisyn— "That these items would be hard to fabricate, well, I concede that at once. But *hard* is not impossible, and a clever individual, let alone a group of people, may achieve much in ten years."

The Master Prime said nothing, but her eye suggested she was growing impatient.

"Very well," said Perriad, smiling complacently. "I move to the items before us. Regrettably, one which has been hailed as the most important is not currently here..."

Evisyn signalled her wish to speak, but the Master Prime waved her down. "Should any of the Masters be unaware, that item has been under examination since yesterday by Senior Tutor Jossena and several of the Librarians. I have assurances that they will bring it, and their reports, to us the moment they are able to give a clear verdict." She glanced at Evisyn, who nodded, satisfied. "Master Perriad, please turn your attention to the items which *are* before us."

Perriad began with the maps. Jerya knew that Evisyn was eager to start work on the 'concordance', but could hardly do so during the Conclave, so all the maps were there on the table.

"Whether they are fabricated or not," said Perriad smoothly, "This is an impressive piece of work. I am not a specialist, of course, but I took the usual courses during my Novitiate. As such I know that the ultimate benchmark by which a map is to be judged is not beauty but accuracy. And there lies our problem, my fellow Masters. We have no way to verify, not merely whether these maps are accurate, but whether they bear any relation whatsoever to the real world. They may, for all we know, be complete fantasy."

Jerya half-expected Evisyn to register another protest here, but she only made a note.

Perriad forged ahead, but could do little more with the maps than restate her point in different ways. Her treatment of the other physical evidence was similar. 'Evidence' was said with a finely-judged hint of a sneer every time. You had to admit she had a sense of theatre. The coins, the unfamiliar cut of Jerya's clothing, were acknowledged only in order to dismiss them. It all seemed to Jerya like thin stuff, but watching the faces among the listening Masters made her feel less secure.

How many of those Masters were aware of the key piece of evidence that had still not been brought before them? Perriad knew, as did Syrtos, Evisyn, and of course the Master Prime. Surely Jossena would be ready to report soon...?

✳

Evisyn rose. "My fellow Masters, I beg your indulgence. I am not so accustomed to addressing you all as Master Perriad. I have not a half of her eloquence; nor, I fear, her elocution. I can only muddle through in my plodding way, and hope that among my rough words you may discern some points of substance."

Jerya kept her face straight with an effort. The insinuation that Perriad had said nothing of substance... that was *exquisite.* She thought there was nothing *plodding* about Master Evisyn.

Evisyn stepped forward to the table in the centre, picked up one of the maps. "I must say, I agree with Master Perriad in one particular: fabricated or not, these maps are indeed impressive. In fact, I'd go further. If they are fabricated, they are remarkable... but if they are a true representation of what lies beyond the Eastern ranges, then we must surely consider them even more remarkable." She paused a moment, let that sink in. "And I will argue shortly that, given what may be at stake, that possibility is one we must take very seriously indeed.

"However, let me first say this. I agree with Master Perriad on the one point, but I disagree with her on many others. And crucially, Master Perriad stated before us all..." She consulted her notes. "In her own words, *We have no way to verify, not merely whether these maps are accurate, but whether they bear any relation whatsoever to the real world.* Masters, it is my duty to tell you that on this point Master Perriad is entirely in error." There was a rustle around the room, people stirring, making notes or whispering to each other. Evisyn allowed it to subside before continuing. "We can very easily verify whether these maps bear any relation to the real world, in the most scientific way... We go and look."

More than a rustle; a suppressed turmoil seethed through the gathering. Evisyn pitched her voice to ride over it. "Masters. By her own account—and I have heard something of it from her own lips—our former Novice, Jerya, has crossed the mountains twice. She did so ten years ago, with the recently Ordained Singer Railu and another companion. She returned little more than a week ago, with different companions."

"'By her own account'," repeated Perriad. "This is not evidence."

Evisyn nodded, to all appearances perfectly humble. "No, Master, and I do not claim it as such... until put to the test. But such a test would be simple—and would confirm the veracity of these maps, too. If her tale is true, then *we know where to look.* A small band of my Peripatetics could make the crossing, far enough to confirm the lie of the land—and the presence of human life—and return within four weeks. In fact they could make the return as far as Delven within three weeks, and let us know their key findings from there by bird." *And I would give my right arm to be with them*, was the subtext which, Jerya thought, must be apparent to everyone in the room. "And here's the beauty of it. If her tale is false, if these maps are fabricated, that too will be clearly demonstrated within the same time-frame." She turned her gaze on Jerya, as if in challenge: *if you're lying, you'll be found out soon enough; why not admit it now?* Jerya returned the look, hoping she appeared calmer than she felt. Evisyn held her regard a moment more, then gave a tiny nod, as if satisfied.

"Masters," she went on, "There is another possibility. We can go looking for verification... or we can sit back and wait for verification to come to us.

"I am sure you have all heard the gist of Jerya's tale, so you will know that the reason she has returned now is that she got wind of a well-resourced expedition being mounted on the other side—yes, Master Perriad, I know this is all based on the word of one individ—*yes*, a renegade, if you will. I am sure our fellow Masters have quite enough wit to have understood that perfectly well the first time you said it. If you will allow me to make my point...

"Consider the scenarios. By Jerya's account, this expedition is looking for a possible crossing further South than the point where she herself has crossed. At this present moment no one, on either side of the divide, knows whether a feasible crossing exists in that region. It is possible that the route Jerya discovered is the only one. But let us consider the possibility that a route *does* exist, that this expedition does find it and make the crossing. Well, my Masters..." A perilous smile, making her look more raptorial than ever. "That is of course another way in which we could receive verification of at least some aspects of Jerya's tale. Well and good... But please, my Masters, consider, and consider well, what else may follow such an eventuality. Consider all that's at stake before you decide how we should act."

She stepped back, and Jerya briefly wondered if she had finished, but Evisyn had merely retreated to a side table where a jug and glasses stood ready. She poured herself a drink, swigged half of it down, then returned to the centre.

"My fellow Masters, our purpose here today is to consider evidence. I won't take up your valuable time with the coins, or Jerya's clothes. All very interesting, but I don't believe they add anything that the maps don't do better. But there is one other source of evidence we would be foolish to ignore... and that is Jerya herself."

Jerya was taken aback, but she had a moment to recover herself as Perriad was on her feet protesting. The words 'Vow-breaker' and 'renegade' were trotted out again, but the Master Prime swiftly cut her off. "We all know Jerya's history, Master Perriad. Your fellow Masters do not need constant reminders." Perriad glowered, but there was nothing she could say.

"Would you stand, please, Jerya?" said Evisyn. "Let the Masters take a good look at you. At your hair and your clothes, since we've heard about them. Now, my Masters, I don't think there's anything to be gained at this time in delving into why Jerya left us; why she turned renegade, if you choose to put it that way. This Conclave may wish to go into that at another time, and that is its right.

"At this time, I deem it more important, more urgent, to hear what she has to tell us of the land beyond the mountains... yes, the *alleged* land beyond. May we take 'alleged' as read from here on? As you said, Master Prime, the Masters can judge for themselves."

The Master Prime gave one regal nod; Perriad made no protest, but equally no acknowledgement. Evisyn turned to Jerya. "Now, Jerya, would you tell us, briefly, what happened to you at your first encounter with people on the other side?"

It was hardly a tale she liked to recall, and already since returning to the Sung Lands she had had to recount it multiple times; once to Evisyn herself. If a trace of emotion showed in her voice as she recounted their capture and the indignities that followed... well, there was no reason to hide it. Maybe it helped her credibility.

"So you discovered, in the rudest possible way, that the society on the other side practices slavery? Can you tell me *why* you and Railu were taken for slaves?"

"Anyone on that side would have taken one look at us and seen us as slaves. In that land a shaven head is the mark of a slave."

Consternation, outrage... there was no Master who was indifferent. Several were shaking their heads, but whether in alarm or disbelief, she could not tell.

Evisyn let the Conclave settle. "Jerya, you just told us a shaven head is the mark of a slave. And you were taken as a slave... but looking at you it's clear your head has not been shaved for... I should say several years, am I right?"

"You are, Master. A good nine years, in fact."

"So you ceased to be a slave quite soon after your arrival. Can you tell us how that came about?"

From the sheer good fortune of their acquisition by the most benevolent owner in the Drumlenn hinterland, Evisyn drew her on to her freedom and the role—roles—she now fulfilled. From there they progressed to a wider account of the Principalities, though Jerya had to concede that she had never travelled beyond the borders of Denvirran. Indeed, most of her life was spent within a small compass, between Duncal and Drumlenn. The last two weeks had rekindled the urge to go further, to see more. She understood very well Evisyn's yearning to make that same crossing.

Hedric could tell them more... Rodal too, she thought suddenly; he had seen Troquharran and Sessapont. How would he like recounting his adventures before the Conclave? Her first inclination was to protect him, and his family, from any such scrutiny, but she had no time to think about it. Evisyn was already asking about the planned expedition.

"It was in preparation when we left," said Jerya. "We were able to move more quickly, because there were only three of us. A large party, with far more equipment, will take longer to assemble, and move more slowly. Still, I expect they're in the field by now."

"Have you any notion how long it might take them to find a crossing?"

"Impossible to say, Master. As you said yourself, there's no way of knowing whether a crossing is even possible in that region."

"But you yourself found a crossing at the first attempt, did you not?"

"Yes, by sheer good luck."

"You seem to have had a great deal of 'good luck'," said Perriad acidly.

"I have never denied it, Master." A little politeness could not hurt. It would hardly make a dent in Perriad's adamant rejection of every single thing Jerya said, but who knew what might count with the rest? "As I said, we crossed further North; on both sides, it's further from centres of population. But from what I've seen, on the ground and on the maps, the peaks there are somewhat lower and less jagged than further South."

"So you think a crossing further South will be harder to find?"

Jerya shrugged. "I can't say that. If you're looking to cross a range, it's not the peaks that matter, it's the passes between them. I suppose..."

"Yes?"

"You and I, Master Evisyn, have already discussed the possibility of creating a concordance between the Eastern maps and the Guild's own. That might give us a better idea." *And a better idea than the Duke of Selton starts out with*, she thought. "But even then, it's only an indication of where best to start looking, nothing more."

"Thank you, Jerya." Evisyn indicated she had no more questions.

The Master Prime turned toward Perriad. "Do you wish to question Jerya?"

Perriad stood up, then waved a hand, sat down again. "Since we can't believe a word she says, I see no point."

The Master Prime's face barely flickered, but Jerya didn't think she was happy with that. All she said, however, was, "Thank you, Jerya. You may retake your seat." As Jerya moved away, she went on, "Anything further, Master Evisyn?"

"A few words, if I may, Master Prime."

"Proceed."

"Conclave," said Evisyn. "That is all I can offer you in the way of evidence at this juncture. I have indicated a way in which we might gather proof incontrovertible, within a few weeks. I humbly submit to you that, whatever else this Conclave may decide, this option should be pursued, and urgently.

"I also submit that it is imperative that, in weighing the evidence, we consider the stakes on each side. Above all, I urge you to consider this. If Jerya's tale is false, then sending Peripatetics into the mountains, either to seek a crossing or to scout for signs of attempts from the other side, loses us nothing of significance."

"Surely it exposes your Peripatetics to considerable risk?" said Perriad.

"My girls are well trained, and they are not fools," said Evisyn, with more heat than she had shown before. "And there's risk in everything. Doing nothing is also a choice fraught with risk. That's the other side of the coin. If Jerya's tale is true, and we do nothing... think about that, my fellow Masters. If it's true, then sooner or later, this year or next, we could find ourselves facing an incursion from the East. From a society which is dominated by men, and which practices slavery. Is *that* a risk you're prepared to take?"

"Anything to say to that, Master Perriad?"

"Thank you, Master Prime. Just one thing. We have heard nothing this morning but supposition and hypothetical eventualities. No evidence beyond a farrago originating with... I can scarcely believe I need to remind the Conclave *again*... originating with a known—a *notorious*—Vow-breaker and renegade. The only business the Conclave should have with her is to consider what penalty to impose for those offences. I move that we close this meeting and waste no more of the Conclave's time on this nonsense." Evisyn surged from her seat, anger creasing her brow, but Perriad had not quite finished. "If there is no more evidence then why do we delay?"

The Master Prime waved Evisyn back. "You know full well, Master Perriad, that we have not seen all the evidence."

Perriad made show of looking about her. "I see nothing more."

The Master Prime frowned, not troubling to conceal her displeasure. "If I did not know better, Master Perriad, I might almost think you were trying to pull the wool over the eyes of your fellow Masters." She reminded the assembly that they still awaited Jossena's report. "I suggest therefore that we adjourn for an hour, take some refreshment. And—" She beckoned to a young Singer standing at the back. "Find Tutor Jossena, and please inform her that her presence is required at the start of proceedings this afternoon, no matter what stage her investigations have reached."

"Pardon me, Master Prime," said another Master Jerya did not recognise. "Master Perriad has moved to close the meeting. I believe procedurally we are now obliged to consider that motion."

The Master Prime sighed. "I fear you are correct, Master Ottenni. Anything to say, Master Evisyn?"

Evisyn stood, drawing herself up to her full rangy stature. "Just this. Master Perriad's motion to dismiss is mischievous and mendacious. She clearly doesn't want us to consider the remaining evidence. I can only conclude she is *scared*... scared of what it may tell us."

Perriad looked furious, but, perhaps wisely, said nothing.

The Master Prime called a vote, reminding the Conclave that the implication of dismissal would be that Jossena would not be heard. Perriad mustered precisely two supporters for this.

The Master Prime signalled that proceedings were in abeyance for an hour. The young Singer scampered off; Perriad stalked out a few paces behind; the others began to move in more leisurely fashion.

And for the first time since the start, Jerya was able to turn and look for her mother.

❋

"You knew all along, didn't you? The very first time I came to your classroom. I didn't understand at the time. It wasn't till much later, on the other side of the mountains, that I got a proper look at myself in a mirror."

Yanil looked almost embarrassed. "I guessed. I didn't know."

"But you know now."

"Sharess showed me your letter. When she came back to live here."

Jerya turned from her. "You kept the letter?"

Sharess smiled. "It is my most treasured possession."

Jerya blinked hard. For a moment she could not speak.

"I hope you don't mind me showing it to Yanil," said Sharess, possibly mistaking the reason for Jerya's silence. "No one else has seen it, but, well, Yanil is my oldest friend here."

"Whatever you choose to do with it." Another thought, her mind racing. "But then you both knew."

She didn't need to spell out what she meant. It had been on everyone's mind all morning.

Sharess nodded. "I carried that knowledge, alone, for some years. Finally I felt I had to share it with someone."

"I have to ask..."

"Why we never told anyone else?" said Yanil. "Yes, well might you ask. For myself, I can only say... well, you've seen today how Perriad can be, especially where you're concerned. I only had to think how the message might be received; and what, really, would I say? *I have seen a letter from Jerya. She says there are people East of the mountains, and that some of them are slaves.* You can imagine how that would go down. And you could just say that I lacked the courage."

"I would never say that."

"*I* lacked the courage," said Sharess softly. "No two ways about it. Perhaps I infected you with my timidity, Yanil." She turned back toward Jerya. "And how could I show the letter to any but those I trusted absolutely? You remember how you began?"

"*My dearest mother.*"

"Just so. Can you imagine how I felt when I saw that? The sense of *forgiveness* that I felt..."

"There's nothing to forgive."

"I can hardly believe that. You had to grow up as a motherless orphan... and then, to pluck you from everything you knew, and despatch you here with barely a moment's notice..."

"Mother," she said, and then she had to pause a moment. "It was the best thing that ever happened to me."

Both Dawnsingers stared at her, and she thought she knew what was in their minds. *If that's so, why did you leave?*

That required either a very long answer, or none at all. And she was pretty sure they already had more than an inkling. Instead she thought about her life. About telescopes and libraries; about riding horses; about standing on the top of a mountain. About Railu and Rhenya; about Embrel. About Hedric. So many things, none of which she would have known but for that moment in the Dawnsinger's chamber atop the tor in Delven. "I don't regret anything that's happened."

CHAPTER 22

JERYA

"Can you say beyond all doubt that this work is genuine?"

"No," said Jossena.

Triumph flared in Perriad's face, but it died almost immediately, as Jossena added, "But I will declare it so beyond all *reasonable* doubt."

"Would you explain, please, Senior Tutor Jossena?"

"Gladly, Master Prime. Perhaps first I should beg the Conclave's pardon for taking so long to deliver our verdict to you. But if I explain the delay... well, the reasons for the delay are closely bound up with the nature of the evidence itself. Both are complex, but I shall try to be as brief as possible."

"Please proceed."

"The first complication is that the scientists of this far land don't use the metric system, as we do, but—like our own common-folk—couch everything in units such as feet and miles. This of course is unnecessarily cumbersome and can sometimes be a positive handicap to progress; I suppose that's why we have kept the metric system to ourselves. Be that as it may, our first task was to track down precise conversion values for the various units. I know the approximate equivalence between miles and kilometres, metres and yards, but we needed to have them as exactly as possible. And then, before we could check any of the calculations, we needed to convert all the distances given in this paper."

She looked up, and presumably saw something in the faces watching her. "I'm sorry, I'm not being as brief as I should be, am I? I'm sure I'm not the only one who's fascinated by all of this, but we can dig into the details later.

"Let me just say that we had similar problems with the calendar, but *without* any readymade conversion tables to refer to. However, fortunately, the paper under scrutiny—of which Jerya herself is listed as an author—is concerned with the moons, and particularly the One. The moons themselves present a kind of calendar, one which of course is exactly the same on either side of the mountains. With reference to Jerya—" Perriad sniffed loudly. "—It was possible to establish the dates concerned, but only after painstaking calculation and reference to the lunar ephemerides.

"And mention of the ephemerides really brings me to my fundamental point, my Masters. How could a paper such as this have been produced? Either it is what it purports to be, a record of genuine observations made late last autumn, or it has been fabricated. But, to fabricate this, and I mean to create a fabrication which stands up to the kind of scrutiny we subjected it to... and I might just say that I enlisted both of my most able assistants, and none of us slept more than three hours last night..." As if to underline that last point, her eyes seemed to lose focus for a moment.

"Your indulgence, my Masters. To create a *plausible* fabrication requires that all the figures given must be plausible, not just approximately, but to a high level of precision. And no one could do that without access to a full set of lunar ephemerides. There are supplementary references to further observations made for calibration purposes, occultations of bright stars. These imply access to at least a partial set of stellar ephemerides also.

"My Masters, for those of you whose acquaintance with astronomical calculation ended with your Novitiate... especially when your Novitiate is as long ago as mine... permit me to remind you that the production of ephemerides requires a great quantity of both observation and calculation. In fact it is the principal work of the custodians of the Kendrigg Observatory. We keep very few copies... copying them is another great labour... and all of them are very carefully looked after. None, I can assure you, has ever gone missing."

Perriad stirred. "I believe that Jerya, during her brief Novitiate, made a visit to Kendrigg? Is it possible that she could have copied the ephemerides at that time?"

Jossena's reaction was brief, but telling. Jerya was sure she was struggling not to laugh. She felt the same herself. *Talk about clutching at straws.*

"No, Master Perriad. For two reasons. No one could copy an entire ephemerides in a few days, especially when she was seldom alone."

"Surely she would only have needed to copy specific sections?"

"You credit her with much greater astronomical expertise than she possessed at that time; she would have had no idea *which* sections to attend to. Further, there is a second, conclusive, objection. Jerya was at Kendrigg ten years ago. The observations in this paper were taken last year. Ephemerides for that date did not exist at that time. We don't work that ahead."

Perriad frowned, but she wasn't quite done yet. "Is it possible, then, that the observations in question are genuine, but that they were taken within the borders of our land?"

This, apparently, was one scenario Jossena had not considered; but she only needed a moment. "In theory, I suppose it might be. But consider what that would imply. Observations were taken simultaneously over several nights at points over three hundred miles—approximately five hundred kilometres—apart. There is space for a baseline of that length within our land, but only in the far South. I suspect both ends would be difficult of access. And every single observation would need to be adjusted by a precise amount to make it look as if it were taken at a different latitude and a different time. *That* would be impossible without ephemerides.

"There is one more thing I should mention, my Masters. Indeed, I should perhaps have mentioned it first. In several respects, this is exceedingly advanced work. Even with the telescopes at Kendrigg, we would find it challenging to equal this level of precision. And those telescopes are emphatically not portable. Some of the theoretical discussion around the observational work embodies ideas which I find both novel and exciting. I do not believe this could be created in isolation; it implies the existence of a larger body of theory.

"Masters—" She did not mention Perriad by name, but her glance was telling. "Are we really to suppose that Jerya concocted all of this on her own? She was an unusually talented girl, certainly; she had deduced a good deal, purely from naked-eye observations, before she arrived here. But she came with no deeper base than that, and of course she was only here a few months. Are we really to suppose that she could have created all this unaided?"

Perriad shrugged, as if to say *who knows what she's capable of?* Jerya saw, as if for the first time, that Perriad was gripped by an obsession. An obsession with *herself*, Jerya, that had burned slowly for a decade.

"But then," said Jossena, "What is the alternative scenario? If we are to believe that these observations were taken, this paper created, within our own land... then we must accept that within our own borders there exists a group—and not just a mere handful of people—which practises observational and theoretical astronomy at a level at least equal to our own. That they can create substantial telescopes and other instruments, travel the length and breadth of the land with them, set them up in remote areas and make observations... without any hint of it reaching any Dawnsinger.

"This volume also suggests that there is equally sophisticated work going on in other scientific disciplines. How could that be? Do we imagine some clandestine group of disenchanted Dawnsingers building what almost amounts to an alternative Guild? Or do we even dare to imagine that this secret association also includes *men*?"

She let them think about that for a moment before continuing in a softer, even a reassuring, tone. "There is a rule in science and philosophy called Occam's Razor. Whoever this Occam was, I take her for a woman of great wisdom. You all know the principle: when confronted with competing explanations, one should prefer that which rests on fewer assumptions. And by that rule, it is absolutely clear, at least to me, that the best and simplest explanation of this volume I hold in my hand is that there is a civilisation East of the mountains.

"One more sentence and I shall finish. I may have had my head buried in this volume, and in the calculations it has required us to make, but even so I have heard that some voices are saying, not only that Jerya's story should be disregarded, but that she should be sanctioned as a Vow-breaker. Masters, this volume convinces me that the central point, at least, of Jerya's tale is true; there *is* a civilisation beyond the mountains. That being so, we need to know about it, and we should not be censuring Jerya but *thanking* her for making us aware of it."

She stopped, bowed her head. Then she looked up again, with an unexpected grin. "Sorry, that was three sentences, wasn't it?"

There was a flurry of whispering as Jossena stepped back. The Librarian, Viveen, came next and the room settled quickly as she began in a dry, quiet, voice. "I have had far less time than I should like with the journal, or the fragment of a newspaper, and I have as yet had no chance to examine the maps at all. Still, even from my initial scrutiny, there are a few observations I can make. The paper, particularly the newsprint, is unfamiliar, as is the binding of the journal. I don't attach great weight to that, but I am rather more swayed by the typefaces. All told there are at least half a dozen, and none of them are familiar to us. Some seem almost... outlandish." She gave a brief, shy, smile. "And this I set alongside what Senior Tutor Jossena has said about the effort required to create the *content* of the journal. Creating typefaces is no trivial endeavour either; it requires sophisticated design, mould-making, and casting techniques."

It seemed anticlimactic after Jossena, but underlined her message effectively enough. The Master Prime asked if anyone had questions or challenges for Jossena or Viveen. No one had; many of the Masters looked almost stunned. Even Perriad was silent, though Jerya could not believe they had heard the last from her. Obsession doesn't merely vanish like smoke in a breeze.

"In that case," said The Master Prime, "I propose we move to a vote on the primary question? Having heard all we have, do we now accept that at least the essence of Jerya's tale is true?"

Perriad had had two supporters in her motion to dismiss the meeting; now she had only one.

"Very well," said the Master Prime. "I suggest we take another recess for refreshment—and for contemplation, perhaps. Shall we resume at the fifteenth hour? Having reached this judgement, we now need to consider what action it calls forth."

CHAPTER 23

JERYA

"If it were possible to establish peaceful relations between the two sides, it seems to me there is much for both to gain. The East seems to me to be more advanced in certain aspects of science and engineering. On the other hand, the West is clearly superior in medicine and the healing arts." Some of the Masters would like hearing that; some wouldn't. It couldn't be helped.

"Be that as it may," said the Master Prime, "We still have to contend with the implications for the position of the Guild itself. As soon as people learn that there is a land without Dawnsong..."

The Masters looked at each other. Jerya knew very well what they were thinking. *No Dawnsong... yet the sun rises there too. People live, and thrive.* What would become of the mystery, the mystique, the power of the Dawnsong when the people of the Sung Lands realised that?

Everyone in Delven knows already, thought Jerya, but she had something else to say. "With respect, Master Prime, have you considered the converse? When people in the East learn that there is a land without slavery..."

She had the satisfaction, for a moment, of seeing the entire Conclave of Masters struck dumb.

Perriad shot her a look even more malevolent than usual. It took much of the strength Jerya had gained in ten years to meet it with apparent calm. *I'm only the bearer of the news, not its architect*, she thought, but that would hardly appease Perriad.

"Masters," said Perriad, "It occurs to me that fostering such rumour is exactly the tactic of one who wished to undermine the Guild."

Yanil protested. "You surely cannot still think Jerya wishes us ill?"

"Perhaps, *Tutor* Yanil, you have never, as I have, heard her decrying the Dawnsong itself as a lie."

It is *a lie. We all know it is.* Saying that would hardly help, though.

"Master Prime," she said, with a respectful nod, ignoring Perriad. *To hell with you...* That casual slighting of Yanil, deliberately emphasising her lower status, was unconscionable. "If I truly wished to undermine the Guild, why would I bring this message *to the Guild?* Surely I would do better, if that were my aim, to spread this tale among the common-folk?"

She saw the Master Prime, and others, considering this. Evisyn, she thought, understood it already. "Indeed, if I wished the Guild to be harmed, I need have done nothing at all; I need only have waited for the Duke of Selton's party to arrive, let the news spread in its own time. I could simply have stayed where I was, gone on with my comfortable life." *Books and telescopes, Hedric and Embrel...* "Why uproot myself, put myself through the risks and hardships of the journey—and the risk that the Guild might choose to sanction me as a Vow-breaker?"

"As is our right," said the Master Prime.

Jerya spread her hands. "I don't deny it. I can only hope for your continued forbearance."

"The problem would not arise," said Kurslan, Master of Husbandry, "If no one came from beyond."

They all—the other Masters, Yanil, Jerya herself—stared at her. It was, of course, perfectly true. It was also—so Jerya thought, at least—breathtakingly naive. *Stupid might be a better word.*

It rather looked as if Master Evisyn had a similar view. "You mean if this Duke of Selton and his company never arrive? How do you suggest we achieve that?"

"I have no idea," said Kurslan frankly, "But at least the question should be considered."

"No harm in that if that's how you choose to spend your time. For myself, I see more gain in thinking about what we do if—*when*—they do come."

"My Masters," said Perriad. "You have chosen in your wisdom to give credence to the tale that Jerya brought us. I argued otherwise but, as always, I accept the verdict of the majority. And I do understand, of course, that if it should prove to be true, even in part, it will be news of great significance to the Guild and to the land that we serve. However, until, and unless, that proves out, we cannot unquestioningly accept her claim that if she wishes us harm she need not have come here. At the very least, if her tale ultimately proves to be a fabrication, then Jerya will have been the cause of severe disruption to the normal operation of the Guild. Disruption that may affect the training of Postulants and Novices, perhaps even cause them to question some of our teaching. That possibility, which as a former Senior Tutor I regard with great concern, must also be considered.

"In any case, Masters, whatever the ultimate outcome, a second question remains... whatever service or disservice she may have rendered, can we afford to overlook the undeniable fact that she is a Vow-breaker? Remind yourselves, my sister-Masters, of what that means. A little short of ten years ago, this g—this young woman stood in front of you, Master Prime, looked you in the eye and repeated the words we all carry in our hearts.

"At the equinox it will be thirty-eight years since I said my own Novitial Vow. I have witnessed every ceremony since then; at almost thirty of them I have watched Novices I trained myself take their Vows. And every time, the Master Prime of the day urged every Postulant who had doubts of her vocation to make them known. Many have done so, and suffered no penalty, no disgrace." *I wonder,* thought Jerya. "Jerya did not do that. She stepped forward when her turn came and she said the words.

"In full understanding and after solemn consideration,
"By my own free choice and absolutely without duress,
"Do irrevocably bind myself and undertake to serve,
"The most perfect and immaculate Guild of Dawnsingers.

"Well, you all know them, and the rest. She said those words yet, less than two months later, she had not only torn them to shreds and trampled them in the dust, she had taken another with her—an Ordained Singer, no less. Not only did she turn renegade herself, she made a renegade of Railu also. I am sure many of you remember Railu, a most promising student with a particular aptitude for healing."

Sudden fury boiled in Jerya. She was on her feet before she could think, and then they were all staring at her.

"Something you wish to say, Jerya?" asked the Master Prime in deceptively mild tones.

"Your pardon, Master Prime." But..." she turned to face Perriad. "Say what you like about me; I'll have my chance to reply in due course. But dragging Railu into this when she's not here to speak for herself... There are people here, now, in this room, who remember exactly how you treated her. It..." *It makes me furious, truth be told.* But she held it back. "I cannot just sit here and let you prate about her 'aptitude for healing', when you—you and no one else—sent her off to be a village Singer, in a place where, as you knew full well, she would have scant chance to exercise her healing skills. You denied her that, then; how dare you claim it as my offence now? How *dare you?*"

They glared at each other, and it felt to Jerya as if the intersection of their gazes must glow before everyone's eyes like a sunbeam in a darkened room.

I'll not be first to look away. Perriad had been an intimidating figure ten years ago, to a girl fresh from the backlands. But Jerya was no mere girl now. She had seen things Perriad had never dreamed of. She hadn't broken when the freebooters took them. She hadn't broken under the indignities of the slave market. She hadn't broken when displayed naked before a crowd, even when she heard what some of them had in mind for herself and Railu. She had endured all that, regained her freedom and built herself a new life.

She told herself all this as she held Perriad's gaze.

It seemed like minutes; probably it was just seconds. Perriad broke away, forcing a laugh. "Have it your way; it matters not. I need not cite Railu to make my case. The facts are well known, anyway. Most of us were here on the day that Jerya took her Novitial Vow. Most of us were here on the day that she left, supposedly to accompany Railu to Delven, make a short farewell visit, and then return. Most of us were here on the day the news arrived that she had broken every promise.

"I must own, my Masters, my personal responsibility. As Senior Tutor I agreed to her request for that visit. I was not without qualms, but I allowed myself to be persuaded. I told myself that the girl's own circumstances were themselves irregular, summarily plucked from her previous life at nineteen. And she herself was... persuasive. She was a glib talker then, as she is now."

And you are not...? Jerya allowed herself a small shake of the head.

Perriad went on, "I have asked myself many times whether things would have been different had I refused that request. Would Jerya have meekly settled to life as a Novice, then as an Ordained Singer, here in the College—as her Vow, of course, required her to do?"

The Vow says nothing about being meek, thought Jerya, but she knew it was a mere quibble.

"For myself," said Perriad, "I doubt it. She knew other ways out of the Precincts. She had the means to disguise herself. And she herself claims that she has crossed the Sundering Wall not once but twice—surely a more demanding journey than from here to Delven."

Yes, but you say you don't believe that story. That, perhaps, *was* a flaw. Though did it matter? Perriad was indulging in speculation here.

It seemed the Master Prime was thinking the same. "This is hypothetical, Master Perriad. Perhaps you could confine yourself to the facts."

"Of course, Master Prime. I apologise for the digression. As you say, the facts. And the facts are well-known. That this person is a Vow-breaker and a renegade is not in dispute. The question, surely, is what we do about it.

"Well, my Masters, you have determined that you do accept her tale, at least provisionally. I have argued against that choice, but I accept the verdict of the majority, and I do understand the precautionary principle. I do understand that, if in the event that this tale should prove to be true..."

Her tone reeked of doubt. "Then she will have done us a service. I do understand that, in any such eventuality, forewarning is of real value. Let that be stipulated also.

"Whatever the truth of this, do we really believe that doing something which may—I stress *may*—have value to the Guild is sufficient to cancel out the breaking of our Vow? Is *anything* sufficient to do that?

"My Masters, more than a hundred years ago, the Master Prime of the time wrote some words which I believe she was wont to say at Vow-taking. I believe they are equally apposite now. *The Vow is what makes you a Dawnsinger. The Vow is what makes the Guild. The Vow is the one thing that all of us, from the youngest Postulant to the Master Prime, share equally.* I cannot say it better than that. The Vow is... everything. How can we ignore a flagrant breach? How can we condone it? I ask—I urge you to ask yourselves—what lesson may be conveyed to impressionable young minds if a notorious Vow-breaker is subject to no sanction whatever? Never mind the possibility, which seems to exercise certain minds, that she might also be not merely admitted to the Precincts, but deferred to, given a place in our counsels, even honoured?"

Perriad looked around once more, then bowed her head. "My Masters, I rest my case."

There was only one way to begin. "I am a Vow-breaker. I cannot deny it. It would be foolish, an insult to the intelligence of every one of you. It is exactly as Master Perriad says. I said the words before you, Master Prime, yet, only weeks later, I walked away from Delven, from the Guild, from all the Sung Lands. I walked out of one life and into another, though I had no idea at that time what that other life would be like.

"I don't deny it and I don't seek to mitigate it. I know what the Vow means. And I know I am in your hands. I ask only a few moments to try and explain, to say a little of why I left... and why I came back.

"I broke my Vow, yes, and perhaps you will think I encouraged Railu to break hers too. If you'd seen what happened to us when we reached the land beyond the mountains, you might think we had been punished already. I don't like to recall those days, I seldom speak of them, but I have done so here. You should know, as far as I can explain, how things are on the other side. But let me tell you now, the thing that weighs heaviest, more than any act of brutality. We were taken for slaves, and we were *sold*." She gazed around and then repeated, "Sold."

The clock ticked.

"So you say," said Perriad finally. "And yet it hardly looks as if you are a slave now."

How would you know what a slave looks like? she demanded in her head. "No, I have my freedom. But Railu does not. She is still a slave.

"There is much more to say about that, about her circumstances. She is not ill-treated in the way that many slaves are... I know that many of you remember Railu, and there are others here who knew her well, who will want to hear how things stand with her. I'm sure this is not the time to go into detail, only to recall the crucial fact. She is, still, a slave.

"Every day, in that other land, I am reminded of that. And when I think that it is only because of me that she is there... I am not sure, Masters, that you could devise any punishment crueller than that.

"Well, enough of that. I need to try to explain to you why I did what I did. Why I felt I could not stay. It was not something I undertook lightly, and I have thought about it many times since...

"You say that the Vow is what makes the Guild. But is there not something else that defines it? Not a Vow, perhaps, but surely there's a promise.

"To me, certainly, growing up in Delven, there was a promise. A promise that I heard in Song every morning; a promise that the sun would rise. But more than that. What we, in Delven, believed was: if the Song was not Sung, the sun would not rise.

"We all know, every one of us here, that it's not true. I did not know that when I swore my first Guild Vow to Sharess. I still didn't understand

it when I said my Novitial Vow. Perhaps the others who swore that day did;
I didn't know. I wonder if you can understand how shattering it was when
I learned the truth. Can you at least grasp a little of how I felt? When I
realised that the promise I had lived with all my life was hollow? If I felt that
a Vow had been extracted from me under false pretences, can you entirely
blame me?"

She paused for a moment, dry-mouthed, and Perriad pounced. "You see,
my Masters, the sense of grievance? Would it now be any surprise if she has
the desire to do us harm?"

Jerya shook her head. "You mistake me, Master. And I may say I am not
surprised; you never understood me. But more than that... if we are talking
about breaches of trust, you yourself were not entirely honest with me, or
with others, on more than one occasion."

"How dare you!"

Jerya was ready for her. "I dare because it's the truth. I have already
mentioned how you deceived Railu over what her future might be... *and*
the cruelty with which you denied her the role she was perfectly fitted for,
as a Healer. Tell me how that benefitted the Guild...

"As for me, you told me many times not what I needed to know, the
truth, but what you thought I wanted to hear. You never even understood
what I really wanted or needed. You never saw that if you'd been honest
with me from the start—fully and genuinely honest—then you could have
made me the Dawnsinger I was ready to become, that I yearned to be. It
was you, Master Perriad, who made it impossible for me to stay.

"You told me once that I had something special to contribute because
I had lived outwith the Guild for longer. I don't know exactly what you
thought that contribution would be, because you never explained. And,
naive backland girl that I was, I had no idea. But being nineteen... maybe
that's why I was able to see through you, your mendacity and your malice."

The silence that followed could well have been described as 'stunned'.
Looking around, Jerya had no idea whether she had saved herself or sealed

her own fate. What she did know was that it had felt good, finally, to tell Perriad exactly what she thought of her.

CHAPTER 24

HEDRIC

It was the first chance they'd had to be alone together since arriving in the city. Though it was a somewhat specialised sense of the word 'alone'. There were always people passing near, but none paid special attention to the young man and woman strolling along the riverside walk.

Certainly Jerya did not look at all out of place. Her tightly braided hair was wound about her head in a sort of coronet, a style rare in the Five Principalities but common enough here. Her skirt, newly acquired, was a light tan colour, with the relatively slim silhouette that prevailed here. It also stopped at her ankle, rather than skimming the floor. He had no objection to the slimmer outline, but the shorter length struck him as less elegant. Then again, her hem must be less prone to sweeping the dust off the street.

No one would notice her in any but the most mundane way; men will look with admiration at a handsome woman; and women will look too, he supposed, whether with fellow-feeling or malicious envy.

Few seemed to have eyes for him, either. Once or twice his spectacles had attracted remark. Horn-rims seemed to be unknown here; every pair of eye-glasses he had seen had the lenses bound in metal, often so fine that it could be called wire.

Anyway, they were not alone, but no one was watching them, no one eavesdropping. He might wait a long time for a better opportunity to broach the subject that had been preying on his mind.

Grasping her elbow for a moment, he gently guided her closer to the balustrade, aiming for a spot between two trees, for shade and for a little more privacy.

Releasing her arm, he leaned on the coping. *Fossiliferous Limestone*, he thought, then scolded himself for succumbing to distraction. Distraction was fuel for procrastination... and procrastination was immensely tempting. He steeled himself, turned toward her, found her eyeing his face expectantly. "Jerya, my dear, there is something I must say."

She smiled. "That's been obvious this past half hour."

"Am I so transparent, then?"

"Let's just say I know you well enough... So, out with it."

He sighed. "Very well. The truth is, I've been considering my obligations. Not my wishes, I hasten to add, but my duties and my... moral obligations."

"You're thinking about going home."

"Again it seems I'm utterly transparent to you."

"As I said, I know you. I know you've been growing uneasy. I'm impatient too; the Masters of the Guild seem in no hurry to make any decision. They have barely resolved whether or not they believe the news we brought—still less how to act upon it. And we both made promises..."

"You know I told my uncle I would be back within six weeks. Perhaps that was rash of me..."

"Perhaps..." Her tone implied something nearer certainty.

"...But at the time I felt it necessary to secure his blessing on the enterprise at all. And... well, you know what he's like."

"Unfortunately." She looked out across the water, and he followed her gaze. The two great bridges blocked passage of larger vessels, upstream or down, so that the reach between was effectively reserved for pleasure craft. Little dinghies with bright sails darted about, while rowing boats proceeded more sedately. In most cases, he saw, the rower was a young man, doubtless seeking to impress the young lady who sat in the stern. Some might have more success than others, judging by the varying levels of expertise apparent even to his unschooled eye.

He tore his gaze away. Jerya was watching him, a faint smile teasing at the corners of her mouth—a mouth he would very much like to kiss, though this was not the moment.

"I said my obligations are at war with my desires. I don't want to leave you, you must know. But if I do not return within the time I stated, he could easily take umbrage. He could disinherit me on a whim. And then what happens to the estates? What's to become of all those slaves?"

"Of course. I understand." She did, yet her face showed how much the words cost her.

"Jerya, dearest. Knowing me, you must know how it grieves me even to contemplate leaving you. It has been a joy, these past weeks, to be with you every day, as if we were wed already. Even the journey, the hardest, roughest, most uncomfortable of my life; even there I cherish every minute."

He tried to smile. "And if that were not enough... how little I've seen of this land, how little I understand. It is like a whole new world to me. A world where women rule, and where there are no slaves." He paused, and she recognised the glint of a new idea in his eye. "Do you think it is possible that there are no slaves *because* it is women who rule?"

She shook her head with a rueful smile. He almost read her thought: how like him to fasten on a new notion even as they faced a terrible choice. A question that would surely fascinate her too; but he knew he must say, "We must settle the question of travel before we turn to any other."

She sighed. "I'm afraid you must go; a lot may rest upon it. And I think I must stay; a lot may rest upon that, too. Even the future of this land, perhaps both lands."

"It may be weeks..." he said sadly. "Or months. I can only hope it does not stretch into years."

"I can't see that. One way or another, it seems to me, we'll have some answers before this summer is out."

"We must hope, I suppose, that Selton's party really are looking in the wrong place. That they do not find a viable crossing before the winter."

"I don't know, Hedric; I'm rather hoping they will appear, and soon. To settle the doubters."

Silence fell between them. He leaned on the coping, looked out again. After a moment she moved closer beside him, her skirt brushing his leg. Her arm was not quite touching his, but then she moved, entwined her fingers with his. "Hedric..."

"Yes?"

"I'm sure I shouldn't need to ask this, but somehow I can't resist. Is that really the only reason?"

He moved his right hand to cover hers. "Of course it is."

"I have to wonder. I know your Uncle has pressured you many times to choose a bride. To *marry well*, by his lights. If he's there and I'm not..."

"I'll do much to retain his goodwill, but I will not marry someone I do not care for."

"But perhaps among the well-bred there are one or two you *could* care for."

"Perhaps, but I have never met any such person. And, believe me, as Skilthorn's heir I've had pretty nearly every eligible young female in Denvirran, and some from beyond, paraded before me at one occasion or another."

She laughed at that, as he had hoped, but when she spoke again her tone was no less serious. "I can't believe they're all entirely empty-headed."

He half-wished he could say that they were, but he—and she—had too much respect for the truth. "Not all, not entirely. No, many are amiable enough as partners at a ball or a dinner. I have met a few whose company I thought might be tolerable in the longer term; even a few who seemed to have some glimmers of curiosity. Though it is often hard to tell... it is, apparently, *unladylike* to display any form of learning whatever. I recall one who apparently believed that the sun revolved around the Earth... and when I corrected the error, appeared to imagine I would be delighted with her ignorance."

She snorted with mixed mirth and disgust, but said soberly. "There are many here who believe that. I suppose I believed it myself at one time..." She sighed. "And the Guild of Dawnsingers allows this belief to flourish."

"It would be much harder to suppose that Dawnsingers have power over the sun if it were generally known that the Earth is the satellite."

"Yes. And yet they castigate me for..." She broke off. "But we've been over this ground before. And I... forgive me, my love, if I seem to doubt you. Probably it's myself I really doubt... It's meant so much to make this journey with you, to have you at my side in these difficult days."

"I haven't been able to be at your side half as much as I might wish." That was part of his frustration; he had given his testimony in the first days, and now the Guild seemed to have no further interest in him. He felt useless.

Jerya, however, saw it differently. "At least you're always there to talk it through with in the evening."

He pressed her hand again. "If it has meant much to you, be assured it has meant no less to me. To be with you all day, every day, on the journey. To be with you every day, at least for an hour, since arriving here... It has only cemented my certainty, Jerya. None of those daughters of Dukes and Barons and Earls can hold a candle to you."

"But they *would* be acceptable to your Uncle. Whereas I... I was once a slave."

"Not so," he protested. "You were once falsely proclaimed a slave, but you are freeborn. I know that for a fact, now."

"But how much weight will that carry with your uncle?" *Little, or none.* "I may be freeborn, but by his lights I am still the lowest of the low. No *connections* at all."

"Jerya," he said vehemently. "I care nothing for my uncle's opinions."

"Oh, but you so obviously do. You must smile and bow and nod when he holds forth. You must sedulously conceal all sympathies for the slaves, your support for their cause. And most of all you cannot let slip why your visits to Denvirran became so much more frequent this past year. And why you always chose the same road..."

He sighed. Every word she said was true. And yet... "My love, I mean it when I say I care nothing for his opinions. No, more than that, many of his opinions, and his actions, are loathsome to me. I conceal my feelings because... well, you know the reason."

"Yes, all those lives that could be changed for the better. How do I... what right, even, do I have to weigh my interests against theirs? Maybe you *should* marry someone tolerable. Someone with *connections,* who can be useful to you in furthering the cause."

"No, Jerya. I will sacrifice much... I *have* sacrificed much already. Am I to sacrifice my chance of happiness also? Throw off the woman I love for someone merely tolerable? No, Jerya, a tolerable bride would surely become an intolerable wife. I told you I would marry no one else, and I meant it. If you will not have me, I will not settle for second best."

He hoped that would cheer her, but her look remained miserable. "Even if we have to wait ten years? Twenty?" She looked away, but he doubted she was truly seeing the bright sails, the sparkling water,. "In twenty years, Hedric, I will be almost fifty." She laughed, but there was no mirth in it. "For the first time in my life I know my exact age, my exact date of birth. Sharess told me."

"That is sad, but you must have all those birthday celebrations to catch up on."

She flashed him a quick smile, recognising his kind intent, but was not distracted for more than a second. "What happens to the estate, to those fifteen hundred souls, after you? What about *your* heir, Hedric?"

He stared at her profile. This was quite unexpected. To the best of his recollection she had never even alluded to children before. *I think I would recall...*

Did she want children? And if she did, would she want them enough to settle, in the end, for someone tolerable—but free to wed whomever he pleased? Someone, in plain words, other than himself.

"Damn it!" he growled, freeing her hand to beat his fists on the unyield-
ing limestone. "I tell you, Jerya, there is one thing that *is* intolerable, and
that is the situation in which we find ourselves."

She said nothing. When he looked at her he saw why.

"Devil take it, Jerya, now I've made you cry. You know that's the last
thing I wanted, don't you?"

"Of course I do," she said, trying to smile. She made searching motions
with her hands at her hips, then waved them helplessly. "Draffing stupid
skirts with no proper pockets."

She wiped at her face with a wide sleeve. He offered his handkerchief,
and she accepted with a wan smile. "You have to go," she said when tears,
and the evidence of their passage, were wiped away. "You have to go, and I
have to stay."

"For how much longer?"

"I don't know. Not too long, I hope. Who knows when snows may make
the pass impossible? I wouldn't much fancy my chances beyond a couple of
months from now." She drew a deep breath, squared her shoulders. "Well,
I must make sure I've done all I can before then. At least I have allies who
do see the need for urgency."

"Like Master Evisyn?"

"Her above all."

They looked at each other, and then both began to speak at once. "Will
you—" "What about—"

"Please," he said. "You first."

"Ladies first, is it? Well, I just wondered if you and Lallon would be all
right going back without me."

He smiled. "And *I* wondered if you would be all right going back alone.
We will have the rope, and each other..."

"I can get another rope. There are ways to protect yourself, especially
going down." She had seen the men of Delven on the crags, but only from
a distance. She had an idea how the business was managed, but it would

need more thought. *And I can ask Rodal...* "I grew up among the rocks. You didn't."

"I know how to do it now. You just have to think of it as a problem in physics."

"And stay off the ice," she said with a brave attempt at a smile.

"You could come back now," he said, surprising himself, certainly startling Jerya. "Surely you have given them all the information you can."

She did at least appear to consider it, before shaking her head. "I wish I could. More than anything. For you, and for my family... but for my other family, the ones who raised me, for them and for everyone in the Guild I ever cared about... For Sharess, for Analind, for Rodal and Annyt and Sokkie, I can't leave till I'm sure I've done all I can."

"Are you sure you *are* coming back?" he said with a bleak hint of foreboding.

She looked back with equal seriousness. "I made a promise to Embrel, and I make the same promise to you. And nothing means more to me than those promises.... Listen, Hedric, when you get back, first thing you do, find Embrel and tell him. I'm going to be a little longer, but I'm coming home."

"I'll tell him. Of course I will."

"Thank you... when are you leaving?"

"If I'm going at all, I may as well go tomorrow." *Or I may not have the resolve to go at all.*

"Then... would you come to my room tonight?"

CHAPTER 25

HEDRIC

Her hair was loose, as he'd never seen it before, streaming over her shoulders. In the candlelight it looked black, only an occasional fugitive gleam hinting at the auburn fire.

She smiled, gestured him to the one upright chair. On the small table by the bed were a bottle and two glasses. "Rodal recommended this," she said. "I have no idea what it is."

She poured a small measure for each, the spirit looking clear in the subdued light. They raised glasses to each other. Jerya took a seat on the bed, arranging her skirts around her.

He sniffed. "There's fruit in this, but I'm not sure what..."

"Well, it'll do." She sipped. "I shouldn't need drink to give me courage, but... Hedric, before anything, there are things I must say. I didn't ask you here just to drink firewater. If you're to leave tomorrow... then I want more than just words to hold on to. I want our promises to be more tangible than that. I... we've spent a long time never quite saying what we feel, never really giving expression to any of it. I don't want to watch you get on a horse and ride away and only then think, 'I wish I'd said this, done that.' But there are one or two things you should know about me first."

She swallowed the rest of the spirit, made a face, refilled her glass. "I have never lain with a man. Not in the... you know what I mean. To put it at its plainest, I am a virgin." She drank again, looked at him under her brows. Her hair hung forward, shadowing her face. With her free hand she hooked it behind one ear, then the other. "I want no secrets between us. With men, I am a virgin... but not with women."

He stared at her. She gazed back, apparently calm, or at least calmer than he felt himself to be. "I don't even know what you mean," he managed at last. "*How*...?" He flung down the dregs, reached for the bottle.

She gave a subtle smile. "I was like you once. Hadn't understood that two women could... but what do you think goes on up there?" She meant up on the hill, he realised, as she went on, "A thousand Dawnsingers up there behind those walls, and not a man in sight... but that makes it sound like it's settling for second-best, and I don't know if it is. How would I? I suppose some would pity me, near thirty years old and never lain with a man, but I can honestly say I never missed it. Not till now.

"But it's always been your mind that draws me to you. Your mind and your heart."

"And I you," he said, for the sake of saying something. He heard how it must sound—stilted, dutiful—and felt his face grow hot, but told himself it would not show in the candle-glow. He lifted his glass again.

Jerya sighed. "It shouldn't be hard, seems to me, but somehow we, people, make it so. Just to say what we really mean..." She, too, sipped her drink once more. "Perhaps that's why... I think if I cannot say what I feel, then I must show you."

"Show me?" Suddenly he could hardly breathe.

"Aye... but still there are a few things I must say." She laughed unexpectedly. "I'm supposed to be good with words. Rhenya says I could talk a bull into giving milk. She might not think so now.... Hedric, I may never have lain with a man, but I know what happens. My oldest friend is a healer, after all... and there are books in the Squire's library that are 'not for the eyes of ladies'. Which, not being a lady, I haven't shied from. I know what happens, and I know what can be the result."

"And that is a risk we cannot countenance," he supplied when she hesitated.

Was there a hint of regret in her eyes, or was it only his imagination, ignited by strong drink? Impossible to tell. He only knew that she shook her head, hair falling over her face, and then said as she brushed it back, "Not now, besure."

They looked at each other and he had to ask, "Then what do you propose?"

She laughed again. She too was a little drunk. "Propose? Hedric, you are... you are so much *yourself*. I do believe that's what I... why I care for you as I do. So what do I *propose*? I told you I have never lain with a man, only with women. I propose that we take guidance from that."

"If you think it..." But what word should follow? Possible? Proper? He could only shrug helplessly, but he began to feel some explanation was needed.

"I am younger than you," he began, because that at least was harmless enough. "But not so very young... and I have lain neither with man nor with woman. 'Tis hardly for want of opportunity; many times in my college years was I invited to join my fellows in visiting the bagnio. I always declined... but I confess I said more than once 'why should I pay...' or some such form of words." He felt heat in his face again, comforted himself it would not show. "They knew I often spent nights away from my lodging. I had said that I was stargazing, but if some chose to think that was cover for something else, I did not try too hard to disabuse them. And if others, knowing my uncle's reputation, imagined that I was emulating him... I would protest, but perhaps not strongly enough. Sometimes you can deceive people even when every word you say is true."

She said nothing, and her face was enigmatic in the shifting light. "I am not proud of these things, Jerya, but you did say no secrets."

"I did... but I wasn't thinking anything against you. I was thinking how what you said about deceit applies to the Dawnsingers... but I mustn't dwell on that now."

"Then what do you *propose*?"

"We need to get rid of some of these clothes."

❋

Hedric wasn't quite the innocent he might have suggested. It wasn't as if he had never seen a naked woman.

When he was sixteen, the son of the neighbouring landowner, his companion in riding-lessons, had ordered a slave-girl, a year or two older than themselves, into an empty barn. Almost before Hedric's eyes had adjusted to the dimness, the girl had shed her garments. But as soon as he could see well enough, he saw the mix of resentment, and, yes, fear, in her eyes. He had burned with shame and pity, but he hadn't found the voice to protest, or the will to walk away. And then, as Favrel ordered the girl to move into a shaft of sunlight, Hedric had seen beauty, and he had felt desire.

He was sure, now, that the utter confusion of emotions he had experienced that day had contributed to the way he had avoided occasions of a similar nature since.

But this was *Jerya*. He had felt even at their first meeting that Jerya was different, in ways he still could not entirely pin down. Jerya was no frightened slave, unable to refuse. This—whatever it was—was happening at her instigation.

And her body was different too. The girl—whose name he had never known—had been, he thought, voluptuous. His uncle favoured the same type, was apt to feed up his favourites.

Not one with the slightest regard for accurate expression would describe Jerya as voluptuous. She was slender to the point of leanness; but not slight. There was nothing insubstantial about her. In fact her presence seemed almost to fill the room.

And she was looking at him now, a smile tugging at the corner of her mouth. Such a familiar look, but so strange to see it above an unclad body.

"You're lagging," she said.

He apologised, and clambered out of his breeches and braies before his nerve could fail him.

Her half-smile became more solid. "I'm glad to see the Illustrations are accurate."

"Illustrations?"

"In anatomy books. I had to..."

"You've never...?"

All at once they were both convulsed with laughter, and the distance between them just dissolved. They tumbled onto the bed together.

❈

Jerya's skin was cool, smooth, both familiar to touch and entirely new. For a time, simply exploring all the new places that were now open to him was enough; and it seemed to be the same for her also. But a kind of heat, or pressure, a feeling he could not quite name, was growing in him. He rolled on top of her.

"Remember," she said, the first clear word either had spoken since they fell onto the bed.

"Remember?" He couldn't quite grasp what she meant.

"There's one thing you can't do." She looked into his eyes. "Hedric..."

He let his weight slip back to the side.

"Try this," she said. "Put your finger there... A fraction lower. Ah. *There.*" He felt a kind of tension in her. "Just there. Move it a little. Yes, like that... Oh." He did as he was bidden, and words seemed to desert her. She began to pant, to moan softly. He wondered if he was hurting her, but the moment he stopped her hand clutched his, urging it into motion again. Her lips pressed his, briefly, but then her head fell back and she breathed in short panting gasps, shorter and faster, until a long shudder convulsed her entire body, her back arched, and he saw she had to bite her lip to keep from crying out aloud.

Jerya slumped back bonelessly. Now her hand found his again, gently moved it away to rest on her thigh. For a moment she lay there, eyes closed, hair strewn across her face, breathing as if she had just run a race.

Finally she pushed her hair away, looked up at him and smiled. "You *are* clever."

He wanted to say something, but couldn't find the words.

"Now," she said after a short pause, "My turn to look after you. But I may need some... guidance."

"I don't know if I..."

"Surely you... don't tell me you never touched yourself in that kind of way. Never gave yourself pleasure?"

"But I was always taught that gentlemen never discussed such matters in front of ladies."

"Well," she said, grinning impishly, "You could always get *behind* me. Or shall we just say—again—I'm no lady?"

He didn't know how to answer that either. After another awkward hiatus, Jerya simply reached out and placed a hand on his manhood. Its reaction, and his, elicited another of her quirking almost-smiles. "There?" was all she asked.

"A little higher," was the last sentence he managed for some time.

❀

"This is a promise," she said, scooping all her hair around to fall over her left shoulder as she crouched, still naked, before the fire. Water for an infusion was heating on the coals. "Most of all it's a promise that there will be a next time."

"I never doubted it."

She glanced back at him over a bare shoulder limned in the glow from the fireplace. He thought it very possible he had never seen anything lovelier. Then the bubbling of the pot snagged her attention, and she threw in a handful of leaves before turning again. "If it was solely a matter for you and me... then there would be no place for doubt."

"I make a promise to you, too," he said, looking at the fall of her hair, the line of her cheekbone. "I will tell my Uncle I have found the woman I wish to marry."

She swung around. "Are you sure that's wise? You're only leaving now to keep in his good books. Telling him you're going to marry a woman of no connections..."

"I will be very careful how I phrase it," he said. "But after this... after our journey, and after tonight... I will not deny you, Jerya."

PART THREE
PARTINGS

JON SPARKS

CHAPTER 26

JERYA

"I can't stay indefinitely," she said. "I made promises..."

Analind gave her a sceptical look. "I can't see the Masters paying much heed to that. To be honest, Jerya, I have some difficulty with it myself."

"Yes, I know. I am a Vow-breaker; how dare I talk about promises made to someone else...?

"Of course, you didn't hear what I said to the Conclave. But I said much the same to you before that. I may have broken my Vow, but only after I learned that the promise the Guild made to *me* was hollow. And, I might add, after Perriad deceived both Railu and myself. *She* is not too particular about keeping *her* promises."

Analind still looked dubious. "I'm sure Perriad would say that a lesser promise is not equal to your Guild Vow."

"I'm sure she would. But is she right? Or does using the Vow as an excuse to discard lesser promises taint the Vow itself?"

When she received no answer, she went on. "Let me tell you something about the promises I made, the people I made them to. Two people in particular. Well, you've met Hedric, perhaps I needn't say too much about him. But the other... is ten years old."

Analind stirred, lifted a brow. "What's her name?"

"*His*, if that makes any difference. His name is Embrel." Suddenly deciphering her old friend's look, she added hurriedly, "Not my own child. No, officially I'm his governess, if you know what that is. But my real relation to him feels closer than that. Closer, besure, than I was with the women, the 'aunts', who raised me in Delven.

"I could spend half an hour telling you about our household, there beyond the mountains, and at the end I'm not sure you'd really... if I have the ability to convey how it feels. But if the word 'family' means anything to you... then my family is there. Embrel. The cook, Rhenya. And Railu."

"You count Railu as family?"

"I think I always did, from the beginning. I was close to others, too, not least yourself, but you know there was a special bond between Railu and me. And... you know what we've been through together."

Analind nodded. "Crossing the mountains... You know, if Evisyn did not like you so much, I think she would hate you. First person in this age of the world to have crossed the Sundering Wall. Can you imagine how much she wishes she could have done that?"

Jerya could, very easily. It matched her own impression of Evisyn, a woman whose urge to explore probably outstripped her own. "But remember what happened next."

Analind blinked, as if she had forgotten, then smiled: she almost laughed. "Indeed. She would not have liked that half so well."

"Nor did we. And we were lucky. Had we been bought by anyone else..." She stopped. Analind had closed her eyes on 'bought'.

Jerya reached out, laid her hand over Analind's. The contrast, tawny brown and almost-black, reminded her of Rhenya. Not that there was much else in common between the slave-cook and the Dawnsinger... not obviously, at least.

"But we *were* lucky," she said.

Analind blinked, then steadied her gaze. "I don't understand. How you can speak of being bought and then in the same breath say you were lucky...?"

"Aye, I can see that's a puzzle. Maybe I can put it this way... being *sold* was the worst thing I have ever experienced. But once we'd reached that point... *then* being bought by those who did buy us was the best outcome we could possibly have."

"I still don't understand a half of what's happened to you. Probably not a tenth."

"Well," said Jerya with a chuckle, "Nothing since has been so... dramatic, moons be thanked."

"Dramatic, or traumatic? The East sounds like a terrible place. I wonder you're so desperate to return."

"Terrible? Aye it is, in many ways. But not everything or everyone. Not my family. Not Hedric. And.. if—when—I go back, I believe I'll have a real chance to make things better. At least a little."

She knew what Hedric would say; had said, more than once. As his wife, and (one day, perhaps) as Countess of Skilthorn, there would be every opportunity to make things better. For more than fifteen hundred people, to start with, and perhaps for many more.

That had been hard to believe even when he was with her; it was harder now he was further away with every passing day. In any case, it was not that thought that truly fuelled her resolve. It was the thought of Hedric himself, of Railu, of Rhenya. And of Embrel.

"You know," she said, "One thing I haven't done nearly enough is to tell what it is really like over there. To you, and anyone who cares to listen."

"It's the Masters who need to know, above all."

"And half of them aren't listening. Perriad is the chief obstruction, with her grudge—her *obsession*—but she isn't the only one. And as long as I'm an outsider, I don't know if they *can* hear me."

"Are you not tempted at all?" said Analind at once. "To come back?"

"At all? No, I'd be lying if I said it had no appeal at all. Especially if I could work with you and Master Evisyn." Seeing hope kindle in Analind's eyes, she hastened to dampen the fire. "But Perriad would have me back only over her dead body. I won't force them to that. Make no mistake, Analind. I mean to go back... to go *home*."

She pressed hands again. "I will miss you, never doubt that. You and others, but you most of all."

"But not Perriad," said Analind with that sudden grin she'd always had, though rarely seen.

"No, not Perriad; most assuredly not Perriad. As long as she's here, a power in the Guild, I could never be comfortable... but most of all, I'm going back because of my family."

As she spoke her mind was running ahead. "I need to speak with Master Evisyn again, if you could convey the message to her..."

"Privately, you mean?"

"Aye, privately."

"I know you're frustrated too," said Jerya. Evisyn gave a small nod. "I've been here over three weeks and apart from preparing the maps, which has gone well... what else has been achieved?

"Remember, I've been *here* three weeks. I left home a fortnight before that, and the news of Selton's expedition was already ten days old. They may have been in the field for a month now. They obviously haven't had the luck we had, ten years ago, finding a route first time. But they have numbers, they're vastly better-equipped, and if there's any viable route in the part of the range where they're working, they'll find it. Is anyone even watching out for them? Ready to respond?"

She thought she knew the answer, but Evisyn surprised her. "Don't tell anyone, but I have put a few of my best Peripatetics in the field, in the areas that look most likely."

"Without the Masters' knowledge?"

"I *am* a Master, you know." Evisyn smiled. "And I might have mentioned it privately to a couple of my fellows... but it would not go down well with some of the others; not well at all. You can guess who I have in mind... I even took your advice."

"My advice?"

"On a few points, but specifically in the matter of covering their heads; having hats or scarves to hand. I took to heart what you said, what befell you and Railu. I don't want any misunderstandings."

It was gratifying to know that *someone* had not only listened but acted on her information, and Jerya said so. "But if they do encounter Selton's party... what then? The Masters will know about your... subterfuge."

Evisyn shrugged. "I'm reckoning if we do have a visitation from the East, the last thing on anyone's mind will be to wonder what a Peripatetic was doing in some far-flung dale."

"I suppose so."

"But it's too little, and it may already be too late." Her amber eyes fixed on Jerya. "I don't suppose you have any suggestions?"

Jerya shook her head. "I'm sorry, it's not like I have influence with the Conclave. And that's not why I asked to see you."

Evisyn shook her head sorrowfully. "Well, then, why did you summon me?"

She softened the word with a smile, but Jerya knew that most Masters would not look kindly on being 'summoned' by a plain Dawnsinger, let alone an infamous Vow-breaker. Evisyn was emphatically not most Masters, of course, but she still had her pride.

"As I said, I share your frustration at the slow progress... It's not what I hoped for. I hardly expected the Conclave would fall over me in gratitude, but I came, above all, to deliver an important message that the Guild needed to hear.

"Well, I've delivered it. And I'm still willing to give whatever help I can. But if I'm just to cool my heels here while the Conclave wrangles endlessly about my fate instead of seriously debating how to tackle the real challenge, I might as well start for home tomorrow."

"Ah," said Evisyn simply, understanding.

"Besides," added Jerya, "As long as there's a chance Perriad might get her wish and put me to some serious punishment... why would I linger waiting for that outcome?"

"I'll try again to speed things up, but I see little chance of putting Perriad off her stride." She smiled sardonically. "Perhaps you should be grateful. So far the Conclave does nothing but talk, and you are still free."

"So far," repeated Jerya with heavy emphasis. "But in any case, no matter what happens, I intend to be on my way before autumn is too far advanced. I daren't risk snow closing the passes."

"You want to go home," said Evisyn simply.

"Yes. Home." She thought of her conversation with Analind. She saw, more clearly than she had at the time, how her talk of 'home' and 'family' must have stung.

"This was my home once," she said. "Not this tavern, but the College. And the Guild, or a few people within it, were my family. It wasn't a long time but it was a very important time for me. The things I learned, the friends I found... I personally couldn't remain within the Guild but, as I've tried many times to explain, I bear it no ill-will. There are far too many people I care about for that." She paused a moment. "I hope I may add you to that list, Master Evisyn."

CHAPTER 27

JERYA

"Jerya of Delven," began the Master Prime as soon as everyone was seated. "Your case is unprecedented. On the one hand, you have brought information which, should it ultimately prove true, is of vast significance for this Guild and for the land we serve. On the other, you are a Vow-breaker—a fact you have never attempted to deny. After much deliberation the Conclave has concluded that the former cannot entirely cancel out the latter.

"The question, therefore, is, what is to be done with you? There are those who contend that, after suitable penance and with appropriate guidance, we should welcome you back into the embrace of the Guild."

Master Kurslan raised a hand. "Might I speak to this, Master Prime?"

The Master Prime looked at Perriad, who gave way with a brusque gesture.

"You swore a Vow, Jerya," said Kurslan. "We all know that you broke it. But now you are here again. And nothing that has happened annuls your Vow. In the words Master Perriad has quoted, *The Vow is what makes you a Dawnsinger.* You are still a Dawnsinger, you only need to live as one again. Do full penance, resume the calling you were chosen for, and make good your error by what I am sure will be valuable service to the Guild."

Jerya was stunned. True, Kurslan had hinted at this once before, but nothing more had been said. *I have to get back to my family, to Hedric.* She felt close to panic, unable to think straight.

Strangely, it was the sight of Perriad's face which restored some semblance of calm. For once, she and Perriad were in full agreement. Perriad did not want her here; Jerya did not want to be here any longer than necessary.

The trouble was, she could not be sure that either of them would get her wish.

The Prime herself was gazing at Jerya as if hoping for some reaction, perhaps even a smile. *What kind of smile?* wondered Jerya? *A grateful one?* She supposed Kurslan's proposal was well-meant, but she found scant gratitude in her heart.

"The alternative view," said Perriad, "Is that, having comprehensively broken your Vow, you can hardly be trusted to honour it in future. Furthermore, having abetted or encouraged another Singer to defect with you, you would be all too likely to exert a subversive influence on others."

The Master Prime looked left and right, then directly at Jerya. "Have you anything to say for yourself at this point?"

Oh, I could say a great deal, she thought bitterly, but she doubted she would be allowed that much latitude. "As you said, Master Prime, I've never denied that I broke my Vow. Nor have I sought to exonerate myself, only to explain. And, as I said to... someone... last evening, I could not remain in the Guild myself, but I bear it no ill-will, and there are many Singers whom I care about. It was for them, and for the Sung Lands, that I came back." *And now it looks like I've thrust my head into the noose.* "Master Prime, you said yourself that the news I brought is of vast significance—"

"—If true." For once, it was not Perriad's voice. Jerya wasn't sure who had spoken. The Master Prime looked around, clearly irritated, made a quelling gesture.

"It is true," said Jerya as calmly as she could manage. "If you still doubt the proofs I brought—despite the verdict of Masters Skarat, Evisyn, and others—you may only have to wait a week or two before there is proof no one can explain away as a cunning forgery.

"And that, Masters, is where I... where I think you are making a grave error. My own fate is important to me and to those I love." Her voice wobbled. "But it is insignificant compared to the future of this land. And yet, so far as I can tell, the Conclave has spent far more time discussing trivial matters like this than resolving what to do. That, Masters, is something you may very well live to regret."

By the decorous standards of the Conclave of Masters, what ensued was uproar. Many of the angry utterances were aimed at herself, but not all.

When the Master Prime finally succeeded in making her calls for order heard, two Masters remained on their feet. Inevitably, they were Perriad and Evisyn. The Master Prime, in a tone almost of resignation, invited Perriad to speak first.

"You see what we are dealing with," she said. "We arraign this... person... on the most serious charge our Code allows, and she turns around and rebukes *us*. The insolence is breathtaking. You can surely now see, my Masters, why the suggestion that she be restored into our ranks is preposterous."

The Master Prime said nothing, simply turned to Evisyn. Her response was even more terse. "My Masters, I have but one thing to say: Jerya is *right*."

Again there was hubbub bordering on uproar. After a minute, the Master Prime said, "You had better explain that, Master Evisyn."

"What's to explain? It's perfectly clear. Ten years ago, Jerya broke her Vow. I do not belittle the seriousness of that offence, but... she came back. She placed *herself* in this position... and why? Because we face a challenge vastly more momentous than any individual misdemeanour."

"*Misdemeanour*," repeated Perriad with all the scorn at her command.

"I call it a misdemeanour, Master Perriad. I call what you are doing something worse." She scanned the room. "If we are not ready to meet the challenge which awaits us, the very existence of the Guild may be under threat. And yet we sit here in our comfortable chairs, take refreshments every hour or two, and we fritter away precious days—*weeks*, now—debating this and that—now including Jerya's future. Masters, if we fail to meet this challenge, it will not be Jerya who has betrayed the Guild, it will be this Conclave."

Perriad's voice cut through a new outcry like a cracking whip. "You would rather be sitting in a saddle, no doubt, galloping off to some remote hillside in pursuit of glory."

"By the Six," snapped Evisyn. "We have disagreed many times, Master Perriad, but I never thought you a fool before."

This time, the Master Prime had to resort to pounding both fists on the table before order was restored.

"Master Evisyn," she said at last, "I invite you to withdraw your last remark."

Evisyn returned a level gaze. "I cannot, Master Prime. The course this Conclave is currently pursuing is, quite simply, folly. And it is Master Perriad, driven by her personal grudge against Jerya, who has led us to it."

"Grudge!" spat Perriad. "I stand for the sanctity of the Vow and you call it a personal grudge. You should be ashamed—"

A sound like a clap of thunder silenced both the warring Masters. The Master Prime had slammed the heavy minute-book down on the table with all the force she could muster.

"Masters," she said, "I have sat in this chair for eleven years, on this Conclave for more than twenty. Never in all that time have I witnessed such scenes.

"The Conclave will stand in recess for one hour, and I urge you all to use the time wisely. Reflect on your own conduct in these past minutes. Reflect also on what may be at stake. When we reconvene I expect debate to continue in full accordance with our usual standards."

"Masters," said Evisyn when the meeting resumed, "I apologise if I over-stepped our normal bounds or spoke intemperately. But I must say that I can neither regret nor retract the *substance* of my remarks. It is my absolute conviction that the Conclave has spent far too much time discussing the fate of one indivi—"

"—Because time and again *you* opposed any meaningf—"

"—Master Prime," said Evisyn. "I believe normal standards in debate do not allow unsanctioned interruption of the current speaker."

"You are quite right, Master Evisyn. I trust you will remember that when it is your turn to listen." Evisyn bowed her head as the Master Prime continued. "Master Perriad, take your seat, and remain silent until called upon to speak."

"Thank you, Master Prime," said Evisyn. "I am aware that I have expressed myself forcefully today. I did not do so casually. You may conclude that my intention was to shock, and I won't deny it. How else, I ask myself—I ask all of you—am I to stir this Conclave into properly and *urgently* addressing the issue of what we are to *do*?"

"If that is your overriding concern," said Perriad silkily. Jerya knew those tones; this was Perriad at her most dangerous. "Allow me to offer a suggestion. Let us resolve the matter of Jerya swiftly and decisively. *Now*, in fact. Thereby clearing our agenda for the matter you consider so vital."

There were immediate murmurs of agreement from several voices, and even the Master Prime was nodding thoughtfully. Evisyn frowned... but what could she say against Perriad's proposal?

And in that moment, the wheel turned. It was clear that the majority of the Conclave were keen to see an end to the discussion over Jerya. Perhaps Evisyn's eloquence on the urgency of action had had some effect; and Jerya herself had said that her own fate was infinitesimal in comparison.

We did it to ourselves, she thought. She saw the irony, but it was small comfort as the proceedings went on.

"As the Master Prime said at the start," purred Perriad, "This case is unprecedented. We have studied the Code and what it says about Vow-breaking. It seems clear to me that the originators of that section were thinking of Singers who... fell short in some relatively minor way. Some deviation from *rules and practices of the Guild*; some shortfall in *deference to duly instituted authority*. In such cases, then the prescribed process— confession, penance, and a return to normal duties under appropriate mentorship—is both wise and compassionate.

"However, with all due respect to Master Kurslan, this strikes me as entirely inadequate for dealing with one who has wholly removed herself from the Guild, who has lived an entirely different life for ten years. Furthermore, nothing Jerya has said in any of our recent encounters leaves me with the slightest hope that she might be willing to be taken back."

You are right there, thought Jerya. Agreeing with Perriad was a rare experience, but gave her no pleasure.

In a brief pause, the Master Prime said, "Perhaps we should vote on whether we proceed according to the Code, or whether we need to use our powers of discretion to enact other measures."

Only Kurslan and one other Master voted for applying the Code. Jerya's eyes sought Evisyn, who shook her head as if to say *I know you wouldn't want this.* Jerya gave a small nod of understanding.

"Therefore," said Perriad, "We must consider other avenues. I have studied the forms of punishment applied by civil authorities. In cases such as fraud and theft, financial penalties including the sequestration of property are common, but hardly applicable here. The other main options are physical punishment, both corporal and capital—" There were shocked gasps, mutters of 'no!'. Perriad glanced around. "Rest assured, my Masters, I suggest no such thing here." *I wonder,* thought Jerya, *if you were planning to say that all along or changed your mind when you saw the reaction?*

"That being so, my Masters, but one choice remains: incarceration."

Impulsively, Jerya raised her hand. At once all eyes were on her. The Master Prime regarded her with surprise, yielding to curiosity. "You wish to say something, Jerya?"

"This is quite irregular," objected Perriad.

"As you said yourself, Master Perriad, this case is unprecedented. I am inclined to allow a little latitude. Speak, Jerya."

"Thank you, Master Prime. I only wished to say that Master Perriad has not actually listed all the possibilities."

"What else is there?"

"Banishment."

A startled silence, then Perriad gave a mocking laugh. "Oh, very good. I commend you, Jerya. You banished yourself ten years ago. Now you ask us to return you to... wherever it is you've been this past ten years. But ask yourselves, my Masters, is this *punishment*?"

The idea had come to her half-formed as she walked up the hill that morning; but now she saw a certain elegance to it. "But that's the exact point, isn't it, Master Perriad? I don't suggest that you just send me away from the city. Take me to the mountains, beyond Delven, see me beyond the watershed. If I've been making it all up, as you insist I have, then I'll be going into the unknown. Possibly a wilderness, possibly the Blistered Lands that I believed in as a girl. Alone, with no more than I can carry on my back... doesn't that sound like a fitting punishment?"

Perriad stared—*glared*—at her for long moments. Between heavy ticks of the clock, the silence was as absolute as it ever could be in a room of close to thirty people. Everyone, thought Jerya, had to see the elegance of the trap: if Perriad had been right all along, and Jerya's tale of another land beyond the mountains was all a fabrication, then exile beyond those mountains would be not only a suitable punishment but an *elegant* one. Jerya would be hoist by her own petard; and, since no one knew what lay beyond, she might pay the ultimate price.

However... if Jerya *had* been telling the truth, then she had only to repeat a journey she had made twice before and she would be home. Hardly a punishment at all... And not only that, Perriad's whole case became suspect and the tale of men arriving from the East suddenly looked not merely plausible but probable.

And the Conclave would have banished the one person who could help them most in dealing with those men...

Perriad was disconcerted, besure, but not for very long. Jerya counted seven ticks before she spoke again. "Take you to the watershed, you say?

And what's to stop you just lurking about somewhere and then just sneaking back in again?"

Jerya was irked by 'sneaking', but she couldn't let that bother her. "Then let someone watch the pass for a while. Until it's no longer passable."

"Why would that be?"

With four words Perriad had revealed her utter ignorance of the mountains. Jerya only needed one word to answer her. "Winter." In the corner of her eye she saw Evisyn nodding.

But Perriad was not deterred. "By the stars, Jerya, you expect much. You expect Dawnsingers, no doubt several, to wait about for months. Winter is a long way off—"

"—Not up there, it isn't. We crossed at the end of Nawvamès, the first time, and there was snow lying only a little higher."

"But we only have your word for that, don't we?"

"Master Evisyn?" said the Master Prime; Jerya realised that Evisyn had raised a hand.

"Thank you, Master Prime. Master Perriad says that this would require Singers to remain up there for months. I have been to the foothills of the mountains in several places, have climbed a little above the highest villages, places like Delven and Blawith. I don't think I boast in suggesting I know more about the mountains than most of you, and what Jerya says makes perfect sense to me. I am confident it would require those Singers to remain only weeks, rather than months." Perriad drew a breath, but Evisyn gave her no chance to speak. "And it seems to me that we could make good use of their time, improving our maps, adding to our knowledge of the land, perhaps even gaining a better sense of what lies beyond..."

Jerya could hear, as she rather thought everyone could, how Evisyn would relish that chance herself. Whether she, as Master, would be licensed to make that journey was another question, and Evisyn well knew it. "I am sure I would have no difficulty finding volunteers among the Peripatetics."

"Well and good," said Perriad, sounding as if she thought it was neither, "But even if you watch one pass, what is to stop Jerya finding another?"

Jerya almost laughed. "If there were passes all over the place, don't you think—"

The Master Prime cut her off. "I've given you considerable latitude, Jerya, but this must not degenerate into a free-for-all. I remind all of you that our protocol is to speak only when I invite you." She looked around the three in turn. "Very well. Master Perriad, have you more to say about this suggestion?"

Perriad considered. She still faced a delicate dilemma: to accept that Jerya's suggestion was no true punishment would come perilously close to acknowledging that there was a land, even a home, beyond the mountains. "Only this, Master Prime," she said finally, "Whatever Master Evisyn may say now, I cannot recall her ever suggesting that any of her Peripatetics should spend any extended period in the mountains, beyond civilised places. Whatever side-benefits to the Guild she may now offer, they have not previously been compelling enough to prompt such a proposal. To do this now would entail very substantial effort, and implicit cost, to the Guild, in provisioning such an enterprise, and in the disruption, taking those Singers away from other important—nay, vital—duties."

"Master Evisyn?"

Evisyn stepped forward, and Jerya saw for the first time that she, too, walked a delicate path. "Master Perriad objects to banishment on grounds of practicality. But she has said nothing about the practical complications of incarceration. Let us consider this... This Guild does not operate a prison. The closest we come is after some minor transgression, when a Sister is required to confine herself to a single cell for a few days. I repeat, to confine *herself*. We do not lock the door; a Singer in this situation is confined by nothing more than her own word. I don't think I take your name in vain, Master Perriad, if I suggest that would hardly satisfy you in this case?" Perriad's silence was as good as an answer.

"My Masters, if you do elect to pursue the option of incarceration, you must find answers to two questions. First, *where* would you keep her? That is not as simple as it might sound. I remind you, thus far, this Conclave has chosen to keep Jerya's return secret from Postulants and Novices, even from the majority of Ordained Singers. Do you think keeping a *prisoner* within these Precincts could remain secret? And..." She smiled. "Perhaps this is a second, or even a third question: *should* it? Perhaps you would prefer the whole story to be known. To make an example, as the saying is. This choice must be made, one way or the other; this Conclave cannot simply say, 'incarcerate her', without addressing the implications or repercussions.

"And then there is my original second question. *For how long* would you keep her? That is a weighty matter also. I am sure we can all agree indefinite detention is inhumane and unconscionable; therefore a limit must be set. A year? Ten years? One month?

"All these present, as I said, knotty problems. For myself, I am not sure that any satisfactory solution can be found. And therefore I remind you, my Masters, of the alternative mentioned by Jerya herself. We never considered banishment before because we never knew there was anywhere a person could be banished *to*. Now we do—and for that we have Jerya to thank. I urge you, my Masters, to give it due consideration. And let me say, in conclusion, if banishment is your choice, I myself would gladly escort Jerya to... to the frontier." She paused a moment and Jerya knew she was tasting that new word: *frontier*. "I would escort her there—and at our parting I would thank her for the service she has done this Guild and this land."

As Evisyn resumed her seat, her eyes again sought Jerya's, and Jerya gave her a nod: *thank you for trying*.

CHAPTER 28

JERYA

"A year," said Analind. "It could be worse, I suppose."

"I suppose so." Jerya was unconvinced. On being escorted to her new home, she had waited until the door closed behind her and she heard the key turn in the lock, and then she had thrown herself down on the narrow bed and cried. She hadn't wept like that since... she couldn't even remember. She hadn't given in to grief even when she and Railu were taken by the freebooters and sold as slaves.

She felt like weeping again, now, but Analind was watching her. She sat straighter, brushed back an errant strand of hair.

"They tell me they're doing something about... sanitary arrangements," said Analind. "And a lock for the outer door. Then you'll have more room to move around."

"How delightful," said Jerya, not troubling to mask her asperity.

"I'm sure it's hateful... I just... I don't know what else to say."

"I'm sorry. I know you meant it kindly..." For the first time she properly met Analind's gaze. "You always were kind to me."

Now it was Analind's eyes that filled with tears. "I don't feel kind," she sobbed. "Knowing that I can get up and walk out of here whenever I choose... and you can't."

Jerya reached for her hand. "It's not your fault. None of this is your fault... But tell me... how do you feel about it? Does this feel *right* to you?"

Analind looked away, but didn't withdraw her hand. "I don't know," she said at length. "It's what the Conclave decided. I can't set myself up to know better than the Conclave."

Else you'd be a Vow-breaker too, thought Jerya. She could still recall the words of her Novitial Vow: *I shall defer at all times to duly instituted authority.*

She framed a new question. "How does Master Evisyn feel about it?"

"Oh, yes, I have a message from her. She'll come to see you as soon as she can."

"At least I'm allowed visitors."

"No one said anything about it, for or against. I thought it best not to ask, in case... there's never been a prisoner within the Precincts before."

"Yes, I'm quite the pioneer, aren't I?"

Analind didn't answer that."You asked me a question: how does Evisyn feel? I only saw her for a moment, but I think... she seemed very angry."

"You should have seen her yesterday morning." Despite her situation, Jerya smiled. "*That* was angry. Truth be told, she was magnificent. *She* doesn't think much of the way the Conclave is conducting itself. At one point she told them what they were doing was folly."

"She said *that*?"

"And a good deal more."

"I suppose it's different when you *are* a Master," said Analind uncertainly. "Then you can challenge the others, to ensure a good debate."

"Do you think she believes it was a good debate?"

Analind only shrugged.

"The problem," said Jerya, "Is that the Conclave's polarised between Perriad and Evisyn. And in the end Perriad's more senior... and I don't believe Perriad's only concerned with good debate. She wants to *win*. And most of all she wanted a win over me. I said my fate was insignificant... but it's significant to her."

"She's still a Master."

"Does reaching the rank of Master confer infinite wisdom? It doesn't look that way to me. And the Master Prime seems more concerned with keeping the peace within the Conclave than reaching the right conclusion."

"Jerya!" Analind, clearly shocked, pulled her hand free. "She's the... but you must be feeling bitter, and who could blame you?"

"Aye, who could blame me? I came back across the mountains for no reason but to warn the Guild of what's coming... and look how they repay me."

Analind had no answer. They sat in gloomy silence for a minute. Faint sounds penetrated, a shuffling and scraping as of heavy objects being moved around in the outer chamber: *sanitary arrangements*, no doubt. Then Analind said, "Is there anything I can bring you? Books, maybe? Or... I don't know, anything."

"Apart from a key to the door, I suppose."

"No, I can't... but anything else."

She thought about it. "You could go to the tavern. Ask Rodal or Annyt for my belongings. Don't tell them I'm *incarcerated*. There's nothing they can do, so why worry them. Just tell them I've moved into the Precincts... it's not exactly a lie, after all."

Analind frowned, but acquiesced. "Anything else?"

"You mentioned books..."

"Yes. I can bring anything that I'm allowed to take out from the Library."

"Truth be told, anything would be better than nothing. Anything you've enjoyed... But perhaps something dealing with the latest learning in astronomy."

❋

After Analind had left, promising to return soon, Jerya paced the room. As she paced, she thought some more about libraries. Her first exposure to books, Delven's single shelf. She actually smiled as she contemplated how *Proceedings of the Denvirran Society for Natural Philosophy* would sit with the rest. Perhaps one day there would be another girl like her, another Jerya. At eleven, the normal age of Choosing, or even at nineteen, she would have understood almost none of it, but it would surely have fired her imagination.

Then she thought of the Guild's own Library, right here in the College. She was hazy about her exact location in the Precincts, but the Library couldn't be more than a few hundred metres away. More than any single lesson she had received, stepping into the Library for the first time had been the moment when she sensed vistas of learning opening up before her. The way the shelves receded in near-endless perspective, the smell of leather bindings, the overlapping aroma of beeswax from the long oak tables. The way light through the rippled panes of glass made the page you were reading look green and crinkled.

Her legs paced mindlessly as her mind roamed the stacks.

When she first began to contemplate leaving the Guild (*Vow-breaker...*), there had been many things that tempted her to remain. Things, and people. Among things, the Library had been far from least. Did anyone, she wondered, truly comprehend what she had chosen to sacrifice to assuage her own sense of integrity? Not Analind, surely, or even Evisyn, for all her attempts to explain. She had embarked, ten years ago, on a course which seemed certain to lead to a life without books. Could anyone know just how much that would have meant? Hedric perhaps; and perhaps Railu.

Had things gone differently she might easily have found herself permanently consigned to the life of a slave. That, too, was a life without books. Instead, she ended up at Duncal. Its library might be modest after the Guild's, but it was a cornucopia compared to Delven's meagre tally. And now she had her own shelf in her attic room there, her own small collection. She remembered the day she had bought her twenty-fourth book. Realising that she now owned more books than she had seen in her first nineteen years had made her dizzy.

As wife of Hedric, she supposed, she would have access to as many books as she could wish. She had heard him speak of the Earl's library, of the thousands of volumes, many of them pristine, their pages uncut. And if any volume she wanted was not there, she could order it.

As wife of Hedric... the words—the *word*—still tasted strange. Never mind the greater strangeness, the *outrageousness* of 'Countess of Skilthorn'.

Working with him, travelling with him, simply being with him; all that had been wonderful, had given some of the happiest times of her life. But to be a wife was something more. Or, perhaps, something less. Even for a Countess...

Now, though... would she ever have that choice? If it was to be a year before she could return... A great deal could happen in a year.

I will not deny you, Jerya, he had said. She had no doubt that he meant it. But still... a year was a very long time. And a year in which he would have no word of her... Would he really put his inheritance at risk? Promises made in the afterglow of love-making were fine things. But she herself had made promises, with equal conviction, and she had not always kept them. She was the Vow-breaker, after all.

She had made a promise to Embrel too. *As soon as I can.* And she still would. But she was a prisoner; the power to keep her promise had been stripped from her, at least for a year. If *As soon as I can* stretched to a twelvemonth... Would Embrel understand? If his parents kept to their intent, he would have been sent away to school by then, and perhaps as unhappy as he expected to be. A twelvemonth might seem as long to an unhappy small boy as to a prisoner. Perhaps even longer.

She had stopped pacing, come to a halt by the single window. Someone had put a plant in a pot on the windowsill, she saw. An act of kindness... She stumbled to the bed, sat heavily, and surrendered to tears once more.

❋

"I had a thought," she said.

Evisyn gave her a curious look. "Please..."

"Well, suppose Selton's party do find a crossing soon. It's high summer, surely the best time. Suppose they do, and we—you—do encounter them. I began to think about that and it occurred to me... if things went well, then perhaps it would be possible to send a message to someone in the East?"

"Like Hedric, you mean?"

"He's one, for sure. Others, too."

"Well, there's a lot of 'suppose' there, but I can't say it's *not* possible... do you have writing materials now?"

"I do."

"Write your letters, Jerya, and if there's any way I can pass them on, I will."

"Thank you," said Jerya with a fervour that made Evisyn blink.

The Master sat a moment, thinking, then abruptly burst out, "Damn it, this is intolerable, Jerya! I know most of all it's intolerable for you, confined here like this... but not to have you at my side when we do meet this Duke... I told the Conclave its course was folly, and this is the worst folly of all."

"But there's nothing we can do about it."

"It may be a weakness in my character," said Evisyn, "But doing nothing never sat well with me."

"I hope I'm doing the right thing," said Analind as she handed Jerya her rucksack.

"Why would you not be?"

"I don't know. No one's told me you can't have visitors, or that I can't fetch your things."

"So, no need to worry."

"But I do. I am a worrier, Jerya."

"Funny. I always thought you were the most serene person I knew."

Analind laughed. "Did I really seem so? I suppose I just kept it inside. And I can't help worrying I may have overstepped the mark... the Conclave may not have explicitly forbidden it, but is it in the spirit of what they intended?"

"Surely it's for the Conclave to make its intentions clear, not expect you to second-guess them."

"I suppose you're right." The tension Analind had been carrying was only clear as it dissipated.

"Did Rodal or Annyt say anything?"

"I didn't see Rodal. Annyt just said she hoped you were well and that you could pay them a visit soon. I couldn't say anything to that... and then she said the baby was kicking and would I like to feel it?"

"And did you?"

"Yes... oh, the strangest thing. To think of a new life growing inside you... Have you?"

"Felt a baby kick? Yes, many times. I've assisted Railu at several births, too." *Though not that of her own son. That doctor wanted us all out of there.*

"That must be extraordinary... but tell me, Jerya, about Railu. You haven't said much about her."

Analind had known Railu since they were new Postulants, Jerya reflected. Eight years. She had every right to ask; but what to tell her? She wondered what Railu herself would say, but there was no way to ask.

"I'm going to tell you something very few people know," she said, deciding. "And you must promise not to tell another soul."

"I promise."

"That's good enough for me.... but first, perhaps we should have some tea?"

A jug of hot water, well-insulated in thick felted wool, arrived with every meal. Jerya supposed she was eating the same food as was served to Novices in Refec. She would not go hungry during her incarceration.

She made tea, then sat down on the bed again, as Analind occupied the only—but surprisingly comfortable—chair.

Analind sipped, murmured her thanks. "So... what's the secret?"

"Railu has a son."

Analind jolted in shock, tea slopping over the rim of her mug. Jerya darted into the other room for a cloth.

"Did I hear you aright?" said Analind when they were settled again. "You did say Railu has a son?"

"I did."

"But no... husband?"

"No... listen, it's best if I tell it from the beginning." Jerya blew on her tea to cool it, sipped quickly. "First let me set your mind at rest. You know when I spoke of how things are over there I said that slaves have few if any rights—and female slaves even fewer. And we of course were taken for slaves as soon as we were spotted."

"Because you were bald?"

"Exactly. And we were handled roughly, but we were not violated. Not then, or at any other time. Many others taken as runaways have been less fortunate."

Analind frowned. "But if you were not... violated, then Railu must have lain with a man of her own free will."

Yes, and so have I, now. Aloud, she said only. "Yes. But he was nowhere about when we realised that Railu was pregnant." That was eliding the truth in a way that might reflect poorly on Rodal; but Analind had no idea it was Rodal they were speaking of, and Jerya had promised not to reveal that particular fact. "When her pregnancy became apparent, our... owners called her in. They had no heir and they proposed to adopt Railu's child, if it was healthy, as their own."

"Adopt?" repeated Analind, and in her incomprehension Jerya had a clear glimpse of the gulf between Dawnsingers, even Peripatetics, and the rest of the population. Not for the first time she wondered just how long the Guild could continue without embracing some sort of change; but that was a conversation for another time. This was about Railu.

She clarified 'adoption', then recounted her own long-simmering fury at Railu's lot, required to act first as brood-mare, then wet-nurse, to her own child. "It was harder for her, of course. Far harder... and I don't know if

I was always as good a friend to her as I should have been. Opportunities arose for me even as everything narrowed down for her. It wasn't that I'd do her any good by refusing what was offered to me, but I got too caught up in things. I'm sure I could have tried harder to support her. It was several years, really, before we felt comfortable with each other again. And in many ways it was Embrel who brought us together."

"Does he look like her?"

"I see it. I'm not sure anyone else does. If she had hair it would be more apparent. But of course it's never come back."

"Yours did."

"I didn't use the lotion for very long. It was uneven at first, but soon grew in well enough."

Analind swallowed the last of her tea and Jerya offered more from the pot. "It's funny," said Analind, "I knew you at once when I saw you in the tavern, and yet you look so different. Strange, I might even say."

Jerya smiled. "I was only ever bald for... less than a year of my life. So which is strange?"

Analind shrugged. "To me, bald is normal; but I see what you mean. So... how is Railu's life now?"

That was easier. "She's very well. They call her housekeeper now, but she also has repute as a healer."

"It was always what she loved best."

"Indeed. It has to be unofficial, because women are not permitted to practise medicine."

Analind was initially shocked, then grew more thoughtful. "I suppose they aren't here, either, outwith the Guild."

That was something Railu had been vexed about; Jerya had always believed that her airing that question was what had got her despatched to Delven. There was a lot she could say about that... but Analind glanced at her watch, then drained her cup. "I'm sorry, Jerya, I must go. Next time I want to hear about *your* life over there."

"I can talk at any length about that. It's not like I have much else to do."

❋

The following day she had another visitor.

"They are afraid, Jerya," said the Master Prime. "To tell you the truth, I am afraid too. And fear often clouds judgement." She smiled sadly. "I seem to be suggesting that I myself may be guilty of poor judgement. You may have your own opinion on that..."

Jerya thought rapidly. It might be a very bad idea to alienate—or further alienate—this woman; but on the other hand, she was here, and she seemed to be calling for honesty. "I would not say poor, Master Prime. I might as well say my own judgement was poor for not leaving sooner, and going back with my friends. I had delivered my message, why not leave it up to you what you did about it?"

"Now I am bound to ask why you did not."

"I suppose I was frustrated that so few of you seemed to grasp the urgency. And I still thought that I could help... with the concordance, for example." She gave a bitter laugh. "Perriad thinks I am arrogant. Perhaps I am, perhaps I thought myself indispensable."

"I hesitate to call anyone, including myself, indispensable; but I am haunted by the thought... if your warning does prove to be true, and especially if we do find men from the East appearing somewhere in our marchlands, we might be wishing you were there."

Jerya hardly needed to voice what she felt about that. Instead, after a momentary hesitation, she dared to say, "As to your judgement, Master Prime, it did seem to me that you might have given too much weight to maintaining harmony on the Conclave, and perhaps not enough to the wider risks to the Guild—and to all of the Sung Lands." *Exactly as Yanil said*.

The Master Prime sighed. "And in the end, I have not been successful even in that lesser aim. Certain Masters are still at each other's throats... you may guess who I mean."

"And you may guess which of them I think you should pay heed to."

"Would that be your advice now? To act as Master Evisyn suggests, and despatch watchers to the regions where they are most likely to appear?"

I think you may find Master Evisyn has taken matters into her own hands, thought Jerya.

Chapter 29

Jerya

There are 31,536,000 seconds in a year.

Jerya knew this already. She'd done the calculation in her head years ago, as soon she knew what hours and minutes and seconds were; and the word 'million', too, which she'd picked up just a few days before.

"Thirty-one and a half million seconds," she said to Yanil now. "That's a lot of time for thinking. But if I just sit and brood I think I'll only spiral down... I have to talk to people, and you always gave me good advice."

"Seems to me you didn't always take it," said Yanil gently.

"No, but I always listened."

"Except at the end..."

"I didn't dare talk to anyone about it, except Railu."

"You didn't trust me to keep your secret?"

"I thought you might feel your Vow obliged you to tell."

Yanil said nothing, just looked thoughtful. They looked at each other, both surely wondering if things would have been different if that conversation had taken place.

"Well," said Jerya eventually, "I can't promise I'll take it now, but I am asking and I will listen."

"What is it you want to ask about, then?"

"When I get out of here, and if I get home, and if Hedric made it back safely, and if he hasn't forgotten me and married someone else..."

"That's a lot of *ifs*."

"I've had a lot of time to think already. Even five days is four hundred and thirty-two thousand seconds."

"Very well, if this and that and the other...?"

"If he still wants to marry me. And I still want to marry him."

"Sorry, was that last sentence a statement or a what-if?"

Jerya took a slow breath. "I do want to. But sitting here for second after second after second, I start to question everything. And I start to ask whether I should have questioned some things before."

"Things like..."

"Whether I *should* marry him."

"Jerya, I've lived in these Precincts for fifty years. I've scarcely ventured Outwith, bar a few trips to Kendrigg. What do I know of marriage, of men?"

"Perhaps enough to help me with this. What troubles me is, if I marry him, then I... enrol myself in the owner-class. And I don't know if I can do that."

"I said I know little of marriage and men; I know nothing whatever of slavery but what you and Hedric—and Lallon—have told us. Mostly you, of course. But did you not say that, as a woman in the Five Principalities, you cannot truly own anything?"

"I own my clothes. Some books. But I can't ever own the horse I ride or the house I live in."

"And you can't own slaves."

"No, not in my own right. But as Hedric's wife, as Mistress of Kirwaugh, and maybe, one day, as Countess of Skilthorn..." It was the first time, she realised, that she'd spoken that title out loud. "I would be complicit in his ownership."

"I wonder, Jerya, if you should talk to someone like... Asutra is our Master of Logics, so philosophy and ethics are her domain."

"I don't want someone I don't know. I want you."

"Well, I don't know if she'd talk to you anyway. She is somewhat of Perriad's way of thinking."

"Then definitely..."

"I shall do my best for you, but I don't know if I know enough. The only slave I've ever even seen is Lallon. But... well, there seems little point in this if I am not candid, and I cannot help wondering... You walked away from the Guild, into the unknown, because you felt you could not be part of what you called the deception. That's the nub, is it not?"

Jerya could only bow her head in agreement.

"Well," said Yanil, "I know nothing of the Five Principalities—everything you want to talk about is something I know nothing of!—but I've listened to everything you've said, all three of you. And it seems to me... well, I ask, anyway: if you have lived there, as a free person, for the better part of ten years... are you not part of it all already?"

For a moment reflections on her lenses hid her eyes, but she shifted minutely and her gaze was clear. again. When Jerya did not immediately reply, Yanil went on, "You are free, but Railu is still enslaved. I have that right, don't I? And you live under the same roof?"

"Yes, you have it right."

"Don't you feel that you—"

"—I know!" Jerya was unable to sit any more, sprang up, began to pace. Four paces one way, four paces back again. She had managed, so far, not to calculate how many paces a woman might take in thirty-one million seconds. It was sorely tempting to work the problem now, but she knew it was pure distraction.

She wrenched herself to a stop, turned to face Yanil, who sat quietly, unmoving. "I know," she said again, flatly now. "I know. I see her every day, and I can't forget that she's only there because I... because I knew better than fifteen generations of Dawnsingers. I had a finer sense of what's right and what's wrong than all those Singers and Masters... finer than *you*..." Tears blurred her vision and she furiously brushed them away with her sleeve. "But what can I do? There's nowhere else to run to."

She felt weary, as if she'd been walking all day, not just a few paces to and fro. She flopped back onto the narrow bed. "All I can do is the best I can."

"I do wonder..." Yanil stopped.

"Yes?"

"I wonder you're so keen to get back. It sounds an awful place."

"It is... and it isn't. You know, it's funny: I never really had a family in Delven. I started to feel like I did when I was here, with some of the other Novices, Railu and Analind and Veradel, but I... well, you know. But for ten years now, the truest family I've ever had has been Railu and Rhenya and Embrel."

Then she had to say a little more about who Rhenya and Embrel were, but omitting as ever one crucial fact that bound Railu and Embrel—and herself—even more tightly.

"I have to go back, for them," she said at last. "And because I made promises." She saw Yanil's face. "Yes, I know, I'm a Vow-breaker. But that's why... once was enough. Maybe too much. I can't be a vow-breaker all over again."

And I made promises to Hedric too, she thought, *and what does he deserve?*

What a mess I've made of everything. She brushed at her eyes again.

"Perhaps there's another way to look at it," said Yanil after a moment. "If you'd stayed here, completed your studies, been Ordained... maybe one day you'd have risen to Tutor, or even to Master."

Her glance was mischievous, and Jerya almost laughed, but she had to say, "That doesn't seem likely."

"Well, one never knows. But my point is, if you'd stayed, you would have had to accept the *deception* that unsettled you so much. To be, in your word, complicit. After all, you're right, we profit from a falsehood even if we don't ourselves promulgate it. We take tithes, you know, and people buy our sand-glasses and so on. We may not live extravagantly, but we're comfortable. A lot more comfortable, I suspect, than many of the people Outwith." Jerya thought of her sleeping-cell in Delven, and nodded. "More comfortable than people who believe in us, in the power of the Dawnsong."

Of course that's why people in the Guild, and not just people like Perriad, are alarmed. You tell us there's a land without Song, without Dawnsingers."

"But it has slavery."

"And perhaps that's worse... but we've had all that wider debate, maybe too many times already."

"You know how I feel. How much time's been wasted."

"And I understand... but you asked my advice on your personal dilemma. And I really don't know if anything I say is of any use, but since you asked... Jerya, if you'd stayed, and if perhaps you'd risen to a position, whatever it might be, where people at least listened to you... wouldn't you be asking, *is there a better way? To keep all the good that the Guild does without the deception?*

"You see, Jerya, what I think of you... what I think I saw ten years ago, and what I still see now, is someone who wants to make a difference. You aren't content just to fit in, to rub along. Whether it's measuring the distance to the moons, or making a second crossing of the mountains to bring us news you believed we needed to hear... you want to do something, something that matters. You want to *act*." She looked around: the small room, the half-open door to the outer chamber. "It must pain you even more than most people to be confined like this.

"Well, my question for you is... which gives you more opportunity to act: returning to your former life, when you get back there, or marrying Hedric?"

"Marrying Hedric," said Jerya as if by reflex, but then she shook her head. "Well, I tell myself it does. But do I tell myself that because it's true, or because it would suit me for it to be true? Because if I was his wife maybe we could do more science together, build an observatory... or maybe I'm even baser than that, because I know that if I was his wife I'd have a very comfortable life. More than comfortable, really."

"It never seemed to me that you were the sort to be overly concerned about comfort."

"Oh, feather-beds and fine dresses, I don't care about all that. I slept on stone all my early life; still can't abide a soft bed... But I think about a library. Maybe even a library that brings together books from the Sung Lands and the Five Principalities..."

"Well, that sounds like a very fine thing. But the value of a library depends who's allowed to read there, doesn't it? We have a wonderful library here, by far the finest in the Sung Lands, but it's only open to Dawnsingers."

Jerya was silent, thinking about that, and after a moment Yanil continued, "Forgive me if I speak out of turn here, but I think there's another reason you find this hard, why marrying Hedric is so... beckoning for you."

"What's that?"

"Hedric." She watched Jerya's face, and after a moment nodded slightly, as if to herself.

Jerya took a deep breath. "Aye, Hedric. I love him, I suppose. At least I think I do." *It certainly felt like it when we lay there flesh to flesh...*

"You *think* you do?"

"Do I love him, or do I love the things that he makes possible?"

"I can't answer that for you. Perhaps if I knew him better, or I'd seen more of the two of you together... But I think being in here is making you question yourself too much. You're second-guessing everything you say, and that's not like you, unless I'm quite wrong in my estimation of you, and I really don't think I am."

"And it's only been five days..."

"So you have to put a stop to it. Maybe there are others you should talk to... I know you've seen Evisyn, and Analind, and there's Sharess too. Or maybe it's just yourself... listen, Jerya, I have to go in a minute, so let me finish what I began to say. I'd almost said it, but we veered off down a side-path. So I'll come back to it: in the end, which gives you more opportunity: your life as it was, or as Hedric's wife?"

"I know what *he* would say."

'What would he say?"

"He went back before me because of his sense of duty. Because he needs to keep his uncle happy if he's to remain heir to Skilthorn. Because if that changes, and his cousin inherits, it'll be so much the worse for all the slaves on the estate."

"I see why that matters to him, but... this is probably my ignorance speaking, but he can inherit whether or not he marries you?"

"Yes, but he needs to marry *someone* so he can have an heir. And anyone else he's likely to marry... would *she* be committed to making things better for the enslaved? Would *she* support him, maybe even push him to go further, or would she sap his resolve?" She felt almost sick at the thought. In a year... how would it feel to go back and find he'd married someone else? She pushed the thought down, hurried on. "I dare say there are good women among the ranks of the eligible, but I'm sure as stone about this: there won't be any others who know what it's like to *be* a slave."

Yanil nodded, and then they were both silent for some moments. Then Yanil looked at her watch, and sighed. "I'm sorry, I really must go."

Jerya accompanied her into the outer chamber and Yanil knocked on the door. As she waited for it to be opened, she turned back to Jerya. "I'll come back whenever I can. And there are others... But you know, it occurs to me, in the end, maybe, it isn't me you most need to talk to, or anyone here. Maybe the person you need to talk to most about this is Railu."

She's right... "But that's not possible, is it?"

"Not right now."

"Well, by tomorrow morning I'll have passed the first half-million seconds."

CHAPTER 30

JERYA

A hand on her shoulder. She came out of a confused dream in which everyone was bowing and scraping and calling her Countess... but doors kept being locked in her face. "What? Who?"

"Quiet..." warned a voice, suitably hushed. "Where's your lamp?"

"Here." Jerya sat up, shaking the hair off her face, fumbled for a light, got the lamp glowing. She looked up into Evisyn's angular face. "What's happening?"

"We need to leave, and we need to leave now."

"But..."

"I can get you out, don't worry about that. And by the time anyone realises you're missing we'll be five hours up the road."

Jerya gave up on objections. *Why should I object? I have no desire to stay here. And no Vow to keep me.* There was still one question. "Why?"

"There's a flag."

"Where?"

"On Keldash Peak. The local Dawnsinger's a good ranger in her spare time. She's been keeping a watch through spy-glasses every chance she gets. I had some girls in the vicinity; she sent a runner to 'em, they confirmed it, sent a bird at once."

Jerya, now fully awake, strove to recall the maps she'd studied with Evisyn and Analind and Skarat. "Keldash Peak' meant nothing to her, but clearly did to Evisyn. "So we know where they're coming?"

"Better than ninety percent chance," said Evisyn. "That's good enough for me. Hope it's good enough for you."

"Give five minutes."

Her rucksack was already part-packed; half of its contents had never been removed since arrival in the city. She dressed quickly, heedless of modesty. Her old familiar riding-habit, a warm waistcoat for the morning chill.

She left the Carwerid skirt and blouse on their hangers.

It was not the first time Jerya had been abroad in the Precincts at night, but never so late (or early?) as this. One or two lighted windows suggested some zealous Novice was studying far too long, or had simply forgotten to douse her lamp. No one was about in the courts as they hurried on. Jerya realised that she had been held in one of the newer buildings, beyond Refec; not somewhere she'd been familiar with in her previous life here. They exited under a broad arch, down a few steps. Gravel crunched under their feet and they stepped quickly onto the grass alongside.

Down below the songstead, round to the right a little. Jerya had never visited the stables before. That earlier Jerya had never been on a horse, only followed behind one in mail-coach or cart. The Jerya of today was a regular horsewoman and often wished she had the opportunity to do more.

The building loomed ahead of them, silhouetted against the glow of a street-lamp or two somewhere outwith the walls. It was only when they were inside, in the horse-scented warmth, that a figure stepped out of the shadows, uncovering a lantern.

"Where are you going?" asked the Master Prime.

❄

Evisyn recovered from the shock first. "Master Prime. I know you are a consensualist. I know you hate even to use your casting vote. But you know what the Conclave decided was folly, and now you must choose."

"What do you think, Singer Analind?" asked the Master Prime. "Should I stand aside, or summon help to apprehend these miscreants?"

Analind, who had appeared a moment after the Master Prime, looked more flustered than Jerya had ever seen her. "It's surely not for me to say, Master Prime."

"Is it not? And yet you know Master Evisyn better than most; and I suspect you know Jerya better than anyone in these Precincts."

"But I am just a lowly Singer."

"We are all lowly Singers. It's well to recall that; some need to be reminded more than others. I needed a reminder myself. What matters is the Guild, and above all our Purpose; the peace and wellbeing of this land. We are all servants of that."

"But my Vow..."

"*I shall defer at all times to duly instituted authority*; I presume that's the line you're thinking of?"

"Yes, Master Prime, and the Conclave..."

"Some of whose decisions, of late, have been folly, if Master Evisyn is to be believed."

"But still *duly instituted authority*," protested Analind. "If I go against the ruling of the Conclave I am in breach of my Vow."

"Yes," said the Master Prime, "The Vow... lately I have begun to wonder why it is that the Vow, as we have it today, binds us to service but says nothing further about the land and community, only about the Guild itself: *rules and practices*; deference to *duly instituted authority*, and more."

"Perhaps," said Analind with desperate stubbornness, "But that is the Vow I swore." She glanced at the others. "That we all swore."

"You're right, of course. And I will say I am bemused to find myself standing here now debating this with you. But a few days ago Master Evisyn said something which lingered with me. *If we fail to meet this challenge, it will not be Jerya who has betrayed the Guild, it will be this Conclave.* I thought about it more in the days that followed, and now, from what you tell me, the challenge is upon us, and we can delay no longer."

"We have dithered too long already," growled Evisyn.

"Five more minutes can make little further difference. Five more minutes to be sure we are doing the right thing. Tell me again, Evisyn, why you need Jerya by your side."

"Because there's a flag on Keldash Peak. Because that makes it very likely that men from the East will be entering the Sung Lands within days, if they aren't already here. Because no one but Jerya knows the first thing about them, how they think, how they may act."

"I know a great deal less than I should like," said Jerya. "But you're right; if ten years in the Five Principalities means anything, I'm better prepared than you."

"If you're right, Evisyn," said the Master Prime, "No one will question our actions. If your prediction is wrong, if no one appears, very likely we will all be arraigned as Vow-breakers, myself included. I have discretionary powers, yes, but discretionary action is always subject to scrutiny after the fact." She turned back to Analind. "You, too, face that prospect. I shall not order you, Analind. I cannot order a Singer to break her Vow, and if you truly believe that the Vow requires you to sound the alarm, then that is what you must do."

Analind stared at her. Nothing, Jerya saw, had prepared her for such a choice.

The Master Prime, it seemed, had made her choice. Evisyn had made hers some time back, while for herself it had hardly been a choice at all. Everything hinged, now, on Analind; both the Master Prime and Evisyn seemed to have said all they meant to say.

Analind turned toward her with a pleading look. For a moment Jerya struggled for the right words. Then, all at once, she knew. "I am a Vow-breaker, it's true. But locking me up for a year does nothing to change that, or to repair any damage I may have done. It serves nothing but Perriad's need for revenge. This, however... This is the best chance—the only chance—I'll ever have to serve the Guild."

The silence stretched. A horse stamped, another snorted sleepily. Lamp-light trembled on Analind's dark face, the curve of her scalp. Finally she shook her head. "Which horse should I take?" she said.

Evisyn grinned fit to split her face. "I knew I could count on you."

"I don't know how you could know before I did."

"I'd thought of your Arrain for Jerya, but you should have the horse you know. Jerya can take Mineas. Have you anything with you?"

Analind shook her head. "I'll have to pick up anything I need along the road."

"Right," said Evisyn, already swinging away to lift a saddle-blanket from a rack. "Saddle up. And we'll muffle their hooves till we're out of the city."

"I can help," said the Master Prime. "I used to be a fair horsewoman myself, once on a day."

"You're coming with us?"

The older woman shook her head. "I'm out of shape for hard riding, and I'm thinking that's what you'll be doing. But I can help you saddle up. And then... well, we'll see. Maybe I can delay the pursuit. And then... I'll have to deal with whatever consequences may follow."

CHAPTER 31

HEDRIC

"He could linger like this for months," said Doctor Aiskin. "Or he might recover, at least partially. It's always hard to tell with apoplexy."

"It definitely is apoplexy, then?"

"No doubt about it. Face all fallen down on the right side, right hand useless. Textbook case... sorry, lad, that might sound callous. I came straight over from setting a broken leg, one of Pethril's boys." The doctor had had precious little sleep last night, he deduced. "I'm a bit worried about complications there, to be frank with you."

"Meaning you ought to be getting back there?"

"More chance I can do some real good there than here." The doctor sighed. "One day I'm kicking my heels and griping there ain't enough work, the next I'm wishing I could be in two places at once."

Hedric thought, *and I know where there's a most capable healer just a day's ride from here.* He wondered how Aiskin might react to being supplanted by a female, and a slave. *Though Railu isn't rightly a slave*, he reminded himself. He hadn't had that conversation with Duncal and his lady yet. He had called there on his way, but had been mostly occupied with reassuring Embrel that Jerya absolutely would return just as soon as she could. The news from Skilthorn had reached Duncal only hours after his own coming, and he had left immediately, putting up at an inn when it grew too dark to ride and leaving again at first light.

He broke his reverie. "You should go... Anything else I need to know?"

"The slaves have all the instructions for his care," said the doctor, before proceeding to list them anyway. But within five minutes he was striding away down the passage, caught momentarily in a succession of gilded mirrors. Hedric turned slowly in the opposite direction, reluctant—almost fearful—to face what awaited him in the Earl's bedchamber.

In truth, the reality was less awful than his imagination had made it... but bad enough. His uncle's face did indeed appear to have slumped on the right side, as if the flesh had melted and recongealed like candle-wax. It took strong effort to muster a cheery tone. "How now, Uncle. What's this I hear?"

The answer was an unintelligible mumble. Hedric, usually one of the best at understanding the Earl's often-slurred delivery, was dismayed. He tried again, but to no better effect. The old man's brow drew down, on the left side, a frown or a scowl. That, at least, was decipherable.

With an impatient snort, the Earl made a gesture with his left hand. Hedric realised he was grasping a small bell, but his fingers were curled around it so as to muffle the clapper. "You want to ring, Uncle?"

The Earl muttered something. It could have been, *of course I do, don't be a damn fool*, but Hedric knew that was guesswork, based on what he was likely to say. He freed the bell from the arthritic grip, rang it.

A moment later a slave-girl came scurrying in. "I'm so sorry, m'lord, I had ter—" She saw Hedric, stopped abruptly. Her face reddened. After a moment she made the hand-opening gesture which, in strict households, was a request for permission to speak.

"Go ahead, please," he said.

"A thousand pardons, sir. I's been here since dawn, and not a moment to..." Her blush intensified.

"I understand," he said. "We all have the same need, at times."

She dipped her head; a grateful acknowledgment, he supposed.

"I've seen you before, have I not?" Round face, vivid green eyes, sandy eyebrows; nothing to suggest she could be one of his unacknowledged cousins.

"Aye, sir, yow have."

"And what do they have you doing for him now?"

Before she could answer, the Earl mumbled something. Hedric could not make out a word, but the impatience was clear. The girl darted forward, bent close and listened to him, his voice barely above a whisper. Hedric couldn't help noticing that her dress was cut low, and shaped to crush her breasts together. He also observed that his uncle's eyes—at least the left—went straight to that glimpse of young flesh.

He was unshocked. The Earl had always had a preference for nubile house-slaves, and had always had them dressed immodestly. One more thing that Hedric intended to amend when the opportunity arrived.

The girl looked up at him and again made the 'permission to speak' gesture.

"Speak freely," he said.

"Thank you, sir. His Lordship says don't talk about him like he's not here."

"You can understand him?"

"Mostly I can, sir. I's been studyin', as yow might say."

He felt a stirring of jealousy—*he's* my *uncle!*—but dismissed it briskly. If the girl could help, all to the good.

The Earl mumbled again. "I'm sorry, Uncle, I didn't catch that."

"He says he can't see yow properly, sir."

Hedric had a sudden thought. "Let me try something, Uncle." He looked around for a clean cloth or bandage. Being a sickroom, he didn't need to look far. As gently as he could, he laid a folded bandage over his uncle's wandering right eye. "Is that any better?"

He didn't need the girl to render the words this time: "Thass mush better."

"We'll have to get you an eye-patch," he said.

Mumble. The girl: "He says where the h... hell have yow been. Sorry, sir."

"Please," he said. "Speak his words exactly as you hear them. If the language is foul, that's his responsibility. Don't waste your breath on apologies."

She nodded once, bent down again as the Earl mumbled some more. "He says answer the damn question."

"Just back from the West, Uncle."

Mumble. "He says oh yes, yowr damn silly expe... exped..."

"Expedition."

"That's it, sir, must be."

Mumble. "He says he reckons yow had a wasted summer."

"Not at all, Uncle, a resounding success."

Mumble. "He says don't tell me—him—yow actually crossed the mountains?" Her eyes flickered in surprise even as she reported the words.

"We most certainly did."

Mumble. "He says and did you beat that damn jack..."

"Jackanapes?"

"Aye, sir. Did yow beat that damn jackanapes Selton?"

"We surely did. At least there'd been no sign of him when I left. No report from any quarter."

"Report?" This was clear enough for his own ears to make out.

"Aye, Uncle. That's the real news. There's life over there. People, towns, at least one city."

The Earl absorbed this in silence a few moments, then *Mumble.* "He says his mouth is dry. He wants brandy."

"And does the doctor admit that remedy?"

"Says it can't do no more harm, sir. In small doses, like. I been givin' him a spoonful at a time." She turned to her patient. "Yow've slid down in t'bed again, yowr Lordship. Can I help you sit yowrself uprighter again?"

There was precious little of helping him raise himself; it was all the girl's effort. The Earl was not as stout as he had been, but he was still no lightweight. The girl must have muscles under the freckled skin that showed at shoulder and wrist. Too late, he realised he could, and should, have offered his help. He'd been distracted by wondering at the tenderness that accompanied the girl's strength.

It moved him remarkably to see such solicitousness from one who had undoubtedly suffered at her patient's hands. The first time he'd seen her, the Earl had abused her disgracefully, reducing her to tears. Hard treatment was commonplace at Skilthorn, and it generally took something beyond everyday indignities to reduce even the youngest to the point of weeping. Even now, when the Earl was helpless, he had her dressed in a costume more suited to a bagnio than a respectable mansion. *And it will be respectable again, when I have the ordering of it.*

He watched as the girl, having got her charge re-settled to her satisfaction, administered a spoonful of brandy. It was full enough to show a distinct meniscus, but it was not a large spoon. And, if the tint of the liquid in the decanter was any guide, it had been watered anyway. Doctor's orders, no doubt.

Next moment the girl was at his side, requesting permission to speak. "Did I not say speak freely earlier?" he responded. "Please, as long as I'm here, feel no requirement to keep asking permission."

"Thank yow, sir. He's dropping to sleep now. A drop o' brandy usually does it."

"How long will he sleep?"

She shrugged. "Never can tell, sir. And I'm no great hand with clocks, neither. Got me into trouble more'n'once, I can—" She stopped abruptly, flushing pink.

"Don't fret about it... shall we step away, so we don't disturb him?"

He took her over to the window-bay, where a shaft of afternoon sunlight slanted through the narrow gap in the curtains, illuminating the smooth curves of her shaven head. He recalled all those bald women in Carwerid—bald and formidable, the very antithesis of slaves. And Jerya had once been one of them...he wondered just how she had looked bald.

But that was profitless distraction. Lallon's words came back to him once more: *Get a grip on yourself.* The memory brought a smile. *Let the girl think it's for her,* he thought. "What's your name, child?"

She lifted her chin, and he realised he'd slighted her; she was too old to care for being called 'child'. "They calls me Dortis, if it please you, sir."

"The truth is what pleases me, Dortis. And what age have you?"

"I dun't rightly know, sir. Se'nteen, they say, most likely."

He sighed. 'Well-regulated' estates registered every slave-birth, and he had no doubt that in this regard Skilthorn was as well-regulated as any. They just didn't bother to keep the slaves themselves informed, and all too often mother and baby would be separated, the young—the cubs, in a particularly hateful idiom—transferred to a creche as soon as they were weaned, to be raised en masse while their mothers were put back to work.

"Seventeen, you say? That's young, I'd have thought, to be given sole responsibility of caring for a difficult patient."

"Seems his Lordship asked for me hisself, sir. S'pose he must ha' liked me... not for me to say, o'course. But I warmed his bed for a while afore this... I were with 'im when he c'lapsed, be the fact."

The image of this young girl in bed with his uncle, even as he'd been before the apoplexy, was not one he wanted to dwell on. It was almost fortunate that she was looking at him in sudden concern; not gazing steadily into his face, but shooting hasty side-glances, as slaves often did. Concerned that she'd said too much, no doubt.

He smiled again. "Whatever the Earl's wishes, I'm sure the doctor wouldn't trust you alone with him if he wasn't satisfied of your competence. From what I've seen thus far, his trust is not misplaced."

She took a moment to work this out. The double negative confused her, he supposed; but then she brightened. "Thank yow, sir."

"It's I who should be thanking you. I'm glad to know my uncle's been in good hands while I was away. Now, Dortis, let me ask you something. Have you cared for the sick before?"

"In th'slave-quarters, sir. Helps out when I can, like."

"Do you like it? Would you like to do more?"

"T's not for me to say, sir."

"Indulge me." *No*, he thought, *put it a way she'll understand better*. "Suppose you were ordered to spend your time—your working hours—caring for the sick, for whoever needed it... Would that please you?"

She hesitated. He could almost read the words *not for me to say* forming on her lips; but he knitted his brows just enough to deter her, to demand an answer. "S'pose it would, sir."

"Well, I'll say no more just for now, but you've given me an idea."

There was one estate, that he knew of, where there was a healer among the slaves. Railu was freeborn, of course; again he thought of the conversation he must have with Duncal and his lady, as soon as he could get away again. Though for all practical purposes, it probably made precious little difference. Slave or free, Railu was female, and females were not licensed to practise the clinical arts in any of the Five Principalities. The fact that she was a better healer than any of Drumlenn's local sawbones would count for nothing.

"Well," he said, "I'll leave you to care for your patient. I need to find myself something to eat."

"Yow only need to ring, sir."

"I know, but I also know my way to the kitchens, and meat's a lot better straight from the spit than plated up and carted round this draughty old place. Have someone call me if he wakes, though, will you?"

"Aye, sir."

CHAPTER 32

JERYA

F our emerged from the dark gash in the rock walls, a fifth, a sixth straggling behind. When no more followed, Jerya glanced at Evisyn. The Master nodded back, looked around at once more to check there were no bald heads showing. Then she gently heeled her mount into a walk.

Well before they reached them, the five men had halted and drawn together into a loose clump. They met on a stony flat, where the stream that issued from the gorge spread into half a dozen braided channels. Hooves clattered and splashed until they halted perhaps ten yards short of the newcomers.

Jerya and Evisyn swung down from the saddle. Jerya handed her reins to Analind. Her old friend was tight-lipped, eyes under the brim of a grey felted cap fixed on the five men.

The two of them walked forward together. Evisyn said nothing, but Jerya sensed she was thrilling to this moment as if she had waited her whole life for it. She made a splendid figure in divided skirt and riding coat, against which long auburn hair almost glowed. Her wig suited her very well, unlike some of the others.

One man advanced to meet them. His face was familiar from the engraving on the newspaper page she'd carried across the divide, but the emblematic moustache was blurred by a week's growth of beard.

They stopped two strides apart, and for a single moment there was silence. Then the breeze rushed in to fill it. Jerya's skirts snapped, and Evisyn's hair blew across her face. She hooked it back behind her ear with what looked like an habitual gesture. *You really can't tell it's a wig*, thought Jerya.

She drew breath, gave a slight bow. "Am I correct in thinking I have the honour of addressing His Grace the Duke of Selton?"

The Duke's eyes widened fractionally, but that was the limit of his visible reaction. With barely a pause, he returned the bow, but deeper, well-schooled and courtly. "You have the advantage of me, madam. Or should I say my lady?"

"Whichever you prefer."

Selton was about forty, she knew. He had the reddish face of a naturally light-skinned man who spends a lot of time outdoors. He looked like an active man, but one who also liked to eat well; lithe but not over-lean, and just a little jowly.

"My name is Jerya Delven," she said. "And may I present Master Evisyn of the Guild of Dawnsingers?"

Selton bowed, and Jerya had the surreal experience of seeing a Master Dawnsinger echo it. All things considered, Evisyn executed the manoeuvre with remarkable aplomb.

Her description of Evisyn made the Duke raise an eyebrow, tilt his head, but he wasn't about to forget his manners. "An honour, madam. May I present my companions, Lords Rafforth and Gallard, and my son, Tavistan." Each, as he was named, made a polite bow. The Duke did not name the other two, standing a few paces back, because they were slaves.

Evisyn named the rest of her company, then said, "I believe we have much to say to each other, but I am sure it would be more comfortable in our camp."

"I must say, madam, I would be very happy to sit down, if your hospitality extends to chairs."

❋

"I have a great many questions, madam, but there is one which occupies my mind more than any other."

"Please," said Jerya, though she had a pretty good idea what the question would be.

"How is it, madam, that you knew my name? That you appeared to be expecting us?"

"I *appeared* to be because I was. I knew of your plans seven weeks ago."

"How so?"

Jerya found she was enjoying herself. "I read about it in the *Denvirran Remarker*."

He absorbed this intelligence in silence at first, only a widening of his eyes betraying any emotion. Then he puffed out a sharp breath. "Forgive me if this is indelicate, but... who by thunder *are* you?"

It *was* indelicate, highly so, by Five Principalities standards, but Jerya was unconcerned. "That is not such a simple question as you may think. For some years I have been secretary, and more recently also governess, in the house of Duncal, in the bailiwick of Drumlenn." She paused a moment, assessing his reaction. He was hard to read, though his mind must be spinning under the urbane facade.

"I may have heard the name," he said, "But I cannot claim acquaintance with your employer."

Jerya shrugged. "It's not important. What's important is who I was before I came to Duncal. I said my name is Jerya Delven, but once I was Jerya *of* Delven—and Delven is a village in the mountains, far North of here... but on this side, in the Sung Lands. And for a brief period, a few months, I was studying to be a Dawnsinger."

"Wait," he said, forgetting his manners in his impatience. "Let me be clear. You are telling me that you originated *here*, in the West; that you crossed the Dividing Range some time ago—how long, to be precise?"

"Close on ten years."

"And then... well, I might at some time request further proof of that, but it certainly does appear as if you *have* been in the Five Principalities; you knew my name, and you are familiar with the *Denvirran Remarker*. These may not be proofs that you have made a prior Crossing, but they look very like proofs that *someone* has."

Jerya was not affronted by his scepticism; it was exactly what she would expect of a scientific mind. "I can furnish other proofs, sir, though not immediately. But there are people here who can testify to my presence in the College of the Dawnsingers ten years ago—not Master Evisyn, but others in this company."

"I did not know Jerya ten years ago," said Evisyn, who had been following the exchange with an air of amusement. "But others did, and I am quite assured that she is the same person who was in our College then, and of whom nothing was then heard until just a few weeks back."

"And if you require evidence that I have been in Denvirran in the interim," said Jerya, "It should take me only a few minutes to find a map which you will recognise as a Five Principalities publication. And if you come to Carwerid—the principal city of the Sung Lands—I can also show you a volume of the *Proceedings of the Denvirran Society for Natural Philosophy*."

There was no mistaking his surprise at that. "A curious choice of baggage, if may say so, madam."

"You're not the only one who requires proof. I had to convince the Dawnsingers... well, I had to start by proving that there is civilisation East of the mountains, not just that I'd been there."

"Still, I wonder at your choice. The *Proceedings* is an admirable publication, of course—"

"—And would be very hard to fake if I was trying some deception. But there was a personal reason. My name is in it."

"*Your* name?"

Jerya understood his surprise, had almost been counting on it. "I appear as J. Delven, co-author of a paper on revised parallax observations for measuring the distance to the One."

"I suppose the editors were not informed that 'J.Delven' is a lady?" He smiled. "I have some recollection of reading that paper, albeit superficially. Astronomy is not my field, beyond what I need to know for practical position-fixing—which involves sighting on stars, not the moons."

He sat for a moment, apparently lost in thought. The youngest Peripatetic, Elifian, slipped quietly in to add fuel to the fire. As the dry juniper stems blazed up, the Duke's face was suddenly illuminated, and Jerya saw how dusk had settled in; only the very highest peaks were still catching the last crimson glow of the Sun.

He startled them all with a great shout of laughter. "By thunder, madam, you have confounded me! Look at us, with all our bandobast; not just us few, but a dozen more, and as many slaves, back in our base camp. Mule-trains for resupply, every comfort that can be contrived, every assistance that modern science can give... and yet you have beaten us to it, not once, but twice." He narrowed his gaze on her. "Though I cannot quite believe you did it entirely alone."

No, but I think I would have tried anyway... "In fact I had two companions each time."

"Well, that softens the wound to my pride, just a little... but if you truly first crossed ten years ago, you must have been very young?"

"I was nineteen."

He chuckled. "Then we may claim one distinction. My son—" A slender figure, darker-skinned than himself, standing a few paces away. "—Can still claim to have been the youngest to make the Crossing... unless your companions were yet younger?"

"One a little younger, but she had turned nineteen. The other was a little older. And that's not the only distinction you can claim. We took an entirely different route... I don't know about yours, but ours has some difficult climbing at one place."

"We shall have to compare notes in detail," he said. "Or, if you plan to return East, you could simply take a look at our route... but I think we pioneers are monopolising the conversation, and as I understand matters, it's you, madam, who are our true host?"

He turned to Evisyn, who gave a grave nod. "I suppose I am."

"If I recall correctly, you are Master Evisyn of the Guild of Dawnsingers?"

"I am. Master of Peripatetics if you want the full title."

He smiled again. "I think we may all be counted peripatetic, else we should not be here at all. But you use the word more specifically... First, however, what exactly is the Guild of Dawnsingers?"

"Simple answers are hardly adequate; I hope things will become clearer soon. For now... we are the custodians of knowledge and scholarship in the Sung Lands; and, I hope, of wisdom. We guard and preserve all the ancient learning we have been able to recover, and through study and research we strive to add new knowledge and understanding."

Jerya did not fail to observe a quickening of Selton's interest, particularly at the mention of 'ancient learning'. "You say 'guard'. Do you, then, keep such knowledge to yourselves?"

Evisyn looked into the flames. "We err on the side of caution. We are very conscious of what too much knowledge, in the wrong hands, once wrought." She gestured to the Three, a handsbreadth above the ragged Eastward skyline. "Still, we are custodians, not hoarders. It is important never to lose sight of all the ways learning can improve the lives of the people of the Sung Lands."

"Forgive me if I am slow to understand," said Selton, "But are you telling me that your Guild *rules* the... Sung Lands?"

"I'd rather say that we guide." *I wonder what Perriad would say?* thought Jerya.

"And... it is obvious at a glance that all your present company are ladies, but a scientist is wary of leaping to conclusions based on a small sample, so may I ask...?"

"All Dawnsingers are female."

"But not all females are Dawnsingers?"

"No, not by any means. There is a Dawnsinger in every settlement, but in villages only one. As you can see tomorrow. There is a village a couple of hours' ride down the strath."

"We are in your territory, madam, so I await your invitation."

"I think I may take it on my own authority to invite you that far. And from there we can send a speedy message to the College, to our Conclave, to request consent for you to proceed further."

"My thanks, madam."

Again Evisyn gazed briefly into the fire before speaking. "We have much more to say to each other, of course, and I hope we shall be able to do so over food very soon... but there is one more thing I should like to make you aware of now. Jerya has informed me that in your land—in the Five Principalities—you keep slaves."

"That is quite so, madam. Indeed, as you may have observed, we have a couple of trusted fellows with us here."

Jerya remembered Hedric's remark to Lallon as they passed the watershed: *you're a free man, lad.* She wondered, for the merest instant, if Evisyn intended to say something similar; but that was not what she had in mind. "I'm also told that in the Five Principalities a shaven head indicates that a person is a slave."

"It does."

"It's different here," said Evisyn, and pulled off her wig.

That, thought Jerya, surprised the Duke of Selton more than almost anything else he had seen or heard.

CHAPTER 33

JERYA

The way Perriad sat a horse, it was obvious she was not used to riding. The ill-concealed wince as she dismounted, the moment needed to straighten, confirmed the impression. It could not have been a comfortable ride, but she was here.

It could not be good news.

"Master Perriad," said Evisyn. "What—"

"It's Master Prime, in fact." Jerya's heart dropped.

For a moment Evisyn appeared lost for words, but she recovered quickly. "A new Master Prime can only be ratified when all Masters are present in Conclave, and that clearly was not so. Besides, we have a perfectly fine Master Prime already."

"A Master Prime who aided and abetted the escape of a convicted Vow-breaker? Not what I would call 'perfectly fine'. She did at least take the honourable course and resign her office. And as for your other point, you are correct that all Masters must be present to install a new Master Prime, but the removal of an existing Master requires only a three-quarters majority of those present."

As Evisyn parsed this, as she realised exactly what Perriad was telling her, Jerya saw muscles bunch in her jaw. Fists clenched.

Perriad watched her, then glanced over at Jerya. The smile that teased at her lips was subtle, but she had to be dancing with glee inside. Doubtless she had dreamed of this moment for a long time.

But Evisyn still wasn't entirely defeated. "So, *Master Prime*, have you troubled yourself yet to notice that we have guests? Have you deigned to acknowledge that the eventuality Jerya warned us about has come to pass? The same eventuality that you said was nonsense, a fabrication? Can you bring yourself to admit that she was telling the truth all along? And it's your prevarication that left us so ill-prepared for—"

"Enough!" They had tasted the momentary satisfaction of seeing the smile wiped from Perriad's face, but she wasn't about to concede any more than that. "I will not be castigated by renegades." She turned to her companions, snapping out orders. "Clear out that tent, strip it of everything, then throw them in there. They will at least have the joy of each other's company for the first days of their incarceration." She stepped closer to the other Peripatetics, who had huddled together in their shock. "There's room for a few more, if anyone else feels inclined to defy the duly appointed Head of your Guild."

No one moved, save to look at each other. No one spoke.

Perriad smiled. "Very wise. I shall assume you were acting under orders from your Master, with no reason to know she had violated her Vow. If you conduct yourselves dutifully from now on, no penance will be exacted."

Already Perriad's cohort were emptying out the tent. Within a minute, no more, it was clear, and Jerya and Evisyn were bundled inside. The last thing Jerya glimpsed as hands closed on her arms was Analind's stricken face.

※

Analind still looked distraught. "I didn't know what to do. But then I thought, the Master Prime... the, the original..."

"The real one," said Evisyn.

"I realised she must not have said anything about me helping you escape. She protected me even when she herself had to resign. It feels like she was sending me a message."

"So here you are."

"Here I am. But I haven't a single idea beyond getting you out of this tent."

"It's a start," said Evisyn, reaching to grasp Analind's shoulder, the two of them mere outlines in the mix of moonlight and fireglow filtering through the canvas. "I'm proud of you."

She turned back toward Jerya. "But we'd better come up with a plan before we move from here."

"Maybe we should go and talk to the Duke."

She had learned to move quietly during early-morning exits from Delven, but it had never mattered more than it did now. Having rolled out through the slit Analind had made in the rear of the tent, she crept cautiously forward, peered round the corner.

Most Dawnsingers were in the habit of retiring early, especially in summer when Dawnsong was in the small hours. Analind had waited for the camp to settle, too. As Jerya had thought, there were few signs of life, but one figure stood before the tent-flaps and another sat near a dying fire. Even in high summer, nights at this altitude could be chilly.

By staying close to the fires, both watchers were compromising their night vision. That was potentially helpful, but she had no doubt that Evisyn and Analind's white garments would still be all too conspicuous. *Pity they didn't throw their cloaks in with us.*

Her own clothes were helpfully darker, but her skin was paler than the other two. A moment's thought joined the dots and she slipped back to where they were now waiting in the lee of the tent.

"Take off my clothes?" Analind's protest threatened to rise above a whisper.

Jerya put a finger to Analind's lips. "Just till we're well clear. I'm not asking you to walk into the Duke's camp in your smalls."

Analind huffed, but she saw the sense in Jerya's plan. Jerya made a bundle of the others' garments and stowed it under her own, then swiftly unbraided her hair and pulled it forward to cover as much of her face as she could.

Then she led them on a wide arc, looping away from both encampments before slowly drawing their course around towards the camp of the Easterners.

Perhaps fifty yards short, they gathered behind a shoulder-high boulder. Jerya handed back the clothes. As the others dressed she raked her hair back and twisted it into a rough knot.

Already she could tell there was still activity in the camp. She could hear voices, an occasional laugh. There was nothing to be gained now from further stealth, so together the three women stepped out from behind the rock and walked steadily down the slight slope.

"Ladies," said the Duke. He had been called from his tent, but he was still fully dressed. "To what do I owe this unexpected pleasure at so late an hour?"

"Unfortunately we couldn't get away earlier," said Jerya.

"I was wondering what had become of you. In fact we've spent most of the evening trying to make sense of what we've seen. As if it were not already sufficiently out of kilter with anything we could have anticipated, this afternoon seemed to change everything all over again... I take it what transpired was discord between Dawnsinger and Dawnsinger?"

"I'm afraid so."

"And the... lady who now appears to command...?"

"She has... seized control of the entire Guild," said Evisyn heavily.

"A palace coup?" said the Duke.

Jerya had read enough Five Principalities history to recognise the phrase. "Something of that kind."

"So you are now out of favour...?"

"For the moment," said Evisyn.

Jerya added, "Master Evisyn and I were confined in a tent. We only escaped thanks to Analind."

"Well," said the Duke, "I condole with your predicament, and if we can offer you better hospitality tonight we will gladly do so... some gin, by the way? Or tea? That much we can certainly do."

He sipped from his glass, held it blindly out to one side. A slave stepped forward to refill it. "And speaking for myself, I find this change regrettable. My discussions with you have been cordial and highly... promising. My first acquaintance with your new leader has been sorely lacking on both counts. However, I am inclined to think it would be unwise for me to take sides in an internal conflict within the Guild of Dawnsingers."

"We could hardly expect you to do that," said Jerya. "However, there may be a way you can still help us."

The rising sun threw long shadows ahead of them as they walked down the faded tan grass of the slope into the Dawnsingers' camp, Jerya and Evisyn side by side, Analind a few paces behind. By the time they reached the main campfire, everyone had gathered.

Perriad—of course—stepped forward. "I see you've decided running away was futile."

"Were you never taught not to jump to conclusions?" said Evisyn.

"There's a whole other land we could make for," added Jerya.

"You will address me as *Master Prime*."

"I think not," said Evisyn. "I think the words would strangle in my throat."

"How *dare* you!"

"I dare because some truths need to be heard. For the good of the Guild, and of the Sung Lands."

"We didn't go far last night, it's true," said Jerya. "We spoke with the Duke and his companions. I think it's fair to say they are dismayed by your first approach to them. They—and we—are very much afraid that you are throwing away all the good work that was done before your arrival."

"Good work?" scoffed Perriad. "Delivering Guild secrets into the hands
of *men*?"

"There you go again," said Evisyn with a theatrical sigh. "Do facts mean
nothing to you?"

"Facts? What facts?"

"First, the fact that we have *not* revealed any Guild secrets. Continue to
maintain otherwise and I will say you are either deluded, or a liar. We have
discussed the possibility of sharing knowledge in future, to the benefit of
both sides. Nothing of substance has been revealed, nor will be, without
the approval of the Conclave of Masters."

"*The possibility of sharing knowledge*," repeated Perriad, curling of her
lip in a sneer. "Shared... with these *men*. And wherever they actually come
from."

"But that's another fact," said Jerya. "However much you or anyone else
may mislike it, your feelings don't change the facts. The fact is that Terith,
Hillya, and Ezryn all saw the flag on Keldash Peak, Blawith's Dawnsinger
too. Any of you can see it for yourselves if you take a glass and climb a few
hundred metres up that ridge."

"A flag proves nothing."

"It proves *someone* was on that peak. Unless you think it blew up on the
wind and somehow got its pole wedged among the rocks?"

Somewhere behind Perriad, someone chuckled. Perriad whirled about.
"Who was that?" No one cared to own up. "I'll have the lot of you thrown
in confinement if no one admits it."

"How?" asked Evisyn, with a smile that made her face more hawkish than
ever.

Perriad spun back to face her. "What?"

"You just said you'll have everyone thrown in confinement. I couldn't
help wondering who's left to do the throwing." Perriad glowered but said
nothing. Evisyn went on, "But we were speaking of facts. There's the fact
that Kestyl observed smoke from beyond the ridge a few miles East of us,

and another fact is that six of us saw the Duke's party emerge from the narrows below what looks like a pass. Ask them."

She named three Peripatetics, now spread out among the Singers who'd arrived with Perriad. They confirmed what Evisyn had just said.

"I've heard more than enough of your renegade nonsense," declared Perriad. "Mazelik, put them back in the tent. All three of them, this time."

A young Singer, looking bloodless under a tan, took a nervous pace forward. "With respect, Master Prime, we haven't repaired the slit where they got out the first time."

"Then fix it now!"

"With respect, Master Prime... what with?"

Perriad hissed in frustration. Sensing that she might be close to cracking, Jerya faced her. "You really haven't thought this through, have you... any of it? Ever since I first arrived you've been casting doubt on the tale I carried, claiming it as mere fabrication. But you haven't been above lying yourself, when it suits your purposes, have you?"

Even though she was half-expecting it, the blow was a shock. Perriad's open-handed slap was delivered with enough force to rock her back on her heels. Through a ringing in her ears she barely heard Perriad say, "I'll take no lectures in truth from a Vow-breaker."

Jerya, shaking her head to clear her thoughts, saw Analind step forward. "It may not be part of the Vow, but one of the first things I ever learned as a Postulant was: *Dawnsinger shall not strike Dawnsinger.*"

"This woman is no Dawnsinger!"

"She was enough of a Dawnsinger when you had her incarcerated back in the College." Clearly this was news to most: Jerya saw startled glances, heard furtive muttering. Analind continued; she might seem calm on the surface but Jerya, who'd known her well, suspected she was seething with agitation underneath. "She was enough of a Dawnsinger to be subject to Guild discipline. I hear you were quite clear on that."

"You can hardly have it both ways, Master Perriad,"said Evisyn.

Analind looked about her, and Jerya saw that she had the complete attention of everyone present. "Sisters," said Analind, effectively ignoring Perriad and speaking past her to the others. Nothing, Jerya thought, could have been more effective. "Sisters, I think I hold my Vow as sacred as any of us. And yet, when I discovered Jerya's escape from confinement, and had the opportunity to prevent it... not only did I not do so, I joined her. I learned in that moment that sometimes there are bigger things than the letter of the law. When obedience to authority may not be in the best interest of the Guild or of the land." She took a breath, looked around again. Jerya was close enough to see that she was trembling, but her voice held steady. "If I had any doubts of that, the last few minutes have removed them. A woman who would strike another Dawnsinger—indeed, who would strike any other woman—is not someone I can willingly serve as my Master Prime."

Perriad was not quite finished yet. "You hear, Singers? Another of these renegades openly confesses to Vow-breaking. Throw them in the tent and watch the rear as well as the front."

No one moved. In the silence Jerya heard the clinking call of a stonechat.

"Do as I command!" raged Perriad.

Still there was no response. Then another young Singer took a pace forward. She could hardly be more than a year or two out of Novitiate, like Elifian; a girl, still, to Jerya's eyes. "Your pardon, Master Prime, but I for one would like to hear if they have anything else to say."

Jerya took that as her cue. She nodded to Evisyn, who turned to give the signal to the concealed watchers.

She smiled at the girl before she began. "We were talking about facts. And there is one fact above all others that Master Perriad has sought to deny. When I first arrived in the Precincts, I brought evidence that satisfied Masters such as Skarat and of course Evisyn, as well as Senior Tutor Jossena. Perriad continued to rubbish it. She used her ancient grudge against me to attack the messenger instead of scrutinising the message.

"There's another fact that comes into play. I was a Dawnsinger, at least a Novice, for a short time. Then I broke my Vow. That's true, and I've never denied it But I did so because, for me, the Guild, and most of all Master Perriad, broke a promise greater even than the Vow; the promise of truth.

"I broke my Vow, I left this land, and for the last ten years I have lived in the East, in the Five Principalities. There is another land there, beyond the mountains, and now we have visitors from there. That is the primary fact that Perriad has sought to deny... and when she could no longer deny it she sought to conceal it. She has deceived you, every one of you, again and again. It seems to me that is a breach of trust equal to any violation of the Vow."

"What would you have us do?" asked the girl.

"Listen to these men," said Jerya. "Just that, for now."

"Listen to Jerya, too," said Evisyn. "Listen, and decide for yourselves who you believe. Then you can decide what you want to do."

She heard footfalls on the gritty ground behind and turned to greet the newcomers. "Dawnsingers, may I present His Grace the Duke of Selton?"

❋

"We need a meeting of the Conclave," said Evisyn. "It's the only way to sort out this mess. But since they removed me, I can't call one."

"Master Vakosh is always fair," said Analind.

"Yea, but I think the safest approach might be to start with an approach to someone we know we can trust. Skarat or Jossena. Vakosh would listen to them. Give, let's say Skarat, the full story, let her decide how to put it to Vakosh."

"And how do we get a message to Skarat?" asked Jerya.

"By bird," said Evisyn. "None left in Blawith, thanks to Master Perriad, but Sarriet, down in Varsett, should have some."

"And where do we want the Conclave to convene?" asked Analind.

"By the Six, the Three and the One, that's a question... Many ways, I want to bring 'em here, best place to see the truth, but it'd take... I know we did it in five days, but not all the Masters could manage that kind o'riding. One or two probably wouldn't take kindly to being shoved in a saddle at all." Evisyn snickered, but her amusement was ephemeral. "But for us to get back, that's still five days. What we need is somewhere in between."

"What about the Observatory?" said Jerya.

Evisyn swung toward her with a grin. "Perfect, Jerya, it's just the place. They can get there in a day, and by carriage for those who don't fancy riding. And we... a few hours down to Varsett, send the message, overnight there; then a long day down to Carevick. Charter a river-boat. Downstream, this time o'year, a fast vessel can make better speed than we could, short of killing the horses. Disembark below Kendrigg... we could walk up to the Observatory if needs be. Still be there by nightfall two days hence."

She whirled back to Analind. "Tell everyone to start packing up, I want to leave for Varsett in an hour. Jerya, let's you and I go have a word with His Grace."

"One question," said Analind.

"Mm?"

"What about Master Perriad?"

"She can stay here and rot, far as I'm concerned. Or she can saddle her horse and come with us."

CHAPTER 34

HEDRIC

To The Editors, Proceedings of the Denvirran Society for Natural Philosophy.

From: The Hon. Hedric of Kirwaugh, A.D.S.N.P.

Written at Skilthorn, in the month of Calorander.

Esteemed Sirs,

I beg leave to lay before your Readers a preliminary account of a Journey of Exploration undertaken in the months of Meadander and Gleander just past. I assure myself, and your selves, that no one, once acquainted with the facts of this Expedition, will accuse me of exaggeration when I say that it is of exceptional significance; presenting, as it does, the answer to a question which has undoubtedly at some time exercised every educated mind in the Five Principalities.

It is my earnest intent, at the earliest possible date, to offer for publication a full account of our Travels and what we have seen, but with the best will in the world I cannot suppose that it will be possible to present a fully corrected Text, and to prepare the maps and illustrations required, before the end of the year. I beg the indulgence of the Society, and of a wider readership, in this, and can only express my hope that this preliminary Digest will convey sufficient of the essential facts to satisfy the most urgent curiosity; Curiosity being, after all, what drives us in the investigation of Natural Philosophy.

He sat back for a moment, looked around. He would far rather be in his own study at Kirwaugh but the Lesser Library had always struck him as the most congenial room at Skilthorn. He wondered whether Jerya would feel the same. He knew her ambivalence about the title 'Countess'; he suspected her equilibrium would be further strained by Skilthorn itself. Perhaps a room like this would help reconcile her to it all.

But that was distraction; he had a job to do, and no more than two hours to complete both draft and fair copy, if the package was to go by today's post.

He finished the covering letter and turned at once to the factual report, reminding himself that it was the barest bones that were needed now.

A Brief Account of a Journey of Exploration. Including the Crossing of the Dividing Range, and Some Remarks on What Lies Beyond.

We departed from Drumlenn on the twenty-fifth day of Gleander, a party of three, plus a couple of slaves tasked to take back the horses from the point where we must continue on foot. The three of us were myself, my attendant Lallon bey-Kirwaugh, and Miss Jerya Delven of Duncal, in the bailiwick of Drumlenn.

I can have no doubt that many readers will be surprised by the inclusion of a young lady in a party of Exploration. Let me at this point simply avow unequivocally that Miss Delven proved herself entirely equal to the rigours of the journey, as will soon become clear. More than this, as will also become clear, she was in many ways the instigator of this adventure.

We proceeded up a long valley, North-West of Drumlenn, unnamed on the regular Principality maps, though I am assured it is known locally as Birkrilldale. We reached its head well into the afternoon of the second day. To my eyes the way onward looked impregnable, the valley ending in a grand Cirque of Crags four to five hundred feet in height. However, Miss Delven stated categorically that, not only was it climbable, she had herself climbed, or rather descended, it on a previous occasion. I had, and retain, full confidence in her veracity, and in any case every assertion she made prior to our Journey was fully borne out in due course. That the Crags were indeed climbable was proven the next morning.

He paused again. That climb would make a full chapter, and an exciting one, in the longer monograph, but for now he must restrain himself. *Bare bones.* It felt wrong to consign the climb to a few dry sentences, but needs must. In similar vein he whisked through the rest of the Crossing, to the point where they topped the second pass.

A short way down from this Watershed, Miss Delven turned to us and said, 'Welcome to the Sung Lands'.

The import of the name, the Sung Lands, will become clear as my narrative proceeds; as it did, indeed, for me early in the morning of the second day following. From a camp on the edge of a moor, the mountains behind and a further declivity ahead, we heard a voice raised in song. A Female Voice: a Dawnsinger.

We met that Singer later that morning: a woman clad all in white and with a perfectly Bald head. I was glad that Miss Jerya had forewarned us that this is how Dawnsingers distinguish themselves.

As I have said already, I rest full trust in Miss Delven, but even if I had harboured any doubts about the stories she had told me, they would now have been banished. The said Dawnsinger was by no means alone in this Place, which is called Delven. Further, it was manifest that she had prior acquaintance with Miss Jerya, and I soon received further, unequivocal, testimony that Delven was where Miss Jerya had been born and raised.

Her full story—and it is quite a tale—is really hers to tell, and I very much hope that she will give us her own account as a Chapter, or perhaps an Appendix, in the full monograph which I purpose to write this Winter.

He stopped again. *I very much hope...* but there was only hope, no certainty. And when he thought of the journey, the passes, the precipice, all of which she would, most probably, have to negotiate on her own...

Hedric shivered, as if the chill of the mountains had invaded the book-lined room with its cheery fire. Riding away from Carwerid, he had almost turned back more than once, wrestling with the nagging sense that he had abandoned Jerya. Even after turning back no longer seemed a viable choice, as when he and Lallon were slithering down the crags, he had felt again and again that he had done wrong in leaving her. That she had made no protest, had even seemed to encourage him, was not enough to assuage his doubt. 'I'm afraid you must go; a lot may rest upon it,' she had said, but had she merely been putting a brave face on things?

His uneasy conscience was bad enough, but behind it there was something else, something starker. He was, when he allowed himself to think of it, terrified that he might never see her again.

But there's nothing you can do about it now... he told himself. *And this still has to be written.* He could chew on his fears later, instead of sleeping.

Dipping the pen, driving his mind back into the task, he resumed. He passed quickly over the journey to Carwerid. There would be plenty to say in the monograph, two or three sketches to accompany it; some more accomplished artist could work them up into something fit for the engraver. For now, the central matter of the whole tale was the College of the Dawnsingers, and what had transpired there.

He thought about them now, those women. They might look alike, with their bald heads and white vestments, but each one he had met was individual and distinct to him. Yanil, the first he had spoken to in that place; Perriad, truculent and suspicious; the Master Prime, the voice of calm; Evisyn, passionate and decisive; Analind... Analind he had found harder to apprehend. She and Jerya had been close, once, but there was a tension between them; he could grasp that much.

Those five, and many more. Names he recalled, names he had never known. Far from alike, yet all with this in common; collectively and individually, they were the real power in the Sung Lands. No woman in the Five Principalities could know how that felt.

He wondered again how Jerya could have borne to leave that behind. Did that add to the appeal of becoming a Countess, or did even that exalted rank seem shabby in comparison?

In the full monograph he could give pen-sketches of each of the key players, but for now he decided it was simplest not even to name them, only to say that there was discord.

In the Five Principalities it is widely believed that there is no life West of the Dividing Range. I can, of course, now categorically state that this belief is erroneous. It may strike my readers as ironic that this belief is exactly mirrored in the Sung Lands, and that a faction among the Dawnsingers clung to it even in the face of the Evidence we presented. Indeed, it remained to be seen, at the point when I was obliged to take my leave, which side of the argument would prevail.

If some there could cling to disbelief, despite physical evidence and the clear testimony of the three of us, I must suppose it probable that there will be some in the Five Principalities, even some among my present Readers, who will respond in like manner.

To all such doubters, I observe, first, that I too have in my possession certain items which I can produce in Corroboration of my account. These include Maps and a pocket-watch, in direct symmetry with the evidence we presented in Carwerid. In the interim, Fellows of the Guild are welcome to examine these if they wish to present themselves to me; I will be found either at Skilthorn or at my own home at Kirwaugh.

I note further than a large expedition led by His Grace the Duke of Selton had also set out seeking a Crossing, in a region somewhat South of ours. Supposing that they do in due course succeed, their return will bring further testimony; is the word of a gentleman of the highest rank in the Denvirran nobility still to be doubted?

I also observe that it is now open to anyone to seek corroboration for himself. The sketch-map accompanying this account will give a general idea of our route, and if anyone wishes to apply to me I shall willingly supply further detail. I caution, however, that there may be little time left this year to make a Crossing, and less still in which to return. Miss Delven, more experienced in mountains than myself, opined that the passes might be closed by snow at almost any time, and thought it unlikely indeed that they would remain viable beyond the end of Veremander.

He stopped again, chewing the end of his pen. Jerya's considered opinion was one thing, but she had also said that mountain weather was fickle. If she left her departure too late… well, she was bold but not, he thought, foolhardy. Surely she would turn back rather than hazard herself unreasonably. In such a case her return might be delayed six months or more, but at least she would return.

But that would mean six months—or seven, or eight—of not knowing, and that would be agony.

He sighed, shook his head, and picked up his pen again.

CHAPTER 35

JERYA

Perriad had been quiet throughout the journey, almost to the point of meekness. Even Jerya, who had less reason than most to care for the abrasive Master, had begun to wonder if something had broken inside her.

Now, as she sat with Analind and the rest of the roving party observing the start of the Conclave, it was clear to her, and probably to all, that Perriad had merely been biding her time.

"Masters," she began with all her usual sonority, "I am sure you need no telling that it is not at my instigation that you have been dragged so far from your usual haunts, foisted with the cold rooms and hard beds which are our lot here." That was empty rhetoric, thought Jerya. Kendrigg's rooms and beds were simple, true, but they had never struck her as either cold or hard. *But empty rhetoric's her stock in trade.*

"Nor do you need me to tell you that I had no hand in instigating this absurd proceeding. I must question whether this meeting has even been convened in accordance with due practice."

"Do not concern yourself on that account," said Vakosh, a short woman with very dark eyes set deep in a narrow pale face. "We have taken great care to assure ourselves that procedure was followed. There are precedents for the Conclave meeting here, not least for the solar eclipse of—"

"Never mind your precious eclipse," snapped Perriad. "I'll take your word for the procedural question. That was always a secondary point. My main question, quite simply, my Masters, is... what is the point of this meeting?" She paused a beat; several listeners leaned closer. "Ten days ago this Conclave met—in perfect accord with procedure—and voted to unseat Master Evisyn—*former* Master Evisyn—and to appoint me Master Prime. What possible justification can there be for revisiting those decisions in so short a span of time?"

"The reason for challenge," said Vakosh. "Is that the Conclave was not fully aware of all relevant facts on the first occasion. Furthermore, and very pertinently, it is alleged that important facts—*vital* facts—were deliberately withheld, by none other than yourself."

"*Vital* facts?" scoffed Perriad. "More vital than the *fact* that a Master of the Guild aided and abetted the escape of a Vow-breaker who had been duly convicted and confined... by the order, need I remind you, of this very Conclave?"

"I think the Conclave may consider that the presence of visitors from beyond the Sundering Wall is of greater impor—"

"—*If* you believe that is what they are."

Vakosh could no longer fully conceal her irritation. "I *believe* that the Conclave needs to see and question these men in order to reach a definitive view. And I will say, Master Perriad—"

"Master Prime, if you please."

"Master Prime, then, if you will. You have consistently sought to deny us any opportunity even to scrutinise the evidence. I assure you now that the Conclave is resolved to consider the evidence in full, but a clear majority takes the view that our first order of business must be to re-evaluate the decisions of our last full meeting."

Vakosh took a sip of water, then picked up a sheet of paper. She glanced at it but did not, yet, read from it. "We have heard a great deal lately about the meaning of the Vow and its central place in the life of the Guild. None of us would deny or belittle it, of course, but perhaps we have lost sight of what the Vow is for—what the Guild itself is for. The Guild does not exist merely to perpetuate itself; there is a higher purpose. I would suggest we need to remind ourselves of that rather more frequently, and more forcefully, than we have been doing. Above all, in the end we are *servants*.

"There is another aspect we may have lost sight of. Here, with the Conclave's permission, I will read some words given to me by Master Evisyn."

"Former Master Evisyn," objected Perriad, but her tone was almost resigned.

Vakosh made no comment, just lifted the paper and began. Jerya recognised the words at once. They had, after all, been crafted by herself and Evisyn, with a few comments from Analind, close to midnight in the inn at Carevick. *"Sometimes the most important things are not spoken, not laid down in Vow or rule. Nowhere is it written in so many words that Dawnsinger shall not raise hand against Dawnsinger, yet it is an imperative we all absorb in the first weeks of Postulancy. Any violation of this principle is deeply shocking, as when Master Perriad, in front of a dozen witnesses, struck Jerya.*

"Another equally fundamental law is also unwritten and—usually—unspoken,. We would argue that it is a promise of the Guild to all its members: Dawnsinger shall not deceive *Dawnsinger.*

"Perhaps these promises should be explicit in our Vow,, but that is a discussion for the future. We would, nonetheless, argue that violations of such principles must be treated with at least equal seriousness as direct violations of the Vow. We would even suggest that, under certain circumstances, adherence to these principles may excuse apparent violation of the Vow. The Vow commands obedience to duly constituted authority... but when that duly constituted authority practices deceit, does that not in itself represent a violation? On such an occasion, we contend, defiance of authority, breaching the apparent letter of the law, may be not only excusable but essential to preserve the higher principle."

Vakosh laid down the paper, its quiet rustle easily audible in the dense silence. "My Masters, I can, if you require, recount for you the full litany of occasions on which Master Perriad has sought to deceive this Conclave. She has attacked and undermined evidence, she has concealed facts, she has made explicit statements which we all now know to be untrue. I only ask if we need to hear the full list again."

"I don't think we need to hear it," said a dark, elderly, Master whose name Jerya did not know, "As long as it is entered into the record in full."

"It shall be," said Vakosh, nodding to the record-keepers. "Very well. I'm sure none of us relish the thought of hearing that sorry catalogue again. May I therefore proceed to the first motion for voting? *Resolved: that Master Perriad be requested to surrender the office of Master Prime with immediate effect.* Masters, how say you?"

There were fourteen in favour, three abstentions, and one opposed. Vakosh, acting the role of Master Prime, did not vote, and Perriad, still claiming the prerogative, also sat mute.

"Master Perriad," said Vakosh, "The Conclave invites you to surrender your office. Will you do so with grace?"

"Grace?" snarled Perriad. "You dare speak to me of grace? I will give you no such satisfaction."

Vakosh sighed, saddened but surely not surprised. "Then I must invoke the provisions of Section 4 of the Articles of Order. I don't believe this has ever before been invoked in the long history of our Guild." *This is a sad day,* her tone said. "Conclave, the supplementary motion is: *Resolved: that Master Perriad be* required *to surrender the office of Master Prime with immediate effect.* Masters, how say you?"

This time there were fourteen in favour, three abstentions, and two opposed, Perriad herself voting this time.

"Master Perriad," said Vakosh, "You are no longer Master Prime. Kindly vacate the head seat."

Perriad, scowling, obviously considered staying put, but after a few agonising seconds gave a heavy sigh and moved to an empty seat at the farther end of the table—actually a hastily-assembled collection of dining tables. The dining room was the only chamber at Kendrigg large enough to hold the Conclave, and even so the observers were obliged to stand against the walls.

"Now," said Vakosh, "We have at least three further questions to consider in relation to the composition of this Conclave, and I suggest we should resolve them all before we turn to other matters. I am unsure, however, in which order these are best taken. There is the question of whether Master Perriad retain her seat on the Conclave—and, if not, who should replace her. There is the question of the installation of a new Master Prime. And—"

"—Forgive me, Master Vakosh," said Kurslan. "You said 'installation of a new Master Prime'. Do we not now know that we perpetrated a great wrong against the former Master Prime? Should we not seek to redress this? Surely our first order of business should be to reinstate her?"

"I entirely agree that a great wrong was done," said Vakosh. "However, Singer Katellen has indicated that she does not wish for reinstatement. She told a few of us that, having served eleven years, she feels she has been in place long enough. I asked if she would return as a plain Conclave member, without portfolio, and she requested some time to consider."

Kurslan nodded. "My pardon for interrupting."

"No matter... The third question we should discuss is the reinstatement of Master Evisyn."

The elderly Master, whose name Jerya did not know, raised a hand. "May I suggest we consider Evisyn's case first? It seems to me we should have all possible seats filled before discussing the Primacy, in particular."

No one objected to that, though Perriad's glare looked fit to ignite the papers on the table..

"I think we are all familiar with the facts of the case," said Vakosh. "Evisyn, is there anything you wish to say?"

Evisyn stood. "Thank you, Master Vakosh. I think the closing lines of the statement you read out are the best expression of my position."

That, thought Jerya, was Evisyn to the core. To some, it might look like arrogance; she hoped none of the Masters would see it that way. For Evisyn, it was simply that she had already expressed herself as well as she could (as *they* could) and didn't see the point in burdening them with more.

Fortunately, the Masters already knew Evisyn's ways, or they had worked themselves into a forgiving mood. The vote mirrored the first: fourteen, three, and one. Evisyn was welcomed back to the table. Jerya couldn't help wondering how many of the Masters now smiling and murmuring greetings had voted in her favour the first time. A minority, besure. *Well, maybe some are genuinely remorseful.*

"There remain," said Vakosh, "The question of the Primacy and the motion for the dismissal of Master Perriad from this Conclave. Can anyone suggest which we should take first?"

"Logically," said Kurslan after an uncomfortable pause, "It seems to me we should consider Perriad's position first. It makes little sense to me that we should allow her to vote on so vital a matter if our very next step is to strip her of the vote."

No one had anything to say against that.

"Very well," said Vakosh, "The motion is: *Resolved: that Master Perriad be requested to surrender the honour of Master with immediate effect.* Master Perriad, have you anything to say?"

"I am sure you have made up your minds already. I doubt very much any words from me will deflect you from your predestined course. And in any case I am not sure I wish to be part of so fickle and reckless a body."

"Has anyone else anything to say?" One hand was raised. "Yes, Master Evisyn?"

"You all know that Master Perriad and I have clashed many times in the past. We disagree profoundly about what is best for the Guild, even about the question you alluded to, Master Vakosh, namely what the Guild exists for in the first place. Given this history, and especially in light of all that's happened in the past couple of weeks, you might expect me to say I would be glad to see the back of her. And perhaps, in my selfish heart, I would... but at the same time I wonder if it is really a good thing to lose dissenting voices. Our thinking is surely better for being robustly challenged."

"Are you saying you would vote against her removal?" asked Kurslan in apparent disbelief.

Evisyn shrugged. "I think I'm saying I could yet be persuaded either way."

"You are more magnanimous than I," said Syrtos. "I'm still enraged at the way we were hoodwinked. I certainly take your point, Master Evisyn, about the positive value of dissent, but I think we must look elsewhere for such voices. I can see no place on this Conclave for one who repeatedly and deliberately misled us."

Evisyn gave a single slow nod. A few other Masters spoke to similar effect. No one else came close to defending Perriad's place. This time there were no opposing votes and fifteen hands were raised for dismissal.

Without a word Perriad rose and left the chamber. If you said nothing else for her, thought Jerya, she knew how to make a dignified exit.

The door had barely closed behind her before Vakosh was inviting nominations for the Primacy.

"I nominate Master Evisyn," said the elderly Master.

"What?" cried Evisyn herself, obviously shocked.

"Would you care to explain, Master Tambren?" said Vakosh.

Tambren spoke quietly, her voice dry as rustling paper. Everyone sat still and silent to hear her. "It had crossed my mind before that she would be a fine candidate. Her courage and resolve, her determination to serve the higher purpose, impressed me greatly. But I wasn't quite convinced until just now, when she spoke about the need to embrace dissent within the Conclave. I believe, though she might have expressed it differently, that is a principle Master Pri—I beg your pardon, Master Katellen—also held dear."

Several others spoke up in support, and no one offered any alternative nominations. Vakosh appeared to be about to move to a vote, when Evisyn herself raised a hand. "My Masters, you do me great honour, but no one has asked me if I am willing to accept."

"It would be a sad day for the Guild if you did not," said Tambren.

Evisyn inclined her head. "Will you allow me to share my thoughts? Perhaps in doing so I can see my own path clearly."

"Please," said Vakosh.

"You'll forgive me if I move around?" said Evisyn. "It helps me think." She began to pace the floor, sandals whispering on the age-dark boards.

"Since I was a young Novice, I knew I wanted to be a Peripatetic. Everything about it seemed to call to me. It almost felt like I was made for it. I suppose I have a restless soul... look at me now." She gave a rueful smile. "I hate to sit, unless on a horse. Seeing new places—and new faces... but I don't think I am simply indulging myself. I believe it is essential that the Guild maintain good contact with all Singers, including the most remote places." Jerya thought of Sharess—and of Marit, too.

"It's equally important that we are aware of all that's going on in our land," continued Evisyn. "After all, the land and the people are the reason we, the Guild, exists. We are servants, not masters. Some—I mention no names—might have lost sight of that.

"As a Peripatetic, as one who loves to roam... well, you can surely imagine how I felt when I first heard the news Jerya brought. We've all looked at the mountains and wondered, haven't we? Now we learn that there is a whole other land there. A very different land, it seems, but that is what fascinates me, what *lures* me. As Master of Peripatetics I could make a good case for being one of the first to visit... I cannot say *the* first, because that distinction was claimed ten years ago." She gestured toward Jerya, flashed an ephemeral smile. "Perhaps the first to visit as official representative of the Guild... As Master of Peripatetics I could, as Master Prime I surely could not. And to my selfish heart that is a powerful reason to refuse the honour you offer me."

She sighed. "But I just said we are servants, not masters. If I meant that, if it's not just empty rhetoric, then I must be guided by what's best for the Guild... I can't judge if I am the best person to lead you. You've heard what I've said, you know how I've acted; I submit to your judgement.

"Just one thing more, my Masters. Master Katellen says that eleven years was enough. I think we might consider whether a shorter term would be even better. If you want me, I will promise you five years, and then both you and I should have the opportunity to think again. I suppose in five years time I'll still be young enough to pick up saddle and harness once more."

Within two minutes of retaking her seat, Evisyn had been elected Master Prime by unanimous vote.

Jerya was startled to receive a fervent hug from Analind. She had never seen her old friend so exuberant.

After a brief ceremony of investiture, Vakosh yielded the chair to Evisyn. "Thank you, Master Vakosh. I hope we can move swiftly on to address the real issue before us; our visitors from the East and all that follows from their coming. But I believe we now have two vacancies on the Conclave: Master of Records and Master of Peripatetics. Has anyone any nominations for the former?"

"May I suggest Tutor Brinbeth?" said Kurslan at once.

"Admirable," said Evisyn. "But since she isn't here we can't proceed immediately. I suppose we can wait till we get back to the city. Very well, then... does anyone have any nominations for Master of Peripatetics? No? Then may I offer a name myself? One who is present among us? She's young for elevation, but I believe she has the right qualities. An able Peripatetic *and* a fine cartographer, but more than that, a woman of true integrity, who wrestled mightily with the fear that she might be breaking her Vow but listened to argument and put the greater interest of the Guild first; and who, once she'd made that choice, followed through with complete resolution. Masters, I unreservedly commend Singer Analind for your approval."

As the speech went on, Analind had gone very still. It was hardly possible for her face to go pale, but colour seemed to leach from her cheeks. Inconspicuously, Jerya grasped her arm.

"Are you willing to be considered?" Evisyn asked her.

Analind took a hesitant step. "I don't feel worthy... I can only repeat what you just said, Master Prime: I can't judge if I am the best person for this; I submit to your judgement."

❋

"I was about to say it's just like old times," said Jerya, "But I never shared a room with a Master of the Guild before."

"Please, Jerya, don't remind me. I know it's a great honour and all that, but... can't we just be ourselves? As if it *was* old times?"

Jerya squeezed her arm apologetically. "Of course we can. Sorry." She looked around the room. "It's much the same size, I guess, but doesn't look much like our old place. Wood everywhere, instead of stone."

"Makes it feel warmer, don't you think? And it smells nice."

"Yes. I remember the first time I was here, how strange it was. I grew up with stone all around. Never saw anything larger than a beehive built from wood till I was nineteen."

Analind looked at her, and suddenly laughed. "What?" asked Jerya.

"I was just thinking how I used to shave you sometimes. And... well, look at you now."

Jerya, smiling, began to let down her hair. Then it was her turn to laugh, Analind's to look quizzical. "I don't suppose you have a hairbrush with you?" she said.

Then they were both convulsed with giggles. There was a lot more behind it than the absurdity of asking a bald woman for a hairbrush. It was a letting-go. They had scarcely been able to relax since the night of Jerya's escape, ten days ago. Perriad's final ousting, Evisyn's election to the Primacy, had closed a chapter.

A chapter, she thought, *not the whole book. But, yes, tonight, we can laugh.*

When she could speak again, Jerya said, "It's a personal thing to ask, with someone you don't know. Draff, I managed half my life with nothing but my fingers. I've grown soft, there in the East."

Analind watched as she finished unpinning her hair, began to run fingers through its tangles. "It seems like it's a lot easier being bald."

"I'm sure it is, especially for Dawnsingers, never having to shave... "

"You said slaves are all bald? Do they have to shave regularly, or do they have something like the cream that we use?"

"They shave. And I'm not sure they'd want the cream even if they could get it." Jerya began to braid one side. Analind, after seeking permission with a look and a gesture, added her own efforts on the other. Jerya explained about the Crest and topknot. "I'm sure Railu would be entitled to wear the Crest, if only her hair would grow."

"So there are distinctions even among slaves?"

"Yes, very m—don't tug too hard, please."

"Sorry."

"It's all right. Yes, Railu would be entitled. She carries a lot of respect." *Not to mention the undying gratitude of her owners for giving them a son...* "Her position in the household is unusual; but then it's an unusual household. If you knew how Hedric's uncle uses his slaves... and he's far from the only one."

The sooner Hedric inherits, the better it will be for all those people. And, one way or another, he needs a wife...

Chapter 36

Jerya

"We need to think about timing," said Evisyn, seated behind the Superintendent's desk. The room felt crowded with eight in it, but Jerya could quite see that all who were present needed to be there. "Your Grace..." The Dawnsingers were growing accustomed to the honorific, though Jerya had heard one or two laughing about it out of earshot of the Easterners. "Remind me, please. You wish to be on your way back across the mountains... when?"

"I would not be confident of the way remaining passable beyond another four weeks, Master Prime. And if we do miss this chance, it might be six months or more before we get another." This time, he made no flippant remarks about daughters and weddings.

Evisyn nodded. "Aye, I've often seen snow well down the mountains when it's still summer in the lowlands. Your caution seems well-grounded."

"You understand, Master Prime, it's not that I'm anxious to leave for any other reason. I cannot fault your hospitality and we are keen to see more of your land."

"And I'm sure we can oblige you in that. It's only a day's journey to Carwerid, after all, going downstream. We should allow a day or two for arrangements to be settled there—I'm sure you'll understand we can't accommodate you in the Precincts. Still, if you have four weeks, we can plan for at least two in the capital."

"That would be most welcome, Master Prime."

"However, you did suggest earlier that you might wish to send one or two of your party back sooner—if I understood correctly?"

"You understood perfectly, Master Prime. I think it would be well to send some word back. To reassure friends and families at home that all is well... and to prepare the ground for what will come as a shock to so many."

"Whom do you propose to send?"

"There is an obvious candidate. My son, Tavy, is due to start his University course soon; a further four-weeks delay would make him late."

"You surely don't mean to send him back alone?"

"No, Master Prime, certainly not. I will send my own attendant with him. Currick is no ordinary slave, I assure you, but a most competent man. I would hardly entrust my son and heir to anyone less able."

"I'm sure," said Evisyn. "But it's often said there is safety in numbers. Would you have any objection to a couple of our people accompanying them?" She looked up, met Jerya's gaze. "Jerya, you have said more than once that you are anxious to return home."

"Yes, Master Prime, and to keep my promises... but I can remain another few weeks if I can be of any further use here."

"You have done inestimable service to the Guild already... and had poor thanks for your endeavours, it seems to me. I'm sure there's much more you could contribute, but you've laid the groundwork so well that we no longer need you quite as we did." She smiled. "And we'll have a few days yet to pump you dry."

Jerya hardly knew what to say. The thought that, in less than two weeks, she might see Hedric again, and Embrel, and the others, was almost too alluring to bear. But it also meant that she would not see Rodal and Annyt again. *Not this time, anyway*, she told herself; surely crossing the mountains would soon become easier, a regular thing. But there was also Sharess. Sharess who, the very first time they had spoken, had feared herself nearing the end of her life. They had so much more to say to each other.

How did she balance them against each other? The man to whom she was, privately, betrothed? The boy who was almost a surrogate son? The mother she barely knew?

She sighed, deciding. "You may wish to pump me dry in the next few days, Master Prime, but I must claim some time for my own. There are several letters I must write, to people in Carwerid, and they won't be brief ones. And if the Duke is willing, perhaps his party, when they do return, can convey any replies?"

The Duke bowed. "If we can do you that small service, my lady, it will give us the greatest pleasure."

"Excellent," said Evisyn. "And I don't propose to send you alone. I think it high time that one of us—one of the Conclave, ideally—see the Five Principalities for herself."

Unable to contain herself, she sprang up, her chair grating on the floorboards. She began to pace, behind the desk, but there was only room for three or four of her long strides. After a couple of turns she gave up, settled for standing behind the chair, gripping hard on the uprights of its back. "It won't surprise any of you if I say I long to go myself. But I knew the price when I accepted the Primacy. Perhaps in a few years... I did say I'd serve for five, after all... In any case, we have to find another, and I don't think we'll find a better candidate than our Master of Peripatetics."

For the second time in two days Jerya saw Analind struck dumb. The previous time, her first emotion had been dismay, if not terror. This time, thought Jerya, it was something very different: yearning, eagerness. But then the new Master shook her head. "How can it be possible, Master Prime? The Duke said, and you agreed, that the pass is likely to be closed for six months or more. I'm barely a day into my... my Mastership. How can I leave those responsibilities for half a year, if not longer?"

"Well," said Evisyn, "The responsibility I'm offering is a greater one, I think. Neither I nor the majority of the Conclave still harbour any doubt that there is life beyond the Sundering Wall, but Perriad clings to her delusion, and she may still find others willing to be persuaded. The best way I can think of to stifle any remaining doubts is to send someone that we all trust, as witness. If it is possible to make the Crossing, see what you need to see, and return before winter, so much the better, but if you have to wait till spring..." She glanced at Jerya. "If you can assure us of her safety...?"

"The Crossing is the most hazardous part, and from what I can gather the Southern route is perhaps longer, but less difficult, than the Northern route I've taken twice now. And, with a few precautions, I see no reason for concern about Analind's—*Master* Analind's—safety in the Five Principalities."

"There's risk in everything," said Analind, moving toward acceptance. "I can fall from my horse anywhere."

"You're a better horsewoman than you've ever let yourself admit," said Evisyn, smiling. "And, well, if it does take six months... I'm sure we can find someone capable enough to take care of things... and if she should need guidance, her predecessor will be always on hand to offer it."

Analind absorbed this, silent for a long moment. Evisyn moved as if about to begin pacing again, but restrained herself, resetting her grip on the chair.

"If you truly think me capable," said Analind, "Then, yes, I accept."

Jerya found herself beaming. The thought that she would have Analind's company on the journey—and perhaps for a good while longer—felt like the best news she'd had in many days.

CHAPTER 37

JERYA

The sun was low in the West when they came over the last rise of pale bare moor and looked down on Blawith in its bowl. Where the light caught the clouds they were the pale gold of buttermilk, but the shadows went from mauve down to indigo.

"Looks stormy," said Analind.

Jerya had seen clouds massed like that many times over the mountains around Delven. Sometimes she'd heard thunder grumbling within them, echoing again and again off the peaks: but more often, she thought, they had been silent. "We'll see tomorrow."

The village Dawnsinger, Sellet, emerged from her cottage, on a rise West of the village, to welcome them. They walked down into the village together. Jerya saw again that Sellet's relations with the villagers were much closer than in Delven. There was still respect, even deference, but no one, not even the children, turned away or fled as Jerya herself had been schooled to do. Which, she wondered, was more typical—or were both outliers, the norm somewhere between?

It would be very easy to yield to anger, she thought; because Delven did things differently, she had been deprived of even superficial acquaintance with the woman who turned out to be her own mother. But she had made peace with that, or at least hoped she had. Instead she told herself *Railu would approve of this.* Thinking of her friend, she carried on into the narrow cobbled alleys of the village with a smile on her face.

It seemed they would all dine together too; the four travellers, Sellet, the Headman and Elderwife, and a few others who seemed to be the notables of the place, two of them women. They were ushered into a sizeable room—she never did quite work out whether it was someone's home or a communal space—lit by a blazing fire at one end and a comfortable abundance of candles elsewhere. The tables were well-lit, but the joists and struts of the roof were only suggestions in flickering shadow.

Familiarity did not quite extend to seating the Dawnsingers at the same table as the others, but after brief discussion Jerya found herself placed with her and Analind. Drinks were fetched at once and toasts went between the tables. Baskets of bread came next; being hungry, Jerya was quick to grab a piece.

In the interval before the meal itself arrived, Sellet leaned closer to the other two. "I heard a rumour, day before yesterday. A couple of the men said they were out in the drumlin country, after hares or whatever they could get, when they saw a Dawnsinger in the distance, walking East. They may have been mistaken, of course. There's no trail there, and there was mist about that morning—and why would any Singer come up this way and not stop by here, if only for some refreshments?"

Jerya and Analind looked at each other, silently wondering.

They departed early and were back at their former campsite by mid-morning. The clouds were shredding in a freshening breeze from the North-West, the peaks emerging as if shrugging off heavy cloaks. They handed the borrowed horses back to the Blawith men, shifted their loads to their own backs, and set off.

This was as far as Jerya or Analind had been. "You've been this way before," said Jerya to Tavy and Currick. "You're in the lead." Currick, a tall, gawky man who made even Lallon seem garrulous, merely looked at his boots. Tavy, on the other hand, was clearly pleased, though he modestly disclaimed, "Well, it's obvious enough at first."

For a while Jerya was preoccupied with the usual business of the start of a trek, getting her pack properly settled, reacclimatising herself to its weight, tweaking the lacing of her boots. Then, as they came over a slight swell of land and got their first clear view of the braided gravel channels that spilled out from the Defile, she saw that Tavy, a few strides ahead, had stopped. She came up alongside him and saw why. "Whose tent is that?"

"I don't know," he said. "Doesn't look like one of ours... and it's a dashed stupid place to pitch. If there *had* been a storm last night they'd have been right in the path of a flash flood. Father said never to go through this first section if there was rain about."

They walked on, curiosity lending haste. As they drew nearer Jerya could see that the tent was small, suited to one or two people, and well-worn. Its canvas might once have been yellow but had faded to a pale parchment hue.

The flaps facing them were not laced, and Jerya had a strong sense of someone within, watching. When they were perhaps ten metres short, a hand parted the flaps, and a figure emerged, crawling as one must from a small tent.

Jerya found that she wasn't surprised. A quick glance at Analind showed that neither was she.

※

The last days had not been kind to former Master Perriad. She wore a gold-trimmed robe, as if she were still a Master, but the thread was fraying at one cuff, and the white wool was grubby, especially around the knees. Jerya wondered exactly what Perriad had been doing to spend so much time on her knees.

But it was the smile that split Perriad's face which sent a chill down Jerya's spine. It was gleeful, even triumphant, but there was something else behind it. A word came to Jerya's mind like a crow she'd once seen, appearing out of the night like darkness becoming solid, settling in a tree at the edge of the firelight.

The word was 'madness'.

A hard word, maybe, but there was definitely something unbalanced, off-kilter, about Perriad now. She slowly looked the two of them up and down before speaking. "I knew *you* would come. But little Analind too... that is a surprise."

"It's Master Analind now."

Perriad blinked, twice, then barked a laugh. "So a Conclave of turncoats is handing out titles to all and sundry now, is it? "

"You were happy enough with the makeup of the Conclave when they named you Master Prime."

"They turned their coats soon enough," said Perriad sourly. She stalked, stiff-legged, away from the tent, a few paces taking her into the sunlight. "What happened to loyalty? What happened to *deference*?"

"They are two very different things," said Analind.

"Maybe... and which is enshrined in the Vow?"

"*I shall defer at all times to duly instituted authority*," Jerya quoted. "It seems to me you sacrificed any claim to legitimacy by repeatedly mislead—"

"You dare to lecture *me* about legitimacy? You, of all people!"

"Yes, I dare. Besides, the Conclave took the same view."

"Whatever the rights and wrongs of Jerya's actions ten years ago," said Analind, "She was a Novice, and new to the Guild. You were a Master, and then Master Prime. You had to be held to a higher standard."

It was as if Perriad hadn't heard a word; almost as if Analind didn't even exist. "I had hopes for you, Novice Jerya. Gave you time and attention like no other Novice. And how did you repay me?"

Jerya reached a conclusion. It was pointless to expect reason to prevail with one who was now operating on the further fringes of rationality, if she could still be called rational at all.

She took a couple of steps closer to Perriad, who was hugging her arms around herself as if cold. despite the warm sunshine. "Singer Perriad," she began.

"It's *Master Prime* Perriad."

Jerya couldn't help recalling Evisyn's response to the same demand: *I think the words would strangle in my throat.* "No, it isn't," she said, "You were installed by *duly instituted authority*—and you were uninstalled the same way."

Perriad's look was almost pleading. "I called you Novice as a courtesy. You could extend me the same courtesy."

What, call you Novice? Jerya quelled a momentary urge to laugh. "Just tell me. What do you think you're doing here?"

"Waiting for you."

"Yes, that much is obvious; but why?"

"To stop you. To return you to custody."

Jerya's eyes strayed to the scruffy little tent. *You can't mean that...* But somehow she was sure that was exactly what Perriad did mean. "You tried to confine me in a tent once before. Remember how that worked out? Besides, how do you propose to do it this time? You're on your own and there are four of us." She glanced round, saw Tavy and Currick still where they had stopped, a few paces back.

Perriad sighed with an air of tragedy, "I had high hopes for you. High hopes. But you threw it all back in my face... what made you hate the Guild so much?"

You did, was Jerya's immediate thought, but it was pointless to say it. And there was another answer, equally true. "I don't hate the Guild. I never did. I came back to *help* the Guild. The Guild needed to know."

"You wanted to make it all a lie."

"No," she protested automatically; then, thinking about it, "I don't believe you've really heard a word I've been saying. Not just today, every time."

With a snarling, wordless, cry, Perriad sprang at her. A fierce swipe made her head ring, then ragged nails raked her cheek; but in a second she had recovered her balance, grabbed Perriad by the wrists.

At once Jerya realised that she was the stronger. She was able to force Perriad's wrists down, hold the woman away from her, not without effort, but without excessive strain.

In that moment, also, she finally knew: *I was terrified of you once, but now... now I think I pity you.*

Perriad made several attempts to free herself, sudden convulsive moves; but each was presaged by a would-be-cunning look from under her brows; and each was weaker than the last. Clearly, Perriad had very little strength left.

"Just stop," said Jerya. "You're more likely to injure yourself than me."

Perriad sagged, and Jerya released her hold. After a moment she saw that the older woman was weeping silently. Gently, Jerya grasped her shoulders. In that moment, Perriad's legs seemed to give way, and Jerya barely had time to shift her grip, hold her up. Perriad slumped against her. Jerya was shocked how light she seemed, how frail.

"Draff!" she said, looking over the white curve of Perriad's head into the shocked face of Analind. "She's skin and bone."

"I'm not surprised," said Tavy, arriving at her side. "There's nothing in the tent but a couple of blankets. No sign she's ever lit a fire. I don't know how long she's been here, but..."

Jerya had a vision of Perriad kneeling by the stream, drinking water from cupped hands. That would explain the state of her knees, she thought. But, however she had travelled to reach this spot, she could hardly have been here more than a couple of days. That fitted, too, with the report Sellet had mentioned; but it needed more more than a few days on short commons to explain Perriad's emaciated state.

She lifted Perriad's chin with one hand. "Perriad, listen to me. You're starving. You can't have been eating properly for some time. You aren't well, you need care. We have to get you to Blawith."

Perriad made no objection, but beside her Tavy stirred. "Um..."

"What is it?"

"That will delay us too long. If we go back, we might as well stay another night and start again tomorrow. And you know the Dawnsinger said there could still be storms..." He broke off; Currick was tugging at his sleeve. The slave spoke to the master, too soft for Jerya to hear. "Currick says the men who are taking the horses back may still be there, they were planning on some hunting. If we took this... lady to them, would that be good enough?"

Jerya exchanged glances with Analind. "If they're there."

"I'll send Currick. He's a fine runner."

A few more words and Currick was off, loping easily even in heavy boots. The others decided to leave their packs, and the best place was in the tent.

Jerya soon knew that she'd been right in concluding that Perriad was incapable of walking down to Blawith under her own steam. They had found her at the very end of her strength.

She and Analind took it in turn to support her stumbling steps. On Jerya's turns, she essayed a few questions about what Perriad had hoped to achieve, and why she was so ill-equipped, but got no intelligible reply.

When they reached the former campsite, they found the horses still there, and a couple of the Blawith men. Even as they were greeting them, a couple more came jogging down the hillside.

The men were evidently disconcerted at having to deal with an ailing Dawnsinger. They balked visibly at the thought of lifting her into the saddle, but there was no possible way Perriad was going to climb up on her own. They rallied when Jerya and Analind moved into position to do it. Then they fretted about the fact that her robe rucked up, leaving most of her legs bare, as well as worrying that she might fall. In the end both problems were solved by draping a saddle-blanket, folded several times, over her legs, with ropes to help keep her secure.

Finally Jerya had a few words with the one who seemed most capable. "Currick has told you what happened?"

"That 'e did, m'lady."

"This Singer is half-starved and not in her right mind. Deliver her to your own Dawnsinger. Tell her what I've told you, and what Currick said."

For the rest, they would have to leave it to Sellet, but Jerya thought Perriad was in good hands; Sellet had struck her as sensible and pragmatic. Analind concurred.

Right now, Perriad seemed beyond causing any further trouble; but when she regained her strength it was all too possible she would regain her malevolence too, and her ability to do harm. Jerya was sure Sellet would send word to the Guild as soon as she could, ideally on the wing; Evisyn would see the need for a timely response. Perriad needed care, certainly, but she would need to be watched too. Whether Perriad would even remember that she, Jerya, and her companions had delayed their journey to ensure she was looked after, Jerya had no way of knowing. *I suppose I'll find out in time*, she thought, though it might be next year at the earliest.

Tavy was looking anxiously at his pocket-watch, a bulky piece which the Guild's horologists would have disdained. "We'll have to move quickly," he said as soon as he caught Jerya's eye.

"Then that's what we'll do," she said, stepping out.

The moment they entered the Defile the temperature of the air dropped sharply. A breeze seemed to spring up from nowhere. Behind, she heard the abandoned tent flap once, forlornly.

There was no chance of sunlight penetrating to the floor of that narrow, twisting canyon; at times they could not even see sky overhead. The light was dim, but Jerya could see that the rocks either side had a slick, smooth look, as if river-worn.

At first the going was easy enough, mostly rough walking with a few short steps of rock to scramble over. Jerya kept a discreet eye on Analind; she knew her to be an experienced traveller, but Peripatetics went mostly on horseback, occasionally by boat. She had no idea how Analind would conduct herself on rock or mountain; but from first indications, she was, at least, more assured than Railu had been ten years before.

Then they came around a slight twist in the line of the Defile and found the floor filled by a long dark pool, a silvery sliver of sky reflected down its centre.

"I should have mentioned this, I guess," said Tavy, a little shamefaced.

"No matter," said Jerya.

"It's not too deep, as I remember. About to here..." he tapped his leg, about the middle of the thigh. "We..." It was hard to see in the light, but Jerya thought there was new colour under the deep honey-hue of his cheeks. "We removed our trousers. But I..."

She felt like laughing, but that would have been unkind. "If you think our legs are not a sight to be borne, go first, and don't look behind you."

"I am sure your legs are very fine, my lady." He was definitely blushing now. "I am thinking only of the decencies."

"Let's think about getting on, first and foremost. And we needn't look at you either."

Jerya and Analind turned their backs until Tavy and Currick were well down the pool, wading steadily away, trailing one hand on the rock wall alongside. As soon as their turn came she understood why. With the heavy rucksack on her back while her legs were both buoyed and restrained by the water, she felt strangely top-heavy.

The water was also icy cold, and their teeth were chattering as they dried their legs as best they could. Movement warmed them a little, but she hadn't fully warmed through before they reached a second pool, shorter but deeper, and with an awkward climb out on steeply sloping rock at the far end. There was no real alternative; someone—Currick—had to climb out unladen and then they would have to hand the sacks up to him. By the time they were all on level ground again, everyone was too chilled to care much about 'decencies'.

Jerya dug in her rucksack for an extra coat, and while she was about it pulled out a packet of dried fruit. Tavy gave her an anxious look. "I'm not sure we have time to stop for food."

"I'll eat as I walk. Going hungry won't help us get on."

Now the going was easy for a good way, rising gently, with only a few innocuous rock-steps or boulder-chokes to negotiate. There was even a little more light, as if the canyon were less deep, though the sky remained a mere pale thread far above. They went in single file, with little conversation beyond immediate practicalities.

In the long easy intervals she thought about Perriad. Perriad had terrified her once, and it had taken all her courage to defy her that first time. But now, in mere moments, she had transformed into an object of pity. As she munched on a handful of raisins, she remembered how thin and frail Perriad had felt in her arms.

There was no doubt that Perriad had been failing to eat properly for some time. The question was *why?* It could be no one's doing but her own. No one had locked her in a room, or excluded her from meals. No one had deprived *her* of her liberty.

Jerya saw only one explanation: Perriad had not been entirely in her right mind for some time. A disquieting thought came to her, unwanted but unshakeable: what if it was her own arrival that had tipped the scale? Perriad's reaction to her first appearance had been strong but not obviously irrational. She wondered if any on the Conclave of Masters had noticed any change, any warning signs, in Perriad before, or indeed after, that day.

Well, she tried to convince herself, *there's nothing you can do about it now.* And Perriad should be under Sellet's care by this time.

It would be inhuman not to wish for Perriad's recovery; but a recovered Perriad could still be a troublesome presence. There might be some who would listen to her extravagant claims, summed up in that one wild cry: *You wanted to make it all a lie.*

No, she thought, *all I ever wanted was the truth.* The truth, however—the full, unadorned truth—could be dangerous for the Guild. *But that's not my fault. Don't blame the messenger because her message is unpalatable.*

She was not much easier in her mind when she rounded a bulge in the rock wall and found Tavy and Currick waiting. There was a fork in the canyon; the way ahead seemed to continue at an easy slope, but grew rapidly darker. On her left was a steeper but brighter way. Without ado, Tavy indicated that this was indeed the way, and led off.

Analind let out a long breath. "I'm beginning to think I could use a rest."

"He's still worried about time. I guess we want to be out of here before dark. Here, have some water."

Part Four
The Five Principalities

CHAPTER 38

JERYA

"If you don't, maybe I will."

Jerya's laugh was rapidly stifled as she registered Railu's expression. "Gossan, you're serious, aren't you?"

"Why not? I'll be certified free soon enough, it seems. Free*born*, no less. Anyway, what happens if you turn him down? You break his heart... but he'll go on. Duty, responsibility... Sooner or later he's going to start thinking, *who inherits after me?* He'll need an heir, so he has to marry *someone*. So who? Some high-bred ninny who thinks slaves only exist when she needs something, or someone who knows exactly what it's like to *be* a slave?"

Jerya had said much the same to Yanil, but then she had been in a mood to doubt herself, to doubt everything. "Draff, it actually makes sense. How long have you been thinking about this?"

Railu's smile flickered momentarily. "Oh, about the last ten minutes... but you know how sometimes a whole story can come clear in a moment."

"Maybe you *should* marry him."

"No, Jerya, that's not what I'm trying to... look, you're what he wants. I'm what he just might settle for. I'm trying to make you *see*." She fixed her gaze on Jerya's face. "You love him, he adores you, and you could do great things together. Are you really going to throw that all away because it's an imperfect world? It's not going to be any more perfect if you do, you'll just make two people miserable. Honestly, Jerya, if you do, you're even crazier than I already thought."

A yelp of laughter escaped Jerya's lips. "You think I'm crazy?"

"I know you are. Mostly it's a good kind of crazy, but... Seriously, what's crazier than two girls—"

"Women."

"We were girls, Jerya, still in our teens—what did we know about anything? Two girls setting out to cross the mountains without a clue what we were going to find. Tell me that wasn't crazy. Tell me..." She stopped, drew a long breath. "Took me a long time to realise this; this isn't anything that came to me in the last ten minutes. But I do think now, I don't see many ways it could have worked out better than it did."

Jerya stared. For some moments she could not speak; then, just as she was about to fumble out a few words, Railu stopped her. "It was still crazy, of course. And just because that crazy choice worked out well enough, doesn't mean this one will. That's what I'm trying to tell you. How is there any better outcome than the one where you do marry him?

"You say you'll feel complicit—well, aren't we all? Aren't I? Every time I treat a slave whose owners wouldn't pay for a doctor, so they can go back to work... Who am I helping then? The owners benefit, don't they... so should I not treat someone who's sick or injured?"

She paused, watching Jerya, perhaps waiting for a response, but Jerya was silent.

"I'm not saying it'll all be skylarks singing and happy ever after. That's for stories, isn't it, not real life? We make the best choices from what's possible, and then we make the best of them. What else are you going to do? If you think you can do more good in the world any other way... how? Where? You did something, back in the West, but what are you going to do, go back and shave your head and put on the white again? Seriously, Jerya? You know you look better in blue or green."

Lost for words, Jerya could only step closer and wrap her arms around Railu.

"All right," she said, some time later. "Tell me one thing, Rai. When we set out, ten years ago... did you think I was crazy then?"

Railu laughed. "Probably. I don't know. I didn't know enough to tell, really."

"But you came, anyway."

"I did. I guess I was crazy too."

They looked at each other again, a look heavy with all the memories of ten years. Then Railu fished her watch from her pocket. "I'd better be getting back."

"Me too. Got to try and get some geometry into that boy's head."

They turned and made their way out of the glade. Once clear of the trees, Jerya came alongside Railu, linked arms. "Tell me one thing. If I did turn Hedric down, would you really marry him?"

"It would rather depend on him, don't you think? But I suppose I could let him know I would be open to an offer. After all..." She gave Jerya a sidelong glance, a quick grin. "It's not the craziest idea I've ever heard."

"All right, but there's one more thing. If I really did turn him down, would you really ... I mean, I never thought you wanted to have another child. But you said 'he'll need an heir'.

"I'll never have a child that will be raised as a slave." Railu's flat tone could not have carried more conviction if she had shouted at the top of her voice. "But as Hedric's wife... that would be different, wouldn't it? Instead of being the wet-nurse, I could employ one, if I wanted."

❋

Embrel hadn't been happy that she was leaving again so soon. "It's only for a few days," she'd promised. "Kirwaugh or Skilthorn, wherever Hedric is. I need to see him."

He'd brightened. "Are you going to marry him?"

She'd grinned back, and deflected the question. "Not this week."

"Couldn't I come with you? You said I could travel with you."

"If I remember rightly, I said *one day, when you're a bit older.*"

"I *am* a bit older," he'd said at once. "That was two whole months ago."

"I can't fault your logic," she laughed, "But I probably meant more like a couple of years than a couple of months."

"A couple of years is more than a bit."

"Well, that's an interesting point... makes you think, doesn't it, how important it is to be clear about what you're saying?"

"You turn everything into a lesson."

He was observing, not complaining, but she'd taken it at face value. "I am your governess, young man. Unless you'd rather have old Stink-Goose back?"

There was no mistaking the fervour of his response. "No, no, you're a thousand times better..."

"Thank you," she said, resisting the urge to hug him.

"But I thought you said you'd tan my hide for calling him Stink-Goose..."

"Hm. I think, if my memory hasn't completely failed me, I said I *ought* to tan your hide."

"Do you often not do things you ought to do?"

"All the time, I dare say."

Then, in the blink of an eye, he was glum again. His moods changed so fast... "Two years, they'll have sent me off to some stinky school and I won't be able to go travelling with you anyway."

"You won't be at school the whole time," she'd said. "Did you think you would? There are such things as holidays, you know. Near enough half the year, I reckon."

That had cheered him somewhat, but the looming prospect of school clearly weighed heavy on his young mind. The thought stayed with her as she set off, always in the back of her mind if not at the fore. Early on the second day, as she passed the outskirts of the town of Wroldham, it came back with full force.

She was riding down a white road when the dust-grey hedge gave way to spiked metal railings. Wide lawns, pleasant in the early sunlight, but beyond them a long dour building of dark brown brick. Alongside a gatehouse, a signboard proclaimed *Venning's Academy for Sons of the Gentry.* There was more, but she did not rein back to read it all.

The thought that announced itself was enough: *schools aren't all going to be alike.*

That gave her an idea. Another thing that involved travel, but that couldn't be helped. And Analind needed to see more of the Five Principalities also. *Two birds with one stone, maybe.*

Then came another thought. She, Railu, and Analind too, had all been 'sent away to school'. She herself had not stayed long, but Railu had been there eight years, and Analind still called it home. Not that there was anywhere in the Five Principalities exactly—or even vaguely—like the College, but still, it might open up a better way to talk to Embrel about it.

Though if I know him he'll probably end up demanding to be sent to the College of Dawnsingers, she thought, smiling behind her veil.

She let the thought play itself through in her mind for a while. Self-evidently impossible, perhaps, but just supposing... That would be a change, and no mistake.

CHAPTER 39

JERYA

All the resolve she'd mustered seemed woefully inadequate as she rode up to Skilthorn. It was close on a mile from the lodge to the main house, the drive winding artfully through a park that seemed devoid of people, populated only by fallow deer that gazed with mild curiosity as she passed. When the main house came fully into view, mirrored for even greater effect in a long winding lake, it was all she could do not to turn her horse right around and scuttle back homeward.

If only he'd been at Kirwaugh. Kirwaugh had not been... intimidating. Kirwaugh was on the same scale as Duncal, perhaps even a little more modest. She knew how houses of that scale worked, and their estates.

More, Kirwaugh had been pretty: soft golden brick, darker bricks picking out a diamond pattern, nestled in a fold of green hills, tall trees on one side, an orchard heavy with apple, pear and quince on the other. 'Mistress of Kirwaugh' did not seem an impossible stretch.

But Hedric had not been there. *If only...* she thought again. The horse, as if sensing the rider's mood, slowed her walk to a mere amble.

"No, girl," she said, "Let's get there before my nerve fails me entirely."

Jerya had occasionally attempted to read what passed for ladies' literature in the Five Principalities; much of it, she suspected, written by men under feminine pseudonyms. Now she distracted herself by imagining how such an author might describe the approach to Skilthorn. Would the sward—it would definitely be a sward—be verdant or emerald? Come to think of it, would 'verdant greensward' be tautological—and would the author care? The lake would be sinuous, and surely it would shimmer as it lapped against its banks.

As for the house, it would undoubtedly be nobly proportioned. And, to be fair, in its basic outline, it was. The architect, whoever he was, had achieved that much. There were well-worn formulae for such things, after all. The problem was, he had clearly had no notion of when to stop adding ornamentation,.

Jerya was well aware that, in some respects, she had led a peculiarly sheltered life. Still, she had ventured a few times onto the streets of Car-werid, and had at least passed through Denvirran. She had seen women she now took to be whores, faces heavily painted. If the intention was to draw attention to themselves, they were entirely successful, but if it was to make themselves more beautiful... she could not begin to fathom what would make them attractive to any man; to *anyone*. Why would they feel such a need to hide their true selves?

Skilthorn was not heavily painted, apart from doors and win-dow-frames, and a sheen of gold on much of the ornamentation that en-crusted the facade. She had only a vague idea of the right names for most of it: pediments, porticos, lintels? All of it seemed to be oversized, and ornately carved into scrolls and curlicues, or stylised fruit and foliage. The parapet was studded with a dozen finials, if that was the word.

As she came up the final approach, another question came to mind. No one was expecting her, though she could hope that Hedric would occasionally think about her. Was it appropriate to present herself at the front door? The portico was wide enough to admit a carriage, so that guests could step from their vehicle to the house with minimal exposure to the weather. To a single horsewoman it was far less inviting. Again she felt the urge to turn her mount around and putting the whole place behind her.

She decided that it made sense to find the stables first, have her horse attended to, and see if she could glean any clues about where to go next. It seemed logical that stables, and no doubt a carriage-house, would be found by following the extension of the driveway that curved around the right end of the frontage.

And so it proved. Passing a walled garden, she soon left the groomed gravel of the drive onto grey stone setts, arranged in fan-like patterns. Two young male slaves came trotting out from a stable door.

"Good morning, my lady," said one as the other grasped the reins. "There's a mounting block just there."

"Thank you, but I don't need it. Just hold her head." She swung down from the saddle, threw back her veil, stood for a moment stretching her back. She wondered if these men, grooms or stable-hands, would know anything about the etiquette of arrival. Doubting it was even worth asking, she sighed and turned toward the house.

Nearing the narrow yard which separated house and walled garden, she spotted a figure striding toward her. A second later she recognised him. Her relief was such she could almost have hugged him, but she knew that would be flouting decorum, and she had to content herself with a broad smile. "Good morning, Lallon."

"Good morning, m'lady." He bowed. "Yow'll be hoping to see Master Hedric." A statement, not a question.

"I am, if that's possible."

Never one to waste words, he merely nodded, gestured towards a door standing open in the back wall of the house. Jerya hefted her saddlebag and he held out a hand. She was perfectly capable of carrying it herself, but she knew that would not be 'appropriate'.

Lallon led her along a passage; through side-doors she glimpsed a gun-room and, a little further on, what she took to be a laundry, where five or six female slaves toiled among clouds of steam.

A few more strides, and then Lallon was bowing again, speaking quietly to a tall free woman in an austere but finely tailored grey dress.

"Miss Delven," she said, offering a small curtsey. "I am Mistress Gillas, second housekeeper. I understand you have business with Master Hedric."

Business, she thought. *Yes, I suppose you could call it that.* "Thank you, yes. Is it possible to see him?"

"I'm sure it will be, as soon as his uncle can spare him. I will have a message sent up immediately. In the meanwhile, may I show you to somewhere you can wait?" She moved off as she spoke, adding, "And will you be staying the night?" Jerya could only answer that she wasn't sure. "I shall have your bags taken to a suitable room."

"Just the one bag," said Jerya. Mistress Gillas looked as if that were beneath the dignity of a lady, but said nothing.

A few minutes later Jerya was ensconced in a sitting room, with the promise that coffee and luncheon would be with her directly. Then there was nothing she could do but wait.

The coffee came, as promised, within a few minutes, and she drained the first cup almost before it had cooled enough to drink. A tray of food came as she was pouring a second. Both, she noticed, delivered by young female slaves in dresses that were cut low and short, scarcely concealing their knees. Sometimes, she knew, slaves' clothes were simply not replaced often enough as they grew, but here she suspected a different agenda. The dresses fitted well enough; one might even say, too well. Someone had deliberately made them that way, and not, she suspected, simply to economise on fabric.

Skilthorn did not seem like the sort of place that economised.

She found that her thirst for coffee was not matched by hunger for food, and picked desultorily at the platter: bread, three varieties of cheese, and some smoked meat. Venison, she thought, remembering the deer she'd seen on the way in.

Putting the platter back on the tray, she filled her cup a third time and took it over to the window. The room was at the side of the house, looking over the drive she had come in by, then across a broad sloping lawn. Beyond was a fence enclosing an orchard, before a more distant rise dotted with tall trees. *More art than nature*, she was thinking, when she heard the door open behind her.

She glanced over her shoulder, expecting a slave come to remove the serving-tray, but it was Hedric. She looked around, found somewhere to set down cup and saucer, faced him as he hastened to her side.

Just as he reached her, and as she was wondering whether they would embrace or merely clasp hands, the door opened again. This time it was indeed the slave who'd brought the tray.

When the girl had gone, they stood gazing at each other. It ran through her mind that, almost the last time she had seen him, they had both been naked. Then, it had been easy. Now, it wasn't.

She sighed. "It's hard to feel alone in this house."

"I know one place, if you would like."

"Please."

He led her back the way she had come in, but then turned off into another passage, unadorned, with floors of board rather than marble. This, she knew, would be mostly for the use of servants and indeed they passed several slaves, arms full of bed-linen, who hastily stood aside with averted gaze as soon as they saw them. They turned onto a steep stairway, ill-lit by flickering oil-lamps. Two more flights followed, another short passage, and then a door disguised as part of the panelling. Hedric opened this with a key and gestured her to precede him. Yet another stair, even darker and much narrower than the others.

At the top, she drew back a bolt, and opened the door onto brightness that blinded her momentarily. They were on the roof. Now he took her hand, drew her forward, until they were standing at the parapet and, she saw, directly above the portico of the main entrance.

"Now," he said, still clasping her hand. "No one will disturb us here. And now perhaps I can truly express how very glad I am to see you." He lifted her hand, held it against his chest, over his heart. "All the time I was travelling away from you I kept asking myself if I was a fool to leave you. Even if... I often wondered if I would ever see you again."

"I thought the same," she said, thinking of how Perriad had had her locked up. Somehow she didn't feel like telling that story just now.

Gently disengaging her hand, she looked out across the park. It was beautiful, she had to admit. Under a stand of oaks she could just make out a few of the deer, their spotted coats almost disappearing in the dappled light.

"What a place for a telescope," she said, for the sake of saying *something*.

He picked up on it enthusiastically. "Indeed. I've been up here many times with a small telescope, but we could... Have you seen Cracoe's ideas about permanent housing for telescopes? Instead of spending twenty minutes every time carrying the apparatus out and getting it levelled, leave it in place and create a shelter that can be moved away or folded back in a quarter of the time."

"At the Dawnsingers' Observatory they have canopies—like very robust tents—that can be lifted clear by four people, in two minutes. I was there just a few weeks ago." She could easily have said more, but reminded herself that she had come to Skilthorn for a reason. Telescopes and ways of housing them was not it.

But how to introduce the subject? It had all seemed much simpler when she left home, even when she was riding up to Kirwaugh.

Ah... she thought. "I went by Kirwaugh first. I hoped I'd find you there."

"Alas..." He shrugged. "I have little choice but to abide here for the time being."

And what choice *will you have when you finally inherit?* she wondered. She left that unsaid, returning instead to Kirwaugh. "All the things I wanted to say seemed much clearer there."

"Should I, then, regret that you did not find me at Kirwaugh? Or is it in the end best that you see all this too? Even if you find it..."

"Monstrous," she said. "That's how I find it."

"Monstrous..." he repeated, musing. "Yes, I see how it would... I've known this house all my life, of course. It would be very easy to take it all for granted. But that is where I value your perspective, in helping me see more clearly."

"Flattery, Hedric?"

"No, the simple truth." He met her gaze a moment, then turned, resting his hands on the parapet, looking out into the pale olive haze beyond the trees of the parkland.

There was a pause. Jerya hoped he would say something, but it didn't seem as if he was about to. And, after all, had she not just said she had ridden here with things to say to him?

I had it all clear, and now it's all confusion again.

Clearly, though, she needed to say something. She stepped up alongside him, leaned on the cool dove-grey stone. "I can't tell you how relieved I was to know that you and Lallon had made it back safely."

"And I you... I don't suppose this is the time, but I must hear all about that other route, the one Selton found."

"I think everyone will be hearing about it soon enough. Tavy Selton came with me as far as Drumlenn, but the very next morning he was off early for Denvirran, to spread—" A thought struck her. "Hedric, what have you done about getting the news out? I haven't seen anything."

"Would you come down again with me? I'll show you what I sent."

Jerya read the draft copy of his letter in silence, almost in disbelief.

Esteemed Sirs,

I beg leave to lay before your Readers a preliminary account of a Journey of Exploration undertaken in the months of Meadander and Gleander just past...

This *'Brief Account of a Journey of Exploration. Including the Crossing of the Dividing Range, and some Remarks on What Lies Beyond'* amounted to five closely-penned pages. There were a few lines crossed out and reworked; he had been anxious to assure her that the copy he'd actually sent was a fair one.

"Does it seem a fair account?" he asked as she laid the paper down.

"Well, yes, I suppose so..." she said, distracted. "But Hedric... the 10th of Calorander; that's almost three weeks ago. Has this been published yet?"

"Another week or two, I think."

She stared at him, seized by the desire to shake him. "And did you think of lodging a report anywhere else?"

"The *Proceedings* is the journal of record for this Principality. How else should I establish priority?"

"Priority? *Priority?*" Never mind shaking, she almost wanted to slap him now. "Do you suppose Tavy Selton's only placed a report with the *Proceedings*? I'd be astonished if there weren't stories in the Denvirran papers already. You know the Duke... Draff, the only reason we made the journey in the first place was because I saw Selton's expedition announced in the paper."

CHAPTER 40

HEDRIC

"I'm sorry," he said. He had only slowly grasped how irate she was. "I should have thought of the general Press, of course. But I... I don't even know how one goes about it. What would you call it? Placing a story?"

"I don't know what you call it, but I reckon I know how Tavy Selton did it. Rode to Denvirran and walked right into the office of one of the papers. The *Remarker*, probably."

"And that would have been two extra days. My uncle was impatient enough as it was."

"Choss, Hedric, does *everything* have to depend on your uncle's whims? Besides, you said the idea of beating Selton was what persuaded him to agree to your coming with me. Isn't he going to be looking for something in the paper?"

"Oh, blight!" In sudden dread he continued, "And if he reads about Selton before there's anything about our Crossing... I'm a fool, am I not?"

"I'll not dispute that, not now. But look, Hedric, never mind your uncle; can't you see what this means to me? Who made the first Crossing of the mountains? The true first?"

"You did."

"I did, with Railu and Rodal. And who made the second? You, me, and Lallon. Is it unreasonable of me to want some recognition?"

"Of course not... but you never made any claim about your true first Crossing."

"No, because no one would believe us. We were no one: a slave, an ex-slave, and a man who doesn't even exist in the Five Principalities any longer. Selton's a Duke and you're the heir of an Earl; it shouldn't make a difference but you know full well it does."

"And you will be recognised, when the *Proceedings* publishes my letter."

Out of the blue, Jerya laughed. "Draff, Hedric, but this is all so much... it's *you*. Look, I have enough pride to want people to know what we did—and not just the subscribers of the *Proceedings*—but I can't stay mad with you."

She stepped closer, around the table that had been between them. "What do you call this room?"

"The Lesser Library."

"There's another one?" She looked around, taking in the shelves of books, the writing desk under the window, the green leather armchairs before the fireplace. "It's nice to know there's at least one room in this place that isn't monstrous."

She came closer again, took his hands. That level gaze, the hazel eyes. "Hedric. You know I love you, don't you? Even when—or maybe especially when—you do something like this. And if you were just a yeoman, if it was just Kirwaugh, it would be so much simpler. But all this..." she made a sweeping gesture, to take it all in; not just the room, but the whole vast house, the demesne that they'd seen from the roof. "*All this* is the obstacle. Those conventional young ladies might throw themselves at you for it, but it's exactly what's holding me back.

"But... I thought I knew, when I set out from home, what I was going to say to you. I spoke with Railu, and she told me I was crazy if I didn't marry you."

He smiled. "I must be sure to thank her at the earliest opportunity."

"Don't be too hasty. I was ready, when I rode up to Kirwaugh. I thought I'd be ready when I turned into the drive here... but I wasn't. I can barely even grasp the scale of it."

"You know how I sometimes think of it all? It's like a machine, some colossal engine of clockwork... but all the moving parts are *people*. Slaves or free, need make no difference to the working of the machine."

"But a machine that's all for the benefit of one man."

"At present, yes... At least, you can look at it that way. But also a machine that gives people purpose. From bakers and brewers to artists and sculptors. Yes, things must change—which they will, if and when I inherit... But there has to be a way to change things without throwing away what's good..."

He straightened suddenly. "Jerya, will you come with me? There is someone I should like you to meet."

※

"I see something in that girl," he said. "Don't you?" To his relief, his uncle had still been asleep, and it had been easy to ask Dortis to step out into the sitting-room.

Jerya screwed up her face, as she did when thinking hard. "Possibly... but at the moment she can't even see it in herself. But that's what slavery does to people... and not just slavery." Her look as she faced him now was almost truculent. "Do you know what I was thinking as I rode over? I've been in this land ten years and I've never seen a school for girls. Have you?" He shook his head. "And then they dare to say women don't have the capacity for abstract thought. It's a miracle any girl gets any kind of education at all... But is there anything to actually stop someone creating a girls' school? A law, I mean, like the one that says you can't teach a slave to read."

"Not that I am aware..." He thought a little more. "You're thinking we... I mean, you're not going to be satisfied with improving the lot of slaves, you want to better the lives of women too... What is it? Jerya?"

Her face, her whole body, had gone strangely still. For a long moment she neither moved nor spoke. Then, suddenly, she seized his hands. "Ask me again."

"Ask you...?"

"You know what I mean."

And suddenly he did. He turned his grip so that it was his hands that were enfolding hers. "Miss Delven... Jerya... would you do me the honour of agreeing to be my wife?"

"Yes," she said. "Yes, draffit, I will."

CHAPTER 41

JERYA

"D *raffit?*" he repeated a little later.

"There's so much that feels wrong about it. This house, the whole insane notion of being a Countess—see, I can barely say it with a straight face. Even the word 'wife', all the expectations that go with it..."

"Then what changed your mind? What was enough to overcome all that?"

"You said 'we'."

"I did?"

She laughed. "You didn't even finish the sentence. *You're thinking we...* but you thought of us, together, and I just saw, in that moment, if we want to do anything in this world, we need to be together."

"I believe it too. I don't think I can accomplish half as much on my own. Or, worse, with some bride who doesn't even understand what I want to achieve."

"And you're going to need someone to tell you when you've been a fool, too." She softened the words with a smile, a brush of fingers against his cheek.

"I don't doubt it."

"And there's another thing I was in danger of forgetting, for a while."

"And that is?"

"I love you, you dunce."

"Ah," he said. "Yes, the other thing." Then they were both laughing, so helpless with it they had to hold each other up.

＊

"Uncle," he said, "Permit me to present Miss Jerya Delven. My betrothed."

Until that moment Jerya hadn't imagined he would present her as his betrothed. *Draff, it's only been five minutes!* She was still trying to come to terms with being thrust into the Earl's presence at all.

Under the circumstances, she thought—or hoped—that she'd controlled her reaction well, but an alert observer would surely have noticed *something*. She could only hope that the Earl was not in the best shape to observe.

And, of course, he was surprised too. His visible eye widened, his head arched back; he uttered an unpleasant sound, a kind of wet bark. Jerya realised he was laughing.

Finally he spoke, though Jerya couldn't get a single intelligible word. Dortis leaned close, listening and watching intently. "He says, *Do young ladies not curtsey before an Earl these days? Or are my eyes worse than I thought?*"

"Your pardon, my lord." The words tasted like chalk, but... Hedric had taken an appalling risk bringing her in at all; she must not make it worse by offending the Earl. *If I could just be sure what* will *offend him...*

She made a deep curtsey. She had had little practise, normally keeping such obeisance to the minimum. Under the circumstances she thought she carried it off well enough.

Another mumble: "*Stand over there where the light's better.*" She complied. The Earl muttered something else, irritable tone obvious even if the words weren't. Dortis didn't repeat this, only making a quick adjustment to his eye-patch.

The good eye, a bright island in the slack ruin of the face, roved up and down her body. She felt a chill along her spine. It was all too easy to imagine how he had looked at women when he had full use of both eyes. She began to feel that Hedric had given her but an expurgated version of the full tale.

"She's handsome enough, lad." Dortis had the grace to look embarrassed as she relayed this. Jerya clenched a flare of rage to herself. *"No, I'll say very handsome... Where did yow find her...? I've never seen yow before, have I, Miss —?"*

"You have not, my lord." 'My lord' almost curdled in her mouth.

"I found her a day's ride from here, Uncle," said Hedric. True, but uninformative.

"And who are your people, Miss... Delven, was it? Not a name I ever heard."

"No, my lord, you wouldn't have." *Unless you perused a certain edition of the Proceedings of the Denvirran Society for Natural Philosophy...*

"Miss Delven hails originally from beyond the mountains, Uncle."

That got a reaction. The eye widened, the brow lifted high. Then he emitted another horrible laugh. *"You didn't tell me... you'd brought back a trophy."*

Again Jerya bit down on her anger. *A trophy, am I? Oh,* that's *insulting... and factually inaccurate.*

The Earl settled back on the pillows, mumbled something. Dortis wiped his brow with a cloth. Jerya was struck by the delicacy of her action. The Earl, by all accounts, treated his slaves appallingly, with particular humiliations reserved for the young female ones. Hedric had said that the first time he'd seen the girl she'd been reduced to tears by his bullying. She'd 'warmed his bed'... perhaps now that was all that was required, but in former days surely it had been a euphemism. The image of the young girl—*seventeen*, by gossan!—lying beside the old man turned Jerya's stomach.

All that, and the girl repaid him with *tenderness*... Dortis, she thought, had a more magnanimous spirit than she herself would ever have. All this went through her mind as the girl mopped the old man's brow again, rearranged the pillows to sit him up a little more.

"I asked who your people were," the Earl said now. *"And you hesitated... yes, missy, I'm sick, not blind... But now I understand... Things are different... beyond the mountains, eh?"*

"Very different, my lord."

"No doubt... and when I am well again... you shall tell me all about it."

That would be interesting, thought Jerya. *Maybe I should have Analind do it. A Master of the Guild of Dawnsingers... What exactly would the Earl make of that? And what would she make of hm?*

Probably it was better if he never did find out too much. And: 'when I am well again'... now she'd seen him, she saw little prospect of that ever coming to pass.

"Aye, Uncle," said Hedric, "When you're well. But we should let you get some rest, now."

You dragged me in here, she thought, *and now you're dragging me out again?* Not that she was eager to linger in that overheated room.

CHAPTER 42

HEDRIC

The moment they were alone again, out in the passage, she spun on her heel, confronted him. "I agreed to marry you. I nearly didn't. I can still change my mind."

"Wh—Jerya?"

She put her hand on his chest, firmly, weight behind it. It felt almost like a blow. "Listen, Hedric. Those days I was locked up in the College, I had all sorts of doubts. Remember, I thought I was going to be there a whole year. Thought I might get back and find you'd married someone else—"

"—No, Jerya, I—"

"—I thought about that and I wondered if I might even feel a sort of relief. That I wouldn't have to worry myself about joining the owner-class after all. Because it was a worry—*is* a worry. But in the end I told myself you were a good man, and we could do great things together." Her gaze, already stern, grew even harder. "*Together*. But together only works if it really means together. If you ever handle me like that again, then it can't."

He began to see. A sick feeling gathered in his gut. "Jerya, I—"

"*I'm* speaking. Bad enough you bundle me into his sickroom without even a by-your-leave. You surely didn't have to drag me in there like a sack of potatoes."

That was a considerable exaggeration, but he was wise enough—just—not to protest. He placed his hand over hers, still resting against his sternum. "Jerya. My love. I swear to you I'll never do such a thing again. Can you forgive me?"

She pulled her hand away. Four long, quick, strides took her to the window. The sun had moved round far enough to angle in, waking the tawny glint in her coiled hair. Her back was very straight.

"Jerya," he said, moving halfway toward her, "It was very wrong of me, I know. It goes against everything... everything I feel about you, about how we... how we mesh together. Believe me when I say I'm sickened by my own action."

She did not turn, said nothing.

"Half an hour ago, perhaps, you accepted me. Forgive the cliché, but in that moment you made me the happiest of men. And to alienate you would make me the most wretched of creatures. I do not expect to exonerate myself, but may I try to explain what was in my head?"

Still she neither moved nor spoke, but she didn't forbid him.

"All my life my uncle has been a... difficult man. As a boy, I feared him; as a man, I've grown to... it's a hard word, but to despise him. A thousand times, it feels like, I've had to stand by and smile while he says or does something that repels me. Say the polite things, the expected things, dance to his tune. Make a liar of myself. All so I should inherit, rather than my appalling cousin.

"I have concealed so much for so long. My thoughts, my true feelings—my true *self*, it feels like. But when we stood in this room, not half an hour ago, and you finally said you would marry me... it's a woeful cliché, Jerya, but you made me the happiest man alive. I could not conceal that.

"I said I'd kept silence a thousand times. A thousand times I've wanted to say, *I hate you, uncle, I hate everything you do, I hate the way you treat people... especially, but not only, slaves.* I wanted to throw it all in his face. I wanted to say, *this is the woman I love, the most wonderful woman I have ever met, a woman who is more than I ever dreamed of. I'm going to marry her whether you like it or not.*

"And I wanted to say, *she is all that... and she used to be a slave.*"

At last she turned to look at him.

"I'm still angry," she said, but her face and her voice gave the lie to her words.

CHAPTER 43

JERYA

"I went away to school when I was... I'd just turned eleven."

Jerya stopped in the doorway. Neither Analind nor Embrel gave any sign of having noticed she was there. Usually Embrel would jump up whenever hooves sounded in the yard, but now he was clearly wrapped up in what Analind was saying. She didn't much like eavesdropping, but she wanted to hear at least a little more. This was *interesting*. She wondered how long Analind had been back from Denvirran. Before her departure, she had been friendly enough towards Embrel, but not close like this.

"You were sent?" asked Embrel now.

Analind shrugged. Her wig, always handy but rarely worn, lay on the table. "Sent, taken... we say *Chosen*."

"A long way away?"

"Actually, for me, not so very far. A day's ride, or a little more."

"So you could go home in the holidays?"

Analind smiled. "That's not how it works, when you're Chosen for a Dawnsinger. I didn't go home again until I was twenty-five, and then..." Her voice tailed off. Jerya had a good idea what might lie behind it. The seasoned Peripatetic, riding into her home-town, would have been a very different person from the girl who'd left fifteen years before.

Embrel was looking worried, and Jerya was thinking about stepping in, but then Analind said, "It's not like that with schools here, is it? The College is different."

"College?"

"That's what we call it. But what I wanted to tell you... when I was Chosen, like I said, I was very young. Just turned eleven. I didn't know much about what it was going to be like. I was bewildered... and, yes, I was frightened. But I wasn't the only one. Even before we got to the city, there were others with me, all feeling the same sort of things. As soon as we arrived, there were lots of us, eighty or ninety. Railu was one of them. "

"And Jerya?"

"Jerya didn't come along until much later." Without turning her head, she added, "Why don't you come in?"

"How long have you known I was there?" asked Jerya, slipping into the end seat, making the three of them the vertices of a roughly equilateral triangle. At the far end of the table, Rhenya looked up from her chopping with an abstracted smile.

"How long have you been there?" asked Analind, smiling. "But we haven't answered Embrel's question yet."

"Yes," said Jerya. "I didn't arrive until years later. Before that I didn't go to school at all."

"Did you have a governess?" asked Embrel.

She had to laugh at that. "If rocks and trees count... No, what education I got I mostly gave myself. I read books, but there weren't many, and I observed, and sometimes I did experiments. Though I didn't even know the word *experiment* then."

"You educated yourself, and you're the smartest person I know. Why can't I?"

"Because if I hadn't come—eventually—to the College of the Dawnsingers, I wouldn't be the person I am now. And from the first moments I was there, I felt like I was running to catch up. I wished so much I'd been Chosen at the same age as the others." *Do I still think so? I'm not so sure.*

"What was it like?" asked Embrel.

"I think that's what Analind was trying to tell you."

Analind smiled. "Yes... where was I? I'd just arrived..."

"You were scared."

"We all were. Didn't know what to expect. But we helped each other, right from the start. Whether it was finding our way around—it's a big place, seemed almost endless when we were small—or shaving each other's heads."

"*Why* do you shave your head? You aren't slaves."

"On this side of the mountains a shaved head is the mark of a slave. But on the other side... well, there are no slaves. There, a bald head is the mark of a Dawnsinger."

There was plenty to unpick here, thought Jerya; what slavery meant; why Railu's hair would never grow back; and much more. But it could wait. "You helped each other," she prompted.

"Yes, and very quickly I... I liked most of the other girls, but within a few weeks I'd found my special friends. And Railu was one of them. You can't imagine how it feels to see her again now, after ten years apart..."

Where was Railu? Jerya wondered. Busy in the house somewhere, or dealing with someone sick or injured? There was little spare time in Railu's life now. She seemed to like it that way.

"I found friends," continued Analind, "And just as important, I found... suddenly I was learning about so many things. It was *exciting*."

"What things?"

"Lots of the things you learn about with Jerya, I'm sure, but going further... I know you said Jerya's the smartest person you know." She smiled. "And maybe she is... but she's only one person, and one person can't know everything. Not even Jerya.

"So we learned... not everything, but a little about almost everything. How the stars and planets move... or seem to move."

"I know that," said Embrel. "It's because the Earth goes round the Sun."

Jerya could see Analind wrestling with the impulse to precision. *Yes, but so do the planets, and the moons go round the Earth, and over a long time the stars do move...* And so much more; so much that was wonderful, fascinating, and so much still unknown—on both sides of the mountains.

Analind contained herself, smiled. "Very good. And we learned what the world is made of, the rocks beneath our feet. We learned... it's such a long list. How our bodies work... Railu was *very* good at that, you know."

"She still is," said Jerya, and was pleased to see Embrel nodding. She wondered again where Railu was. It would be good if she could be part of this conversation, but she didn't want to break its momentum by searching for her, especially when she could be away from the house.

Embrel listened as Analind enumerated more of the subjects they'd studied. *Wish I could always get him to listen that closely*, thought Jerya. But that was hardly fair, at his age. Then, all at once, the lad sat up straighter, a new light in his eye. Jerya knew the signs; it could be good, or bad, but it was unlikely to be dull.

It certainly wasn't that. "Could *I* go to the College of Dawnsingers? I'm not quite ten and a half. Could *I* be... Chosen?"

Jerya might have laughed, but Analind appeared stunned. Giving her a moment to regroup, Jerya said, "There might be one or two... practical difficulties. It's a very long way, a difficult journey."

"*You've* done it."

"Yes, I have." *Three times*, she thought, *and no one else can say that*. She'd never claimed to be immune to pride. "That's how I know how hard it is." Spotting the first signs of a pout, she quickly added, "I'm not saying you couldn't do it. But there wouldn't be any coming home for the holidays."

"I think I said, didn't I?" added Analind. "Not till I was twenty-five."

That made an impression. From a ten-year-old's perspective, twenty-five looked impossibly far off. *And when you look back, it seems like no time at all...*

"There's another problem," said Analind. "You know I'm a Peripatetic...?" A strange look flickered across her face; Jerya thought she might be reminding herself that she was in fact *Master* of Peripatetics. She wondered how that felt: perhaps rather like when she tried to imagine herself a Countess. "You know what Peripatetic means?"

Embrel screwed up his face, nose wrinkling prettily, which meant *No*.

"In general, it means someone who travels around a lot, who does their work in many different places."

"Like the knife-grinder," said Jerya, naming the first familiar example she could think of. Analind looked slightly askance; perhaps she found the comparison less than flattering. Jerya was ready to defend it; she'd found the knife-grinder fascinating to watch, hands tenderly caressing the blade, scant millimetres from the spin-blurred grindstone and the flying sparks. She was always impressed by people who displayed skills that she had no grasp of.

Analind shrugged slightly. "Among Dawnsingers, Peripatetics are the ones who go around... we visit resident Singers in the villages and towns, check on their welfare. And as we travel we do our best to keep our maps up to date."

Embrel brightened."I know about making maps." He glanced at Jerya.

"You do? That's good. Well, Peripatetics do various things but the most important is Choosing. And in Choosing we must look very closely at every candidate. We look for the best and brightest, of course... above all, we look for *inquiring* minds. And I think you might do very well on those tests. But... there is something else. We're only looking for girls."

"*Only* girls?"

"Dawnsingers are female. Well, you can see, Railu and Jerya and I are all female, aren't we?"

"Of course I can see," said Embrel indignantly. "But that's only three of you. I bet there are hundreds of Dawnsingers."

Jerya wanted to applaud his reasoning, the recognition that a sample of three was too small to be significant, but Analind was already responding. "Thousands, in fact. But every one is female."

Embrel had his deep-thinking face on, lips pressed firmly together. "I knew there must be girls in the College," he said at last. "But that's why... every school I ever heard of is boys only. I thought it might be... *nicer.*"

I wonder if it would, thought Jerya. *How would I know? How would any of us know?*

"I'm sorry," Analind was saying. "That's just the way it is." It sounded to Jerya uncomfortably like her aunts' old refrain: *it's the way things are....*

"Besides," she said, hoping to console Embrel, "You'd have to get up every morning to Sing. Like Analind's done every day she's been here. How often have you got up to listen? How often have you even heard her?"

Even as she spoke, another thought was blossoming in her mind. *Every school I ever heard of is boys only*, Embrel had just said. Was that true? She had wondered before about schools for girls: but girls and boys together? And if not, why not? Was there some statute forbidding it, or was it simply that no one had ever thought to start one?

In a kind of daze, she got to her feet, went to the range. "Who wants coffee?" Rhenya and Analind both accepted enthusiastically, so she filled the second-largest coffee-maker, set it on the hotplate. She stayed there as it began to make spitting, bubbling, sounds, thinking. *Maybe girls and boys together would be too much, at least to start with... Maybe there is a good use for a monstrous big house after all... I need to talk to Hedric again soon.*

At that moment there was a clatter of hooves in the yard. The timing, just as she thought of him, made her heart skip, but it *couldn't* be; that would be too much like a miracle. Embrel dashed out to see, and Jerya was only held back from following by the sound of the coffee-maker changing to a sullen hiss; the reservoir was dry. If she didn't take it off the heat right away, the coffee would become acrid.

Embrel came back in, leading Railu by the hand. Seeing what Jerya was about, she grinned. "I hope you're making enough for me too."

"When I was a Dawnsinger," said Railu, "I did as I was told—"

"More or less," said Jerya. Analind suppressed a smile.

"I'm being serious," said Railu. "I did as I was told, mostly, and I went where I was sent. Sent to be the next Dawnsinger in Delven, and that was the end of that. Except it wasn't, but only because I broke my Vow. Draff, I didn't have a choice about becoming a Dawnsinger in the first place. I was Chosen, and that was all there was to it."

"You *should* have had a choice," said Analind. "In my training as a Peripatetic, Master Evisyn was always very clear: if a girl seems unwilling or uncertain, take note. We can persuade, encourage, reassure, but we don't compel."

"All I know is I had no sense of choice. I was barely eleven years old, everyone was telling me what a great honour it was, how proud they all were... Maybe I could have refused, but how was I to know? How could I have found the capacity to refuse?"

"*I* was nineteen," said Jerya. "And I'm not sure I had a choice either." Then she remembered Sharess saying, months later, *but you* have *chosen*. That was true; she had chosen, but only by breaking her Vow. She fell silent.

"And you choose again when you take Novitial Vows, and Final Vows, of course," said Analind.

"What choice?" said Railu. "To serve the Guild in a different way; not to walk away altogether. And you can't believe... how easy would it be, really, to stand there in front of everyone and say, I won't take the Vow? Seems to me that might take more courage than what we did."

Analind looked troubled, but gave a thoughtful nod.

"What I know is, I was told I was going to be Delven's Singer. Probably for the rest of my life, or at least till I got too old. Forty years, fifty? It wasn't what I wanted or what I was best fitted for, but they—*she*—gave me no choice." Neither Jerya nor Analind needed to ask who *she* was. "Whereas, here, now... Everyone outside this house looks at me and sees a slave; in the eyes of the world, that's what I am. And yet I have... at least I have a life that is *nearer* to what I'm best suited for. Is recognition as freeborn going to change that? Maybe if women were permitted to train, to *practise* as doctors—as chirurgeons..."

"You're better trained than most of them already," said Jerya.

"*I'll* not dispute it. But I'm a woman; I can't be a doctor."

"I sometimes think being a woman in this land is halfway to being a slave anyway."

"Unless you marry the right man," said Railu. "And there aren't many of them, not that I've seen."

"I wish you could find one..."

"Thank you, but... but I'm trying to tell you. These things make me angry, but I'm not *unhappy*. I told you; my life is nearer to what I'm suited for. More than it ever would have been as a village Singer, I'm sure. I've made *something* of my life, just as you have. I don't mean that being officially freeborn isn't welcome, but I don't know that it's going to change anything."

"It's different for me," said Jerya, reminding herself how little she had to complain about. "If I am to marry Hedric and... and all that goes with it, then it'll go a lot easier if I'm recognised as freeborn."

"I've seen something of slavery now," said Analind. "I know I've been no further than Denvirran..."

I should have taken you with me to Skilthorn, thought Jerya. She might have said it, but Analind hadn't finished. "And obviously I don't know it like you do, but still... How do you live with it? Either being a slave or just being part of this society?"

Jerya and Railu looked at each other, and to everyone's surprise it was Rhenya who answered first. Having just taken the jam-pan off the heat and set it to cool, she'd come to stand behind Railu. "I been a slave all my life so mayhaps I don't know no different. But I dares say I do know summat 'bout bein' a slave. Only thing I can say is, I don't see as how bein' free'd make my life any better'n what it is."

Railu picked up. "I ask myself the same question. What would I do, what would I have, if I were free, that I don't have now? I still couldn't own the horse I ride... and I still couldn't practise openly."

Jerya nodded along. She knew that feeling very well. Even a Countess could not legally own a horse, or a house.

Or a slave.

Still, when I marry Hedric, I'll be part of the owner class. She had almost drawn breath to say it when Analind picked up on Railu's words. "You could come back to the Guild. Then you could practise."

Railu gazed at her, startled into silence.

"Are you sure?" asked Jerya. "If I was classed as a Vow-breaker and renegade, surely Railu will be too. You can't have forgotten what happened to me."

Analind was indignant. "I'll *never* forget. But we have a new Master Prime now."

"I can hardly imagine that everyone will welcome me back with open arms," said Railu, who'd heard the full tale of Jerya's travails. "But even if it always has to be clandestine, there are people here who... I don't want to sound vain, but people who need me. People who wouldn't be seen at all otherwise, or at best would have to wait hours till the doctor had seen everyone *more important.*"

Analind blinked at the acerbic tone of the final words. "But at least you don't have to be a slave any longer. Not only can you be declared free, you can actually get redress. I can't help thinking that these people have had you working for them for ten years without paying you a penny."

Jerya and Railu regarded each other. Jerya, who kept the accounts for the household and the wider estate, probably had the better idea what ten years' backdated salary would amount to. It wouldn't bankrupt them, but Embrel's school fees would be in jeopardy. The lad himself might welcome that...

"I'll not do that," said Railu. "I remember what would have become of us if they hadn't..."

"Bought you?" Analind turned to Jerya. "I've heard you speak about it; about being bought."

"And I've been free most of the past ten years. I think it's for Railu to say what she thinks."

Railu sat back, spreading her hands in a kind of helpless shrug. "What else can I say? Being bought... it's not a happy memory, of course it isn't.

But if they hadn't... quite likely we wouldn't even be here to tell the tale. I'm not going to punish them for wrongs done by others. I suppose..." She looked at Jerya. "If we could penalise that slave-market..."

"That bastard Keeving..."

"Aye, and him... if we could do that, then maybe... but only if we could do it, for sure, *without* involving the Duncals. Without harming this place."

She looked at Jerya, at Analind, turned to look round and up at Rhenya. "It's my home, after all. Free or not, where else am I going to go?"

CHAPTER 44

HEDRIC

The Earl's left forefinger stabbed at the paper, came away smeared with newsprint. "Look at that," he growled, clear enough that Dortis could stay silent.

CROSSING OF THE MOUNTAINS
DIVIDING RANGE BREACHED
<u>TRIUMPH FOR HIS GRACE'S EXPEDITION</u>
EXTRAORDINARY DISCOVERIES

The headlines alone told him all he needed to know.

The Earl gave him a moment, then snarled something. *"You told me..."* relayed Dortis, *"You beat that... jackass."* Hedric suspected his uncle had actually said 'jackanapes', but couldn't blame the girl for picking the simpler option. *"You swore... you'd made the crossing... first."*

Hedric had a sick feeling. Dread. Had Selton flouted his tacit agreement with Jerya? *If only I'd made an announcement the day I got back...*

Well, there was no gain in second-guessing himself. He lifted the paper from the bedside table, went over to the window, quickly scanned the body of the story.

"Here you are, uncle," he said, returning. *"His Grace's spokesman also informed us that another crossing, by a different route, has been accomplished by The Honourable Hedric of Kirwaugh and Miss J. Delven. It is our firm intention to bring you full details of this endeavour shortly."*

The Earl grunted, unimpressed. *"You told me you were first... Doesn't say that anywhere... You're not... even on front page."*

Selton, or his son, had not entirely concealed the truth. All very well, but it had been done in niggardly fashion. Hedric felt a flare of resentment on his own behalf, doubly so on Jerya's.

The Earl was labouring to speak again. *"And you told me... you found that girl... on the other side. Says here you... both crossed together."*

"I don't believe I did say that," he protested. "I found her a day's ride from here." *All those times I went to Duncal for 'better atmospherics'...* "You want the full story, Uncle? You want to know who crossed the Divide first? 'Twasn't me. It was Jerya."

The Earl laughed, a dry rasp today. *"A girl...? You expect me to believe... some slip of a girl... crossed the range on her own...? Strong men have failed... a hundred times."*

"She's a woman, not a girl," he said, anger overriding caution. An insult to himself was one thing; an insult to his beloved was another. "And I tell you this, I know what she has achieved, what she's capable of. When we crossed, she knew the way. She led me, uncle, that's the fact of it. And I saw where she grew up, met people who knew her as a child. There's no doubt." *Oh, and she wasn't alone, the first time, but you don't need to know that.*

The Earl was silent for a few seconds, considering this, or merely gathering his strength to speak again. Hedric had time to wonder what he might pick out. He'd said too much, he was almost sure. When his uncle did speak, all doubt vanished. *"She led you...? That's no way for a man to live..."* He paused, wheezing. Eight words in one breath was a big effort for him. *"Never let a woman... command you... Once, and she gets... the taste for it... Take charge... or you'll be henpecked... to the end of your days... And your own fault..."*

This was irritating, but he had long experience of shrugging off his uncle's occasional offerings of advice.

What came next, after a bout of coughing, after Dortis had given him more watered brandy... what came next had the reek of disaster.

"I've had enough of you, boy... Aye, you'll always be a boy... Never a man... if you let a woman... command you... Get out... find Dillick... send him to

me... No, you've worn me out... Do it yourself... Send for Ferrowby... And for Veeks."

The last thing he saw as he left the room was Dortis. Her eyes followed him with what seemed to be sympathy.

❋

Miss Jerya Delven
    Duncal
    Via Drumlenn
    My beloved
    I beg your indulgence for substandard penmanship, this being written in haste, with borrowed materials, at the mailing office in Skilton. And when you know the reason why this is so... I can hardly think what your reaction will be. But I must not prevaricate.

My uncle has dispatched me to the town to summon his attorney. The man was occupied with another client this afternoon but has undertaken to present himself at Skilthorn tomorrow. Another message has been sent to my cousin Ferrowby.

I can see but one explanation for this; he intends to change his will. Whether he intends to cut me out entirely, I know not, but I fear the worst.

I must tell you the reason for this, or at least the circumstance of immediate provocation. It was not my absence over the summer, nor was it linked, as far as I can tell, with my introducing you. I rather fancy that, in his way, he rather approved of you, though that would not stop him advocating for a more advantageous match. No, the sticking point is that Selton's 'triumph' is blazoned across the front pages of several newspapers, and we are reduced to a footnote on an inner page.

You told me this would happen, and you were quite right. I have been naive, a fool, and now it seems I shall pay for it; though, as I am sure you will appreciate, many hundreds of other souls will pay a much higher price. My hold on Kirwaugh is entirely secure, and I shall not suffer personally, but the thought that I may have squandered the chance to do good for so many torments me; as does the implication that I would have lost nothing by remaining in the Sung Lands to be at your side, as much as I could be, during the challenging weeks you endured.

And yet I dare, now, to wonder if we may not yet find some crumb of comfort in all this. If I am no longer to be forever, as you put it, referring everything to my uncle's whim, then dare I think there is no further impediment to our marriage? Might I anticipate the joy of making you Mistress of Kirwaugh within a few months rather than some unknown number of years? And would we not then be free, both to do whatever remains open to us in the cause of the enslaved, and to devote more of our joint time to endeavours in science and discovery? I thought again, as I rode here on my unwelcome errand, of the urge that, I am sure, arose in you as much as it did in me when from our peak we saw the glint of sunlight on the glaciers.

I will write again as soon as I have more certain news.

With fondest love,

Hedric.

❋

The Hon Hedric of Kirwaugh

Skilthorn

My dearest Hedric

That is indeed dismaying news, and I take no satisfaction in recalling that I predicted it. I'll say no more, because I know you will torment yourself quite sufficiently without my adding to it. You are absolutely right to say you were naive, but naivety is no crime; your heart is in the right place, always, even if your head is sometimes in the clouds. And did I not say that all of that is who you are, and so must be why I love you? If not in those exact words, that's what was in my heart, besure.

As to 'the joy of making me Mistress of Kirwaugh'; my dear, it is very tempting to say yes, let us be married just as soon as may be; but there is one thing, or rather one person, that holds me back. I have told you how deeply Embrel detests the idea of being sent away to school. If you had seen his face when I told him I was going away for the summer... well, I said a little about why I was late for our rendezvous on the first day. I made promises to him then, and you know how I feel about promises.

The Squire and Lady Pichenta are adamant that he will go to school before his twelfth birthday. Assuming they adhere to their intent, and supposing they would not wish him to start late in the school year, it can be little more than twelve months before he goes.

I feel strongly that I should remain as his governess until then; to do otherwise would feel like an abandonment. I think you know how little he thought of any of his tutors before I took responsibility for his education. This may be a reflection of their shortcomings rather than any great virtue in me, but he has blossomed since then, although I think he will never be intellectual in the way that you are.

I did promise Embrel that he and I would take a journey together, and perhaps one such journey could bring us to Kirwaugh?

Well, all this is speculation; I suppose that before you read this—perhaps even now, as I write—you will have learned what your uncle's intent was. I am sorry I can't be there to offer some comfort in what surely will be (has been?) a trying time. I'm sorry, too, that I can't cheer you by agreeing to wed you sooner; but once we have a firm date for Embrel's start at school, we can make our plans, and surely our wedding can soon follow. I hope that isn't unendurably far off.

I suppose the news, regarding your uncle's will, must be bad; he would hardly have summoned his attorney unless he meant to make a substantive change. I shall hold out hope as long as I can that it is at least less dire than it might be, though I am not sure how that might be. He's hardly likely to divide the estate, is he?

Please write (I know you will!), or better still, send a bird, as soon as you have definite news for me.

Assuring you of the best wishes of all here at Duncal—though I have told no one of the latest development, and won't do so without your permission.

Again, I wish I could be with you, but it cannot be. Whatever happens/has happened, I hope you can find your way here very soon.

With all my heart,

Jerya

His full name was Veekaratelim, but the Earl, even when in full possession of his faculties, had steadfastly refused to countenance the inconvenience of wrapping his tongue around five syllables. Veeks he had become, and would forever remain.

Esric Veekaratelim was one of the palest men Hedric had ever seen, barring two spots of cherry-red on his cheeks, as precise as if they'd been painted. As a small boy Hedric had been scolded more than once for staring; as an adolescent he'd had to suppress a snigger at the thought that Veeks only needed to colour his lips to resemble a whore.

Now he looked at him, and his cousin, with nothing but dread.

If you were picking an heir on the basis of resemblance, he thought, Cousin Ferrowby would win hands down. The broad, jowly, features; the dark, hooded, eyes; the predator's glare: he was far more obviously the Earl's kinsman than Hedric could ever be.

True, the likeness was less clear than it had been a few years ago. The Earl seemed almost shrunken now, his opulent silken dressing-gown obviously made for a bulkier frame. The jowls were loose, no longer cushioned with fat. He sat, propped among cushions, in a high-backed armchair, close to the crackling fire that made the whole room uncomfortably hot and stuffy, at least to Hedric's mind.

He wished he could shed his coat, but that might too easily be taken amiss. He suspected the Earl had made up his mind already, but if there were any chance that he was still undecided...

Hedric avoided Ferrowby's baleful gaze, instead watching Dortis administer a few sips of the usual pale, diluted, spirits. Under most circumstances, Ferrowby would have been giving the girl's under-dressed form a lascivious examination, but today he had barely spared her a glance. *He's anxious,* Hedric realised. *He's not sure.*

Finally the Earl was ready to speak. He made an ugly sound which might have been an attempt at clearing his throat. "*I named Hedric... as my heir... when he came of age.*" Briefly, as the old man drew a shaky breath, Hedric saw Dortis's eyes flicker toward him. "*What was it, five years ago?*"

"A little more, uncle."

A vague gesture of the good hand might have meant almost anything, but Hedric knew his uncle well enough to be confident it was *don't quibble.*

"*I've always been clear... one thing... I'll never divide... this estate... All goes to... one or other of you.*"

The Earl gestured again; Dortis gave him a little more brandy.

"*Veeks,*" he resumed, "*The devil is... can't use... my writing hand... Can't sign papers... that a problem?*"

Devil yourself, thought Hedric, *you're dragging this out. Keeping us both in suspense.* Ferrowby was tapping a foot impatiently. The sound was muffled almost to nothing by the thick carpet, but the Earl had noticed, he was sure. Something that might have been a smile lifted the right side of the old man's mouth. *You old devil...*

Veeks answered in his driest lawyer's voice. "Nothing of significance, my Lord. A probate hearing, should such be required, would address two key questions: was the testator of sound mind? and: does the document accurately represent his wishes at the time it was drawn up? There are three of us here who can testify to the first. Whatever... temporary physical inconvenience you may be faced with, your mental faculties are manifestly unimpaired." Ferrowby quirked an odd smile, as if he had no high opinion of his uncle's faculties at the best of times. That was rich, thought Hedric, but he knew that Ferrowby despised anyone less intelligent than he believed himself to be, and at the same time was deeply suspicious of anyone who might be cleverer. He had expressed his opinions about 'perfessors' and 'stuffy scholars' often enough. Anything he didn't understand was 'high-falutin' nonsense'.

"I am entirely confident, my Lord," continued Veeks, "That if you make whatever mark you can, and we three all witness it... Perhaps, to be absolutely ironbound, we should invite some other disinterested person to be a witness also."

There are four witnesses in this room, not three, thought Hedric. He knew, of course, that slaves were deemed second-rate witnesses at best... and she could not fairly be classed as 'disinterested'. What member of the household did not have reason to care who their next Lord might be? Especially when the alternatives were as starkly different as Ferrowby and himself?

As Veeks spoke, Ferrowby's restlessness had visibly increased; and the Earl had shown signs of impatience too. It was fine to drag things out as long as he was the one doing the dragging... and Hedric was well aware that in his present condition he had very little stamina.

He demanded a little more brandy, then trained his good eye on each man in turn: Hedric, Ferrowby, finally Veeks.

"*Heed me,*" he said at last. "*This is my...*". A rasping cough shook his body; he slumped a little lower among the cushions. Dortis solicitously wiped his lips, propped him straight again. The Earl said something.

Dortis frowned. "I'm sorry, my lord, but I din't follow that." The Earl tried again. "*You want to...* forgive me, my lord, I think it is the long words..."

A third attempt was no more successful. Ferrowby's foot was almost beating a drum-roll on the carpet. Abruptly he could stand it no longer. Striding forward, he shoved Dortis aside so forcefully she almost fell, which would have landed her dangerously close, if not actually in the fire.

"Your pretty little slave is too stupid for gentlemen's affairs," he said, grasping the chair-arms and leaning close, looming over the sick man. "Tell me, uncle."

And the best of luck with that, thought Hedric. He wondered briefly if his cousin might be tempted to interpret the Earl's mumblings as suited himself, but the Earl would not stand for that. He could still refuse to 'sign' any document so created.

"*Write... this... Veeks,*" he managed. The Earl gave a small nod. But there Ferrowby's efforts also stalled. "Devil take it!" he muttered after a moment. His complexion, always ruddy, darkened, a threatening sign that Hedric knew only too well. Further attempts, a couple of false readings, got them no further.

To anyone who knew Ferrowby even slightly, it was obvious his temper was about to ignite. In a convulsive movement, he pushed himself upright. The Earl's chair rocked fractionally, and Dortis took a step forward, an anxious look on her young face.

Ferrowby had lost control. "Speak clearly, you old fool!"

The Earl's face turned purple. At least, Hedric saw, it did where the blood supply was good. For a terrible moment he wondered if his uncle was about to suffer another apoplexy. *Not now, uncle,* he pleaded silently.

The Earl pounded his good hand on the bedside table, twice, three times. Glassware rattled. Then he pointed at Ferrowby. His hand trembled and the gouty swelling of the knuckles was all too obvious.

This time there was no need for Dortis to translate. "Get. Out."

"No, Uncle, wait. I'm sorry, I was ang—"

"Shut... Up... Leave." The Earl licked his lips. "Fuck... Off."

There was nothing for Ferrowby to do but leave, clinging to whatever shred of dignity remained to him. At the door, already half out of the room, he turned, looked back. "You'll regret this, Hedric," he said.

"Regret what, exactly?"

"Don't play the fool with me."

Too long had he concealed his privately-cherished detestation of the man. "You're very ready to call other people fools, Ferrowby. And when you stop and consider what actually happened here, you'll have to see that the real turning point was when *you* called our uncle an old fool."

"Damn... Right," rasped the Earl, needing no translation.

Ferrowby went. The door was so stiff and heavy, he hadn't even the satisfaction of slamming it behind him.

A clotted silence filled the room, broken only by the incongruously cheery crackle of the fire.

Then the Earl wheezed arduously, a mirthless imitation of a laugh. He gestured, and the girl darted back to his side. "*You're quite the lucky lad,*" she relayed. "*All set to tear up... my old will... I was.... If I'd got the words out... if this wench... had understood me...*" Hedric had his own suspicions about that, but the 'wench' was not meeting his gaze.

"*Like you said... Ferrowby... very ready to... call other people fools... But who's the fool now... I'd like to know...? At least you... show some respect.*"

"I was raised that way, uncle."

"*Aye, your mother... had her faults... but she always... had nice manners.*"

And a great deal more, he thought, but the Earl was still speaking. Though only to say, "*Enough,*" then mutter something that Dortis did not relay. The girl scurried into the other room, leaving an awkward silence. Everyone, he thought, was glad when she returned, pushing a wheeled chair.

"Yow should go, m'lord an' sir," she said as she began preparations to transfer her patient from one chair to the other.

"Do you require assistance?" asked Hedric.

"Thank yow kindly, m'lord, but we've done this often enough. We know how it goes. And I'm stronger'n I might look."

She flicked a glance over her shoulder, and again he wondered, but he certainly wasn't going to ask when there was any other audience.

And if I did ask, he thought, *you'll either have to lie to me... or make me complicit in your deception.* It was most convenient that the one time she completely failed to understand the Earl should be just then. It stretched one's belief in coincidence... but even the unlikeliest of coincidences can happen. There was no doubt Ferrowby had made up his mind that there was more than coincidence about it. For himself, Hedric knew that there had been no collusion. On that, his conscience was clear. *Don't ask, and it can stay that way.*

He knew one thing, however. *I have to tell Jerya.*

CHAPTER 45

JERYA

Analind turned to Jerya. "I heard the Duke and his men are back. I think I must decide very soon if I'm going back this autumn or staying till spring."

Jerya looked at her in sudden dismay. "I hadn't thought..."

"You know, in lots of ways I'd like to stay. Selfishly, for more time with you and Railu. And, more practically, because I can learn more. But it could be the thick end of six months. And how much can I really achieve here, on my own? You know what the main objectives were: first, to verify beyond all doubt that there really is a land here. A civilised land... well, civilised in some ways. So that no one, not even Perriad, could keep on claiming that you'd made it up and Selton and the others were somehow in league with you."

"Does anyone apart from Perriad still believe that?"

Analind shrugged. "Hard to see how anyone could. But we're here and Perriad's there and if she's recovered... You know she'll only hate you the more for being kind to her at the end there."

Jerya hadn't considered that angle, but she could see how it might be true. "But however much she hates me, can she really go one denying plain facts?"

"Facts are slippery. It seems to be a 'fact' here that women aren't capable of serious scientific work. You know you had to publish masked by an initial."

Veiled, thought Jerya. In a dishonest world, even the most honest are forced into deceit sometimes.

"So," said Analind, "I can go back now and settle that question once and for all."

"Unless Perriad decides you're also part of the conspiracy..."

"I'm a Master of the Guild." Analind blinked once, twice. Jerya knew she was still barely acclimatised to her elevated status. "Perriad can believe what she wants—and she will—but I can't see many others denying the sworn word of a Master."

Jerya nodded thoughtfully. "You said there was a second thing?"

"Yes; if I go back now then we have months to prepare for a larger... Visitation... next year." They both smiled at the new use of the word. "Now we're reasonably sure we'll get some kind of civilised reception."

"You took some risk coming on your own, didn't you?" Jerya realised afresh. "Considering what happened to Railu and me."

"I suppose I did. But a letter from Selton with the... what did he call it?"

"The Ducal Seal."

"Aye. That counted for something. Like having the seal of a Master on a letter at home."

"All right," said Jerya. "Two reasons to head back soon. Reasons to stay longer?"

Analind smiled. "More time with you and Railu. That's one."

Jerya blinked away what felt very like the threat of tears. *I'm sure I've wept more in the last half-year than the ten years before.* "You weren't so thrilled about spending time with me when you first saw me in the tavern."

"Maybe not. And part of me still wishes you'd stayed, ten years ago..." Their eyes met, full of unspoken thoughts about what might have been.

Jerya decided that the look said all that needed to be said. "What else?"

"More fact-gathering. And, to be honest, it's just very enticing to stay, long enough to travel further. Troquharran, Sessapont..."

"You know I've been here ten years and I've never seen those places? Never been further than a day's ride: Denvirran-city one way, Skilthorn the other."

"I'd be fascinated to see Skilthorn," said Analind pensively. "From all you've said, it's the darker side of the Five Principalities."

"Not worth the risk. But come back in a few years and it may be different."

"I fully intend to." Analind grinned at her. "When you're a Countess... Whatever that means."

"Whatever it means," echoed Jerya. "I'll have to figure it out some day. I'm hoping for a few years as Mistress of Kirwaugh first. That sounds like enough to be going on with. But then I think that's more time that all the slaves there are still under his regime, and am I being selfish?"

"You're no good to anyone else if you don't look after yourself."

"I suppose not... Well, are you anywhere near a decision?"

Analind sighed. "I think... in many ways I *want* to stay longer, but I probably *need* to be heading home."

Her words so echoed what Hedric had said on their last night together in Carwerid that Jerya was silenced for a moment. Finally she managed, "Are you happy making the crossing on your own?"

"Well, I know the way." Again she held Jerya's gaze. "But then again I was wondering if you might come part of the way with me."

"When were you thinking of leaving?"

"In a few days."

CHAPTER 46

HEDRIC

He'd sent on the wing, and she had come as soon as she could, but it had still been the greater part of two agonising days. It was a joy to see her warming herself before the great fireplace in Kirwaugh's hall, still in her blue riding outfit. However, joy soon gave way to anxiety at how she would react to the news he had just imparted.

"I left the Guild because I didn't want to be part of a falsehood," she said. "Now... it seems like we're going to profit from another one."

"You call it profit? You've never seemed much enamoured of the title, of becoming a Countess."

"You must have your own doubts, else why did you summon me?"

"Summon?" he repeated, trying to laugh. "I'm sure my message *requested* your presence."

"*At my earliest convenience*," she quoted back at him. "But let's not get sidetracked. You must have some misgivings...?"

"I am not entirely easy in my mind, no. But more importantly, I knew you would not... I must confess, Jerya, it did cross my mind not to mention it to you at all."

"A good thing you didn't," she said, stern. "We can't start out, before we're even married, keeping secrets from each other."

"Of course not. I only said it crossed my mind... I didn't let the thought linger. I don't want secrets. And so often I know my own mind better after I've talked things through with you." She relaxed a little, even proffered a small smile.

The door opened and the housemaid, Safiri, entered with a tray. "I took the liberty of orderin' coffee as soon as I heard yowr horse, m'lady," she said. "I thought yow'd 'preciate somethin' hot after a chilly ride."

"Thank you. It *is* fresh out," she said, smiling at the young slave.

"D'yow need anything else, m'lady?" the girl asked. "Cook says dinner will be about an hour."

"Thank you, no, I can wait an hour to fill my belly."

Once Safiri had left, Jerya saluted him with a steaming mug. "I see slaves here are allowed to speak without waiting for permission."

"Of course," he said. "Since my father's time. I've taken things further, given them more initiative. Especially in the last year and a half." He was sure she would take his meaning: *since I became a regular visitor to the house of Duncal.*

She nodded. "Glad to hear it... but we're getting sidetracked again."

"Think about this," he said. "If you—or I—do call out the deception... and remember, we don't absolutely know for sure, it's only my intuition... if we did, what happens to Dortis?"

"What *could* happen?"

"You know the law, Jerya. An owner can do pretty much anything they like to a slave; nothing short of killing them outright is likely to attract judicial penalty. And my uncle... he may not have been as bad as some, if only because mutilation reduces the value of an asset, but he never shrank from it when he deemed it necessary. I can well imagine for this offence he'd see tonguing as a fitting—Jerya?"

She shuddered violently. Coffee slopped from cup into saucer; perhaps a few drops escaped onto the floor. Under the brown, and the cold-blush of her cheeks, her face had gone bloodless.

With exaggerated care, she set the cup and saucer back down on the tray. As she stepped back, he was there, and she leaned into his arms. "Jerya, what is it?"

"A memory," she said, then drew a long, shaky breath. "When we were first taken—Railu and I—taken by the freebooters." A tear escaped one eye.

"You don't have to tell me anything you don't want..."

"I think I do. You should know, anyway. I said *no secrets*, didn't I?" She looked up with a watery smile.

"If you're sure..."

"Yes. They brought us to their chief... we'd already been roughly handled, thrown over horse's arses for an hour or two... Well, you know that much already. But the reason I... the reason I reacted like that was, when they dragged us in front of him, one of the first things he asked was *Hab they bin tongued?*" She mimicked the rough accent with an accuracy he would have admired under kinder circumstances. "I hardly knew what he meant, then... but I suppose I could guess, and it was close enough to the truth, and that was when I began to grasp just how... how dire our predicament was."

He pressed her to him, feeling as if he never wanted to let go. "Well," she said, voice muffled against his shoulder, "I found that man, later. Best part of a year. What was his name? Barek, that was it."

"Why would you...?"

"I wanted to know exactly where they'd found us. And it turned out..." She gently pushed away, far enough to look him in the eye. He kept his hands around her back; hers rested against his breast. "It turned out I felt better. He was drinking himself into an early grave, didn't seem so fearsome after all. But still, that first memory..." She stiffened for a moment under his hands, then shrugged. "I'm not sure I can explain..."

"You don't have to. The mere thought of you being treated as you were... I feel *angry*... like I should have been able to prevent it. It makes no sense. I didn't know you..."

"It's ten years ago. How old were you?"

"Sixteen," he said, "And no fighter. What could I have done? But I just feel such things should never happen to you, so I must have failed you in some way."

"Such things should never happen to *anyone*," she said firmly. She disengaged herself, stepped away. "Draff, I've spilled some... I should go find a cloth."

"It won't harm those tiles. Let it be for now."

"All right." She turned away, stepped closer to the fire, stretching her hands toward the flames. He took a step, close behind her, but did not touch her.

After a little time, she sighed. "You're right, of course. We can't expose Dortis to that risk. It doesn't mean I have to feel *comfortable* about it."

"No, I understand. But, Jerya... I hesitate to ask this, but you did say *no secrets*..."

"What?"

"There is another deception that you... participate in. Have done for many years, unless I am very much mistaken."

"You mean Embrel," she said. He was relieved that she didn't seem angry at him for mentioning it. Her tone was... resigned. "How long have you known? I didn't tell you, and no one else would."

"It just seemed obvious, when I saw him and Railu together. She had to be either his mother, or his sister... the age-difference is large, but hardly impossible."

"Yes, of course. She's his mother. And I am not *comfortable* with this deceit either. Doesn't Embrel deserve to know? If not now, when he's older? And there's his father, too..."

"You know who the father is?"

"I do. And I've had more than one opportunity to tell him... and, believe me, I was sorely tempted. Does he not deserve to know? Such a wonderful boy..."

"He is a very fine lad. But what would it do to him, to be told? Especially at such a tender age?"

"I don't know." Jerya sighed again, heavily. "And that's one reason... but also, Railu has always been adamant."

"But she loves the boy."

"Aye, well, we all do. She's good with him, and she does love him, but... I think, sometimes, the three of us, Railu and Rhenya and I, are like the 'aunts' who raised me, in Delven. But he does have his parents too... his *official* parents." Her face twisted a little as she finished, and he saw how much the deception pained her. He saw, too... it had long been obvious, if only he'd seen it clear... who Embrel loved best, and, possibly, who loved him most dearly in return.

"Well," he said, thinking she might welcome a change of subject, if only a partial one, "Are we agreed to say nothing about any deception Dortis may—*may*—have engaged in?"

"You know," she said. "Maybe there's another thing. You didn't tell Dortis to do it, did you?"

"Absolutely not."

"That was a rhetorical question, not an accusation. And no one else would even have thought of it. So... we have to assume it was all her own idea. She knew what she was doing."

He laughed suddenly. "Ferrowby would never believe it. His dream dashed by a slave."

"And by his own stupidity, by your telling."

"Yes, that too. But you're right. Dortis knew who she wanted for the next Earl of Skilthorn. For herself, and for every other slave on those estates too."

"You can't know that."

"All right, I choose to believe it. I choose to believe she was thinking further than her own interest."

"But even if she wasn't... if there was deception in that room that day, it was her own doing, her own choice. I think I can live with that."

"I think so too. Now, you didn't manage to throw *all* the coffee on the floor..."

CHAPTER 47

JERYA

Embrel was actively looking about as they rode. Jerya was happy to see his keen curiosity, and did her best to answer any questions sparked by his observations. Higher up the valley, however, there were long stretches through thick forest, and the lad had no great interest in the difference between fir and pine. Nor did he give more than a dutiful nod at the fact that the larches, already starting to turn to gold, would lose their needles in the winter.

He was only ten, and this was his first journey into 'uncivilised' country. He would see, and learn, plenty: no need to force education upon him.

As the forest crowded the track once more, Embrel moved up alongside Analind, and soon he was once again plying her with questions about the College. He had been very taken with the realisation that in the Sung Lands girls his own age were regularly Chosen for the life of a Postulant. Indeed, as he soon established, many would be making their journeys to Carwerid right now. Or as Analind, ever the stickler, qualified, 'I'd be very surprised if they weren't'.

This led Analind into a discussion about equinoxes, and Jerya was pleased to see that Embrel recalled at least the main points of that lesson, delivered at the last spring equinox.

His fascination with the College was understandable, and she had every sympathy, but it could lead nowhere. Embrel could not change sex even if he really wanted to, and it was scarcely more likely that the Guild would suddenly ditch a rule that had endured for centuries. Even allowing that,

Jerya could not imagine that parents who had been desperate enough to adopt the child of a slave would ever allow that child to leave them so irrevocably.

There was no way in this world that anyone could change sex... But perhaps you *could* change its meaning. In the Sung Lands, only women could be Dawnsingers; in the Five Principalities women could not attend universities or own any substantial property. Railu, though at least as able as any doctor they'd seen this side of the mountains, could only practise clandestinely. These things could change, and if she had anything to do with it, one day they would.

It was not why she was marrying Hedric, but it was the consideration that most effectively reconciled her to the otherwise appalling prospect of becoming Countess of Skilthorn. A Countess could do things that the Mistress of Kirwaugh could not; and the Mistress of Kirwaugh could do things that Miss Jerya Delven could not.

It was not fair, and it was not right, but it was—in the phrase that had once made her burn with irritation—the way things were.

It was not indignation she felt now. It was resolution.

They spent the night with the herders at the high meadows. The men made a great fuss of Embrel: *of course*, thought Jerya, *they'll have families they probably hardly see for three or four months.*

Next morning they left the horses there and hiked on up, a steady climb for the most part, interrupted by just a couple of easy bands of rock. Jerya let Embrel find his own way up. He was fearless enough, and agile enough, practised in climbing trees. A governess in full skirts might have had some trouble following; Jerya of Delven, in divided skirt and good boots, had none.

The last of the trees were behind them, save a few dwarf specimens huddling in sheltered spots. The Sun, cloud-dimmed, was past the zenith.

A cool breeze slithered down from the heights that massed ahead of them. A boulder the size of the Duncal carriage gave shelter while they ate a frugal lunch and prepared to say their final farewells.

Embrel gave Analind a fierce hug. It surprised Jerya to see it, but it surprised Analind more; she seemed frozen for a moment before she returned the embrace. When—if ever—had she last embraced a child? wondered Jerya.

"I'll miss you," said Analind, and it was clear that she meant it, and that she had surprised herself.

Then it was Jerya's turn. She took Analind by the shoulders, looking into her eyes, and said, "If I'd got nothing from it but seeing you again, it would have been well worth the Crossings."

Analind laughed gently. "I think you had more to contend with than the effort of the Crossings."

"Aye, but I gained more, too. But I mean what I say. I'm truly glad to have seen you again, and maybe begun to repair the hurt I caused you ten years ago."

Analind waved a hand. "It's behind me now. I'm just happy we're friends again."

"I hope it won't be another ten years..."

Analind shrugged. "I don't know how much freedom a Master of Peripatetics can really have. I'm sure I won't be able to come back every year. And..." She smiled. "For all I know there've been another three or four changes of Master Prime while I've been away."

"Let's hope not."

There wasn't much more to say. Sometimes an embrace said far more than any words could.

Jerya and Embrel stood for a long time watching the small figure, half-hidden by her own pack, only the white of her pants standing out against the dull greens and greys and splashes of heather-purple as she steadily climbed the slope. Not until Analind vanished over the crest of the rise did they gather themselves and turn to descend.

❄

"Are you really going to marry Hedric?"

Jerya smiled a little at the bluntness of the question, but held it to herself. "I really am."

"Why?"

This time she wanted to laugh, restrained it with effort. "Because I love him, I suppose."

Embrel walked on eight or ten paces, lips pressed together, before he spoke again. "If you love him, it's right that you marry him... but why do you have to go and live at Kirwaugh?"

Thank you for approving my marriage, she thought, but it was his question that she responded to. "We need to live somewhere, and I don't have a house. Kirwaugh's where his property is."

"You've got a home. Duncal. Why can't you live there? I'm sure Mama and Papa would like it."

I'm not so sure about that—but that's another story. "Listen, Embrel, I said I don't have a house. You know I can't own a house, don't you? I can't even own the horse I ride."

He looked at her, cocking his head on one side. "But she's your horse."

"No, she belongs to your father." She felt the usual guilty stab at saying 'your father'. Rodal was his true father, but... *the way things are.* "He allows me to ride her as if she were my own. You know it's the law, don't you? You know why I can't own a house, or a horse?"

He tilted his head the other way. "Because you used to be a slave?"

It was wrong, but not a stupid suggestion. Her status as a freedwoman had its own consequences, but it bore no such legal impediment. "No, because I'm a woman."

He frowned. They walked on. The trees sighed in the soft cool breeze that slid down from the heights.

At last he said, "So if I was a girl I couldn't ever own a horse?"

"Or a house." *Or slaves...*

"So if I went to the College—"

Jerya stopped abruptly. Embrel had gone on a couple of paces before he realised. He turned back with a startled face.

"Embrel," she said. "Come here." When he obeyed, she dropped to one knee to bring their faces level, grasped him by the shoulders. "Listen to me. First of all, I just said goodbye to a very dear friend. I hadn't seen her for ten years and I can't be sure I'll ever see her again. So I'm feeling quite sad at the moment. Can you try and remember that?

He nodded solemnly.

"And because I'm feeling sorry for myself, it's a bit harder than it should be to feel sorry for you. No—" She lifted one hand to forestall him. "Let me finish, please. I just need a minute. I understand why you're so interested in the College, I really do. I was there for four months and there'll always be a part of me that wishes I could have stayed. But if I'd done that, I'd never have met Hedric... and I'd never have known you." *Actually, if I'd stayed, you wouldn't even exist.*

It was a difficult thought. Actions had consequences, but mostly it was the consequences for herself and Railu that she thought about. Yet she'd made one choice and it had rippled out into the world. *I'd never have met Hedric, and Embrel wouldn't exist...* and that wasn't even the half of it.

She clamped down on wandering thoughts. "One day, perhaps, there'll be a place like the College here in the Five Principalities. Not exactly like, maybe, but closer. And maybe, maybe, marrying Hedric gives me a chance to bring that day nearer. I can't do it on my own, I know that.

"But there isn't anywhere like that for you now. You hate it, I know. I hate it too. But you can't go to the College. Even if you were a girl, do you think your parents would let you go? And anyway, would you *really* want to? You know it would mean never seeing them again. Never seeing me, or Rhenya, or Railu..."

"Analind came back... well, not back."

"Analind is a Master of the Guild, and even she doesn't know if she'll ever be able to come across again. And let me tell you something else about Dawnsingers. You know I said a girl can't own a horse?" She waited for his nod, watching his face, the dark eyes intent on her. *How can everyone not see he has Railu's eyes?* "Dawnsingers can't own horses. They don't really own anything. Not even the clothes they wear. And... they have a saying: *we do what we're told, we go where we're sent.* Even someone like Analind, a Master, can't just go where she likes."

Put it that way, it sounds a lot like being a slave, she thought. She hoped Embrel wouldn't draw the same parallel, because she wasn't sure she could explain just *how* it was different.

"Embrel," she said instead, holding his gaze. "A year from now, you'll be going to school. You may not like the idea, not right now. I don't suppose all the girls who're Chosen for Dawnsingers are filled with joy either. Analind said she was terrified, didn't she? I was pretty terrified when it happened to me, and I was a lot older. But you going to school isn't the same as them being Chosen. Most of them will never see their parents again, or the place they came from. Most of them will spend their entire lives in the College, studying, teaching, researching. And they'll get up before dawn every single day, spring, summer, autumn, winter, to Sing... how many times when Analind was here did you get up to hear her Sing?" They both knew the answer to that.

"It's not going to be like that for you. For us. Kirwaugh's a day's ride from Duncal. And when your parents settle on their choice of school for you, it's pretty near certain it'll be nearer than that. And you can write letters, can't you?"

"Write to you?"

"To me, to your parents, to Railu, to Rhenya, anyone you like."

"Rhenya can't read, she's—"

"She most certainly *can* read. Who do you think writes the shopping lists?"

He grimaced, scrunching his lips as far to one side as they'd go. "Would you put red lines through all my bad spelling?"

Jerya laughed. Suddenly she powerfully wanted to hug him. "These are letters, not school tasks. Though of course it'll be easier for me to read if you keep working on your spelling." *And your handwriting*, she added privately. "But we've time for that. I'm not getting married till the spring."

He looked like he was still minded to grumble. "What, you want me to get married sooner now, do you? Sooner I'm out of the way the better?"

He protested, just as she'd thought; just as she'd hoped. "It's just... spelling."

Jerya released his shoulders and got to her feet, making a performance of it. "These ancient knees can only take so much of that." She gave him one of her fiercest grins. "Do you suppose you wouldn't have to do spelling at the Dawnsingers' College? What d'you think they teach there anyway?"

CHAPTER 48

EPILOGUE

Jerya

In Drumlenn or Denvirran, it was wearing a veil that got you noticed. In Sessapont the opposite was true. Since their arrival, rather late the previous night, and more particularly on this morning's get-your-bearings walk, she didn't think she had seen a single free woman without a veil. Many were flimsy things, it was true, the merest gauze, but it appeared that no woman, no girl over the age of ten or so, would go about bare-faced.

"It's funny," she said to Hedric as they strolled arm-in-arm down the wharf of the inner harbour, the view to their right more like a great river, not the sea... *not yet.*

"What's funny?"

"Back home, hardly anyone wears a veil, and I like it. Here, everyone does—every free woman, I mean—and I feel like I want to tear it off."

He laughed. "Doesn't surprise me in the slightest."

"What? Why?"

"Because you like to be different."

"And you're mean," she said, lightly punching his arm with her free hand.

"Mean? Do you think that was censure? Why do you think I married you?"

"Oh..."

"Yes, Mistress Jerya of Kirwaugh, if I'd wanted someone commonplace, I could have wed five years ago."

"I'm sorry. I'm still getting used to—" And then, passing near one of the great statues, they rounded a curve and the words died on her lips. They halted.

The water spread before them, glittering in the morning Sun, and alive with shipping. Vessels the size of houses glided past under many-coloured spreads of sail; smaller craft, driven by oars, dodged and darted between them. The keen breeze carried a dozen scents she could not name. Whatever convention might decree, she could not resist briefly lifting her veil to take it all in more fully.

When Hedric had first asked where she might wish to go for a sweetmoon, her immediate response had been a blank stare. She hardly knew what a sweetmoon was, and, though she had considered many things that might follow from marrying a gentleman, that had never been among them. Recovering her composure, she had considered for a moment, and then made one decisive response. "I've never seen the ocean, save as a gleam on the horizon. It's time to put that right. Apart from that, wherever you think best."

And so, five days after the wedding, on a bright crisp morning in Pulluander, here they were in Sessapont, the greatest port—the greatest *city*—in the known world.

As her eyes adjusted to the dazzle of the water, she saw that they were not truly looking out over the open ocean. Several islands, all roughly conical, like the hills over which the city sprawled, rose from the water; and most of them were linked by barriers of some sort, mere dark lines against the light, occluding any true horizon. There were but two places where gaps remained, and after a moment she saw that one was used by ships coming in, and the other by vessels leaving.

She sighed, a little disappointed not to have the unobstructed view of the ocean she had hoped for. There would be a wider view from the hills behind them, of course, but what she really wanted was to stand on the shore, see and hear and feel the waves crashing in, let her gaze range slowly out to the edge of the world.

Well, there must be a way... She pressed gently on his arm, and they moved on together. *Husband and wife. Wife and husband... Do I feel any different? Should I feel different? Are we still Jerya and Hedric?*

Their course weaved around heaps of net, cargo-crates awaiting shipment, mooring-bollards—if that was the word. Twice they paused to avoid obstructing—or being overrun by—gangs of hurrying men hauling heavy carts. One gang were all slaves, the other free. There were only a few spots along the wharf where it seemed safe to stand and look.

They found one such place at the base of another of the colossal figures. Its stone legs were densely painted in overlapping layers, a palimpsest of names. Suddenly she recalled something Rodal had said, one night in the tavern in Carwerid. *Almost the only time we really got to talk...* He had been here, of course, ten years before her. He'd left his name... Doubtless it had been painted over many times since, and she had no idea if this was even the right statue, but she looked anyway.

Then she looked out into the water, looking more closely at the boats that lay out there, moored to buoys that carried green-and-red flags. What had he said the name of the ship was?

They walked on, but a few minutes later she stopped again. "Hedric. That ship out there... the name on the, what do you call it, the stern... does it say *Levore*?"

He squinted obligingly, but, "Even with the glasses, my eyes aren't as good as yours."

"Maybe you need new glasses."

"I shall pursue it when we're home. But I *can* see this..."

"What?"

He pointed almost directly downward. Below them, several small boats were tied to a narrow jetty that protruded from the angle of the wharf. One had '*Tender to Levore*' painted on its stern.

"'*Tender to Levore*'," she repeated. "Sounds like a poem. But do you know what it means?"

"It's how they get ashore when the ship's moored out there. And that means at least some of the crew are ashore right now. Way I heard it, when I was here before, business gets discussed in the wharfinger's office, but mostly in the taverns."

"Then do you think we could find them?"

"I think these taverns are not very welcoming for ladies," he said. He obviously knew she wouldn't like that, seemed almost surprised when she reacted with no more than a resigned look. "I'll leave Lallon and Safiri with you."

"If they're such rough places, you'd better take Lallon with you. Safiri and I will be fine by ourselves."

When they first planned the trip, she had failed to see the necessity of bringing an attendant for herself (she flatly refused to say 'body-slave'). Hedric had explained that things were different in the Principality of Sessapont, and that travelling without at least one attendant would make things 'awkward', especially in the inns and hotels where they would be staying. Jerya had briefly considered offering the position to Railu or Rhenya, thinking they might like to travel, but a moment's thought had shown her that it would be intolerable on both sides. She could not ask her dear friends to *wait* on her.

Instead, Hedric had suggested Safiri, who he described as the brightest of the younger slaves around Kirwaugh. She was about nineteen, the exact age at which Jerya had first encountered the world beyond Delven. She had a great deal to learn about being a lady's maid, but then Jerya had a great deal to learn about being a lady.

As Hedric and Lallon disappeared, ducking under the low doorway of the nearest tavern, Jerya motioned Safiri to her side. The girl bobbed a swift curtsey.

"You really don't need to do that when we're alone."

"Beggin' your pardon, m'lady, but we ain't rightly alone."

Then she looked shocked at herself, but Jerya only smiled. "I dare say you're right. And never be afraid to tell me if you think I'm in error."

Within only a few minutes, Lallon reappeared. "Master says you can go in, m'lady."

"You'll stay with Safiri?" He nodded. She wondered if they would find something to talk about, or if Lallon was equally taciturn with his fellow enslaved.

Crossing the rough setts of the quay-road, she wondered briefly at Hedric's luck in finding someone from the *Levore* in the first tavern he tried. But then, she reflected, it was the closest to where they'd tied the 'tender'.

The interior was dim after the morning brightness; it took a moment for her eyes to adjust before she spotted Hedric waving from a corner table. The veil didn't help, but it seemed best to keep it lowered.

Hedric and the man with him both stood as she approached. "May I present my wife, Mistress Jerya of Kirwaugh." *Draff, will I ever get used to it?* "Jerya, this is Haulton Filder, Master of the *Levore*."

"An honour to meet yow, my lady," said Filder, then looked surprised as Jerya extended a hand. The hand that—after a moment—grasped her own was huge, gnarled, and seemed to have a dark intaglio in every seam and wrinkle. Not mere dirt, she thought: perhaps tar. She'd already pegged the smell of tarred rope as a major element of the quayside cocktail.

"So, m'lady," said Filder as they all sat. "How might I be of service to yow?"

"I'll begin at the beginning, if I may, Mr Filder."

"Folks just calls me Skipper, mostwise."

"Whatever you prefer, Skipper. May I ask if you were Master of the *Levore* ten years ago?"

"I was, m'lady, it's bin eighteen year since I took her on."

"Then I bring you greetings from an old friend. I believe you sailed here with him, among other places... I mean Rodal."

A broad grin split the weatherbeaten face, revealing a couple of missing teeth. "By the four winds... Rodal, is it? I'm right glad to hear tell of him, m'lady, I've often wondered how he fared."

"He's very well. Has a daughter now, and another child on the way." *Should be born by now*, she realised.

The grin got even broader, which she wouldn't have believed possible. "Yow couldn'a brung me better news, m'lady. He... he tole me he had a promise... no, what'd he say, he had an *understandin'* wi' a girl, back wherever he were from. Would it be th'same one, would yow happen to know?"

"It certainly would."

The Skipper shook his grizzled head, plainly delighted. "That lad..." he said in a musing tone. "When he came aboard, first time, he din't know the stem from the stern. Six month later I were ser'ously thinkin' 'bout takin' him into partnership. Never seen anyone learn so fast. Not to mention... did he tell yow how he beat off a couple o'thieves as were fixin' ter strip my lady *Levore* o' whatever they could grab? Blocks an' shackles, if not the cargo."

"He didn't mention that," said Jerya, amused but not surprised. "But he spoke very highly of you."

"M'lady," said the Skipper suddenly. "I may be speakin' out of turn, and maybe it's not my place... but I'm proper made up wi' this news yow brung me, and I'd be honoured if yow'd permit me to buy yowrself and yowr husband a drink."

"And I'd be honoured to accept," said Jerya, "But it's a little early in the day for a proper drink." *At least for a fine lady like me...* "And in any case you may be able to do me a favour that means a lot more than any drink... than a whole case of wine, indeed."

"If it's in my power to oblige yow, m'lady..."

"Then tell me, please, do you ever carry passengers?"

"Aye, sohappen we do, time to time. Someone wants a trip up-river to Troqu', or wherevers, and can't stump for carriage-fare, we can carry 'em for less'n'half. But..." He looked at her as if peering through the veil. *In this light*, she thought, *it's nothing but a damn nuisance.* "It's not what yow'd call comfortable. We keeps the cabins for th'crew, yow see. Passengers—supernum'ries, we calls 'em—sleep on th' cargo, if it's summat like fleece or cloth, or find a corner up on deck if th'weather's fair. It'd be a far cry from what yow're 'customed to."

"You might be surprised what I'm accustomed to," she said.

Hedric grinned. "No 'might' about it, Skipper. I guarantee you'd be surprised."

"E'en so, m'lady... there are other vessels, yow know. Well, yow must know. Vessels fitted out to carry passengers. Yow could charter one o'them, if that's what yow're after. I could give yow a name or two, belike."

"No doubt I could," she said. "But I don't think that'd be half as much fun. The question I have for you is are you free... for the next week, shall we say?"

"Free? I am that, m'lady. That's why I were sittin' here, yow see. Lookin' out for th' shippin' agents and suchlike."

"And if we made it worth your while, could you make us a little more comfortable? There must be space in the... the hold, you call it? When you've no cargo... Nothing fancy. A couple of mattresses, a little privacy..."

He was thinking. "I'm wond'rin if it'd be best if yow come aboard now. Take a look around, like. I'd want yow to be *sure*, yow see."

"I think that's an excellent idea, Skipper. And at the very least I get to see the *Levore*."

"When exactly did this little scheme come to you?" asked Hedric privately as they followed the Skipper out.

"About the time I sat down," she said.

"But you sent me looking for him before that..."

"Yes, but then I was just thinking of giving him the news of Rodal. The rest just came to me... I hope you don't mind?"

"Mind?" He chuckled. "I'm reassured. I was beginning to worry marriage had turned you into a fine lady after all."

"There's no danger of that. I'll play the part when I have to, but that's all."

❋

Hedric

"How high above the water do you reckon the deck is?"

"Here? About ten feet."

"Three metres, Hedric. Plus a metre and a half; eye-level four metres and a half. We must be able to work out how far it is to the horizon."

"We could just ask the Skipper. He's bound to know: they'll need to. Or you can do it the hard way."

She laughed. "I'm on my sweetmoon. I think I can do things the easy way."

"But only while you're on your sweetmoon?"

"We shall see." She turned, leaning back against the handrail. She was as far forward as they could get, almost wedged into the angle between the rail and the bowsprit. He knew he'd barely begun to learn all the names for parts of the ship, but bowsprit was one he was sure of.

Jerya was looking up now. "How high do you suppose the mainmast is?"

"Sixty feet?"

"Metres, Hedric."

"Twenty metres?"

"Twenty metres is nearer seventy feet than sixty."

"Yes, but when both are approximations... and also both guesswork, I think I may be forgiven."

"And that bit like a barrel, almost at the top?"

"They call it the crow's nest," he said.

"Why crow, I wonder? Why not a gull's nest, or a petrel's, or any other sea-bird?" She shrugged, laughed lightly, pushed back the hair that the constant breeze was teasing free of its restraints. She had discarded her veil before they passed the island-gap into open water. "And that's *not* the question I want answered first. How much wider is the horizon from up there? That must be what it's there for."

"I'm sure they'll know that, too."

"More than one way to skin a cat," she said, and slid past him.

When he caught up she was standing beside the Skipper, who was at the wheel.

"*Yow*, m'lady?" was the first thing he heard, a tone of incredulity.

"The next time we are safely moored, or anchored, I'll tell you something about where I came from. For now, just this: I grew up amongst rocks; I was scrambling on them almost before I could walk. All the children did. I just never stopped. Trees, too. And H—my husband can tell you I've climbed things far higher and more precarious than the *Levore's* rigging."

"That's true," he confirmed. "Hundreds of feet of rock. Some of it almost defeated me, but Jerya went up like a cat."

"We didn't have cats in Delven," she said. "We'd say someone climbed like a squirrel."

"Well, m'lady," said the Skipper, "Happen yow knows better'n'me what yow're capable of. And yow've chartered us, so yow're th'boss. But I wouldn't care to be held respons'ble, if'n anything should happen..."

"I'll sign something for you, if it makes you easier in your mind. And I'll change into my riding-habit..." She grinned at Hedric. "For some unaccountable reason I forgot to pack trousers for this trip."

The Skipper blinked at this, but only said, "Well, m'lady, if yow're set on it, best make it soon. Water's calm enough here, but once we're yond shelter of th'Isles it'll be a diff'rent story. Climbin' th'riggin' when th'ship's pitchin' and tossin' ain't anythin' to laugh at e'en for experienced men."

She nodded, already heading toward the companionway.

Hedric smiled at the Skipper's bemused expression. "She did warn you, you know. Said you might be surprised what she's accustomed to."

"She ain't like most ladies, that's clear enough."

"No," he agreed. "I wouldn't have married her if she were."

❋

Jerya

It *was* easy climbing—but easy climbing on holds that sagged and swayed as she moved her weight onto them. If a piece of rock moved, even slightly, under hand or foot, you looked for another hold. And in a tree, when branches start to dip significantly under your weight, you start to think about the chances of a break. Added to that, the ship's motion became more apparent with every metre she climbed. The Skipper had called the sea 'calm enough', but all things were relative.

Jerya didn't look anywhere but where she needed to plan her next moves, until she was safely ensconced in the crow's nest. She heard a faint cry—a cheer?—from below, wondered how easy—or not—it was to communicate with the deck, especially when the wind was up or the sea was rough. *They must have signals.*

She looked down and was startled to see how small the whole ship looked. The upturned faces were little more than blobs. Lallon was identifiable by his bald head, Safiri by that and by her darker skin, Hedric by his russet coat; but it wasn't so easy to tell the ship's company apart. She counted three, so they were all there, and she supposed the Skipper was still at the wheel, but telling Grauven's dark face from Philliter's heavily-bearded one was not so easy.

And anyway, she hadn't come up here to look at people she could see up close any other time.

Jerya turned to face the bows, to the East.

Rationally, she knew that even from this height the horizon could not be that far away. She knew she had seen much longer horizons from high in the mountains.

She knew all that, but this was a horizon without limits.

Jerya thought suddenly of an evening in the Kendrigg observatory, herself holding a globe, the Sung Lands a mere sliver of paint on its surface. Since then, since last summer, the known world had doubled in size, but there was still so much more to discover.

"Let's just keep sailing, Skipper," she said, but the wind carried her words away, and not even the kittiwakes could have heard.

ABOUT THE AUTHOR

Jon Sparks has been writing fiction as long as he can remember, but for many years made his living as an (award-winning) outdoor writer and photographer, specialising in landscape, travel and outdoor pursuits, particularly walking, climbing and cycling. He lives in Garstang, Lancashire, UK, with his partner Bernie and several bikes.

If you enjoyed this book...

There are several more volumes to come. To be the first to hear about these, and to get other news and insights, please consider signing up to my mailing list: go to tinyurl.com/4dvf7pt. There's a free short story as a thank you.

The Shattered Moon website is at https://www.jonsparksauthor.com. I also have a Facebook Page at https://www.facebook.com/profile.php?id=100089266940531, and I'm on Substack too: http://tinyurl.com/3nmm msm4

Finally, a small plea. Reviews and ratings are really valuable to indie authors like me. If you can find a moment to leave a few thoughts, or just to add a star rating, it all helps. You can do this on whatever platform you got the book from, and there are also general review platforms, notably Goodreads, where my profile is at https://tinyurl.com/2p9znuhh. Thank you.

ACKNOWLEDGEMENTS

Terry Pratchett once said, "Writing a novel is as if you are going off on a journey across a valley. The valley is full of mist, but you can see the top of a tree here and the top of another tree over there. And with any luck you can see the other side of the valley. But you cannot see down into the mist. Nevertheless, you head for the first tree."

This perfectly encapsulates what writing a novel feels like for me. But what Terry didn't say, at least on this occasion, is that few, if any, writers undertake the journey entirely alone.

As with *The Sundering Wall*, parts of this story deal with mountain journeys, and again, I'd like to mention some of the people with whom I've shared great mountain days over many years, including members of Clwyd Mountaineering Club especially Judith Brown, Ian Nettleton, and Pat Cossey. Thanks too to several generations of Lancaster University MC, notably Jonathan Westaway, Colin Wells, and the late Matthew Walsh. For sharing the first tentative forays on rock, thanks to Robin Taylor and Mike Thompson.

I reiterate my thanks from Book One to all who've read and commented on my work, notably Marion Smith and Jago Westaway. Thanks to the many excellent editors I've worked with in my non-fiction career, particularly Ronald Turnbull, Sue Viccars, John Manning, and Seb Rogers. Many other members of the Outdoor Writers and Photographers Guild have helped me too.

First, last, and always, I cannot overstate what I owe to my partner Bernie, with whom I've shared unforgettable experiences from Morocco to New Zealand, as well as a host of hikes, climbs and treks in the Lakes, Scotland, and across the UK. She's also my principal beta-reader, and so much more besides. Our conversations on walks and in pubs and cafés have helped refine my ideas and I'm sure this book, and this series, are much the better for them.

Of all the places we've had such conversations, none means more to us than Cobblers Bar and Bistro in Garstang. Passages from all the books have been written or edited here too. It's a particularly welcoming and nurturing place.

It's very likely I wouldn't have been around to bring this book, and this series, to fruition without the amazing work of many dedicated health professionals. Deepest thanks to all of them, notably Dr David Howarth and Dr Scott Gall.